THE *Best* AMERICAN SHORT STORIES 1955

THE *Best* AMERICAN SHORT STORIES 1955

and the Yearbook of the American Short Story

Edited by
MARTHA FOLEY

HOUGHTON MIFFLIN COMPANY · BOSTON
The Riverside Press Cambridge
1955

LIBRARY OF CONGRESS CATALOGUE CARD NUMBER: 16–11387

The Riverside Press
CAMBRIDGE • MASSACHUSETTS
PRINTED IN THE U.S.A.

TO

AUGUSTA WALLACE LYONS

ACKNOWLEDGMENT

GRATEFUL ACKNOWLEDGMENT for permission to reprint the stories in this volume is made to the following:

To the Editors of *Accent, The Atlantic Monthly, Botteghe Oscure, Fantasy and Science Fiction,* Harcourt, Brace & Company, *Harper's Bazaar, Harper's Magazine, The Hudson Review, The Kenyon Review, Ladies' Home Journal, Mademoiselle, New Mexico Quarterly, New World Writing, The New Yorker, The Paris Review, Partisan Review, Prairie Schooner, Shenandoah, The University of Kansas City Review,* The Viking Press, Inc., *The Western Review;* and to Robert O. Bowen, Nancy Cardozo, Nancy G. Chaikin, John Cheever, Evan S. Connell, Jr., Joe Coogan, Daniel Curley, William Eastlake, George P. Elliott, Mac Hyman, Oliver La Farge, Bernard Malamud, Judith Merril, Elizabeth H. Middleton, Marvin Mudrick, Howard Nemerov, Flannery O'Connor, Irwin Shaw, Wallace Stegner, David Stuart, Harvey Swados, Mark Van Doren, George Vukelich, and Eudora Welty.

FOREWORD

THE SHORT STORY is the oldest form of literature. Many thousands of years ago men sitting around campfires after a day's hunting or fishing told one another stories. Women beating linens white on the rocks of a stream or stopping at the well-side for water told one another stories. Later were to come poems and, much later, novels.

The Bible is full of short stories. One of the finest short stories of all time is the Book of Ruth. And in the New Testament Jesus used short stories in the form of parables to illustrate His teachings.

In medieval times, along with the singing poets called troubadours, storytellers roamed among castles and marketplaces. With the coming of the printing press countless numbers of stories have been printed all over the world.

In this country the short story not only has flourished but renewed itself. It started out by being used for religious and political purposes. The New England preacher, Cotton Mather, is probably the first American short story writer. First, he wrote The Political Fables. These were three stories which were circulated in manuscript form in 1692, warning the Colonists against internal dissension. But Mather really soared off into fiction when, in a frenzy of witchcraft hunting in 1693, he wrote *Wonders of the Invisible World*. This volume is so full of fantastic accounts, so abounding in witches, devils, and weird spiritual manifestations that few of the so-called "fantasy fiction" writers of today could hope to equal it.

In 1774, two years before the Declaration of Independence, Francis Hopkinson Smith wrote a popular short story which had a profound effect on this nation's history. It was called "A Pretty Story" and put into short story form a narrative of the events leading up to the meeting of the first Continental Congress. George the Third, King of England, was pictured as a villainous father and his wife, Parliament, as a debauched woman who oppressed by various evil acts some of their children whom they had permitted to settle on a farm they owned which is America. Things became rougher and rougher for the children and they became angrier until . . . here the story breaks off into a row of thirteen stars.

Today, however, such stories as those by Mather and Smith are of historical interest only. Stories remembered most are those in which people come alive rather than the moral or political points they make. That is why we remember Naomi and Ruth from the Bible, or the Prodigal Son. It is why, when we think of early American writing, we remember Ichabod Crane, the Yankee schoolmaster in "The Legend of Sleepy Hollow," or the rapscallion Rip Van Winkle, and the doomed brother and sister in "The Fall of the House of Usher" and consider their authors, Washington Irving and Edgar Allan Poe, our first really great short story writers.

Since their time thousands of short stories have been written and published in this country. Beginning with Poe, especially, their effect on the writing of other nations has been tremendous. Poetry, in contrast with its blooming in the nineteenth century and again in the middle nineteen-tens, does not attract as many readers as it should. A few good novels appear and there is an abundance of magazine articles which, with a few outstanding exceptions, are mostly superficial. The short story still holds its own as our most important literary form.

Forty years ago this series, *The Best American Short Stories,* was founded to provide readers in book form the excellent stories published each year. Over the years some mistakes may have been made, a few stories which should have been reprinted have been omitted, a few stories which have been included may not seem so important in the long run. But I do believe the over-all intent of stressing good, interesting writing has been achieved.

I often wish, personally, the word "Best" were not in the title. For what is "best" at one time will not seem so at another. I once stood in the Bodleian Library at Oxford University and looked at the few pathetic relics the great library of a great university exhibited in its foremost place of honor. They belonged to a poet the university had expelled. His name was Shelley.

And I am old enough to remember when the only great writer of sea stories was considered to be Joseph Conrad. He still is a fine writer. But there was a writer named Herman Melville who wrote *Moby-Dick,* which nobody read at all, and all but a very few scholars had forgotten.

It is incredible also to think that there was a period when no plays by William Shakespeare were performed on the English-speaking stage. It was a production on the Continent which caused a sensation that drew England's attention again to its greatest playwright and poet.

More than anyone else, critics of writing and editors must be humble. We may have been right many times but we can be very, very wrong.

As I compiled this year's list of contents I have worried more than usual and done much more rereading than ever before. To be frank, there really have been two lists of selections for this year's book. The first list was all prepared and I was about to mail it to the publisher when, glancing for what I thought was the last time over it, I noticed a peculiar fact. Almost every story in the list was about a child or an aged person.

Somehow it did not just seem possible that a really representative collection could contain stories so limited in characters. I should be the last person to cavil at stories about the very young or the very old. The first story of my own that was ever published was about an old man and I have written many stories about children. But for an entire collection, representing American short stories from many magazines for a whole year, to be only about the two extremes of life did not seem right.

Yet the magazines in the past year have overflowed with such stories. One magazine, for instance, published five stories in an issue, four of which were about children. I have been trying to find a reason why this is so. The only conclusion I can come to is that the modern adult exhibits a frightening complexity of traits caught in a web of appalling circumstances. The very young and the very old are usually harmless. Writers and editors both would like to avoid the kind of adult we have today.

There are still some stories about children in this collection, such as the wonderful assortment of small boys in William Eastlake's "Little Joe," those in Flannery O'Connor's "A Circle in the Fire" and the children in "The Decline and Fall of Augie Sheean," by Joe Coogan.

Speaking of the last story, I would like to point out that it has a religious background. Much religion that has been prominent in magazine fiction the past year should be called religiosity because of its artificial nature. What religion there is in Mr. Coogan's story falls naturally into place as an important part of the story.

One of the rarest kinds of writing in America in recent years is a love story with literary distinction. The slick magazines, of course, publish many stories which are supposed to be about love but are mainly props for illustrations of beautiful girls and handsome men.

This year's collection of *The Best American Short Stories* has more love stories of merit than I ordinarily am able to find. Among them are the excellent study of autumnal passion in "Country Husband," by John Cheever; really and truly young love in "The Day of the Equinox," by Daniel Curley; the nostalgic "Maiden in a Tower," by Wallace Stegner, and "I Got a Friend," by Mark Van Doren.

There is "romance" in "Yore," by Howard Nemerov but the kind of romance it is I shall let the reader find out for himself. For this is a remarkable story of many dimensions.

But short stories should be read instead of talked about. Story-telling may have begun as a communal activity around the campfire or at the well-side, but since the invention of the printing press, it has become more like the act of love. It takes place between two people, the writer and the reader.

I wish to acknowledge the assistance of David Burnett and of Terry Southern. And, as always, to pay tribute to the memory of Edward J. O'Brien, the founder of this series.

MARTHA FOLEY

CONTENTS

(From Prairie Schooner)

A MATTER OF PRICE

BY ROBERT O. BOWEN

AFTER they were through cutting the whole course of pathology samples out of him, and they had got most of the steel out, and the scars were coming all right, they used to bring other doctors, sometimes civilians, into the ward to see Carson's case. Only with him it was not simply a case. It was the man. The new ones always paused at the foot of the iron VA bed and studied him with a drawn, unprofessional pinch at the outer corners of their eyes while Major Kimmel spoke the prefatory, unheard, "This is Doctor So-and-so, Carson, come to look in on your case." The little major had been very patient with him in those days, treating him with deft routine efficiency, not stiff but not particularly bending either.

There had been a time when the major's guests had swung quickly from Carson's look to the clip-boarded charts and safe prognostic gibberish, and he had marked the cowed eyes of each in the examination, and after, propped and motionless, watched their consciously professional backs as they left the ward, chatting as in an unpeopled and painless hall. At each of those early visits he had drawn a pleasure from thrusting toward their second's subjective eyes his protest at their violation of his ruin. He despised in them the same curiosity that fetched clerks and housewives to theatres where they cheaply thrilled at other deaths and agonies in photoed news and called their thrill an interest in the world.

He had not learned this hate in the hospital; rather he had survived there on its strength. He had earned it slowly and at great cost through months of frostbite and combat stench and frozen rations, through ammunition shortages and being those several times cut off completely when confusion had become more total than even he had thought a war could breed. In those months he had learned to enjoy killing. He had killed for two years in the ETO, but it had taken Korea before he enjoyed it. In Europe that element of action had been a numb thing, firing on a target, always *the target*. In his mind he had never recognized it *man,* and with the others in his squad, gabbing, he phrased it *one*. "I got that one." When the war had been over for almost a year, it occurred to him that he had never seen the face or looked closely at the body of a man he had killed. In Europe this idea had not surfaced in him, and when he did think of it later, it seemed an odd quirk of his mind, an evasion to no purpose he could understand.

In Korea the last several men he killed he had watched fall and cease, and once, taking a loner in a little draw, had let him close to within ten yards of his bush so he could get the full kick of smashing the guts out of him. He had not understood this but had wished it, knowing it his reward for enduring the frostbite and the grenade-stiffened elbow and the bitter of his own past-harvest life. It was the look of this that he had turned on the major's neurosurgeon colleagues as they stood defenseless in their curiosity by his bed in the long ward with the nineteen other patients that he had never spoken ten consecutive words to.

He was alone within himself, almost beyond physicality, so lone that he did not resent even the nurse's prodding his depleted butt with needles or the one noticeable ward boy's mumbling about the ward with the adolescent surliness that comes out on some noncombat medics. Since the first weeks, after they had flown him back and got him in a decent hospital, the pain had held him like a tentacled thing, from his head downward through his neck and across the shoulder and swathed along his side and back, tapering out into the right thigh; and in the beginning he had felt, with constant shock at its continuance, the pulse of the pain. Major Kimmel had told him that the pulse was his own, his blood throbbing the damaged nerve at the back of his head, but he had denied this for long, believing the pain to be alien, invading, not of himself. The doctors who had come on the guided tour then had been as part of the pain, a tangible part that he could look his defiance on though he could not harm them, being still in the big cast.

His hate was real enough. He did not simply daydream of attacking them. With a weapon in his hands or with strength enough, he would have killed any of them. Back in the ETO, a long way back, he had seen a black-white difference between soldiering and murder. There he had been even less likely to murder than he would have in college before the war. Until he had got his field commission in Germany, he had been a BAR man, a good one; and in the scramble of rummaging Germans out of town after town, door-by-door and room-by-room, he could have killed officers or anybody else and never been caught up on it. But no.

His sergeant then had been a Bronx Irishman, the political type, loud and beefy and backslapping and shrewdly yellow. Going through towns they had always worked in pairs; and, because Carson had been what they called "dependable," the yellow sergeant had partnered with him, sidling up and saying: "What about you and me, Car?" and tailing him up the road, though it had been an order, not a question. When they had gone through one house, there was always the next. They would break for the front and flatten out, one on each side of the door. Then you had to move fast because the man going in has motion to make him faster, and a German in a room somewhere is a second slow because he's sitting. But if you loaf at the door, the German can get nerved up. The second at the door, between the time you hit the wall outside and the first guy on the team goes in, is very precious. It's your handicap over the German.

The yellow sergeant with the blue eyes and black hair let Carson take the first house. The next was the sergeant's. That was the system. But at the second house, stiff against the wall, the sergeant didn't move. Carson jerked his head toward the door, but the sergeant wouldn't take it. That first time Carson saw in the man's face the yellowness. Not fear only, the simple paleness around the mouth and the dry swallowing. Not only that, but the cornered habitual lack of control over the fear and the recognition of Carson's contempt, but no shame at that, only a touch of a don't-give-a-damn privilege to be yellow behind his stripes. When too much time had passed for them to have cleared the building, a three-story French hotel, the sergeant had got control enough to use his politician's voice again and said casually, "Go ahead, Car," ironically even. There was no argument; it was an order. Carson went. He went again and many times, always at the sergeant's ironic Irish smile, always wishing he could gun him down in some hall or alley.

They were together on the sergeant's buddy-buddy orders through a whole campaign; and through all that Carson thought of killing him, not pondering it really or plotting, but in each high-ported rush into a house wishing it. When he steadied afterward, he always remembered that he was alive because he was dependable and he was dependable because he never let down. To kill the sergeant would be letting down a long way. Once he'd done it, he might take to officers. By then, with the general sloppiness of his technique, he'd be sure to get casual about keeping his butt down, or maybe he'd just quit digging in when they stopped in the dark and the 88's would get him. Carson kept his discipline, and finally, one cold afternoon by a watering trough in a village, the sergeant took two machine-gun slugs in his right thigh. Lying on the litter, he was so blatantly glad to be out of it alive that he giggled and repeated over and over like a kid at Christmas, "Class B, Class B."

Carson had gone on, not so much pleased at having the sergeant unhooked from him but satisfied at his own handling of their relation, his control of himself, proof of his competence. There were bits of style that went into soldiering, the tight circle the muzzle of his BAR always swung in so he could snap a shot off at any point from a start already made in that slight weaving, other touches that a man had to teach himself. But it had been the yellow sergeant that put the polish on Carson's military education in the ETO. Before the sergeant he had been a good armed fighter; after, he was a soldier.

In his high VA bed now with the pain that companied him, he could remember the campaign with that sergeant nostalgically. He recalled sitting against a stable wall one afternoon, waiting for ammo to come up so they could push over a little river and on across the hedge-rowed fields. It had turned warm after a spell of rain, and he sat sunning and smoking for an hour until they moved out. A moment only, of springtime pleasure, but he remembered many like it in that war. It had been a good war, that one, a sensible war with clean issues that you could believe in. It didn't poison a man's insides to want to knock out the Germans and break up the gas chambers. The world had needed it. At the end of that war he had felt proud, not noisy but satisfied, and he had written to his mother simply, "I have fought the good fight, and I have kept the faith."

From his bed, where he looked across the ward through the window and out over the brown hills to the mountains twenty miles away at the state line, he remembered his campaigns, those first sane ones in Europe when he had been young, then the Korean affair. He thought that most of the other guys in the ward were Korea cases, but he did not talk to them. That had not been his kind of a war. Only his own doctor, Major Kimmel, struck him as an ETO soldier, and though he did not allow himself consciously to like the doctor, he did not resent him. He had learned not to be fond of people. That was a point of style. Still, there were other points: you trusted a dependable man.

At sick call the major managed always to see him alone before he left the ward. Nothing buddy-buddy, only a word sometimes, no sympathy, no encouragement about the pain, only the calm questions and the steady cut of his gray eyes, and the nods to Carson's terse answers about the pain, and those not encouraging either. Dependable was what the major could be called. Carson had never been ugly with the major. Even before he realized that to irritate this doctor would let him in for twists of agony when they changed his dressings, even back then he had not stared at him sullenly. He was a pretty good doctor at that. Dried up and thin, wiry, hard. It had been Major Kimmel who told him straight about his case, with no Gray Lady crap. In his own field the major was a very competent soldier. Often now as Carson waited the days past until they released him, he went over that interview with the little major.

He had been two days out of the big cast, technically ambulatory, and was sitting on the bed, dangling his legs to get some strength into them. The surly ward boy, the one who disliked combat men because he was jealous of them and so figured they despised him, the blonde, acned one, came down to his bunk and said: "Get in the chair, Carson. You gotta see Major Kimmel."

"Captain Carson," he said, and the punk echoed it as if he could have got up and wrung it out of him. He groped into the wheelchair, and they moved off, and the pain sawtoothed and peaked each time the medic accelerated the chair or swung it hard on a turn in the terrazzoed, institutional corridors, and through the pain

Carson thought of a time when his strength would fill back, and he did not complain. In the dressing room, waiting for the major, he watched the ivoried door in front of him and flexed his hands and counted the pain down silently with that mental trick the major had taught him, focussing on his tally to lull the shoulder and side and today the arm. Across the room at the glazed instrument cabinet the surly medic asked him something that he let slide unrecognized beyond his count. The medic repeated it in his adolescent superiority, but Carson held on, . . . "twenty-three, twenty-four, twenty-five . . ."

The medic came over to the wheelchair to yell whatever he had asked, and he got out, "When I . . ." Then the major pushed open the door, checking him. Carson lost count.

"You can go," the major said over Carson's head to the medic.

From the other side, the medic, "Shall I wait outside, sir?"

"Go back to your ward."

Carson flexed his hands and watched the open door. He never looked up at talk that wasn't his, and he spoke only to answer questions. The door closed behind the medic, and alone with the major he stopped flexing his hands.

"Turn around, Carson."

He labored the chair around, very weak still, and faced the major on the white stool by the washbowl. He was in suntans as always, his tie tucked in like a soldier's and his face lined as if weathered though he never seemed to leave the actual hospital building to sniff air, let alone get marked by it.

"Carson, you've never asked me anything about your case. You listen when I talk to you, but never ask a question. Do you realize that?"

The remarkable thing about the major was that his expression never changed. Looking at him, Carson wondered whether it had been this that checked him from staring him down as he had the others. They'd been soft for a second, vulnerable in their gawking, and he'd gotten to them. None of that stupidity had ever come out on the major, and he didn't slide off behind any GI bedside manner. He was himself, alert, alive, uncallused, but tough. Yes, Carson thought, it's maybe the toughness. He looks at a thing head-on so he can see it. The others skulk around being clever, or they gush, but they never see anything the way it really stands.

"Why haven't you asked, Carson?" curious, non-professional.

"What d'you tell a guy like me?" looking up at the major. "When I first came here, you explained how close I was to it. 'A good sneeze,' you said; one good sneeze would shake my head apart and I'd be done."

"You don't like doctors?"

He worried the question a moment. "It's not the profession, Major. I'm tired. I hurt. I was worn out before I got this." He jerked his hand awkwardly toward the shoulder and head. "You know how tired I am."

The major nodded.

"I want rest, peace. You know how I relax. You write the orders. They knock me out in there three hours a night. It helps, but it's not rest. It's just a blackout. I don't exist in it."

On the stool a few feet away the major leaned with his forearms on his knees and looked steadily into Carson's face. "Carson," his voice was very low, as it was with those little questions he asked each sick call and didn't write any notes on. "I told you when we first patched you up how badly you were hit. That was so you'd be careful and not kill yourself falling out of bed or getting hysterical about your pain."

He reached some Chesterfields out of his shirt pocket but seemed to change his mind and offered them to Carson instead of taking one himself. When Carson got lit up, he went on, "The only difference between you now and when you came in here is that a bump won't damage you much now. Otherwise you're almost as bad off."

Carson looked a question but didn't speak.

"It's not a particularly rare case as these things go. Unusual that they got you to a hospital intact, but not a rarity. I've told you enough about it in the ward, the nerve damage and the other. Would you like me to go over the records with you?"

Carson puffed the cigarette. "I wouldn't understand the technical stuff anyway, Major."

"Well, it's unusual in a case of this type to get the patient healed at all. You're the first I've had that lived more than nine days." He stopped.

"It's better than two months." Carson raised his eyebrows for corroboration on what he was thinking, but the major gave him nothing back to that.

"I don't know whether the two months are lucky or not. The

condition is degenerative. It's advancing now. The pain aggravates it. It keeps you exhausted. The drugs push it along that much faster. As I told you, it's rare that you're alive this long, but the condition isn't rare. Any neuro-surgeon would confirm my diagnosis. I'll get others for you. The ones who've come in to see you have more or less accepted my diagnosis without any real examination."

"Yeah." Carson reached out with the cigarette butt, and the major said: "Throw it in the sink."

"The thing is, Carson, you don't have very much time. I don't know how much yet. Several years, possibly only a year." He slid the cigarettes out again and this time lit one for himself as well as Carson.

They smoked, and in the wheelchair Carson's face did not change. He sat patiently, unshocked at the death he had foreknown. Beneath his listening he felt himself a part of death already, like any combat soldier who knows grief but not the lamentation of a workaday world where men die seldom, die then in age or ill, rarely in strength as soldiers always do, leaving comrades but neither kin nor home, having lost them already miles, months, and lifetimes back. Like that he knew death, had not time enough and life since the Korean hills to unlearn, perhaps undesire it. In the major's low, clipped tone he heard it not as a sentence but as an old soldier takes a briefing on a patrol, not that each patrol is death but that the total is, and each is a part; and in times of steady combat, when all go early to it, death seems past and not future, already accumulated and waiting issue like one's pay. Carson had rated it so long that he simply marked it down as an incidental in the plotted advance of the condition building it. A problem of logistics, one expendable immortal soul to be replaced by issue.

The major went on in that personal but not familiar tone, explaining the tests he wanted to run, the series of pathology samples spanned over the months so he could gauge the rate of degeneration and estimate the time. He glossed over a possible recovery as too rare to hope on. His last point was simple. The lobotomy. It was optional.

"Actually," he said, "none of us know what pain is like to someone else. I have a reasonable idea of what you feel, but that's a guess. If the condition goes beyond your endurance, we can do the lobotomy. It won't stop the pain, but it will cut off the part of your mind that the pain troubles. You'll feel easier because your worry will be cut off. It's a matter of how much you want to pay to control the pain."

Carson flexed his hands very slowly on his lap. "You said it was a kind of mental castration."

"That's the simplest way to describe it."

"What about the other? Cutting lower down so I can't feel?"

"We can do that. You'll have an arm and a leg that you won't feel at all. If you lay your hand on a stove, it can burn to the bone and you won't know it unless you smell it. The pain in your head, that can't be cut out."

There in the tile-sterile dressing room, in the wheelchair with his hospital gown tucked around his sick-bony frame, Carson had a flickered memory of that last Chinese he had killed: the quilted field-coat and brown face with the eyes shut and the mouth hardly open as he slid sideways at the burst from the BAR. There had been something very clean about that, complete. Less a job than a pleasure, that one, but a very efficient piece of workmanship anyway.

"Think about it," the major said. "If you get troubled, I'll talk to you." He got up and slid the white stool back in the corner by the sink and stood there a minute, saying what he'd held back. "About the lobotomy. It'll help in one way, but I can assure you that it'll make you careless about a lot of things. No philosophy, no moralizing. You won't care much what people think any longer." He caught Carson's eyes. "If I were you, nothing would make me request the lobotomy."

He had wheeled Carson back to the ward silently, not helping him into the bed, just giving him a tight-lipped nod and turning on his heel.

That had all been months ago, and the tests were run and the "guesswork," as the major called it, tallied up. Carson had about four years. He had the pain, of course; there were four years of that. He could get it out of his mind if he wanted, cut the wires to the frontal lobes and have . . . what? Not rest, more like as tired and not able to care. Not peace of mind, have in a way none of the good of mind. Be like an old, blind, and asthmatic dog, too gone to live, too animal to know it. Through the long nights until his shot at three each morning he learned to weigh it all, looking at each dawn to come as the lingering dawn that had fetched to him behind an overturned jeep the shell that maimed him, recalling the slow clenching of hate in those months before, and the encumbering weariness that leached through him, striated beyond physicality; and often in the long pain-pulsing hours, among the sleeping patients to whom he never spoke or even turned aside, he felt that he recalled in the falling face of that last Chinese a great and lasting peace.

The Korean thing had not been a war that he could take pride in or find order in. The shortage of experienced infantry officers out there and his old field commission had guaranteed him his captaincy, but there had been little pleasure in the bars. There seemed nothing behind him as there had been in Europe, and no real object in front. They killed gooks and they helped gooks. He had not liked World War II for itself, but it had been needful to wipe out the Nazis, and after it, back in the States, when he saw how the fast bucks had been handled, he had not soured on his belief in an ideal in that war. In Korea he had no such constancy. The Commies he could feel as a proper enemy, but the field was never clearly sided. He located nothing that he could stretch into decency in Rhee's mob. From what he saw of that he got the same impression the yellow sergeant in Europe gave. Rotten to the bone and beyond giving a damn for the contempt of a whole world. The Commies up north were bad, but they weren't Nazi-bad so far as he could judge, and he felt no deep faith in the rightness of his fighting them. Rhee's people questioned prisoners with gun butts too, and left them often in a Commie peace, dead. Carson felt lost among it all, killing and dying purposelessly, evilly.

The various contingents that he touched confused him. On one ridge his company had shared holes with some Turks, and once a slender Turk corporal had shown him with mimetic explanation a trophy. A tobacco pouch crudely worked from the flayed hide of a North Korean. Carson had been too long at war to be repelled physically; but after, as he looked out over the frozen valley to the Commie lines beyond, he thought on that drying skin, seeing in it, beyond the simple proof of killing, a more subtle Turkish pleasure in cutting off the flesh and barrening the land. He remembered now the confusion of that winter after Yalu, among the polyglot packs that roamed the iron earth and as often killed South as North Koreans and were not above ambushing a quartermaster truck in their scavenging. In those months the wrinkled brown leather that the Turk had secreted within his blouse came to be a symbol of the fight to Carson: the end of ordered future. A real war forced order, was fought for that purpose; this marred it in anything it touched.

He had known in Korea, among survivors of those early days, many who were skilled killers, black, white, and brown, men with the hardness to squat on raw earth and eat frozen rations without turning their lean backs on those they had killed in the same hollow; men who endured pain and privation and despair, whose flesh would knit without rest or warmth or a full belly; men from whom all the honor and the pride and purpose that a war is fought for were shorn; godless men whose real hate was turned, not forward against the brown peasants that they shot or stabbed or trapped with mortars, but back toward the white Christmas-card churches and the thoughtless home-people that leched and marketed and bitched at taxes and offered neither ammo nor ideal to an unrelieved and weary mob on the Korean peninsula, to the armed victims caught in a shifting rush of pure attrition from which all must suffer, none gain. Hard men in a hard land, and he among them.

In his VA bed, months from it, but never to unhitch himself from the pain it taught him, Carson lay silently from day to day, brooding out over the hills his window framed, and wondering always whether the spawn of that winter's chaos would multiply itself, or whether, like the Turk's tobacco pouch, it would one time come to be a curio to men, harmless of reprisal, abstracted from the past and dried of living warmth and pain, resting, almost forgot, in an enduring calm. A time when men might cease to kill, when men might think and war be a matter for scholars only. A dream which a wise and tired man could meditate without the need of hoping.

As his last days in the hospital checked off and his weight bulked out his uniform, Carson lost the look he had once turned on those doctors who drifted in to study Major Kimmel's case and paused that human moment to see the face of the man. Now, in the mirror as he shaved, it was an old face, gray-templed, with fixed lines creased deep around the eyes and across the forehead, heavy-featured but almost gentle with fatigue. Now, too, these final days, the major's friends did not turn from the eyes. They were not embarrassed, touched, puzzled. They were like city-bred hunters scanning a slope on which an antlered buck stands clear, and stands unseen.

On the morning of Carson's discharge, the major walked with him down the long drive to the cab at the gate, slowly but like two well men, for it was not the flesh but the nerves that withered within Carson. They walked pleasantly through the May sunshine and the breeze from the wooded valley below on the left. The hills were green now, and far back toward the mountains moist air dimmed the ridges, softening them. Carson and the major smoked a cigarette together in silence at the gate, and across the road the cabby slouched impatiently against a fender.

The major tossed his cigarette out on the cropped grass, watched it smolder out from dew, and swung back to speak. "Carson, I appreciate your decision against the lobotomy."

"Yeah." He measured the hills slowly. They had been his view for most of a year, and he had watched them come alive this spring. "I can handle the pain all right now." He put out his hand and, as the major took it, said: "That cutting wouldn't be the right thing for me."

"Yes." The major's gray eyes were hard and steady as always. "Pain isn't the worst thing in the world." Then abruptly, "Good luck to you, Carson."

They left it at that, and Carson crossed the road.

(From Mademoiselle)

THE EXCURSIONISTS

BY NANCY CARDOZO

THE *MAN* and the woman stand at the rail of the ship. The wind that blows upriver whips her silk scarf against his cheek. His coattails flap against his legs. He holds his brown hat crushed to his chest. The woman's short auburn hair blows across her forehead. Shoulder against shoulder, hip to hip, through layers of tweed and cloth, they are together among the crowds on deck.

"I don't believe it," says the man. "You're not leaving. It's all a mistake—a dream."

The woman slips her hand into his pocket and grips his fingers. Her small white face, lifted toward his, is twisted, crinkled as if she would laugh or cry. No, she is not really leaving him. They are leaving each other. But it is too difficult to explain this, what with the clamor of voices and machinery and the wind in the ears like the sound of blood itself. It is easier not to speak. Any moment now (the desire to pull at his sleeve and look at the watch she had given him on his birthday is almost too much), any moment now the bells will ring and he will be gone, back on the pier, and she will be here still, and alone. "Oh, why, Natalie?" he says. "I will miss you so."

Natalie clenches her fist inside of Willard's pocket. If only the bells would ring now. Of all common, familiar occurrences good-bys are the most trying. She is drained, exhausted, as if she has been explaining her departure forever.

"Cable as soon as you get to Southampton," Willard is saying against the top of her head. "I want to know the moment you're settled, especially in a place I've been in too. You'll love Florence."

Beside them, three women dressed in black like somber birds are weeping and embracing each other. "Oh, my, darling," Willard shouts into her ear.

She will not say good-by at all. She is not responsible for all this pain. "I remembered the dictionary," she shouts at him, "but your Baedeker is still in my desk. If you go to the apartment sometime you might ask them to give it to you—second drawer on the right."

"I'll hardly need it now. Besides it might be indiscreet. . . ." He does not smile. The bells are ringing. The crowd pushes, jostles. They meet in a rough, untidy embrace. In a few minutes he is going down the gangplank. There is the back of his narrow blond head, a little taller than the others. Now he is on the pier, his face lifted searchingly till he finds her again. They wave at each other. He moves his lips, saying something she cannot understand. She throws her hands up helplessly, pulls her scarf off and lets the wind catch it. He has put his hat on. Now he turns away. Perhaps he is crying. There is a feather of pink confetti around his neck. The moments are endless, almost grotesque but still so familiar. Even now she could change her mind and stay with him. But look—they have wheeled the gangplanks away. In the lounge on A deck the ship's band is playing the "Londonderry Air."

In the peach-colored stateroom Natalie lies on her bed, her feet, black suede pumps slipped off, propped on a hatbox. Silently after all the ship and the shore are parted. Willard's face has become part of the white face of the crowd on the pier and then the pier becomes part of the shadow under the serrate towers of the city; and that too dwindles away into the past.

All around her now suitcases, flowers, books in colored wrappings wait like offerings in a tomb. Tears run from the corners of her eyes and spread coldly among the roots of her hair.

Still it was her own decision to visit her cousins in London this spring and see those parts of southern Europe she had not seen before. And why not, everyone agreed enviously—while one was free, before another catastrophe. At the last even Willard urged her to go for her own sake. She can imagine him headed cross-town for the office in a cab, his large torso edged forward on the seat, cursing the traffic, thinking of the morning mail unattended. Natalie moves her head against the stiff, ribbed bedspread. Silly. He must be long since out of the cab, up in the elevator, past Miss Wiley's desk and the other offices. Still for her he is transfixed in the cab, his back turned, going away from her forever. The cold air of distance seems to blow on her wet cheeks.

She remembers how after the Christmas holidays she waited with her father in the very early morning for the train that would take her back to school in Boston. The giant locomotives hissed and sent white, impersonal flags of steam out into the frozen world. The two of them, she in tan woolen stockings and blue reefer, he muffled in a green scarf, stood, not talking, stamping their feet on the drab, splintery board of the platform to rouse the blood, while the winter sun burst fool's gold over the black backs of the coaches in the yards. Finally her train slid into the station and the conductor whooped like a bird in the thin air. It was time to say good-by. She lifted her face for his kiss. There was the rough, cold stubble on his cheek. Upsy-daisy! Her father lifted her, bag and all, onto the steps of the coach. Settled in the green plush seat, she pressed her face against the cold-smelling windowpane to watch him walk back to the car, his figure sparse as the leafless landscape seen through the tears of soot on the glass. Did he miss her? There was no telling. What was it he always said when she dreaded leaving him (or had it been when she was only five and her mother had died)? All things in life must end—the good as well as the bad. The words and the sorrow in his face struck terror in her again and again, and even now, remembering his small, stiff figure, the flimsy yellow station house behind the moving windowpane, blurred by tears as if a face gigantic as the sky were weeping there.

Twenty years ago—but no matter how old one was, no matter how many partings one had endured (and she had endured plenty), farewells were all unbearable. Was all of life then a monumental work of leave-taking? . . . Out in the passageway there are footsteps hurrying, a woman's laughter. The trip has begun.

And what of those farewells that are not partings in reality but only flights of the spirit, when it turns away fearfully? Now, hearing the voices dwindling down the passageway, Natalie remembers that summer in Mexico twelve years ago.

It is difficult to recall our appearance in youth. We are not familiar with our faces then. Mirrors, friends and lovers cannot be trusted. We seek an image that does not yet exist. That summer, when she was eighteen, it is certain that she wore her reddish hair long and caught up in a ridiculous blue elastic snood. It was heavy on her neck, but because Carlos liked it that way, to please him she did not cut it despite the heat. She had a rather Grecian profile, sloping shoulders, a small waist, long, thin hands and feet.

"*Rubia,*" the Mexicans whispered, staring at her in the street; "*Gringo,*" the soft voices called from the black interiors of shops, from the ornate caves of doorways, from white balconies as she passed; from benches under the palms in the Zócalo, from the darkness behind the stalls in the market that smelled of bruised leaves and decayed flesh. She blushed and lowered her head beneath the weight of shining hair. She swung her market basket in one hand and with the other clutched her tooled leather purse to her breast. She was too tall, too pale in the merciless light and dark of that city. The soft voices, whether obscene or kind, embarrassed her, but she was not afraid of them. She moved holding the hand of a guardian angel, as it were, along these streets with memorable names, because then always there was Carlos. For him she picked over the pink and gold and spoiling fruits in the market, walked dreaming from one plaza to another to meet his friends, waited beside dry fountains where the plane trees and acacias sang in verdure overhead, sat at the mouths of cathedrals next to the beggars and the beggars' milky-eyed children.

All week long Carlos worked in his studio on his mammoth, brilliant canvases, and she ran errands, studied Spanish or wandered through museums and slept away the dizzying white afternoons until the rain, regular as hunger, beat on the tin roof of their flat. Sundays were their holidays. They would go on an excursion, to the pyramids or Taxco—or take a picnic out to the lake. But they would never go alone. There were Ignacio, the Catalan musician; his friend Anita, the dancer; Simon, the English boy—and sometimes Suzy, the little French milliner, and the schoolteacher from Nevada, Margaret Smith, and others, Ramon, the novelist, Bloch. They were mostly expatriates, like Carlos, who had been born Charles Neilsen in Los Angeles, and exiles and refugees. Every evening four or five of them would sit in the Café del Chino drinking chocolate or bitter coffee, while she gazed sleepily at their faces, bemused by the strange accents, and held Carlos' hand beneath the zinc-topped table. Later they would walk homeward along the Reforma, the men dark, attenuated figures ahead, the women lagging, gossiping under the moving dark of the sky. Everything she and Carlos did was shared by these others, who clung together, it seemed, with the rapacity of the homeless and uprooted. She rarely complained. Spellbound, she moved through all their days and nights.

Was it love that put a trance upon those months when she lived with Carlos in Mexico? First love, with its great powers of transformation, gave the present the stature of the past, larger than life. Then she seemed to move against a splendid landscape. The arch of the sky above the outskirts of the city, with cumulus clouds raising angelic monuments behind the mountains, was higher than any sky ever seen and toward evening was as intensely blue as the backgrounds of those religious images in the smaller churches. The canal they walked beside some nights shone amber where the jewel of the watchman's lantern touched it; rivers tumbled gloriously down the ravines, lakes dreamed beneath the breasts of strange waterfowl, the purple of bougainvillaea about the windows was as moving as the sight of blood. Love created its own beautiful scenery.

But it had been illusory. It could not last. Natalie opens her eyes. Above is the dull pink ceiling, the grille of the ventilator. She is aware for the first time of the vibrations, undeviating, of the engines, the pulse of the ship, which for all she can tell without benefit of landmark or horizon might be carrying her forward or backward or not at all. Looking back, it seems as if she had known from the beginning that summer ends and the tourist boards the train. Natalie raises her head on her arms as though telling Willard a story.

That Sunday morning long ago in Mexico a dove in gray walked on the sill of their window. The breakfast rolls were stale, the mangoes bitter. Carlos made a joke of everything. But she raved at him, saying he did not really love her. How could she marry him, trust him? She wept when he tried to embrace her. Only his paintings and his friends were important, she said; he ignored her half the time; they were never alone. As if in proof the bell rang before she was dressed. The morning was ablaze with light and other people's laughter. The picnic at Maximilian's palace was Anita's idea. "But you must see it, darlings." She clapped her hands for attention. "It is so romantic!"

Natalie, lying so still talking to the air in her cabin, remembers just how the camion to Cuernavaca skirted the flanks of the hills in clouds of dust and leaves. The bus was a small boat on an ocean of earth, carried on as much by the current and prevailing wind across the blue-covered landscape as by any skill or intention of the driver, who sang while he pretended to swing the wheel around precipitous curves. The passengers, mostly Mexicans, ranged on the wooden benches swayed resignedly, as if with the rocking of the sea, and gripped the floor with dusty bare feet. In their skirts and in the folds of their rebozos the women carried fowl with loose, stringy necks, melons, handfuls of grain. Behind their watchful faces, now the blue sky, now green and umber tapestried hillsides showed in the windows.

"Mira!" said Carlos. "The orchids!" He tapped the glass behind Natalie's head. *Mira,* look, they were always saying to each other; do you see what I see, do you feel as I feel?

She turned. The topmost fronds of evergreens descended in shaggy ranks the side of a gorge. Here and there, like dull stars in the crotches of branches, she saw the pale green flowers.

"The beautiful parasites," said Carlos. His breath moved harshly in her ear. The next moment the bus hurled itself down the mountain road, the festooned trees vanished and they were being tossed across a green mirage of a valley. Natalie reached for his hand, ruddy and large for a painter, with golden hairs at the knuckles. (If it had not been for his red hair and beard he would be more Mexican than the Mexicans. They called him "*Huero.*") "Ah," Carlos kissed her neck, "so you're not angry any more."

On the opposite bench Ignacio was winking at them above the picnic basket balanced on his knees. He held the lid down with his chin and his round brown face shone under his black beret with an approval that was at once benign and lascivious. Beside him, Anita, regal in the voluminous brown skirt and black shawl she affected, sat with her eyes closed, her beautiful dancer's ankles showing and her strong white feet in leather sandals pointed firmly outward.

The other members of their party, Suzy, Margaret and Simon, were seated at the rear of the bus. Simon, who was only nineteen, had fought in Ignacio's battalion in the Spanish war. He had a thin, white, uneven face and a great shock of brown hair.

They seemed more vivid than usual, perhaps by contrast with the dark, quiet Indian faces around them. What an odd assortment of friends they were, together as much by circumstance as by choice—strangers in a strange country. And none of them drifters but driven by some other purpose (she herself, after her father's death, had managed to see France and England and the Far West, where she had met Carlos). Natalie felt a pang of compassion and exchanged weary smiles with the little blond French milliner. She wondered if her nose was shining. Her yellow dress was wilted already; the bottles of beer that Carlos carried wrapped in towels and bathing suits must be warm by now.

Outside of Cuernavaca, on the road of the Tres Marias, the brakes screamed and the bus stopped lurchingly. Two boys in white, who apparently had been clinging to the rear, ran past, their foreheads bandaged, their black hair upright in the wind. The driver shouted and shook his fist at them. They leaped, one, two, over a crumbling stucco wall and disappeared. A tattered poster flew up, waved desultorily after them and fell again in the roadside weeds—the head of a bull.

"We're almost there," whispered Carlos. His eyes, pale blue, the irises rimmed with black, met hers secretly, eagerly, as if they were going to make love, as if they alone were to visit the ruins of the palace where those other lovers, Maximilian, emperor and exile, and his mad Carlota, had waited briefly for their awful, half-foreseen parting.

The gray and pink ruin of the summer palace, scabrous with white lichens and the droppings of doves, as they approached it that afternoon down a long promenade rank with weed and briar and neglected cypress, seemed the recreation of all the ruined castles of the mind: Avalon, Sleeping Beauty, the lost Atlantis (and indeed, sea-shell-hued, it seemed as if it had been washed up on the central plain of Mexico and then abandoned). Natalie felt she might recognize the doorways along the galleries and the views from every window—yet how little of it remained after less than a hundred years in a country where the stones of antiquity were present. The desecrators, the heedless children of countless excursions had carried out time's despoilment. It was a home of scorpions and bats. A vulture circled high overhead as they left the bus and straggled across the grounds.

As if she flew with him, Natalie can imagine how they looked. Suzy held her wide straw hat down on her bangs against the breeze that had crept unwanted into the picture. Simon swung his walking stick into a swarm of gnats that hovered above his head like a gauze halo. Anita's brown skirt looped and belled as she strode beside Ignacio, who was almost running to keep up with her. His white sneakers flashed in the sunlight. Margaret read the guidebook aloud. But no one listened. Carlos and she, in her yellow dress, pulling back on his arm, lagged behind the others. "*Mira!*" Carlos murmured, pointing at the bird. "*El zopilote!*" Natalie shivered.

They avoided the palace itself. The obscenities scratched on the walls, the papers and shards of fruit and the smell of desecration were too repellent. "We will go to the waterfall," said Ignacio. "*Vámonos.*"

He and Anita, arms linked, led the way along the maze of paths. On either hand groups of feathery acacias silvered the light. In the vestiges of the formal gardens lovers lay together, families ate and slept. Children rolled in the grass along the crumbled terraces. The lizards flicked like drops of water running away. Above them all the Mexican sky brooded like an azure bird and in the west the convoluted clouds moved ominously closer.

"Wait," said Natalie. "Please, Carlos, let them go on without us. Listen! Do you hear?"

The sound was more liquid than the blowing of leaves in the rising wind. "The waterfall? It's artificial, you know," said Carlos. "Maximilian was copying a baroque nightmare of Europe. Homesick, I guess. It's a pathetic place in a way. He called it El Olvido."

"El Olvido," she echoed. "The place of forgetfulness."

Carlos set the bundle of towels on the grass and took her in his arms. "Funny girl. Look at me. Why are you always on the verge of flight—my little wild bird?" The roar of the wind and the waterfall rushes over them. Don't ever leave me, don't ever leave me. Which of them had spoken?

If she had stayed, if she had married Carlos as he had begged? The otherwise of life stands in the cabin with her, sweet, tantalizing, as if a thrush or nightingale had sung of the meaning of love to them in the ruined garden that afternoon. Natalie swings her legs over the edge of the bed and sits up, a little dizzy. She should go up to the bar for a drink, find someone to talk to. Someday she would write Willard about that summer. From a pension, perhaps on a hill above Florence. She would explain how chance sent one onward through recurrent cycles of experience.

She remembers how her heart beat, as if in fear, as she clung to Carlos. She must tell him yes or no. If only something, some sign would tell her what to do. But at that moment Simon came crashing through the grove, brandishing his stick. They broke apart. He stopped a little way off and stared at them like a sheepish child, with a bunch of violets in his hand.

Natalie was relieved by his intrusion. She took the flowers from him and hid her face in them. They had the secret odor of water. "They must make you think of England," she said.

Simon shrugged his shoulders. "We've found a place to eat. Very bucolic, I'd say."

They followed him between the trees. "When I was home from school," Simon continued, "we used to go on the most god-awful picnics, all of us, two brothers and three sisters and innumerable aunts and uncles. Piles of biscuits and jam and always some calamity —wasps or someone falling out of a boat."

Natalie thought of the pastures above Lowell—"And nothing but brambles and stone walls. And we'd come home with burrs in our stockings and spend hours on the back porch taking them out of the dogs. I guess picnics everywhere are much alike. Only this, I think, is different."

Carlos, who hated reminiscences, began to sing "Guadalajara" in a loud, sweet tenor, imitating the quavers of the *mariachi*. Simon decapitated a daisy with his stick.

Natalie wondered what would become of him. They stood on the edge of a brown stream. Just above, on some flat black rocks that overhung the falls, Suzy and Margaret were unfolding a white tablecloth, waving it like a flag in the dappled sunlight.

"Oh, there you are," Margaret called down. "We thought you were lost."

"We did not," said Suzy slyly.

Carlos and Simon went on downstream to find the pool where Ignacio wanted to swim. Natalie climbed up to the rock. Suzy opened her arms, extending the palms of her hands, lifting her pretty monkey face to the light that drifted like leaves through the leaves of the willows. "Is it not beautiful?" But even as they unpacked the picnic the quality of the light was changing. It wove in and out unsteadily. The clouds had come over earlier than usual. The trees were feverish in the wind.

Natalie was shivering again. She helped Suzy unwrap the tortillas and the cold sausage. Margaret sliced a pineapple, wielding Ignacio's bone-handled knife with the same precision with which she must have pointed the ruler at the blackboard or placed the pencil correctly in the small pink fist of a pupil. In that archaic setting Margaret, in tweed suit and dusty leather brogues, looked quite out of place, and Natalie, watching her, thought how out of place they all were, spreading their picnic on the safe island of rock.

From below the falls came the hubbub of the men bathing in some hidden pool. Suzy looked uneasily at the changing sky. "How can they bear to swim?" she asked, hugging herself and grimacing so that she looked more than ever like a bleached monkey.

The three of them crept to the edge of the rock and leaned over. The water, falling in black and silver ropes, was ice to touch. Directly beneath them the beer bottles set to cool glinted in the spray like stationary goldfish. Beyond, through willows turned yellow by the ominous light, the naked figures of the men were now visible, now hidden, pink, brown and white, wet marble in motion. Once, in the center of the pool, Natalie saw Carlos' head and his red beard floating out from his chin.

"Ignacio cannot swim," said Suzy. "Therefore he makes, like a walrus, a great noise to distract everyone." They giggled.

"Those funny white behinds," said Margaret. "Like little boys."

"For shame!!" cried Anita, coming up behind them. "Like three little girls." Her skirt was filled with oak leaves. She sat down and began to weave them into a crown as another woman might take up her knitting.

"Oh, I want to do that too," said Natalie.

"Help yourself." Anita did not look up. "Make a crown for your love."

They sat waiting for the men to come and eat, threading the juicy stems in and out as each of them had learned to do when they were children in different places. The milliner's fingers were the most deft. *"Une jolie petite cloche."* She placed the green cap on Margaret's rough gray curls. Margaret was humming softly to herself—what was the tune? "Just like a tree that's standing by the water, we shall not be moved." But even now above their heads the sky was moving, evil clouds tore across. The men's voices were drowned out. A bird shrieked from the ruins.

"I wish they would hurry," said Natalie.

"It's going to pour," said Margaret. But still they sat there waiting.

Huge drops of rain fell singly upon their heads, chilled their bare arms—then rattled on stone and water. The thunder enfolded them in panic. Natalie stood up and called, "Carlos! Carlos!" Nothing answered.

The four women threw the food all helter-skelter into the baskets and gathered it up in the tablecloth as in a giant kerchief, and, each holding a corner, scrambled, shrieking, laughing, down the rocks, along the narrow footpaths, among flying trees, while the rain dragged their wet clothing heavy as metal around their limbs. All over the darkened grounds, seen through a screen of water, other figures were running, bent beneath the blows of the wind under the black, crusted sky. They found shelter on a porch of the palace.

A few minutes later the men climbed up across the terraces, their intent faces illuminated by tremors of lightning. Simon limped behind. What violences out of the past or future were contained for him in the storm? Ignacio ran about the porch, spreading garments to dry, trying to salvage the food, as if he would save their foundered picnic. Carlos stood just under the eave, head back—triumphant. He reveled in the fury and the noise.

Natalie went to him and pressed her head against his shoulder like a child seeking consolation. His flesh was warm through the wet cotton shirt. He did not put his arm around her—he did not speak. He seemed unaware of her presence but watched the storm through the gray arch with an artist's self-conscious concentration. Natalie understood. This was the sign she had waited for. She could not marry him. She stood apart from him and, all alone, saw the storm drive itself out, the clouds lift and rend like worn flags revealing an utter void, and knew in her heart that this was not her place, that the end was beginning and she must say good-by to Carlos before it was too late.

Slowly they made their way out of the grounds under that empty sky. They moved like waders in the sea, weighed down as much by weariness as by their sodden clothes. Carlos took her arm but Natalie shrugged his hand away. What a pathetic, ragged band they seemed now against the impervious landscape.

By the time they reached the road of the Tres Marias, where eventually the bus would come along to take them back to Mexico City, she was on the verge of tears. She sat down on the wooden bench and covered her face with her hands. She heard the others making plans for an outing the following Sunday. They would take her to Xochimilco, where every tourist must go. But already she was saying good-by in a way, seeing herself in Carlos' room packing her cotton dresses, her good silk, the few pieces of silver and semi-precious stones he had bought her, a sketch of her head, the bowl from Oaxaca, her dictionary and books. Even then, while the others complained, impatiently swinging their arms and jigging on the dirt road to keep warm as night came on, even then it was as if she were in the station and the wheels of the train that would take her away from Carlos were shaking her.

Natalie reaches for her pocketbook. She will go up to the lounge, but first she must fix her face. One never knows whom one might meet. And she must see that Willard's flowers get put in water. They are roses, red ones. Is he thinking of her now? Does he miss her, and for how long? Two months, perhaps, for Willard is young, and by the time she returns with a dress from Paris, Venetian glass, perfume and some anecdotes, he will have someone else. It is inevitable. It has all happened before.

Natalie snaps her compact shut on the image of her crimson lips. And meanwhile she must be the traveler who cannot be made quite welcome, or easily loved, requiring too much, longing still.

She goes to the porthole and pulls open the flimsy plastic blind. The room is flooded with an exquisite cold blue light. The ocean is, in the porthole, the blind eye of the future, unknown, unknowing, from which there is no escape.

(*From The University of Kansas City Review*)

BACHELOR OF ARTS

BY NANCY G. CHAIKIN

FROM the window of her dormitory room, Anne Lupoff could see across to the windows of the faculty offices in Mackey Hall, those little cubicles of light and dark that even in the nighttime smelled comfortably of tobacco and old books. She had got into the habit of looking across every night, as she sat at her desk, to see whether Russell Slater was working late; and now, on the night before graduation, she noted, with a sudden electric shock at her stomach, that the light was on in his office. She had promised herself that she would not go through the foolishness of trying to see him that night, that her eagerness was all out of proportion to what she had a right to expect from him—that there was, in fact, nothing to expect. But as surely as she had resolved and known, even while she was doing it, that she was deceiving herself, she felt now the old, strong impulse driving over her; it was the last night, the very last night. Slowly she turned from the window and took the pins out of her hair, walking toward the dresser where she had left her comb. It had been a simple, if fond, professor-student relationship—absolutely nothing more. But now the comb was racing through her hair, and her heart was beating audibly, and she was thinking, "What if he leaves before I get there, what if he leaves, what if he leaves?"

The final, irrevocable, beautiful, warm spring night on this campus. The air flowed softly around her head as she left the dormitory, and there was the slightest sound of it in the trees; and over in the bell tower, a darkening shaft against the late spring sky, the carillonist was playing "Gaudeamus Igitur." She looked up again at the office window—she knew so well which one, counting from left to right until she hit number four—the light was still there, all alone, surrounded on either side by long dark rectangles, the windows of deserted rooms. The others had all gone home—indeed, there was no reason for anyone to be there now; the grades were in, most of the students had left. Why should Russell be working at night in his office? Perhaps he knew, perhaps he had known all along that she would have to come; perhaps that was why he had said nothing, not a word, up to now.

The elevator was closed down for the night and she walked the two flights of stairs slowly, hearing the echo of her footsteps carrying hollowly into the halls, thinking that maybe he could hear them too, there in his office—would know that it was she, and smile to himself, that strange reluctant half smile that did not quite close his small dark eyes. But when she reached his office there was no sign that he had expected her. His head was bent over some papers—familiar, ugly, balding head that inclined itself to one side when he lectured—and his chair creaked back and forth, back and forth as he read. She knew that she could have stood there for some time while he read, could even have turned and left and he would not have noticed. But, having done the foolish, childish, inevitable thing, she wanted it now to be inescapable. So she stood there only for several seconds before she made the final, efficient, deliberate sounds which would give her away. It was silly—as silly as a grammar school adolescent waiting around the corner for her crush—but she was too close to the end of it to care how it looked, what he would think or had been thinking. She wanted only to know whether he welcomed it, whether there was anything there at all.

At last he looked up, and smiled the smile she had imagined, predicted, craved. At last the head came up from the papers, the eyes half closed, and the large dry lips said quietly, "Please come in."

"I can't imagine why you're working tonight," she said, annoyed with herself because, as usual, the words came out flippant, intrusive —not gentle, and softly sympathetic, as she had wanted them to sound. "Everyone else has gone home."

"Everyone else has less to do," he said, offering her a cigarette across the desk, then leaning back and waiting for her to speak.

She shifted uncomfortably in the chair she had taken automatically, and wondered what on earth, what in the name of heaven she could possibly say now that would make sense. In a panic of foolishness, she realized that there wasn't anything at all.

"Out late tonight, aren't you?" he said.

"It doesn't matter the night before graduation—no hours at the dorm. I could stay out and sleep anywhere tonight." My God, of all the things to say! But he spared her any signs of misapprehension.

"Of course," he said quietly. "The night before graduation. At last. Have you stopped mourning?"

She was determined to disregard his amusement. "I'll never stop mourning," she said quickly. "I want to stay here, dammit all. I don't want to graduate."

"So you've said. But, as I've told you, there's nothing to stop you from coming back eventually. They might even give you a teaching fellowship."

"Eventually," she said with disgust. "By the end of the summer I'll have gone crazy."

He laughed out loud, holding his cigarette up in the air in front of him, leaning way back in his swivel chair.

"This is most unwholesome of you, my dear. You're supposed to *want* to graduate. But that's nothing," still laughing, with his ridiculously short legs coming up in front of him, "you'll find out what you want—one of these days."

She grew hot and red under his "my dear," his paternal amusement, his fifteen years of seniority, and hated herself for even hoping that he might have known how important he was to the whole thing.

"I don't know," was all she could say. "I just don't know." And, after a long silence in which he simply pulled on his cigarette and she thought of all the crazy stories in which she might have thrown herself upon his gentle, true, unrevealed love for her—"My parents will be here in the morning. They'd like to meet you. Will you have lunch with us after the exercises?"

"Of course I will, Anne. And thank you."

She got up and went to the door. "Good night then," she said, turning for just a minute on the threshold. "Good night, Professor Slater."

He blew her a kiss with his small hand, and she ran down the hall like a little child, her head pounding, not wanting to give him a chance to spoil that tiny, harmless gesture.

Back at the dormitory she stopped for a moment before going in. The air was cooler now, and the carillon had stopped playing. But she imagined that she could still hear the strong prophetic chords of its clear, sad music—"Gaudeamus igitur, juvenes dum summus . . ." She rubbed the remembered echo of it like salt into her consciousness and wished that she could cry loudly, uncontrollably, as she had cried in her bed when she was a little girl. But nothing would come, except the realization that this, at last, was it—that tomorrow she would have to leave, with her regret sifting inside of her like grey ashes—a strange combination of incomprehensible fears and longings. She did not even know what she wanted from Russell; surely there was nothing she could rightfully expect. She did not know where along the way he had come to represent some sort of solution—a last desperate straw at which she might clutch. But that was what had happened, and now, looking back over it, she saw that it was an empty, innocent way—a filmy world of literature and abstraction—and that there was nothing she could hope for from it to sustain her. The world, the real world, loomed like an ugly unpassable giant and now, after all the years of loving school, her only refuge from it, she was being cast forth against it—out of this balmy, unreal, spring-washed campus, into its evil, waiting arms. Russell had refused to be the slayer—had he offered, she realized now, she did not know what she would have done. And she did not know now, what she would do, how she could bear it. Perhaps that was the way people died, too, crying to life "Keep me, keep me," but finding no refuge anywhere. Suddenly she felt cold and tired, so she opened the door to the dormitory and went in.

Inside the halls were strangely quiet and empty, with the voices of the few graduates who were in their rooms scarcely able to break the unaccustomed silence. She knew that they were playing bridge down the hall on her floor, and one of the girls had a turkey which she had been invited to help eat. But she did not go down the hall at all. Instead, she lay awake for a long time, hearing their voices.

"I pass." The slap of the cards on the floor of somebody's room.

"Oh no you don't! That's my trick!"

"My God, fellers, think of getting out of here at last!"

"Tomorrow, no less, my fine feathered graduate!" And all the others laughed loudly, genuinely, feverish in the excitement of having finished the four years.

You see, she thought to herself, I'm unnatural. I'm probably the only one in the whole place who doesn't want to graduate. They don't even *care,* they don't even care. They'd think I was crazy. I can't even explain it to myself—how could I explain it to them?

She fell asleep long after the bridge game had broken up, after the turkey had been noisily eaten. When one of the girls came down the hall yelling, "Lupoff, hey Anne—your turkey!" she closed her eyes and breathed deeply and loudly, until the girl went away. Finally it was all over, the doors closed on the other rooms, and there was only the heavy silence in which she fell asleep at last.

In the morning, with the sun slanting hotly across the floor of her room, she put on her cap and gown and stood before the mirror looking at herself, pleased with how right they looked on her—how sensible and bright and wise they made her seem. She could never remember which way the tassel went, but she'd see when she got down to the procession. Now she would only have to come back to this room to collect her bags—they were all packed—and they stood alone in the middle of the floor of the half empty room, with its stripped bed and cleared, glass topped dresser, and dust covered study lamp. She looked across to Mackey Hall, but the window glared in reflected sunlight and hurt her eyes—then, down to the street, where the black-robed figures were already hurrying to have breakfast before the procession formed.

She thought of calling the Union, where her parents had presumably spent the night after arriving very late, but decided, instead, to go directly over there and meet them for breakfast. They had said that they would be sitting in the lobby that morning, before the exercises, but she was afraid they would get mixed up and go to the wrong place.

She knew they would expect her to be excited and pleased and loving, that they would not understand. She prayed for patience with them, but knew, even before she went to meet them, that she would not have it. To them, her degree was their stamp of having succeeded in the demanding, difficult New World to which they had come together thirty years ago. She was their only child—the next best thing to a son; if she could not be a professional (my son, the doctor . . .) she could at least be a Bachelor of Arts. In their letters to her—long, affectionate, awkward letters which begged her silently to fulfill their hopes and prayers—they had betrayed their longing for a tall capable son who would do them honor in a profession. And she, with the academic honors which came to her as a by-product of her furious love for the place and the life, had given them the next best thing. They were unbearably proud of her, and she was embarrassed by their open, unashamed European pride, their overstated affection, their naïve conviction that in giving her a college education they had attained the peak of parental obligation. Instead, she thought sadly, they had driven her further and further from them—with their strange emotional way of life, their pathetic ignorance of everything she had come to love. She was not ashamed of them—she had never attempted to cover up for their uncertain, fumbling ways—but they had widened the gap immeasurably, and she was ashamed, not of them, but of herself, for having betrayed them by growing so unattainable, by spending these years in slipping further and further out of their reach. And now, the cruelest blow surely, that she could not honestly say she was glad to be going home with them, could not even try to fool them by celebrating, savoring, loving the meaning of this day.

She walked slowly over to the Union Building, feeling the unfamiliar folds of the black robe about her legs, the pressure of the four-cornered hat upon her brow. And they were there in the lobby of the tall white building, huddled close to one another on a leather sofa, watching anxiously for her through the crowds of noisy alumni and polished, expectant looking fathers and mothers, and eager black-gowned graduates. Her mother looked beautiful—that dark Balkan beauty seeming out of place amidst the athletic trophies and plaidy, collegiate trimmings which characterized the big room; the dark blue eyes looking very deep and sorrowful under the pale brim of her hat, the black hair curling softly all around her face, the white of her blouse pointing up the incredible, natural foreign coloring. Her father, small and very white-haired, turning his summer hat around and around in his fingers, looked only worried and afraid, as he always looked in a crowd. But when they saw her, when they saw her, they clasped their hands simultaneously in front of them, like one person, and smiled broadly, looking slowly down her, from the stiff top of her cap with its ridiculous displaced tassel, to her shoes, just showing from beneath the gown —their glance sweeping with love and wonder over her face, her body, her hands, tentatively outstretched to them. Then they were kissing her and saying the things she had known they would say.

"My Anna—" they would never call her Anne—"our own girl—to think this day would come, that we are here, so far away, to see you with your college graduation."

"Hello Momma—Pa. Did you have a good trip?"

"Such a long trip. You never told us how long—and we sat up all night." Her mother shook her head slowly.

"Well my gosh, you should have taken a Pullman. I *told* you to take a Pullman, Poppa."

"I didn't know. The man said the chairs were comfortable. It wasn't so bad, Momma, was it?"

"I don't know, I don't know. I only know we're here—and soon our girl will graduate." It was all that mattered. She looked eagerly around the crowding room. "You want breakfast first, yes Anna?"

"Yes, Momma, first we have breakfast and then I'll tell you where to go for your seats and where to meet me afterwards."

They had their breakfast in the big oak-paneled dining room of the Union, but no one was very hungry. Her parents simply kept shaking their heads and looking curiously, proudly, about the big room. And for Anne, it was an intolerable imposition of one of her worlds upon the other—they simply did not go together; they had nothing to do with one another. She did not even know what there was for her to say to her parents—but they did a good deal of the talking themselves. She had almost forgotten how odd their conversation could sound.

"You know, Anna, what a great day this is for us—our own daughter graduating. We want you to know how proud it is for us." Her father laid his cool, old hand over her perspiring one, then passed it swiftly, lightly over her cheek.

"Yes, Pa, I know, *I* know." She was stifling with their pride, their misplaced joy.

"And we want, your momma and I, you should come home now and rest and read and do whatever you want till the fall. All summer you shouldn't work. You should just stay home with us and be—" he laughed loudly—"a loafer!"

It was an attempt, a pitiful attempt. And an image of the long, unfilled, intolerable summer days consumed her, filled her eyes with tears. Her mother saw them and turned to the little man, with bewilderment in her own eyes.

"Leave her, Joe," she said, "plenty of time for talk later."

Later, later, later—the shocking, desolating recognition of how much time there would be, how much of later, sent her sobbing out of the dining room. After several seconds of hesitation, the other two people followed her, and they all walked together in silence to the point at which the academic procession was to start. She left them there, indicating the building to which they were to go and arranging to meet them again at the Union for lunch. She hoped they remembered that Russell would be with her—they had told her to invite him, as many as she wanted, they had said—but she did not want to bring it up now. So she stood in line with the others, under the blazing sun, her head throbbing beneath the cap—and watched their figures disappear toward the doorway of Blane Auditorium, their legs very short, moving quickly, firmly, their hands clasped together between them. Then the procession started and she felt nothing except the burning of the sun through her gown, the hot pavement through the soles of her thin summer shoes.

She was grateful that, in the huge auditorium, with the visitors all sitting behind the graduates, she could not see the faces of her parents or hear their murmured wonder and pride when the honors were announced. But on the platform she could make out Russell's face, saw the familiar, noncommittal half smile when her name was announced for the work she had done under his tutelage. At least she had done him proud—at least that; it meant a lot to a man appointed as a Special Studies Tutor to have his student come out on top. Even now some silly, overeager, bright young sophomore was plotting to take her place. And maybe he was thinking that there would be others who would do just as well as she had—someone else he could treat to lunch and Aristotle. She brightened a little—he *had* treated her to lunch, hadn't he—often. And today, today at least was hers. She would make the most of it.

Then, at last, they were singing the Alma Mater—and she sobbed as if she were a slobbering old alumnus at a reunion dinner who had too much to drink.

When the ceremonies were over, she stood outside in the milling mixed throng of graduates and parents, all of them kissing, calling, perspiring—caught in the only half-understood moment of having just received a diploma, a degree, the sad consummation of sixteen years. The high noon sun was incredibly strong, a summer sun now, sudden, uncompromising, with no hint of the balminess and promise of spring in a college town. She stood there for some time, waiting for the faculty to file out, hoping to catch Russell before he started for the Union. Then she spotted him, talking over in a corner to Bill Daimler, a young teaching fellow who was always following him around. Wondering whether he had forgotten, she hurried over to them.

"Behold," shouted Bill, when he saw her coming, "the sweet girl graduate."

"Who mourneth as she comes," said Russell, holding out his hand in a congratulatory gesture.

She shook his hand, and Bill's. "My parents are going to go on ahead and meet us at the Union," she said. "I hope you'll have lunch with us too, Bill. They'd be happy to meet you."

"I'll come gladly—if nobody minds—provided you promise to smile all the way there." Bill looked at Russell sternly. "One thing you haven't taught your prize student, Professor Slater, is how to accept the facts of graduation."

Russ rolled his tongue over into one cheek and looked at her carefully. "She doesn't want to learn," he said at last.

Anne felt terribly foolish again now, and turned her head away quickly. But Bill grabbed her shoulder and was steering her out of the crowd. "Enough of such trifling conversation," he said cheerfully, "on to the Union and the parents of the sweet girl graduate."

She looked around to be sure that her parents were not waiting in front of the auditorium, but she did not see them anywhere. So they walked together, the three of them, down the suddenly busy, crowded excited streets of the town to the Union Building. Now everything was beginning to lose its meaning, and the only thing, in all this strange turmoil, that seemed to have any real relation to her was the sight of her parents, small and anxious, standing together near the front entrance to the Union lobby, looking once again for their daughter. She felt a renewed sweep of pleasure in her mother's beauty, as she introduced them to her, and in the way her father, suddenly secure in the pride of his daughter's success, shook their hands quietly and firmly, looked brightly into their faces.

"We have heard so much about you—all of you professors," her mother said.

"The faculty, no less," her father said, laughing, his too even false teeth showing in the pink face. "If you love her like she loves you. . . ."

"Poppa! Oh Poppa!" She made a gesture of impatience, and the rest of them laughed with the old man.

Then they climbed the marble stairs to the busy dining room and took seats together at a table near one of the big windows. The dining room was almost filled already, and it was some time before their orders were taken. Waiting there at the table, only half-hearing her parents' questions and the answers, some flippant, some serious and respectful, which came from Russell and Bill, she began to feel again the misery of being wedged between two clashing worlds. They were all strangers now, and there was nothing she could say to any of them that would bring them together, or her closer to them. Slowly she allowed herself to be wrapped again in self-pity, wanting to cry out to them that one of them—one of the two worlds, lives, homes—should claim her, keep her, hold her safe against the other. But there was no sign that anyone knew what she was thinking, could have understood what she meant; and the meal was miserable, confused ceremony of farewell.

"When does your train leave, Mrs. Lupoff?"

"Soon, I think. What time, Joe?"

"This afternoon, three o'clock. Maybe you and Anna should go ahead back for her bags, Momma, there's not much time."

Anne looked at her watch. It was true, there wasn't much time.

"No, no. We'll all go," her mother said.

But Bill had to leave before dessert had been served. To her great relief, Anne noted that Russell was making no move to leave with him. She wanted him with her until the last possible minute. And, thank goodness, he knew it.

"If nobody minds," he said, "I'll string along until train time. Can't see my best pupil leaving without a proper send-off."

Both parents laughed with pleasure.

"Mind?" her mother said, inclining her head slightly toward him, "Why I think we love having you. Isn't it, Poppa?"

"Delighted," said her father, with a funny little bow from the shoulders.

Her mother and father waited in the parlor of the dormitory, while she and Russell went up to get her bags. He had never seen her room before—but now there was nothing of her left in it

—not the cute little cartoons she had tacked up on a bulletin board near the door, or the snapshots stuck under the glass dresser top, or the sonnet from Keats, framed delicately on the wall. Only her bags—sitting miserably, coldly in the middle of the floor —and a coat for traveling flung across the stripped bed.

Russell looked around the room carefully, as if he could see it all, all that had been there—then walked slowly over to her desk— empty, dusty, untelling—near the window.

"And this," he said, running a finger over the surface, "is where you sat, turning out those themes of yours." She nodded. "And there—" he looked out the open window and pointed across the street—"is where I sat and read them." He turned and faced her again.

"So you knew that I could see your window from here."

"You forget that as a member of the faculty, I know everything." He smiled at her—but softly, gently, touching her chin lightly with his finger. "Someday you'll know everything too. And you'll see what a little goose you're being and how important it is for you to leave now and give yourself a summer to think things through." He did not say what things—only "things. . . ."

Then, unexpectedly, he drew out of his pocket a small volume— a thin edition of Shakespeare's sonnets, bound in rich red supple leather.

"From me to you," he said, handing it to her.

She opened to the flyleaf. "For Anne, my favorite," he had written, "to remind her gently of her salad days." Then, after watching her as she read the inscription, he walked out of the room. Slowly, closing the book without a word, she followed him down the stairs to where her parents waited.

In the taxi, on the way to the station, she watched her town rush by, wondering how she could be expected to throw it over, demolish it, forget it, after four years of living only from semester to semester, return to return. As the familiar streets and structures stretched out behind them, she found herself coping unsuccessfully with that incomprehensible prospect—that she would not ever see them again and that they, in turn, would go on about their business of standing, being, aging, as if she had never been there at all. She remembered how ugly they had all seemed at first—the streets busier than she had thought college-town streets should be, and the buildings, old and baroque, spread out all over them. And now, how beautiful, with their smell of pipes, their old halls and rooms, their windows and mottoes and walls.

She turned to Russell, who sat beside her holding her small traveling case.

"You're used to graduations by now, aren't you." He was something like the buildings—a permanent, steady figure, unmoved and unmoving against the incoming and outflowing tide of students.

"I'm used to them. But some I regret more than others."

"Oh—you'll have another Honors student. Next year it will be someone else to do you proud. You're used to that too, aren't you?"

"Perhaps," he said. "But by next year that won't matter to you."

She wanted to say, "Will it matter to you?" But she only sat there silently, until the cab pulled up in front of the station house, at the foot of a long sweeping hill. From the bottom, you could see only the bell tower and the wonderful blue sky behind it. She had had her last glimpse of the buildings now, and of the town.

While her father paid the driver, her mother waiting beside him, she and Russell went into the station house with her bags. He set them down near the door to the tracks and pulled her over into a corner, near a candy machine.

"Never mind, Anne honey," he said. He put a nickel into the machine and pulled the plunger under a chocolate bar. "Sweets to the sweet," he said, handing it to her.

"Hardly worthy of you, that old cliché," she said. She could feel the tears starting to roll softly down her cheeks.

He swept his fingers lightly over them—first one side, then the other. "Or of you," he said.

They shook hands slowly, and she felt that his hand, like hers, was warm and sweating.

Her parents joined them, then, looking embarrassed and outcast, and there was the sound of the train, eastbound, rushing in upon the track. They all walked silently out of the station house and, as she mounted the steep little flight of steps to the coach, she could hear him saying goodbye to her parents. They were telling him over and over how much he had done for her, how he must visit them if he ever came east, how much, how very much, they knew she would miss him. He thanked them and helped them on to the train.

As the train quickly gathered its speed, she could see him standing on the platform—still waving—his small form becoming smaller and smaller—his hand at last going down to his side.

She pressed her head hard against the window then, sobbing softly, letting the wetness and the smooth pane of glass cool her flushed face. In the seat in front of her, her parents sat wordlessly together, looking at each other and at her. Finally, when the sobbing had stopped, her mother turned around tentatively, apologetically.

"Such a nice man," she said. "So brilliant. How lucky for you to have him."

And her father turned around too. "You are spoiled by such smart men," he said. "You only shouldn't look for too much now in the ones at home."

"Oh Poppa, Poppa." It was too much.

"Never mind, never mind." Her mother slapped her father impatiently on the shoulder. "Poppa will see now if we can get berths for the night. Go, Joe. When we get home we talk—when we get home."

Anne turned her head again toward the window, renewing the effort to escape the bewilderment in their eyes. Now she resented having to cope with it, with any of it, and she tried hard to push herself once again back into the world in which she had so recently succeeded. Silently she reviewed the last few days and hours, flushing again under the triumph of her oral examination, feeling again the weight of her thick, careful thesis manuscript as she handed it to the head of the department, accepting again, from a high, crowded platform, the academic honors which had come to her. She thought of everything Russell had said, everything he might have meant to say; and she stood with him again in her empty, bereft room, taking from his hands the smooth, leather-covered volume with his farewell on the flyleaf. But something had changed, thinned, lost its earlier impact; and against the even mechanical counterpoint of the noisy eastbound train, the meaning seemed to slip away from her. She was again strongly conscious of her mother's eyes upon her.

The older woman turned further around in her seat. "Anna," she said quietly, "Anna." She waited for her daughter to look at her. "We think now we should fix up the house for you—the way you want it. Then maybe you can entertain all your friends."

Anne smiled briefly at her. It was natural, after all, that even as she had been looking backward, in a last desperate effort to hold on, her parents, with the same measure of desperation, were looking ahead to home, the only place they understood, the only place in which she was—or seemed to be—wholly theirs.

Now she thought of her home, substantial, middle class brick house that stood solidly on the corner of a city street, having nothing to do with classes or Honors or midnight discussions of philosophy—but only with the strong rich smells of foreign cooking, the sounds of steady, quiet domesticity, the small passing exultations of family life. It was, after all, the only place to which she had always been able to return. Now, suddenly, she felt curiously relieved by its simplicity, its lack of complication, its demonstrative, basic, unashamed warmth. For the first time in her life she was not embarrassed by it.

She wished that there was something she could say to her parents to make up for the last few hours. But she knew that they did not expect any such compensation from her—and that their surprise and delight at getting it would be more than she could bear, would only push her back again into her shell of remorse and longing for something else.

So she sat there alone, saying nothing, struggling with the changing tides of her emotions, pressing hard against the images which had so easily brought tears. At last, after a long time, with the flat landscape darkening against the sky of summer evening, she was able to picture, clearly and with a sudden sharp knowledge of how it felt to be there, her own room at home—with its windows wide and flung open over a long, green lawn, its bed, large and soft, that had stood there, in that corner of that room, as long as she could possibly remember.

(From The New Yorker)

THE COUNTRY HUSBAND

BY JOHN CHEEVER

TO BEGIN at the beginning, the airplane from Minneapolis in which Francis Weed was travelling East ran into heavy weather. The sky had been a hazy blue, with the clouds below the plane lying so close together that nothing could be seen of the earth. Then mist began to form outside the windows, and they flew into a white cloud of such density that it reflected the exhaust fires. The color of the cloud darkened to gray, and the plane began to rock. Francis had been in heavy weather before, but he had never been shaken up so much. The man in the seat beside him pulled a flask out of his pocket and took a drink. Francis smiled at his neighbor, but the man looked away; he wasn't sharing his pain-killer with anyone. The plane had begun to drop and flounder wildly. A child was crying. The air in the cabin was overheated and stale, and Francis' left foot went to sleep. He read a little from a paper book that he had bought at the airport, but the violence of the storm divided his attention. It was black outside the ports. The exhaust fires blazed and shed sparks in the dark, and, inside, the shaded lights, the stuffiness, and the window curtains gave the cabin an atmosphere of intense and misplaced domesticity. Then the lights flickered and went out. "You know what I've always wanted to do?" the man beside Francis said suddenly. "I've always wanted to buy a farm in New Hampshire and raise beef cattle." The stewardess announced that they were going to make an emergency landing. All but the child saw in their minds the spreading wings of the Angel of Death. The pilot could be heard singing faintly, "I've got sixpence, jolly, jolly sixpence. I've got sixpence to last me all my life . . ." There was no other sound.

The loud groaning of the hydraulic valves swallowed up the pilot's song, and there was a shrieking high in the air, like automobile brakes, and the plane hit flat on its belly in a cornfield and shook them so violently that an old man up forward howled, "Me kidneys! Me kidneys!" The stewardess flung open the door, and someone opened an emergency door at the back, letting in the sweet noise of their continuing mortality—the idle splash and smell of a heavy rain. Anxious for their lives, they filed out of the doors and scattered over the cornfield in all directions, praying that the thread would hold. It did. Nothing happened. When it was clear that the plane would not burn or explode, the crew and the stewardess gathered the passengers together and led them to the shelter of a barn. They were not far from Philadelphia, and in a little while a string of taxis took them into the city. "It's just like the Marne," someone said, but there was surprisingly little relaxation of that suspiciousness with which many Americans regard their fellow travellers.

In Philadelphia, Francis Weed got a train to New York. At the end of that journey, he crossed the city and caught, just as it was about to pull out, the commuting train that he took five nights a week to his home in Shady Hill.

He sat with Trace Bearden. "You know, I was in that plane that just crashed outside Philadelphia," he said. "We came down in a field . . ." He had travelled faster than the newspapers or the rain, and the weather in New York was sunny and mild. It was a day in late September, as fragrant and shapely as an apple. Trace listened to the story, but how could he get excited? Francis had no powers that would let him re-create a brush with death—particularly in the atmosphere of a commuting train, journeying through a sunny countryside where already, in the slum gardens, there were signs of harvest. Trace picked up his newspaper, and Francis was left alone with his thoughts. He said good night to Trace on the platform at Shady Hill and drove in his second-hand Volkswagen up to the Blenhollow neighborhood, where he lived.

The Weeds' Dutch Colonial house was larger than it appeared to be from the driveway. The living room was spacious and divided like Gaul into three parts. Around an ell to the left as one entered from the vestibule was the long table, laid for six, with candles and a bowl of fruit in the center. The sounds and smells that came from the open kitchen door were appetizing, for Julia Weed was a good cook. The largest part of the living room centered around a fireplace. On the right were some bookshelves and a piano. The room was polished and tranquil, and from the windows that opened to the west there was some late-summer sunlight, brilliant and as clear as water. Nothing here was neglected; nothing had not been burnished. It was not the kind of household where, after prying open a stuck cigarette box, you would find an old shirt button and a tarnished nickel. The hearth was swept, the roses on the piano were reflected in the polish of the broad top, and there was an album of Schubert waltzes on the rack. Louisa Weed, a pretty girl of nine, was looking out the western windows. Her younger brother Henry was standing beside her. Her still younger brother, Toby, was studying the figures of some tonsured monks drinking beer on the polished brass of the wood box. Francis, taking off his hat and putting down his paper, was not consciously pleased with the scene; he was not that reflective. It was his element, his creation, and he returned to it with that sense of lightness and strength with which any creature returns to its home. "Hi, everybody," he said. "The plane from Minneapolis . . ."

Nine times out of ten, Francis would be greeted with affection, but tonight the children are absorbed in their own antagonisms. Francis has not finished his sentence about the plane crash before Henry plants a kick in Louisa's behind. Louisa swings around, saying *"Damn* you!" Francis makes the mistake of scolding Louisa for bad language before he punishes Henry. Now Louisa turns on her father and accuses him of favoritism. Henry is always right; she is persecuted and lonely; her lot is hopeless. Francis turns to his son, but the boy has justification for the kick—she hit him first; she hit him on the ear, which is dangerous. Louisa agrees with this passionately. She hit him on the ear, and she *meant* to hit him on the ear, because he messed up her china collection. Henry says that this is a lie. Little Toby turns away from the wood box to throw in some evidence for Louisa. Henry claps his hand over little Toby's mouth. Francis separates the two boys but accidentally pushes Toby into the wood box. Toby begins to cry. Louisa is already crying. Just then, Julia Weed comes into that part of the room where the table is laid. She is a pretty, intelligent woman, and the white in her hair is premature. She does not seem to notice the fracas. "Hello, darling," she says serenely to Francis. "Wash your hands, everyone. Dinner is ready." She strikes a match and lights the six candles in this vale of tears.

This simple announcement, like the war cries of the Scottish chieftains, only refreshes the ferocity of the combatants. Louisa gives Henry a blow on the shoulder. Henry, although he seldom cries, has pitched nine innings and is tired. He bursts into tears. Little Toby discovers a splinter in his hand and begins to howl. Francis says loudly that he has been in a plane crash and that he is tired. Julia appears again, from the kitchen, and, still ignoring the chaos, asks Francis to go upstairs and tell Helen that everything is ready. Francis is happy to go; it is like getting back to headquarters company. He is planning to tell his oldest daughter about the airplane crash, but Helen is lying on her bed reading a *True Romance* magazine, and the first thing Francis does is to take the magazine from her hand and remind Helen that he has forbidden her to buy it. She did not buy it, Helen replies. It was given to her by her best friend, Bessie Black. Everybody reads *True Romance*. Bessie Black's father reads *True Romance*. There isn't a girl in Helen's class who doesn't read *True Romance*. Francis expresses his detestation of the magazine and then tells her that dinner is ready—although from the sounds downstairs it doesn't seem so. Helen follows him down the stairs. Julia has seated herself in the candlelight and spread a napkin over her lap. Neither Louisa nor Henry has come to the table. Little Toby is still howling, lying face down on the floor. Francis speaks to him gently: "Daddy was in a plane crash this afternoon, Toby. Don't you want to hear about it?" Toby goes on crying. "If you don't come to the table now, Toby," Francis says, "I'll have to send you to bed without any supper." The little boy rises, gives him a cutting look, flies up the stairs to his bedroom, and slams the door. "Oh dear," Julia says, and starts to go after him. Francis says that she will spoil him. Julia says that Toby is ten pounds underweight and has to be encouraged to eat. Winter is coming, and he will spend the cold months in bed unless he has his dinner. Julia goes upstairs. Francis sits down at the table with Helen. Helen is suffering from the dismal feeling of having read too intently on a fine day, and she gives her father and the room a jaded look. She doesn't understand about the plane crash, because there wasn't a drop of rain in Shady Hill.

Julia returns with Toby, and they all sit down and are served. "Do I have to look at that big, fat slob?" Henry says, of Louisa. Everybody but Toby enters into this skirmish, and it rages up and down the table for five minutes. Toward the end, Henry puts his napkin over his head and, trying to eat that way, spills spinach all over his shirt. Francis asks Julia if the children couldn't have their dinner earlier. Julia's guns are loaded for this. She can't cook two dinners and lay two tables. She paints with lightning strokes that panorama of drudgery in which her youth, her beauty, and her wit have been lost. Francis says that he must be understood; he was nearly killed in an airplane crash, and he doesn't like to come home every night to a battlefield. Now Julia is deeply committed. Her voice trembles. He doesn't come home every night to a battlefield. The accusation is stupid and mean. Everything was tranquil until he arrived. She stops speaking, puts down her knife and fork, and looks into her plate as if it is a gulf. She begins to cry. "Poor Mummy!" Toby says, and when Julia gets up from the table, drying her tears with a napkin, Toby goes to her side. "Poor Mummy," he says. "Poor Mummy!" And they climb the stairs together. The other children drift away from the battlefield, and Francis goes into the back garden for a cigarette and some air.

It was a pleasant garden, with walks and flower beds and places to sit. The sunset had nearly burned out, but there was still plenty of light. Put into a thoughtful mood by the crash and the battle, Francis listened to the evening sounds of Shady Hill. "Varmits! Rascals!" old Mr. Nixon shouted to the squirrels in his bird-feeding station. "Avaunt and quit my sight!" A door slammed. Someone was playing tennis on the Babcocks' court; someone was cutting grass. Then Donald Goslin, who lived at the corner, began to play the "Moonlight Sonata." He did this nearly every night. He threw the tempo out the window and played it *rubato* from beginning to end, like an outpouring of tearful petulance, lonesomeness, and self-pity—of everything it was Beethoven's greatness not to know. The music rang up and down the street beneath the trees like an appeal for love, for tenderness, aimed at some lonely housemaid—some fresh-faced, homesick girl from Galway, looking at old snapshots in her third-floor room. "Here, Jupiter, here, Jupiter," Francis called to the Mercers' retriever. Jupiter crashed through the tomato vines with the remains of a felt hat in his mouth.

Jupiter was an anomaly. His retrieving instincts and his high spirits were out of place in Shady Hill. He was as black as coal, with a long, alert, intelligent, rakehell face. His eyes gleamed with mischief, and he held his head high. It was the fierce, heavily collared dog's head that appears in heraldry, in tapestry, and that used to appear on umbrella handles and walking sticks. Jupiter went where he pleased, ransacking wastebaskets, clotheslines, garbage pails, and shoe bags. He broke up garden parties and tennis matches, and got mixed up in the processional at Christ's Church on Sunday, barking at the men in red dresses. He crashed through old Mr. Nixon's rose garden two or three times a day, cutting a wide swath through the Condesa de Sastagos, and as soon as Donald Goslin lighted his barbecue fire on Thursday nights, Jupiter would get the scent. Nothing the Goslins did could drive him away. Sticks and stones and rude commands only moved him to the edge of the terrace, where he remained, with his gallant and heraldic muzzle, waiting for Donald Goslin to turn his back and reach for the salt. Then he would spring onto the terrace, lift the steak lightly off the fire, and run away with the Goslins' dinner. Jupiter's days were numbered. The Wrightsons' German gardener or the Farquarsons' cook would soon poison him. Even old Mr. Nixon might put some arsenic in the garbage that Jupiter loved. "Here, Jupiter, Jupiter!" Francis called, but the dog pranced off, shaking the hat in his white teeth. Looking in at the windows of his house, Francis saw that Julia had come down and was blowing out the candles.

Julia and Francis Weed went out a great deal. Julia was well liked and gregarious, and her love of parties sprang from a most natural dread of chaos and loneliness. She went through her morning mail with real anxiety, looking for invitations, and she usually found some, but she was insatiable, and if she had gone out seven nights a week, it would not have cured her of a reflective look—the look of someone who hears distant music—for she would always suppose that there was a more brilliant party somewhere else. Francis limited her to two week-night parties, putting a flexible interpretation on Friday, and rode through the weekend like a dory in a gale. The day after the airplane crash, the Weeds were to have dinner with the Farquarsons.

Francis got home late from town, and Julia got the sitter while he dressed, and then hurried him out of the house. The party was small and pleasant, and Francis settled down to enjoy himself. A new maid passed the drinks. Her hair was dark, and her face was round and pale and seemed familiar to Francis. He had not developed his memory as a sentimental faculty. Wood smoke, lilac, and other such perfumes did not stir him, and his memory was something like his appendix—a vestigial repository. It was not his limitation at all to be unable to escape the past; it was perhaps his limitation that he had escaped it so successfully. He might have seen the maid at other parties, he might have seen her taking a walk on Sunday afternoons, but in either case he would not be searching his memory now. Her face was, in a wonderful way, a moon face—Norman or Irish—but it was not beautiful enough to account for his feeling that he had seen her before, in circumstances that he ought to be able to remember. He askd Nellie Farquarson who she was. Nellie said that the maid had come through an agency, and that her home was Trénon, in Normandy—a small place with a church and a restaurant that Nellie had once visited. While Nellie talked on about her travels abroad, Francis realized where he had seen the woman before. It had been at the end of the war. He had left a replacement depot with some other men and taken a three-day pass in Trénon. On their second day, they had walked out to a crossroads to see the public chastisement of a young woman who had lived with the German commandant during the Occupation.

It was a cool morning in the fall. The sky was overcast, and poured down onto the dirt crossroads a very discouraging light. They were on high land and could see how like one another the shapes of the clouds and the hills were as they stretched off toward the sea. The prisoner arrived sitting on a three-legged stool in a farm cart. She stood by the cart while the mayor read the accusation and the sentence. Her head was bent and her face was set in that empty half smile behind which the whipped soul is suspended. When the mayor was finished, she undid her hair and let it fall across her back. A little man with a gray mustache cut off her hair with shears and dropped it on the ground. Then, with a bowl of soapy water and a straight razor, he shaved her skull clean. A woman approached and began to undo the fastenings of her clothes, but the prisoner pushed her aside and undressed herself. When she pulled her chemise over her head and threw it on the ground, she was naked. The women jeered; the men were still. There was no change in the falseness or the plaintiveness of the prisoner's smile. The cold wind made her white skin rough and hardened the nipples of her breasts. The jeering ended gradually, put down by the recognition of their common humanity. One woman spat on her, but some inviolable grandeur in her nakedness lasted through the ordeal. When the crowd was quiet, she turned—she had begun to cry—and, with nothing on but a pair of worn black shoes and stockings, walked down the dirt road alone away from the village. The round white face had aged a little, but there was no question but that the maid who passed his cocktails and later served Francis his dinner was the woman who had been punished at the crossroads.

The war seemed now so distant and that world where the cost of partisanship had been death or torture so long ago. Francis had lost track of the men who had been with him in Vésey. He could not count on Julia's discretion. He could not tell anyone. And if he had told the story now, at the dinner table, it would have been a social as well as a human error. The people in the Farquarsons' living room seemed united in their tacit claim that there had been no past, no war—that there was no danger or trouble in the world. In the recorded history of human arrangements, this extraordinary meeting would have fallen into place, but the atmosphere of Shady Hill made the memory unseemly and impolite. The prisoner withdrew after passing the coffee, but the encounter left Francis feeling languid; it had opened his memory and his senses, and left them dilated. He and Julia drove home when the party ended, and Julia went into the house. Francis stayed in the car to take the sitter home.

Expecting to see Mrs. Henlein, the old lady who usually stayed with the children, he was surprised when a young girl opened the door and came out onto the lighted stoop. She stayed in the light to count her textbooks. She was frowning and beautiful. Now, the world is full of beautiful young girls, but Francis saw here the difference between beauty and perfection. All those endearing flaws, moles, birthmarks, and healed wounds were missing, and he experienced in his consciousness that moment when music breaks glass, and felt a pang of recognition as strange, deep, and wonderful as anything in his life. It hung from her frown, from an impalpable darkness in her face—a look that impressed him as a direct appeal for love. When she had counted her books, she came down the steps and opened the car door. In the light, he saw that her cheeks were wet. She got in and shut the door.

"You're new," Francis said.

"Yes. Mrs. Henlein is sick. I'm Anne Murchison."

"Did the children give you any trouble?"

"Oh, no, no." She turned and smiled at him unhappily in the dim dashboard light. Her light hair caught on the collar of her jacket, and she shook her head to set it loose.

"You've been crying."

"Yes."

"I hope it was nothing that happened in our house."

"No, no, it was nothing that happened in your house." Her voice was bleak. "It's no secret. Everybody in the village knows. Daddy's an alcoholic, and he just called me from some saloon and gave me a piece of his mind. He thinks I'm immoral. He called just before Mrs. Weed came back."

"I'm sorry."

"Oh, *Lord!"* She gasped and began to cry. She turned toward Francis, and he took her in his arms and let her cry on his shoulder. She shook in his embrace, and this movement accentuated his sense of the fineness of her flesh and bone. The layers of their clothing felt thin, and when her shuddering began to diminish, it was so much like a paroxysm of love that Francis lost his head and pulled her roughly against him. She drew away. "I live on Belleview Avenue," she said. "You go down Lansing Street to the railroad bridge."

"All right." He started the car.

"You turn left at that traffic light. . . . Now you turn right here and go straight on toward the tracks."

The road Francis took brought him out of his own neighborhood, across the tracks, and toward the river, to a street where the near-poor lived, in houses whose peaked gables and trimmings of wooden lace conveyed the purest feelings of pride and romance, although the houses themselves could not have offered much privacy or comfort, they were all so small. The street was dark, and, stirred by the grace and beauty of the troubled girl, he seemed, in turning in to it, to have come into the deepest part of some submerged memory. In the distance, he saw a porch light burning. It was the only one, and she said that the house with the light was where she lived. When he stopped the car, he could see beyond the porch light into a dimly-lighted hallway with an old-fashioned clothes tree. "Well, here we are," he said, conscious that a young man would have said something different.

She did not move her hands from the books, where they were folded, and she turned and faced him. There were tears of lust in his eyes. Determinedly—not sadly—he opened the door on his side and walked around to open hers. He took her free hand, letting his fingers in between hers, climbed at her side the two concrete steps, and went up a narrow walk through a front garden where dahlias, marigolds, and roses—things that had withstood the light frosts—still bloomed, and made a bittersweet smell in the night air. At the steps, she freed her hand and then turned and kissed him swiftly. Then she crossed the porch and shut the door. The porch light went out, then the light in the hall. A second later, a light went on upstairs at the side of the house, shining into a tree that was still covered with leaves. It took her only a few minutes to undress and get into bed, and then the house was dark.

Julia was asleep when Francis got home. He opened a second window and got into bed to shut his eyes on that night, but as soon as they were shut—as soon as he had dropped off to sleep—the girl entered his mind, moving with perfect freedom through its shut doors and filling chamber after chamber with her light, her perfume, and the music of her voice. He was crossing the Atlantic with her on the old *Mauretania* and, later, living with her in Paris. When he woke from this dream, he got up and smoked a cigarette at the open window. Getting back into bed, he cast around in his mind for something he desired to do that would injure no one, and he thought of skiing. Up through the dimness in his mind rose the image of a mountain deep in snow. It was late in the day. Wherever his eyes looked, he saw broad and heartening things. Over his shoulder, there was a snow-filled valley, rising into wooded hills where the trees dimmed the whiteness like a sparse coat of hair. The cold deadened all sound but the loud, iron clanking of the lift machinery. The light on the trails was blue, and it was harder than it had been a minute or two earlier to pick the turns, harder to judge—now that the snow was all deep blue—the crust, the ice, the bare spots, and the deep piles of dry powder. Down the mountain he swung, matching his speed against the contours of a slope that had been formed in the first ice age, seeking with ardor some simplicity of feeling and circumstance. Night fell then, and he drank a Martini with some old friend in a dirty country bar.

In the morning, Francis' snow-covered mountain was gone, and he was left with his vivid memories of Paris and the *Mauretania*. He had been bitten gravely. He washed his body, shaved his jaws, drank his coffee, and missed the seven-thirty-one. The train pulled out just as he brought his car to the station, and the longing he felt for the coaches as they drew stubbornly away from him reminded him of the humors of love. He waited for eight-two, on what was now an empty platform. It was a clear morning; the morning seemed thrown like a gleaming bridge of light over his mixed affairs. His spirits were feverish and high. The image of the girl seemed to put him into a relationship to the world that was mysterious and enthralling. Cars were beginning to fill up the parking lot, and he noticed that those that had driven down from the high land above Shady Hill were white with hoarfrost. This first clear sign of autumn thrilled him. An express train—a night train from Buffalo or Albany—came down the tracks between the platforms, and he saw that the roofs of the foremost cars were covered with a skin of ice. Struck by the miraculous physicalness of everything, he smiled at the passengers in the dining car, who could be seen eating eggs and wiping their mouths with napkins as they travelled. The sleeping-car compartments, with their soiled bed linen, trailed through the fresh morning like a string of rooming-house windows. Then he saw an extraordinary thing; at one of the bedroom windows sat an unclothed woman of exceptional beauty, combing her golden hair. She passed like an apparition through Shady Hill, combing and combing her hair, and Francis followed her with his eyes until she was out of sight. Then old Mrs. Wrightson joined him on the platform and began to talk.

"Well, I guess you must be surprised to see me here the third morning in a row," she said, "but because of my window curtains I'm becoming a regular commuter. The curtains I bought on Monday I returned on Tuesday, and the curtains I bought Tuesday I'm returning today. On Monday, I got exactly what I wanted—it's a wool tapestry with roses and birds—but when I got them home, I found they were the wrong length. Well, I exchanged them yesterday, and when I got them home, I found they were still the wrong length. Now I'm praying to high Heaven that the decorator will have them in the right length, because you know my house, you *know* my living-room windows, and you can imagine what a problem they present. I don't know what to do with them."

"I know what to do with them," Francis said.

"What?"

"Paint them black on the inside, and shut up."

There was a gasp from Mrs. Wrightson, and Francis looked down at her to be sure that she knew he meant to be rude. She turned and walked away from him, so damaged in spirit that she limped. A wonderful feeling enveloped him, as if light were being shaken about him, and he thought again of Venus combing and combing her hair as she drifted through the Bronx. The realization of how many years had passed since he had enjoyed being deliberately impolite sobered him. Among his friends and neighbors, there were brilliant and gifted people—he saw that—but many of them, also, were bores and fools, and he had made the mistake of listening to them all with equal attention. He had confused a lack of discrimination with Christian love, and the confusion seemed general and destructive. He was grateful to the girl for this bracing sensation of independence. Birds were singing— cardinals and the last of the robins. The sky shone like enamel. Even the smell of ink from his morning paper honed his appetite for life, and the world that was spread out around him was plainly a paradise.

If Francis had believed in some hierarchy of love—in spirits armed with hunting bows, in the capriciousness of Venus and Eros—or even in magical potions, philtres, and stews, in scapulae and quarters of the moon, it might have explained his susceptibility and his feverish high spirits. The autumnal loves of middle age are well publicized, and he guessed that he was face to face with one of these, but there was not a trace of autumn in what he felt. He wanted to sport in the green woods, scratch where he itched, and drink from the same cup.

His secretary, Miss Rainey, was late that morning—she went to a psychiatrist three mornings a week—and when she came in, Francis wondered what advice a psychiatrist would have for him. But the girl promised to bring back into his life something like the sound of music. The realization that this music might lead him straight to a trial for statutory rape at the county courthouse collapsed his happiness. The photograph of his four children laughing into the camera on the beach at Gay Head reproached him. On the letter-head of his firm there was a drawing of the Laocoön, and the figure of the priest and his sons in the coils of the snake appeared to him to have the deepest meaning.

He had lunch with Pinky Trabert, who told him a couple of dirty stories. At a conversational level, the mores of his friends were robust and elastic, but he knew that the moral card house would come down on them all—on Julia and the children—if he got caught taking advantage of a baby-sitter. Looking back over the recent history of Shady Hill for some precedent, he found there was none. There was no turpitude; there had not been a divorce since he lived there; there had not even been a breath of scandal. Things seemed arranged with more propriety even than in the Kingdom of Heaven. After leaving Pinky, Francis went to a jeweller's and bought the girl a bracelet. How happy this clandestine purchase made him, how stuffy and comical the jeweller's clerks seemed, how sweet the women who passed at his back smelled! On Fifth Avenue, passing Atlas with his shoulders bent under the weight of the world, Francis thought of the strenuousness of containing his physicalness within the patterns he had chosen.

He did not know when he would see the girl next. He had the bracelet in his inside pocket when he got home. Opening the door of his house, he found her in the hall. Her back was to him, and she turned when she heard the door close. Her smile was open and loving. Her perfection stunned him like a fine day—a day after a thunderstorm. He seized her and covered her lips with his, and she struggled but she did not have to struggle for long, because just then little Gertrude Flannery appeared from somewhere and said, "Oh, Mr. Weed . . ."

Gertrude was a stray. She had been born with a taste for exploration, and she did not have it in her to center her life with her affectionate parents. People who did not know the Flannerys concluded from Gertrude's behavior that she was the child of a bitterly divided family, where drunken quarrels were the rule. This was not true. The fact that Gertrude's clothing was ragged and thin was her own triumph over her mother's struggle to dress her warmly and neatly. Garrulous, skinny, and unwashed, she drifted from house to house around the Blenhollow neighborhood, forming and breaking alliances based on an attachment to babies, animals, children her own age, adolescents, and sometimes adults. Opening your front door in the morning, you would find Gertrude sitting on your stoop. Going into the bathroom to shave, you would find Gertrude using the toilet. Looking into your son's crib, you would find it empty, and, looking further, you would find that Gertrude had pushed him in his baby carriage into the next village. She was helpful, pervasive, honest, hungry, and loyal. She never went home of her own choice. When the time to go arrived, she was indifferent to all its signs. "Go home, Gertrude," people could be heard saying in one house or another, night after night. "Go home, Gertrude." "It's time for you to go home now, Gertrude." "You had better go home and get your supper, Gertrude." "I told you to go home twenty minutes ago, Gertrude." "Your mother will be worrying about you, Gertrude." "Go home, Gertrude, go home."

There are times when the lines around the human eye seem like shelves of eroded stone and when the staring eye itself strikes us with such a wilderness of animal feeling that we are at a loss. The look Francis gave the little girl was ugly and queer, and it frightened her. He reached into his pocket—his hands were shaking—and took out a quarter. "Go home, Gertrude, go home, and don't tell anyone, Gertrude. Don't—" He choked and ran into the living room as Julia called down to him from upstairs to hurry and dress.

The thought that he would drive Anne Murchison home later that night ran like a golden thread through the events of the party that Francis and Julia went to, and he laughed uproariously at dull jokes, dried a tear when Mabel Mercer told him about the death of her kitten, and stretched, yawned, sighed, and grunted like any other man with a rendezvous at the back of his mind. The bracelet was in his pocket. As he sat talking, the smell of grass was in his nose, and he was wondering where he would park the car. Nobody lived in the old Parker mansion, and the driveway was used as a lovers' lane. Townsend Street was a dead end, and he could park there, beyond the last house. The old lane that used to connect Elm Street to the riverbanks was overgrown, but he had walked there with his children, and he could drive his car deep enough into the brushwoods to be concealed.

The Weeds were the last to leave the party, and their host and hostess spoke of their own married happiness while they all four stood in the hallway saying good night. "She's my girl," their host said, squeezing his wife. "She's my blue sky. After sixteen years, I still bite her shoulders. She makes me feel like Hannibal crossing the Alps."

The Weeds drove home in silence. Francis brought the car up the driveway and sat still, with the motor running. "You can put the car in the garage," Julia said as she got out. "I told the Murchison girl she could leave at eleven. Someone drove her home." She shut the door, and Francis sat in the dark. He would be spared nothing then, it seemed, that a fool was not spared: ravening lewdness, jealousy, this hurt to his feelings that put tears in his eyes, even scorn—for he could see clearly the image he now presented, his arms spread over the steering wheel and his head buried in them for love.

Francis had been a dedicated Boy Scout when he was young, and, remembering the precepts of his youth, he left his office early the next afternoon and played some round-robin squash, but, with his body toned up by exercise and a shower, he realized that he might better have stayed at his desk. It was a frosty night when he got home. The air smelled sharply of change. When he stepped into the house, he sensed an unusual stir. The children were in their best clothes, and when Julia came down, she was wearing a lavender dress and her diamond sunburst. She explained the stir: Mr. Hubber was coming at seven to take their photograph for the Christmas card. She had put out Francis' blue suit and a tie with some color in it, because the picture was going to be in color this year. Julia was lighthearted at the thought of being photographed for Christmas. It was the kind of ceremony she enjoyed.

Francis went upstairs to change his clothes. He was tired from the day's work and tired with longing, and sitting on the edge of the bed had the effect of deepening his weariness. He thought of Anne Murchison, and the physical need to express himself, instead of being restrained by the pink lamps of Julia's dressing table, engulfed him. He went to Julia's desk, took a piece of writing paper, and began to write on it. "Dear Anne, I love you, I love you, I love you . . ." No one would see the letter, and he used no restraint. He used phrases like "heavenly bliss," and "love nest." He salivated, sighed, and trembled. When Julia called him to come down, the abyss between his fantasy and the practical world opened so wide that he felt it affect the muscles of his heart.

Julia and the children were on the stoop, and the photographer and his assistant had set up a double battery of floodlights to show the family and the architectural beauty of the entrance to their house. People who had come home on a late train slowed their cars to see the Weeds being photographed for their Christmas card. A few waved and called to the family. It took half an hour of smiling and wetting their lips before Mr. Hubber was satisfied. The heat of the lights made an unfresh smell in the frosty air, and when they were turned off, they lingered on the retina of Francis' eyes.

Later that night, while Francis and Julia were drinking their coffee in the living room, the doorbell rang. Julia answered the door and let in Clayton Thomas. He had come to pay her for some theatre tickets that she had given his mother some time ago, and that Helen Thomas had scrupulously insisted on paying for, though Julia had asked her not to. Julia invited him in to have a cup of coffee. "I won't have any coffee," Clayton said, "but I will come in for a minute." He followed her into the living room, said good evening to Francis, and sat awkwardly in a chair.

Clayton's father had been killed in the war, and the young man's fatherlessness surrounded him like an element. This may have been conspicuous in Shady Hill because the Thomases were the only family that lacked a piece; all the other marriages were intact and productive. Clayton was in his second or third year of college, and he and his mother lived alone in a large house, which she hoped to sell. Clayton had once made some trouble. Years ago, he had stolen some money and run away; he had got to California before they caught up with him. He was tall and homely, wore horn-rimmed glasses, and spoke in a deep voice.

"When do you go back to college, Clayton?" Francis asked.

"I'm not going back," Clayton said. "Mother doesn't have the money, and there's no sense in all this pretense. I'm going to get a job, and if we sell the house, we'll take an apartment in New York."

"Won't you miss Shady Hill?" Julia asked.

"No," Clayton said. "I don't like it."

"Why not?" Francis asked.

"Well, there's a lot here I don't approve of," Clayton said gravely. "Things like the club dances. Last Saturday night, I looked in toward the end and saw Mr. Granner trying to put Mrs. Minot into the trophy case. They were both drunk. I disapprove of so much drinking."

"It was Saturday night," Francis said.

"And all the dovecotes are phony," Clayton said. "And the way people clutter up their lives. I've thought about it a lot, and what seems to me to be really wrong with Shady Hill is that it doesn't have any future. So much energy is spent in perpetuating the place —in keeping out undesirables, and so forth—that the only idea of the future anyone has is just more and more commuting trains and more parties. I don't think that's healthy. I think people ought to be able to dream big dreams about the future. I think people ought to be able to dream great dreams."

"It's too bad you couldn't continue with college," Julia said.

"I wanted to go to divinity school," Clayton said.

"What's your church?" Francis asked.

"Unitarian, Theosophist, Transcendentalist, Humanist," Clayton said.

"Wasn't Emerson a transcendentalist?" Julia asked.

"I mean the English transcendentalists," Clayton said. "All the American transcendentalists were goops."

"What kind of a job do you expect to get?" Francis asked.

"Well, I'd like to work for a publisher," Clayton said, "but everyone tells me there's nothing doing. But it's the kind of thing I'm interested in. I'm writing a long verse play about good and evil. Uncle Charlie might get me into a bank, and that would be good for me. I need the discipline. I have a long way to go in forming my character. I have some terrible habits. I talk too much. I think I ought to take vows of silence. I ought to try not to speak for a week, and discipline myself. I've thought of making a retreat at one of the Episcopalian monasteries, but I don't like Trinitarianism."

"Do you have any girl friends?" Francis asked.

"I'm engaged to be married," Clayton said. "Of course, I'm not old enough or rich enough to have my engagement observed or respected or anything, but I bought a simulated emerald for Anne Murchison with the money I made cutting lawns this summer.

We're going to be married as soon as she finishes school."

Francis recoiled at the mention of the girl's name. Then a dingy light seemed to emanate from his spirit, showing everything—Julia, the boy, the chairs—in their true colorlessness. It was like a bitter turn of the weather.

"We're going to have a large family," Clayton said. "Her father's a terrible rummy, and I've had my hard times, and we want to have lots of children. Oh, she's wonderful, Mr. and Mrs. Weed, and we have so much in common. We like all the same things. We sent out the same Christmas card last year without planning it, and we both have an allergy to tomatoes, and our eyebrows grow together in the middle. Well, good night."

Julia went to the door with him. When she returned, Francis said that Clayton was lazy, irresponsible, affected, and smelly. Julia said that Francis seemed to be getting intolerant; the Thomas boy was young and should be given a chance. Julia had noticed other cases where Francis had been short-tempered. "Mrs. Wrightson has asked everyone in Shady Hill to her anniversary party but us," she said.

"I'm sorry, Julia."

"Do you know why they didn't ask us?"

"Why?"

"Because you insulted Mrs. Wrightson."

"Then you know about it?"

"June Masterson told me. She was standing behind you."

Julia walked in front of the sofa with a small step that expressed, Francis knew, a feeling of anger.

"I did insult Mrs. Wrightson, Julia, and I meant to. I've never liked her parties, and I'm glad she's dropped us."

"What about Helen?"

"How does Helen come into this?"

"Mrs. Wrightson's the one who decides who goes to the assemblies."

"You mean she can keep Helen from going to the dances?"

"Yes."

"I hadn't thought of that."

"Oh, I knew you hadn't thought of it," Julia cried, thrusting hilt-deep into this chink of his armor. "And it makes me furious to see this kind of stupid thoughtlessness wreck everyone's happiness."

"I don't think I've wrecked anyone's happiness."

"Mrs. Wrightson runs Shady Hill and has run it for the last forty years. I don't know what makes you think that in a community like this you can indulge every impulse you have to be insulting, vulgar, and offensive."

"I have very good manners," Francis said, trying to give the evening a turn toward the light.

"Damn you, Francis Weed!" Julia cried, and the spit of her words struck him in the face. "I've worked hard for the social position we enjoy in this place, and I won't stand by and see you wreck it. You must have understood when you settled here that you couldn't expect to live like a bear in a cave."

"I've got to express my likes and dislikes."

"You can conceal your dislikes. You don't have to meet everything head-on, like a child. Unless you're anxious to be a social leper. It's no accident that we get asked out a great deal. It's no accident that Helen has so many friends. How would you like to spend your Saturday nights at the movies? How would you like to spend your Sundays raking up dead leaves? How would you like it if your daughter spent the assembly nights sitting at her window, listening to the music from the club? How would you like it—" He did something then that was, after all, not so unaccountable, since her words seemed to raise up between them a wall so deadening that he gagged: He struck her full in the face. She staggered and then, a moment later, seemed composed. She went up the stairs to their room. She didn't slam the door. When Francis followed, a few minutes later, he found her packing a suitcase.

"Julia, I'm very sorry."

"It doesn't matter," she said. She was crying.

"Where do you think you're going?"

"I don't know. I just looked at a timetable. There's an eleven-sixteen into New York. I'll take that."

"You can't go, Julia."

"I can't stay. I know that."

"I'm sorry about Mrs. Wrightson, Julia, and I'm—"

"It doesn't matter about Mrs. Wrightson. That isn't the trouble."

"What is the trouble?"

"You don't love me."

"I do love you, Julia."

"No, you don't."

"Julia, I do love you, and I would like to be as we were—sweet and bawdy and dark—but now there are so many people."

"You hate me."

"I don't hate you, Julia."

"You have no idea of how much you hate me. I think it's subconscious. You don't realize the cruel things you've done."

"What cruel things, Julia?"

"The cruel acts your subconscious drives you to in order to express your hatred of me."

"What, Julia?"

"I've never complained."

"Tell me."

"You don't know what you're doing."

"Tell me."

"Your clothes."

"What do you mean?"

"I mean the way you leave your dirty clothes around in order to express your subconscious hatred of me."

"I don't understand."

"I mean your dirty socks and your dirty pajamas and your dirty underwear and your dirty shirts!" She rose from kneeling by the suitcase and faced him, her eyes blazing and her voice ringing with emotion. "I'm talking about the fact that you've never learned to hang up anything. You just leave your clothes all over the floor where they drop, in order to humiliate me. You do it on purpose!" She fell on the bed, sobbing.

"Julia, darling!" he said, but when she felt his hand on her shoulder she got up.

"Leave me alone," she said. "I have to go." She brushed past him to the closet and came back with a dress. "I'm not taking any of the things you've given me," she said. "I'm leaving my pearls and the fur jacket."

"Oh, Julia!" Her figure, so helpless in its self-deceptions, bent over the suitcase made him nearly sick with pity. She did not understand how desolate her life would be without him. She didn't understand the hours that working women have to keep. She didn't understand that most of her friendships existed within the framework of their marriage, and that without this she would find herself alone. She didn't understand about travel, about hotels, about money. "Julia, I can't let you go! What you don't understand, Julia, is that you've come to be dependent on me."

She tossed her head back and covered her face with her hands. "Did you say that *I* was dependent on *you*?" she asked. "Is that what you said? And who is it that tells you what time to get up in the morning and when to go to bed at night? Who is it that prepares your meals and picks up your dirty closet and invites your friends to dinner? If it weren't for me, your neckties would be greasy and your clothing would be full of moth holes. You were alone when I met you, Francis Weed, and you'll be alone when I leave. When Mother asked you for a list to send out invitations to our wedding, how many names did you have to give her? Fourteen!"

"Cleveland wasn't my home, Julia."

"And how many of your friends came to the church? Two!"

"Cleveland wasn't my home, Julia."

"Since I'm not taking the fur jacket," she said quietly, "you'd better put it back into storage. There's an insurance policy on the pearls that comes due in January. The name of the laundry and the maid's telephone number—all those things are in my desk. I hope you won't drink too much, Francis. I hope that nothing bad will happen to you. If you do get into serious trouble, you can call me."

"Oh my darling, I can't let you go!" Francis said. "I can't let you go, Julia!" He took her in his arms.

"I guess I'd better stay and take care of you for a little while longer," she said.

Riding to work in the morning, Francis saw the girl walk down the aisle of the coach. He was surprised; he hadn't realized that the school she went to was in the city, but she was carrying books, she seemed to be going to school. His surprise delayed his reaction, but then he got up clumsily and stepped into the aisle. Several people had come between them, but he could see her ahead of him, waiting for someone to open the car door, and then, as the train swerved, putting out her hand to support herself as she crossed the platform into the next car. He followed her through that car and halfway through another before calling her name—"Anne! Anne!"—but she didn't turn. He followed her into still another car, and she sat down in an aisle seat. Coming up to her, all his feelings warm and bent in her direction, he put his hand on the back of her seat—even this touch warmed him—and, leaning down to speak to her, he saw that it was not Anne. It was an older woman wearing glasses. He went deliberately into another car, his face red with embarrassment and the much deeper feeling of having his good sense challenged; for if he couldn't tell one person from another, what evidence was there that his life with Julia and the children had as much reality as his dreams of iniquity in Paris or the litter, the grass smell, and the cave-shaped trees in Lovers' Lane.

Late that afternoon, Julia called to remind Francis that they were going out for dinner. A few minutes later, Trace Bearden called. "Look, fellar," Trace said. "I'm calling for Mrs. Thomas. You know? Clayton, that boy of hers, doesn't seem able to get a job, and I wondered if you could help. If you'd call Charlie Bell—I know he's indebted to you—and say a good word for the kid, I think Charlie would—"

"Trace, I hate to say this," Francis said, "but I don't feel that I can do anything for that boy. The kid's worthless. I know it's a harsh thing to say, but it's a fact. Any kindness done for him would backfire in everybody's face. He's just a worthless kid, Trace, and there's nothing to be done about it. Even if we got him a job, he wouldn't be able to keep it for a week. I know that to be a fact. It's an awful thing, Trace, and I know it is, but instead of recommending that kid, I'd feel obliged to warn people against him—people who knew his father and would naturally want to step in and do something. I'd feel obliged to warn them. He's a thief . . ."

The moment this conversation was finished, Miss Rainey came in and stood by his desk. "I'm not going to be able to work for you any more, Mr. Weed," she said. "I can stay until the seventeenth if you need me, but I've been offered a whirlwind of a job, and I'd like to leave as soon as possible."

She went out, leaving him to face alone the wickedness of what he had done to the Thomas boy. His children in their photograph laughed and laughed, glazed with all the bright colors of summer, and he remembered that they had met a bagpiper on the beach that day and he had paid the piper a dollar to play them a battle song of the Black Watch. The girl would be at the house when he got home. He would spend another evening among his kind neighbors, picking and choosing dead-end streets, cart tracks, and the driveways of abandoned houses. There was nothing to mitigate his feeling—nothing that laughter or a game of softball with the children would change—and, thinking back over the plane crash, the Farquarson's new maid, and Anne Murchison's difficulties with her drunken father, he wondered how he could have avoided arriving at just where he was. He was in trouble. He had been lost once in his life, coming back from a trout stream in the north woods, and he had now the same bleak realization that no amount of cheerfulness or hopefulness or valor or perseverance could help him find, in the gathering dark, the path that he'd lost. He smelled the forest. The feeling of bleakness was intolerable, and he saw clearly that he had reached the point where he would have to make a choice.

He could go to a psychiatrist, like Miss Rainey; he could go to church and confess his lusts; he could go to a Danish massage parlor in the West Seventies that had been recommended by a salesman; he could rape the girl or trust that he would somehow be prevented from doing this; or he could get drunk. It was his life, his boat, and, like every other man, he was made to be the father of thousands, and what harm could there be in a tryst that would make them both feel more kindly toward the world? This was the wrong train of thought, and he came back to the first, the psychiatrist. He had the telephone number of Miss Rainey's doctor, and he called and asked for an immediate appointment. He was insistent with the doctor's secretary—it was his manner in business—and when she said that the doctor's schedule was full for the next few weeks, Francis demanded an appointment that day and was told to come at five.

The psychiatrist's office was in a building that was used mostly by doctors and dentists, and the hallways were filled with the candy smell of mouthwash and memories of pain. Francis' character had been formed upon a series of private resolves—resolves about cleanliness, about going off the high diving board or repeating any other feat that challenged his courage, about punctuality, honesty, and virtue. To abdicate the perfect loneliness in which he had made his most vital decisions shattered his concept of character and left him now in a condition that felt like shock. He was stupefied. The scene for his *miserere mei Deus* was, like the waiting room of so many doctors' offices, a crude token gesture toward the sweets of domestic bliss: a place arranged with antiques, coffee tables, potted plants, and etchings of snow-covered bridges and geese in flight, although there were no children, no marriage bed, no stove, even, in this travesty of a house, where no one had ever spent the night and where the curtained windows looked straight onto a dark air shaft. Francis gave his name and address to a secretary and then saw, at the side of the room, a policeman moving toward him. "Hold it, hold it," the policeman said. "Don't move. Keep your hands where they are."

"I think it's all right, officer," the secretary began. "I think it will be—"

"Let's make sure," the policeman said, and he began to slap Francis' clothes, looking for what—pistols, knives, an icepick? Finding nothing, he went off, and the secretary began a nervous apology: "When you called on the telephone, Mr. Weed, you seemed very excited, and one of the doctor's patients has been threatening his life, and we have to be careful. If you want to go in now?" Francis pushed open a door connected to an electrical chime, and in the doctor's lair sat down heavily, blew his nose into a handkerchief, searched in his pockets for cigarettes, for matches, for something, and said hoarsely, with tears in his eyes, "I'm in love, Dr. Herzog."

It is a week or ten days later in Shady Hill. The seven-fourteen has come and gone, and here and there dinner is finished and the dishes are in the dishwashing machine. The village hangs, morally and economically, from a thread; but it hangs by its thread in the evening light. Donald Goslin has begun to worry the "Moonlight Sonata" again. *Marcato ma sempre pianissimo!* He seems to be wringing out a wet bath towel, but the housemaid does not heed him. She is writing a letter to Arthur Godfrey. In the cellar of his house, Francis Weed is building a coffee table. Dr. Herzog recommended woodwork as a therapy, and Francis finds some true consolation in the simple arithmetic involved and in the holy smell of new wood. Francis is happy. Upstairs, little Toby is crying, because he is tired. He puts off his cowboy hat, gloves, and fringed jacket, unbuckles the belt studded with gold and rubies, the silver bullets and holsters, slips off his suspenders, his checked shirt, and Levis, and sits on the edge of his bed to pull off his high boots. Leaving this equipment in a heap, he goes to the closet and takes his space suit off a nail. It is a struggle for him to get into the long tights, but he succeeds. He loops the magic cape over his shoulders and, climbing onto the footboard of his bed, he spreads his arms and flies the short distance to the floor, landing with a thump that is audible to everyone in the house but himself.

"Go home, Gertrude, go home," Mrs. Masterson says. "I told you to go home an hour ago, Gertrude. It's way past your suppertime, and your mother will be worried. Go home!" A door on the Babcocks' terrace flies open, and out comes Mrs. Babcock without any clothes on, pursued by her naked husband. (Their children are away at boarding school, and their terrace is screened by a hedge.) Over the terrace they go and in at the kitchen door, as passionate and handsome a nymph and satyr as you will find on any wall in Venice. Cutting the last of the roses in her garden, Julia hears old Mr. Nixon shouting at the squirrels in his bird-feeding station. "Rapscallions! Varmits! Avaunt and quit my sight!" A miserable cat wanders into the garden, sunk in spiritual and physical discomfort. Tied to its head is a small straw hat—a doll's hat—and it is securely buttoned into a doll's dress, from the skirts of which protrudes its long, hairy tail. As it walks, it shakes its feet, as if it had fallen into water.

"Here, pussy, pussy, pussy!" Julia calls.

"Here, pussy, here, poor pussy!" But the cat gives her a skeptical look and stumbles away in its skirts. The last to come is Jupiter. He prances through the tomato vines, holding in his generous mouth the remains of an evening slipper. Then it is dark; it is a night where kings in golden suits ride elephants over the mountains.

(*From The Paris Review*)

THE FISHERMAN FROM CHIHUAHUA

BY EVAN S. CONNELL, JR.

SANTA CRUZ is at the top of Monterey Bay which is about 100 miles below San Francisco, and in the winter there are not many people in Santa Cruz. The boardwalk concessions are shuttered except for one counter-and-booth restaurant, the ferris wheel seats are hooded with olive-green canvas and the power-house padlocked, and the rococo doors of the carousel are boarded over and if one peers through a knothole into its gloom the horses which buck and plunge through summer prosperity seem like animals touched by a magic wand that they may never move again. Dust dims the gilt of their saddles and sifts through cracks into their bold nostrils. About the only sounds to be heard around the waterfront in Santa Cruz during winter are the voices of Italian fishermen hidden by mist as they work against the long pier, and the slap of waves against the pilings of the cement dance pavilion when tide runs high, or the squeak of a gull, or once in a long time bootsteps on the slippery boards as some person comes quite alone and usually slowly to the edge of the grey and fogbound ocean.

The restaurant is Pendleton's and white brush strokes on the glass announce *tacos, frijoles* and *enchiladas* as house specialties, these being mostly greens and beans and fried meat made arrogant with pepper. Smaller letters in pseudo-Gothic script say: *Se Habla Español* but this is not true; it was the man who owned the place before Pendleton who could speak Spanish. From him, though, Pendleton did learn how to make the food and this is the reason a short fat Mexican who worked as a mechanic at Ace Dillon's Texaco station continued eating his suppers there. He came in every night just after eight o'clock and sat at the counter, ate an astounding amount of this food which he first splattered with tabasco sauce as casually as though it were ketchup and then washed farther down with beer. After that he would feel a little drunk and would spend as much as two or even three dollars playing the pinball machine and the great nickelodeon and dancing by himself, but inoffensively, contentedly, just snapping his fingers and shuffling across the warped boards often until Pendleton began pulling in the shutters. Then having had a suitable evening he would half-dance his way home, or at least back in the direction of town. He was a squat little man who waddled like a duck full of eggs and he had a face like a blunt arrowhead or a Toltec idol, and he was about the color of hot sand. His fingers were much too thick for their length, seemingly without joints, only creases where it was necessary for them to bend. He smelled principally of cold grease and of urine as though his pants needed some air, but Pendleton who did not smell very good himself did not mind and besides there were not many customers during these winter months.

So every evening shortly after dark he entered for his food and some amusement, and as he appeared to contain all God's world within his own self Pendleton was not disinterested when another Mexican came in directly behind him like a long shadow. This new man was tall, very tall, possibly six feet or more, and much darker, almost black in the manner of a sweat stained saddle. He was handsome, silent, and perhaps forty years of age. Also he was something of a dandy: his trousers which were long and quite tight revealed the fact that he was bowlegged, as befits certain types of men, and made one think of him easily riding a large fast horse, not necessarily toward a woman but in the direction of something more remote and mysterious—bearing a significant message or something like that. Exceedingly short black boots of finest leather took in his narrow trouser bottoms. For a shirt he wore long-sleeved white silk unbuttoned to below the level of his nipples which, themselves, were vaguely visible. The hair of his chest was so luxuriant that an enameled crucifix there did not even rest on the skin.

These two men sat at the counter side by side. The tall one lifted off his sombrero as if afraid of mussing his hair and he placed it on the third stool. His hair was deeply oiled and comb tracks went all the way from his temples to the back of his thin black neck, and he scented of a kind of green perfume. He had a mustache that consisted of nothing but two black strings hanging across the corners of his unforgiving mouth and ending in soft points about an inch below his chin. He seemed to think himself alone in the restaurant because, after slowly licking his lips and interlacing his fingers, he just sat looking somberly ahead. The small man ordered for them both.

After they had eaten supper the little one played the pinball machine while this strange man took from his shirt pocket a cigarillo only a little bigger than his mustache and smoked it with care, that is, he would take it from his mouth between his thumb and one finger as if he were afraid of crushing it, and after releasing the smoke he would replace it with the same care in the exact center of his mouth. It never dangled or rolled, he respected it. Nor was it a cheap piece of tobacco, its smoke ascended heavily, moist and sweet.

Suddenly the fat Mexican kicked the pinball game and with a surly expression walked over to drop a coin into the nickelodeon. The tall man had remained all this time at the counter with his long savage eyes half-shut, smoking and smoking the fragrant cigarillo. Now he did not turn around, in fact his single movement was to remove the stump from his lips, but clearly he was disturbed. When the music ended he sat totally motionless for several minutes. Then his head began to sink and was almost touching the counter before its direction reversed, and when his face was against the ceiling his throat began to swell like that of a mating pigeon.

Pendleton, sponging an ash tray, staggered as if a knife had plunged through his ribs.

The Mexican's eyes were squeezed altogether shut. His lips had peeled back from his teeth like those of a jaguar tearing meat and the veins of his neck looked ready to burst. In the shrill screams was a memory of Moors, the ching of Arab cymbals, of rags and of running feet through all the market places of the East.

His song had no beginning; it had no end. All at once he was simply sitting on the stool looking miserably ahead.

After a while the small fat Mexican said to Pendleton, "Be seeing you, man," and waddled through the door into darkness. A few seconds later the tall one's stool creaked. Without a sound he placed the high steepled sombrero like a crown on his hair and followed his friend through the door.

The next night there happened to be a pair of tourists eating in the back booth when the men entered. They were dressed as before except that the big one's shirt was lime green in color and Pendleton noticed his wrist watch, fastened not to his wrist actually but over the green cuff where it bulged like an oily bubble. They took the same stools and ate fried beans, tacos and enchiladas for almost an hour after which the short one who looked like his Toltec ancestors gently belched, smiled in a benign way and moved over to his machine. Failing to win anything he cursed it and kicked it before selecting his favorite records.

This time Pendleton was alert: as the music ended he got ready for the first shriek. The tourists, caught unaware, thought their time had come. When they recovered from the shock they looked fearfully over the top of the booth and then the woman stood up in order to see better. After the black Mexican's song was finished they could hear the incoming tide, washing softly around the pillars of the pavilion.

Presently the two paid their bill and went out, the short one leading, into the dirty yellow fog and the diving, squeaking gulls.

"Why that's terrible," the woman laughed. "It wasn't musical." Anyone who looked at her would know she was still shuddering from the force of the ominous man.

Her husband too was frightened and laughed, "Somebody should play a little drum behind that fellow." Unaware of what a peculiar statement he had made he formed a circle of his thumb and forefinger to show how big the drum should be.

She was watching the door, trying to frown compassionately. "I wonder what's the matter with that poor man. Some woman must have hurt him dreadfully."

Pendleton began to wipe beer bracelets and splats of tabasco from the lacquered plywood counter where the men had been. The restaurant seemed too quiet.

The woman remarked cheerily, "We're from Iowa City."

Pendleton tried to think of something but he had never been to Iowa City or anywhere near it even on a train, so he asked if they would like more coffee.

The husband wondered, "Those two fellows, do they come in here every night?"

Pendleton was seized with contempt and hatred for this domestic little man, though he did not know why, and walked stiffly away from their booth without answering. He stood with both hairy hands on the shining urn while he listened to the sea threshing and rolling under the night.

"Who?" he said gruffly. "Them two?"

A few minutes later while pouring coffee he said, "Sometimes I feel so miserable I could damn near roll up in a tube."

The couple, overpowered by his manner, looked up uneasily. The woman ventured: "It seems terribly lonely around."

On the third evening as they seated themselves before the counter Pendleton said to the one who spoke American, "Tell your friend he can't yowl in here any more."

"He's not my baby," this short fat man replied, not greatly interested. "Six tacos and four beers and a lot of beans."

"What do you think, I'm running a damn concert hall?"

For a moment the little Mexican became eloquent with his eyebrows, then both he and Pendleton turned their attention to the silent one who was staring somberly past the case of pies.

Pendleton leaned on his hands so that his shoulders bulged. "Now looky, Pablo, give him the word and do it quick. Tell him to cut that noise out. You understand me?"

This enraged the small man whose voice rose to a snarl. "Pablo yourself. Don't give me that stuff."

Pendleton was not angry but set about cleaving greens for their tacos as though he were furious. While the blade chunked into the wood again and again beside his thumb he thought about the situation. He did not have anything particular in mind when all at once he banged down the cleaver and with teeth clenched began bending his eyes toward the two.

"No debe cantar," the little one said hurriedly, waggling a negative finger at his companion. No more singing. *"No más."*

"That's better, by God," muttered Pendleton as though he understood. He wished to say something in Spanish about the matter but he knew only *mañana, adios* and *señorita* and none of these seemed to fit. He resumed work, but doubtfully, not certain if the silent one had heard either of them. Over one shoulder he justified himself: "Folks come here to eat their suppers, not to hear any concert."

Abel W. Sharpe who had once been the sheriff of Coda City and who now ripped tickets for a movie house on Pacific came in the door alone but arguing harshly. The Toltec had started playing pinball so Sharpe took the vacant stool, looked up twice at the man beside him, and then dourly ordered waffles and hot milk. It was while he was pouring syrup into the milk that the nickelodeon music died and that the black Mexican did it again.

Pendleton was exasperated with himself for laughing and almost choked by trying to stop.

"Heh?" asked the old man, who at the first note had jumped off his stool and now crouched several feet away from the counter, a knife in one hand and his mug of sweet milk in the other. "I can't hear nothing. The bastard's deefened me."

The Toltec had not stopped playing pinball and paid none of them the least attention because he had lighted four pretty girls which meant he would probably win something. His friend now sat motionless on the stool and looked ahead as though he saw clear into some grief-stricken time.

Not until the eighth or maybe the ninth did Pendleton realize that the restaurant was drawing more people; there would be six or eight or even as many as a dozen in for dinner.

There came a night when the fat Toltec entered as always but no one followed. That night the restaurant was an uneasy place. Things spilled, and while cleaning up one of the tables Pendleton discovered a menu burned through and through with cigarette holes. By 10:30 the place was deserted.

Pendleton said, "Hey, Pablo."

The Toltec gave him a furious look.

"All right," Pendleton apologized, "what's your name?"

"What's yours?" he replied. He was deeply insulted.

"Whereabouts is your friend?"

"He's no friend of mine."

Pendleton walked down the counter behind a damp rag, wrung it over the sink, then very casually he did something he never did or never even thought of doing: he opened a bottle of beer for the Mexican and indicated without a word that it was free.

Toltec, though still grieved, accepted the gift, saying, "I just met the guy. He asked me where to get some decent cooking."

Pendleton wiped a table and for a time appeared to be idly picking his back teeth. When he judged the interval to be correct he asked, "Got tired of the grub here, I guess."

"No, tonight he's just drunk."

Pendleton allowed several more minutes, then, "He looks like a picture of a bullfighter I saw once in Tijuana called Victoriano Posada."

And this proved to be a shrewd inquiry because after drinking some more of the free beer the fat Mexican remarked, "He calls himself Damaso."

Pendleton, wondering if something else might follow, pretended to stretch and to yawn and smacked his chops mightily. He thought that tomorrow he would say, when the tall one entered, "Howdy, Damaso."

"Know what? He goes and stands by himself on the sea wall a lot of times. Maybe he's going to knock himself off. Wouldn't that be something?"

"Tell him not to do it in front of my place," Pendleton answered.

Through the screen door could be seen a roll of silvery yellow fog and above it the moon, but the water was hidden.

"These Santa Cruz winters," Pendleton said. Opening the icebox he selected a superior beer for himself and moved his high stool far enough away that his guest might not feel their friendship was being forced. Peeling off the wet label he rolled it into a soggy grey ball which he dropped into a bucket under the counter. "Singers make plenty money, I hear."

The Mexican looked at him slyly. "What are you talking about?"

Pendleton, scratching his head, sighed and yawned again. "Huh? Oh. I was just thinking about what's-his-name. That fellow you come in here with once or twice."

"I know it," the Mexican said, laughing.

For a while both of them drank away at their beers and listened to the combers, each of which sounded as if it would smash the door.

"Feels like there's something standing up in the ocean tonight," Pendleton said. "I could use a little summer."

"You want our beach full of tourists? Those sausages? Man, you're crazy. You're off the rocks."

Pendleton judged that the Mexican was about to insult the summer people still more so he manipulated the conversation once again: "Somebody told me your friend got himself a singing job at that nightspot near Capitola."

"Look," said the Toltec, patient but irritated, "I just met the guy a couple of weeks ago."

"He never said where he's from, I guess."

"Chihuahua, he says. That's one rough town. And full of sand, Jesus Christ."

Breakers continued sounding just beyond the door and the fog now stood against the screen like a person.

"What does he do?"

The Mexican lifted both fat little shoulders.

"Just traveling through?"

The Mexican lifted both hands.

"Where is he going?"

"All I know is he's got a pretty good voice."

"He howls like a god damn crazy wolf," Pendleton said, "howling for the moon."

"Yah, he's pretty good. Long time ago I saw a murder down south in the mountains and a woman screamed just like that."

Both of them thought about things and Pendleton, having reflected on the brevity of human affairs and the futility of riches, opened his icebox for two more drinks. The Mexican accepted one as though in payment for service. For some seconds they had been able to hear footsteps approaching, audible after every tunnel of water caved in. The footsteps went past the door but no one could be seen.

"Know what? There was an old man washed up on the beach the other day."

"That so?" said Pendleton. "Everything gets to the beach sooner or later."

The Mexican nodded. Somewhere far out on the bay a little boat sounded again and again. "What a night," he said.

Pendleton murmured and scratched.

"Know something, mister?"

Pendleton, now printing wet circles on his side of the counter, asked what that might be.

"Damaso is no Mexicano."

"I didn't think so," Pendleton lied.

"No, because he's got old blood. You know what I mean? I think he's a gypsy from Spain, or wherever those guys come from. He's dark in the wrong way. He just don't *feel* Mexicano to me. There's something about him, and besides he speaks a little Castellano."

Both of them considered all this.

"I suppose he's howling about some girl."

"No, it's bigger than that."

"What's the sound say?"

But here the little Mexican lost interest; he revolved on the stool, from which only his toes could reach to the floor, hopped off and hurried across to the nickelodeon. Having pushed a nickel through the slit he studied the wonderful colors and followed the bubbles which fluttered up the tubes to vanish, next he dialed "The Great Speckled Bird" and began shuffling around the floor snapping his fingers and undulating so that in certain positions he looked about five months pregnant.

"Who knows?" he asked of no one in particular while he danced.

The next night also he entered alone. When Pendleton mentioned this he replied the dark one was still drunk.

And the next night when asked if the drunk were going into its third day he replied that Damaso was no longer drunk, just sick from being so, that he was at present lying on the wet cement having vomited on his boots, that probably by sunrise he would be all right. This turned out to be correct because both of them came in for supper the following night. Toltec, smiling and tugging at his crotch, was rumpled as usual and smelled human while his tall companion was oiled and groomed and wearing the white silk again. A good many people were loitering about the restaurant —every booth was full—because this thing had come to be expected, and though all of them were eating or drinking or spending money in some way to justify themselves, and although no one looked up at the entrance of the two Mexicans there could be no doubt about the situation. Only these two men seemed not to notice anything; they ate voraciously and drank a lot of beer after which the one went across to his game, which had been deliberately vacated, and Damaso remained on the stool with his long arms crossed on the counter.

Later the nickelodeon lighted up. When at last its music died and the table stopped there was not a sound in all the restaurant. People watched the head of the dark man bow down until it was hidden in his arms. The crucifix disentangled itself and dropped out the top of his gaucho shirt where it began to swing to and fro, glittering as it twisted on the end of its golden chain. He remained like that for almost an hour, finally raised his head to look at the ticket, counted away enough money, and with the sombrero loosely in one hand he stumbled out the door.

The other Mexican paid no attention; he called for more beer which he drank all at once in an attempt to interest a young girl with silver slippers and breasts like pears who was eating supper with her parents, but failing to win anything at this or again at the machine he suddenly grew bored of the evening and walked out.

The next night he entered alone. When asked if his companion had started another drunk he said that Damaso was gone.

Pendleton asked late in the evening, "How do you know?"

"I feel it," he said.

Big Pendleton then stood listening to the advancing tide which had begun to pat the pillars like someone gently slapping a dead drum. Taking off his apron he rolled it tight as he always did and put it beneath the counter. With slow fingers he untied the sweaty handkerchief from around his neck and folded it over the apron, but there his routine altered; before pulling in shutters he stood a while beside the screen and looked out and listened but of course received no more than he expected which was fog, the sound of the sea, and its odor.

Sharply the Toltec said, " I like to dance." And he began to do so. "Next summer I'm really going to cut it up. Nothing's going to catch me." He read Pendleton's face while dancing by himself to the odd and clumsy little step he was inventing, and counseled, "Jesus Christ, he's gone. Forget about it, man."

(From The Ladies' Home Journal)

THE DECLINE AND FALL OF AUGIE SHEEAN

BY JOE COOGAN

I *WAS* thirteen years old on the day that Augie Sheean sold his soul to the devil. Augie, a short, stocky boy with a round, cheerful face was an eighth-grade classmate of mine, who lived four doors away from me in an old two-story row house on Eighteenth Street in Philadelphia. He was a newcomer to our neighborhood. At just about the time the new school term was beginning, Augie and his widowed mother arrived from Tinahely, a small Irish village, and moved into the house left vacant by the death of old Matt Harvey, a bachelor who had lived in the old house on Eighteenth Street for twenty years. It seems that the Sheeans were cousins of his, and old Matt—who had been a saving and fairly prosperous plumber—used to send money to them when he was alive; when he died, he left them the house and a small legacy.

"It's a mystery to me," my mother said, "why he didn't send for them long ago. Rattling around by himself in that big house when he could have had a fine woman to take care of it for him."

The mystery was cleared up when we got to know Margaret Sheean. A tall, heavy-set woman with an air of brisk, determined piety, she was, in her rather breezy way, what my father called a "great frowner." One of the things she frowned on was America. "A land of flappers, gangsters, bootleggers and drunkards," she called it. Old Matt would have had no living with her. Matt drank.

Augie was a year older than I and had graduated from school in Tinahely, but it was decided that he'd have to repeat the eighth grade at St. Anselm's grammar school to qualify for admittance to the Catholic high school. St. Anselm's school was a squat, brick building which huddled self-consciously against the stone, majestically sprawling church. It was only about five blocks down the street from our house, so I was commissioned to take Augie there on the first few mornings and see that he got to know everybody.

As I came out of the house on the first day of class, Augie was standing on his front doorstep waiting for me. He was dressed in a dark-blue coat and knickers, high black shoes and stockings. I was wearing what everyone wore that year—brown corduroy knickers and knee-length boots with a penknife jammed in the top of them. Augie pointed to my boots.

"Is it hunting you're going?"

I decided to dislike him. "These are lumberjack boots. I'm going to be a lumberjack in Canada. A bunch of us are."

"They're lovely things."

I decided to like him. "Maybe you can get a pair and come along. Canada needs good men."

"It's not for me. I'm going to be a priest."

I stared at him in awe. He looked a little like a priest at that, with his large Irish face and dark clothes. "You've got a vocation?"

"My mother's been praying for it. Everything my mother prays for comes true." He crossed the index and middle fingers of his right hand. "She and Saint Joseph are just like that!"

"Don't you *want* to be a priest?"

"Ah, I suppose so. But a fellow has no say in it. The saint has never refused her a thing in his life. She lights the candle every morning, and whatever she wants she gets. It's hard to believe."

It was. It was especially hard for me to believe that Mrs. Sheean could get prompt, efficient service from such a busy, high-level, heavenly executive. Although Joseph was my patron saint, I rarely prayed to him. I was then working on the theory that if you really wanted anything done you should go to someone who had, as it were, less paperwork. I had great devotion, that year, to Saint Polycarp.

I was about to mention this to Augie, when Mrs. Sheean loomed up in front of us.

"Hello, me buckos." Mrs. Sheean had a deep booming voice and a figure like an uptilted dirigible. She stared at my boots. "Did you join up with the Army?" she asked me.

"They're lumberjack boots."

"A small, skinny thing like you a lumberjack? With a fine name like Joseph, it's a priest you should be. I'll say a few prayers for you."

"No, don't!" I said quickly.

"Well, you needn't shout, lad. If I can't help your soul, perhaps I can perform a corporal work of mercy. Drop by with Augustine after school, and I may find a little something to fatten you up." She waved cheerily and floated up the street.

"Augie," I said when she left, "if your mother likes Saint Joseph so much, how come she christened you Augustine?"

Augie scratched his head. " 'Tisn't too sure I am, but I think at one time she was very fond of Saint Augustine. Then she found out a few things about him she didn't like and turned pretty cool. You know, those are lovely things, those boots."

After school, Augie reminded me of his mother's invitation. We found Mrs. Sheean in the kitchen, cutting a large chocolate cake.

"Sit down and eat up, boy," she said. "Don't stint yourself. You're not Jerry Clarke, praise God." Jerry Clarke, Mrs. Sheean went on to explain, was a miserly atheist who lived near her when she was a girl.

"Scrawny and mean he was. Came to a bad end. Said he'd prove there was no God. Ran into the chapel during Mass one morning, and let loose a string of blasphemies." She smiled. "He burst into flame."

"Was he hurt?" I asked.

"Ran screaming from the church and collapsed on the steps, burnt to a crisp. When they stirred the ashes the one thing left of him was a small pool of melted gold. It was the only good thing the little blackguard ever did—God rest his soul. There was enough gold there to repair the steps. Have another piece of cake."

I ate a good bit of Mrs. Sheean's cake in the next month or so and heard a good many of her stories. The cake was always chocolate and delicious; the stories were always bloodcurdling and moralistic. I became quite fond of Mrs. Sheean.

I became fond of Augie too. Everybody did. He was a friendly, easygoing kid and within a few weeks he was one of the most popular boys in the neighborhood.

Mrs. Sheean's reception was more mixed. No doubt, everyone agreed, she had her good points. She was very nice to Augie (she bought him the boots right off) and she was always cruising forth to nurse at a sickbed or mourn at a wake. Yet she dispensed this spiritual largess with an irritating, hearty aloofness. She may have had good cause for her exalted attitude. It turned out to be amazingly true that every prayer Margaret Sheean made was immediately answered. For didn't Annie Brophy, whom the doctors had given up for dead, recover when Mrs. Sheean gave the nod to Saint Joseph? And when she predicted that Corny Hughes (who hadn't seen a sober day in fifteen years) would lay off the hooch, didn't he come down with a liver complaint and have to give up the bottle entirely? Mrs. Sheean had only to mutter a request as she lit her morning candle and the thing was as good as done. Corny Hughes never forgave her for it.

As a matter of fact, Mrs. Sheean's morning devotion became something of a parish scandal. The vigil lights in front of the statue of Saint Joseph were placed in diminishing rows, like racked billiard balls, in an ascending brass triangle. The red one at the apex of the triangle was Mrs. Sheean's. Every morning after eight-o'clock Mass she'd kneel for a few minutes at the *prie-dieu,* then light the candle. If it had been already lit by some lesser suppliant, Mrs. Sheean would pinch it out before relighting it, then light the usurper's candle farther down the line. This caused a great deal of talk, but nobody tried to do anything about it.

Augie's piety was a little less manifest. He regarded his ordination as a *fait accompli* and, like any good priest, he was in church more often than most of us, refused to listen to the mildly irreverent stories that sometimes made the rounds, and had a tendency to spot virtue in everything. It was when he began to spot the virtue in Doris Clooney that all the trouble started.

Doris Clooney, another Eighteenth-Streeter, was the Clara Bow of the eighth grade. A plump, flirtatious girl, she wore longer hair and shorter skirts than any other girl in the class, and there were occasional rumors of cloakroom kisses with Lindy Geoghegan, her steady boy friend. Lindy, a tall, slow-spoken kid who was in the eighth grade for the second time, always wore a black imitation-leather flier's helmet. He was mad about Doris Clooney, and although he lived in the opposite direction he carried her books up Eighteenth Street every day.

Augie and I frequently walked behind them, and when we did

it was hard to get a sensible word out of him. He looked like a man walking underwater; he inched along with his eyes blurred and his lips contorted into a large, rubbery smirk. Then one day Doris smirked back.

I don't know exactly how it happened, but pretty soon Augie and I started walking home with Doris and Lindy. Lindy and I never said much, but Doris—who, it appeared, had developed quite an interest in religion—kept chattering to Augie about sacramentals and church ceremonies and what a noble life priests lead. What he saw in her was beyond me. I thought Doris Clooney was fat and dumb.

It wasn't a completely compatible quartet, and it broke up on the last day of our October retreat.

Sister Mary Rita had just told us about a Belgian peasant girl who was possessed by the devil. When the devil took over, this girl would turn black, float twelve feet in the air and tell off-color stories in Ancient Assyrian. She became the talk of the eighth grade.

"I'd call it," Doris Clooney said as we walked up the street, "a truly awe-inspiring story." That's what sister had called it.

Augie was about to answer when Lindy cut him off: "I'd call it a lot of junk."

"Lindy Geoghegan, that's blasphemous!" Doris said.

"Twelve feet in the air? I don't believe a word of it."

I decided to come to Christianity's rescue. "I jumped from a twelve-foot diving board last summer," I said. "Twelve feet isn't so high."

"It's not bad for such a short take-off," Lindy said.

Doris giggled; Augie frowned; Doris turned prim.

"Come on, Augie," she said, pulling him ahead, "let's not associate with these heathens."

From then on, Augie and Doris walked home alone together. Or rather, Doris walked Augie home. He and Doris would stop and chat when they reached Augie's house; then, as I approached (I always followed a block behind) Doris would smile, blow him a kiss and saunter up Eighteenth Street.

I was a little hurt about all this. I couldn't understand why she should be sore at me. She wasn't, Augie explained; but a wonderful thing had happened. Doris had discovered that she, too, had a vocation; she wanted to be a nun, but she was constantly bothered by worldly thoughts. It did her good to tell Augie about them.

Doris started calling Augie her "dear, dear friend," and wouldn't so much as pass the time of day with poor Lindy Geoghegan.

Augie's spiritual work of mercy came to an abrupt end on a snowy day in mid-November. When I started up Eighteenth Street, I was surprised to see Augie and Doris still standing in front of his house. Mrs. Sheean, who suddenly appeared on the front steps, was even more surprised than I. I couldn't hear what she said, but I saw her right arm come up and make a slow rigid arc until it pointed due north. And I saw Doris bundle her books under her arm and flee into the storm. As I came closer, the thunder of Mrs. Sheean's voice rumbled around my head, and the compasslike arm swung in my direction.

"You're to come in here, too, young man. It's time you learned about things."

I walked up the steps. She put one arm around me, the other around Augie, and pushed us ahead of her into the kitchen. Mrs. Sheean stood in the center of the room, flushed, silent and swaying violently. Then suddenly:

"What's her name?" she bellowed.

"Doris Clooney," Augie muttered.

Mrs. Sheean stopped swaying. She stood stock-still, dropped both hands to her sides and threw back her head.

"I'll tell you a few things about your friend Miss Clooney. I know her type well, and a bad type it is. All satin and Satan and hanging around in low dens with gangsters and sailors with their slick patent-leather hair." (*Lindy's helmet?* I thought.) "Oh, sure, she'll say to you, 'Come on, it won't matter. What difference will it make?' " Mrs. Sheean imitated what she thought was Doris' voice. It came out a kind of mincing boom. " 'Sure it can't make any difference, dearie. Who'll see us?' " Her fist banged on the table. "I'll tell you who will see you. There's the cherubim'll see you, and the seraphim, and all the saints in heaven, and God, and the good Saint Joseph himself." Unperturbed by this unorthodox billing, Mrs. Sheean went on. "But, no! She'll tell you it won't matter."

Just *what* wouldn't matter wasn't very clear to either Augie or me.

"I don't know about the young narrowback here," Mrs. Sheean continued, "but as for you, Augustine, you have a mother's curse if you come near that flapper again. It'll be part of me general intention when I talk to the good saint tomorrow."

That was enough for Augie. After that, he might have been deaf and dumb for all the attention he paid to Doris Clooney. Doris didn't seem to mind, though. She and Lindy Geoghegan became chummier than ever.

I thought when Augie found out Doris didn't have a real vocation after all, he'd feel relieved. He didn't; when I mentioned it he called me a "meddlesome little prattler" and told me to stop bothering him. And he took to going to church more often than ever.

As I came from the confessional one Saturday afternoon, I saw Augie kneeling before the statue of Saint Joseph. The burning vigil lights sent bright flashes of colored fire flickering across his forehead. His lips moved rapidly and his face had the desperately cordial look of one who is doggedly and unsuccessfully trying to get a word in edgewise.

I waited on the church steps until he came out. "Guess what?" I said. "We decided that the first thing we'll do when we get to the woods is clear out a space for the chapel." Augie was supposed to be the lumber camp's chaplain.

"God of Virtues!" he said. "Will I never hear the end of your silly, childish brillabralla?"

"I just wanted to tell you."

"You told me. Now must you be forever tagging after me? Sure I'm sick of listening to you and your plans. I'd appreciate it if you didn't come near me again."

This was the beginning of a lonely time for me. I got so mad at Augie that I almost didn't invite him to my birthday party.

The birthday parties that my mother threw for me came fairly close to being a racket. I was born on the twenty-sixth of December and although the party was the only gift I got from the family, I usually wound up with a fair share of the neighborhood Christmas loot.

I didn't see Augie from the afternoon school closed for the holidays until two days before Christmas, when I went down to learn if he could come to the party. I found him and his mother in the kitchen. Augie was eating a piece of chocolate cake and his mother was telling him something about the specter of a bad priest that had to say Mass every night in the middle of a great bog. She stopped short when she caught sight of me. Augie didn't even look up.

"Och, boy," she said. "Did somebody steal the bell from the door?" Mrs. Sheean wasn't too friendly with me these days either.

"I'm going to be thirteen on the day after Christmas. I'm having a party and I wonder if Augie could come?"

"Well, now, he might," Mrs. Sheean said in what she thought was a sweet voice. "Who all will be there?"

"Oh, the whole gang."

"And will Miss Clooney be making her appearance?"

"I don't know. Maybe. I guess so."

"Then I'm sure Augustine has no desire to be there. Do you, aroon?"

Augie didn't answer.

"If he did," Mrs. Sheean said, "he'd call down the wrath of the angels, and the devil himself would surely take possession of his soul." It seemed unlikely that Augie would attend.

He did, though. The party had been going on for about an hour when I had to leave a game of Pin the Tail on the Donkey to answer the doorbell. It was Augie.

"I stopped by to say hello," he said.

"Could you come in for a minute?"

"Well, I'm not dressed at all." He had on the boots and knickers he wore to school.

"As much as I am," I said, pointing to the shiny new boots that were my favorite Christmas present.

"But I have no gift. I'm sorry about that. And about other things."

"Forget it," I said. "I'm glad you could make it. I never thought your mother would let you."

"She didn't. I told her I was going to church to visit the crèche."

"You lied to her?"

"She believed me. The woman has never been crossed."

It wouldn't have surprised me at all to see him turn black and float twelve feet in the air. It was a terrible price to pay for a bit of ice cream and cake.

But Augie not only managed to keep his footing, he appeared to be having the time of his life. After winning first prize in the treasure hunt (a fifty-cent piece which he gave me as a present) he did a funny jig, sang a few Irish songs, and was, in general, the life of the party. Not once, however, did he speak to Doris Clooney, and she acted as if she weren't in the same room with him.

Then, as usual, just when the party was getting good, some girl interrupted the fun by suggesting a game of Post Office. I started to object, but my older sister, Kathleen, grouped the boys and girls at opposite ends of the room and began giving out the numbers.

"You won't like this," I told Augie. "It's a kissing game."

He took it philosophically. "No matter. It'll be over soon, and we may as well be polite about it."

Kathleen had finished with the girls and came over to us. Just as she was telling Augie his number, Doris Clooney popped up out of nowhere.

"I'm sorry," she said, "but I can't seem to remember mine."

"Thirty-two," Kathleen said.

Lindy Geoghegan must have overheard, for he called out "Thirty-two" the first time he was up. Doris walked over to him, turned her face and let him kiss her on the cheek. Lindy returned to his place looking a little disappointed.

Doris stood in the center of the room smiling at Augie. "Thirteen," she purred. It was Augie's number.

Doris half closed her eyes, leaned back her head and moistened her lips with the tip of her small pink tongue. Seeing her waiting there like that, I felt a warm, sweet cloud filling my chest as if my heart were dissolving in a mist of honey. For the first time in my life, the game made sense to me.

Augie stood up. He was having a terrible time trying to be polite. He stumbled awkwardly toward Doris; then, just as he was a shadow's breadth away from her, he let a wild, unearthly shriek out of him, wheeled around and raced out the front door.

Doris Clooney jumped back, and everybody laughed and yelled. I grabbed my coat and took off after him.

When I reached the street he was a block away from me, running like a man possessed. I would never have caught up with him if he hadn't turned up the steps of the church.

When I arrived, panting, at the church vestibule, I could see Augie kneeling before the statue of Saint Joseph with his bent head cupped in his hands. As I debated whether to leave or stay, Augie stood up, leaned forward and blew out the top vigil light.

I could have sworn that every light in the church went out, and a fierce, joyous terror surged up in me. Augie strode toward me and would have passed by if I hadn't reached out and grabbed his shoulder.

"Augie," I whispered, "you'd better go back and light it."

"Not a bit of it," he growled. "Those two have made life miserable for me long enough."

I said a quick prayer to Saint Polycarp. Augie marched out and I followed slowly.

"Come on," he shouted, "let's get back to the party." He walked ahead a few steps and waited for me to catch up to him. "By the way," he said, "that number Geoghegan called. It was thirty-two, wasn't it?"

"It was twenty-three," I said.

"That's odd. I could have sworn—" He broke off when he saw the smirk on my face. "Why, you sly little rogue! You wanted to keep it for yourself?" He laughed and gave me a playful punch on the arm.

Then suddenly, for no reason at all, we ran madly up Eighteenth Street, laughing like lunatics, our boots clacking against the brick pavement like the sound of cloven hoofs.

(From New Mexico Quarterly)

THE DAY OF THE EQUINOX

BY DANIEL CURLEY

IT MAY seem strange that Michael Pegnam was glad he was asked to work on Saturday for no pay except a meal on the company. But he was glad. It was something different, something that would set this week apart from all the other weeks of his first winter in New York, and might even divide the winter from the spring.

He was automatically aware of the weather when he came out of the subway that morning. It was obviously a fine day, and he looked on this as a hopeful sign. The sun was higher than it had been at nine o'clock for a long time—or at least he guessed it was by the glow in the sky and on the buildings. All winter he had watched the glow getting higher and higher each day and brighter and brighter as the sun approached the end of the street. All winter he had waited for the morning that the sun would rise squarely in the end of the street, but somehow he had missed the day. Perhaps it was that rainy week. Perhaps he was late and in a hurry. Perhaps he just didn't notice. And now the sun was rising behind the buildings to the north of the street, higher and higher each day at nine o'clock, but each day farther and farther to the north of the street.

As soon as he turned from the street into the empty building, he felt strangeness and expectancy. He had been instructed to use the freight elevator, but even so he felt like a conspirator. The freight elevator was bound up in his mind with being late for work and trying to sneak in without being seen and then in the afternoon sneaking out for a quick one just to get over the horrible butt end of the day after the three-thirty deadline.

When he opened the door to the Webster Corporation's fourteenth floor offices, he thought at first that the great newsroom was empty, but then he heard the soft clear voices of Jimmy Schuyler, his boss, and Joe Black, the district supervisor; and as he came out of the short end of the L-shaped room, he saw them standing near the files talking to a group of girls. Joe Black looked at his watch when he saw Pegnam, undoubtedly a pure reflex. "Right on the dot," he said.

"That's my boy," Jimmy said.

Pegnam felt ridiculous to be so patted on the head, and some of his joy in the day vanished. They seemed to forget about him, however, and went on explaining the exact procedure to be followed in weeding out the files.

He didn't try to understand what was being said because he was there only for the dirty work. The only thing he had to hear was that he was supposed to make a pile of the old reports at the end of the hall near the freight elevator. He went out to take a look at the place and stayed to smoke a cigarette. He looked up and down the elevator and up and down the stair well and out the window at the fine spring day. He couldn't see the sun itself, but he could see the buildings to the west shining, and even the deep small streets were bright with an indirect light.

By the time he finished the cigarette and got back into the office, the girls had already filled their wastebaskets with discarded material, and the floor was littered with paper. He never did catch up all morning, and the only thing that saved him at all was that every once in a while the girls would remember they were working in the office, and they would pick up their purses and twitch off to the ladies room just as if all the reporters were sitting at their desks to look up after they had passed. Pegnam looked up, of course, and went on snatching reports from the floor.

By noon he was soaked with sweat, for he had literally moved a mountain, and he was ready for a break when Joe Black said, "Let's get cleaned up for lunch, everybody."

Joe Black herded them all into the freight elevator and directly across the street into the bosses' restaurant. He talked over their heads to the head waiter. "The big table," he said. "The big table for my big family." That was a part Joe Black didn't know how to bring off, but he didn't know it so there was no harm done.

"Yes, sir, Mr. Black," the waiter said. "This way, please." They followed him into a kind of back room with one big table in it. The room was so dim that they could barely see at first, and Pegnam found himself at the foot of the table beside Nancy Hatcher, a reporter from the construction news division.

Nancy was beautiful. He saw her every morning through a glass partition while he was sorting the morning mail, and he couldn't be mistaken about that, but he just didn't believe in beautiful women. When he was a kid he had believed in them. He had looked at magazines and seen movies and told himself, That is what it will be like to be grown up: there will be women like that. (He had also thought there would be money like that and success like that, but those were other stories although they ended up the same way.) After he grew up he looked around for those women for a while and then forgot about them. Of course now he saw them every day on Fifth Avenue and in Rockefeller Plaza and almost everywhere he went, but he didn't believe in them. He didn't believe in Nancy either although he had known from his very first day with the company that she was not only a beautiful woman but a good kid as well, because she kept suggesting things for him to do so it would look as if he were taking hold.

Even knowing she was a good kid, he had never allowed himself to think about her, but now impulsively on this strange day he believed in her, if not as beautiful, at least as a woman.

"Hello, Micky," she said.

"Hello, Nancy," he said. He was going to ask her to call him Mike, but Joe Black was rapping for attention.

"We're all going to have a drink while we study the menu," Joe Black said, and everyone applauded. The waiter began taking orders for drinks.

"When he comes around," Nancy said, "tell him I don't want any."

"Don't let me down, buddy," Pegnam said. He had seen Nancy stop in with the boys for a couple of quick ones after work.

"My mother says I shouldn't drink before four o'clock," she said.

"Where'd she get that?" Pegnam said.

"She read it in a book," Nancy said. "She thinks you shouldn't drink so much either. She worries about you."

"Bless her heart," Pegnam said.

"I tell her everything," Nancy said.

"What's yours?" the waiter said to Pegnam, perhaps because he was wearing a sweater with no shirt.

"Bourbon," Pegnam said. "Water chaser. The lady will have the same."

"My mother won't like this," Nancy said.

"You aren't even going to see it," Pegnam said.

"I mean," Nancy said, "she isn't going to like to hear what a sot you really are."

"Janitors can drink any time," he said. He was already high just on the thought of the drinks and the general excitement that accompanies drinking. Joe Black looked almost pleasant. Jimmy was laughing and joking with the girls, who were gentle now, somehow attractive. And Nancy—well, she was still Nancy. And they were all of them such wonderful people that Pegnam wanted to make a speech before he had had even one drink. The tears were beginning to come to his eyes foolishly.

"Nancy," he said, "what does your mother think of McSorley's?"

"McSorley's?" she said.

"Where I drink my ale. Two-hour lunch hours on working days and noon to midnight on Saturdays."

"Oh," she said. "McSorley's. I'd like to see that place."

"No women," Pegnam said. "They don't allow women."

"Is that why you go there?" Nancy said. Then she reddened. Her eyes opened just a little and her lips parted as if she were about to put her hand over her mouth.

"I just like it there," Pegnam said a little shortly.

"My mother thinks a man should spend a certain amount of time at his club," Nancy said, and Pegnam knew that a girl whose mother was that intelligent must be more than just beautiful. "But she doesn't think a man should overdo it."

"Moderation."

"Moderation in all things, my mother believes, and no drinking before four o'clock."

"I'll see you then," he said. The waiter set her drink in front of her. Pegnam downed it at once. He was ordinarily a leisurely drinker although often in the long run immoderate.

Joe Black stood up and everyone was quiet at once. He said, "For your loyalty and co-operation, to you." He raised his glass.

"My big family." He had to do it.

Then Pegnam jumped up. He didn't know why. It wasn't the kind of thing he did. He wasn't really like that. "To you, Joe Black," he said, "and all these beautiful people." He didn't ordinarily make that kind of fool of himself. But at least he tossed off his drink and sat down without suggesting For He's a Jolly Good Fellow. Joe Black waved across the table at him, and Jimmy grinned openly and indeed even foolishly at him.

The waiter was going around taking orders. You would have thought the office girls were all pregnant the way they were ordering the fruit salad bowl that Joe Black ordered. But Pegnam was listening to Jimmy, so Nancy and he had the roast beef special. Good old Jimmy. Good old Nancy.

Just as the waiter was leaving, Jimmy called, "Another round for everybody while we're waiting."

"Make his a double one," Joe Black said, pointing at Pegnam. Pegnam waved at him and he waved at Pegnam.

So all in all Pegnam had five shots on an empty stomach, and he felt so wonderful that he hated to begin his lunch. But Nancy poked him in the ribs and said, "Eat something before you fall into your plate."

"I feel wonderful," he said.

"Eat up," she said.

"Your mother wouldn't approve, would she?" he said.

"Oh, she always says, Better a happy sinner than a sullen saint."

"Good old mother," he said. "Let's go see her." He started to get out of his chair.

"We've got to work," Nancy said. "Eat your lunch."

"Yeah," he said. "Sure."

"Eat your lunch, Micky," Nancy said, so he began to eat his lunch.

"Feel better now?" Nancy said.

"No," he said. "I felt wonderful."

"You shouldn't drink so much on an empty stomach," Nancy said.

"Does your mother really want to know why I drink so much?" he said.

"She's sincerely interested," Nancy said.

"Let's go see her," he said, but he didn't have the drive to get even half out of the chair.

"Not now," Nancy said.

"You come with me tonight," Pegnam said, "and I'll tell you everything while we eat. Then you can tell your mother."

"Fine," Nancy said. "I'll call my mother and tell her not to expect me." He was still drunk enough so that it all seemed perfectly natural. If he had been sober he would never have asked her.

Even after Joe Black paid the check and they were ready to go back to work, Pegnam still had enough of that good feeling left so that he hated to let it go. "You go on ahead, Nancy," he said. "I'll catch up. I have to get cigarettes."

He got cigarettes and another double shot at the bar. That really held him right up there, so he moved another mountain and sweated another gallon without being particularly aware what he was doing.

At about three o'clock he went down for another drink because he didn't want to lose that fine casual feeling he would have to have to ask Nancy to slip out for a quick one at four o'clock. But as it turned out he could have been cold sober. He was rushing around to get a little ahead so he wouldn't be missed when he saw her ringing the buzzer by the freight elevator. She held up four fingers and he heaved his trash box at the pile and went with her.

"Your mother would be proud of your self-control," he said.

"No," she said, a little sadly it seemed, "she expects it." They had one and then a cigarette and then another one and went back with the comfortable knowledge that they could last until five.

And last they did, very handsomely, but five minutes past five found them back again at the same spot. Nancy was paying for her own, and it was just as well, because Pegnam never carried too much money on him.

Almost the first thing they did was decide to go to Chinatown for dinner, but it took them a long time to get started. Nancy had to call her mother and one thing and another. They ate potato chips and boiled eggs and pickled pigs feet and herring and the sort of stuff you can find in bars to hold you just a little longer.

"Tell me, Micky," Nancy said. She showed no signs of being ready to go to Chinatown or anywhere else. "There's something I'd like to know."

"What's that?" he said.

"What do you do when you ride me home on the subway and then stay on after I get off?"

"You really want to know?"

"When I called my mother this is one of the things she particularly asked me to find out for her."

"Bless her heart," Pegnam said. "Well, I tell you. I just ride to the end of the line and get off and walk around. Then I find a place to eat and have a couple of beers. One Friday night I was in a diner with some truck drivers and they gave me a ride to Manchester, New Hampshire, and back the next night. Some nights I ride over to Jersey or Brooklyn with some of the other guys. I've seen a lot like that. Two nights a week I go right home after work and write letters."

"And on Saturday you go to McSorley's, right?"

"As soon as I get up. I usually get there between eleven and eleven-thirty for a big corned beef and cabbage feed, and I stay until they close up at midnight."

"I'd sure like to see that place," she said.

"No women allowed," he said.

"I know," she said. "I guess that covers it."

"I guess it does," he said. "How about you?"

"We've got to decide what to do after we finish here. I don't really feel much like eating."

"Me neither," he said, "and it's just as well because we don't have much money. We could do something cheap like go to Coney and walk on the beach."

"Not tonight," Nancy said. "Some other time but not tonight. How about the Staten Island Ferry?"

"Is that good?"

"It's one of New York's most famous cheap dates," she said.

"Sounds OK to me," he said.

"First, we have to get to the Battery," she said, pushing back her chair and starting to get up.

"Wait till I look at my map," he said. "The Battery isn't in my territory." She settled back and he took out his city map—he never took a step without it. "From where we are," he said, "it looks easy."

"It is easy," she said. "Let's go."

But if the Battery wasn't in his territory, Staten Island wasn't even on his map. At the bottom of the map was only a dotted line that ran right off the edge. Printed beside this line was the legend: To Staten Island.

As they stood at the rail waiting for the voyage to start, he said, "It's wonderful already." In his mind's eye he saw the ferry boat plunging off the edge of the map. Then the boat began to move and they were indeed cut off from the land.

"There's nothing like a sea voyage," Nancy said.

"Nothing," he said. "Smell the salt spray."

He inhaled deeply and flung his arms out wide. In dropping his arms he let one of them fall, as if by accident, on Nancy's shoulders. She wasn't in the least deceived and leaned against him. "It's about time," she said.

For some time after that they said nothing but remained in the classic grouping at the boat's rail, their backs to the land and even to the boat, their faces looking, not at horizons, but down at the water sliding directly beneath them. It would have been nice if there had been the arched backs of porpoises and phosphorous reflections of stars and hammered moon path, but there was only the black water sliding hypnotically below, carrying unidentifiable objects into their narrow range of vision and swiftly out again.

Nancy turned her face against his shoulder. "The water almost put me to sleep," she said.

"Me too," he said. He looked down at the top of her head. He had long forgotten that she was the most beautiful girl he had ever seen. It was dark. She was in his arms. He felt strong, gigantic even, protective, yet on the verge of tears.

"We should be looking for the Statue of Liberty," she said without moving.

"Hush," he said. "I'm too comfortable." That was an outright lie. His feet were killing him, and he was getting a stitch in his side from maintaining his position, but he had no intention of giving her an occasion to move away.

"Yes," she said. This time she straightened and took her arm away from around his waist. "Yes, we must. We must always say goodbye to the old lady on the outward voyage."

"We really must," he managed to say although he actually wasn't at all happy about this turn of events. The pain in his side and having lost his grip on her did nothing for his disposition. He would much rather have sulked, but fortunately it was so dark that his sulky attempts at dissembling succeeded.

When they raised their eyes and looked outward, they couldn't very well miss the Statue. "Goodbye," Nancy called, waving to the Statue.

"Goodbye," Pegnam shouted. Nancy began to wave her handkerchief and dab at her eyes. Pegnam shredded a couple of Kleenex and let the pieces float over the side. Then he tore up a cigarette package and threw the pieces into the air. He held the last few cigarettes in his hand.

Near them somewhere a great whistle cut loose with a blast that shook the whole boat. They looked at each other. He could see her laughing but couldn't hear her. He was laughing too. She made a little gesture with both hands and he jumped at her. She met him—at least—and they kissed very hard. The hand that was holding the cigarettes freed itself behind her back simply by opening and letting the cigarettes fall into the water.

At that moment, however, another couple came toward them. Nancy saw them over his shoulder. At first he was glad she saw them, and then he was a little resentful that she should have seen anything just then. She drew away a trifle—just the trifle that made the difference between passion and romance.

"What's all the shouting?" the girl said as the couple came up.

"We were just saying goodbye to the Statue of Liberty," Nancy said.

The boy and the girl turned toward the Statue, which was by then almost out of sight. "Goodbye, goodbye," the boy said.

"Goodbye, aloha," the girl whispered.

"Aloha, aloha," the boy whispered. He drew himself up as if he were about to sing an aloha song the way they do in the movies, but he only kissed the girl, and for the rest of the crossing they stood there hung at the lips, eyes closed, oblivious. Nancy and Pegnam could have acted as if there was no one there at all, but for some inscrutable reason they chose to hold tight to each other and whisper together making fun of the other two. When they tiptoed away and got off at Staten Island, the boy and the girl were still standing there.

Once they had landed, Pegnam discovered that Nancy had no more idea than he did where they were. She had never before got off the ferry but had always ridden directly back across. All around them people were running toward buses lined up in the terminal. "What shall we do now?" he said.

"I don't know," Nancy said. She drooped a little against him.

"Well, let's go," he said and pulled her arm until she was running along with him. He passed up the first two buses because they were almost empty and jammed her ahead of him into the third bus. "All these people have to be going somewhere," he said into her ear. He had one arm around her to hold her up because there was no grip for her anywhere. She just stood there with her arms down and her head against his chest. He would have been completely embarrassed except that he hadn't—and he didn't think anyone else in the bus had—ever seen such a pretty girl acting like that in public.

Now it was his turn to keep his eyes open, for she seemed scarcely aware where they were. "Are you all right?" he whispered.

"Are we in heaven yet?" she said. He flushed, for she said it quite distinctly and several people near them smiled.

Fortunately his rash guess about the crowded bus paid off when several people got off at a kind of square where in one quick glance he could see a diner and a drugstore still open. He helped her off the bus, and when they were alone he shook her gently and said, "Are you all right?"

"Yes, Mickey," she said. "I'm floating."

"Call me Mike," he said.

"Yes, Mike. I'm floating."

"OK," he said. "Let's get something to eat."

"We don't have enough money," she said, which was a strange thing for an enchanted girl to say.

"Lots of money," he said because he had a reserve fund in the bottom of his billfold, a ten-dollar bill that was so much an emergency reserve that he had once walked from 7th Street to 92nd Street rather than break into it. He hadn't really lied to her before when he told her he didn't have any money. He just never thought of that ten-dollar bill as money, but now he took it out and showed it to her.

"Let's eat then," Nancy said. He led her into the diner because she was still not exactly all there. Then she said, "But we ate just a little while ago."

"That was on the other side of the water," he said, "and besides it wasn't really a meal. Do you know what you want?"

"Yes, Mike," she said, but she didn't say any more about it.

"Give us two of your special ham and eggs," he said. "Hash brown potatoes, toast, and coffee."

"So much?" she said.

"This is the best time to eat," he said. "If you can't sleep, you got to eat." So they ate.

He swabbed the last of his toast over his plate and ordered more coffee. "Now, Nancy," he said, "what are your plans for the evening?"

"I don't know, Mike," she said. Her plate was as clean as his.

"Will your mother be worrying?"

"When I talked with her on the phone, she said she was going to take seconal. She hasn't been sleeping well lately."

"I'm sorry," he said.

"She'll be out now until noon," Nancy said.

"Then we can do as we please," he said.

"Yes," she said.

"Well, then," he said between sips of the hot coffee, "let's see about finding a place to stay."

Discreet inquiry at the diner and the drugstore uncovered a rooming house in the next block. And most discreet rapping at the door resulted in the porch light's being turned on and the door's being opened on the chain. "Could we have a room for the night?" Pegnam said into the opening of the door. "We're exhausted from sightseeing and can't make our way back to our hotel or the place we parked our car." He put that last in so that his accent would suggest that he was a traveller from Boston or—if the person behind the door was naive enough—from England. At all events no one could mistake him for a native of the place.

A streak of old face with no teeth and white hair in curlers appeared in the opening of the door. "Step back both of you so I can get a good look." They stepped down two steps and stood still. The door opened and the old lady said, "Come in, come in. It's my business to know good people when I see them even if it it late and they are tired. Come in, come in. I have a bed all turned down for you."

She led them up the stairs to a large room with a connecting bath. "This used to be our room," she said, "but I don't need such a large room any more or such a large bed." She pressed lightly on the bed to show the softness of the mattress. The whole bed shook gently but didn't creak or rattle.

"We are very sorry to have disturbed you," Pegnam said.

"It's quite all right," the old lady said. "Sleep well." She left quietly.

When they at last woke up in the morning and thought about getting home, they had little to say to each other. After paying for the room, they had, deducting the bus, ferry, and subway fares, just enough for two cups of coffee and one doughnut. That was nowhere near enough, for Pegnam was ravenously hungry. As a result of his hunger he was disagreeable—or would have been if he had had to say anything—but the normal sadness of such a morning made it easy to avoid talking, although he meticulously put his arm around Nancy on the ferry and even gave her a little squeeze as they passed the Statue of Liberty.

"Hello, Statue of Liberty," she said. "We're back."

"Hello," he said. But they didn't wave or shout, and no one came out to salute the Statue.

"Do you have money at home for your breakfast, Micky?" Nancy said without removing her head from his shoulder.

"Yes," he said.

"Well, why don't you come home with me for breakfast anyway?"

"I don't want to meet your mother like this," he said. "You're going to have trouble enough."

"It's all right," Nancy said. "I live alone. I don't have any mother."

"But—"

"It's all a game," Nancy said.

So they went to her house for breakfast. Then they lay down for a nap and decided to get married. In the long run nothing came of it, but that was what they decided that day.

(From Accent)

LITTLE JOE

BY WILLIAM EASTLAKE

I *THINK* we all realized that nothing, nothing at all, would ever stop Little Joe; not the drought even, because he, or his father Jonathan rather, had thought of it, but Joe executed it—the damming up of the small spring above Rye Hill, so that they had at least one crop (the oats below) when no other farmer had anything except the orchard crop; nor the mortgage foreclosure when Little Joe took his turn with the rifle because his father couldn't stay awake all the time to fend off the sheriff (who never arrived, however, because the bank had good farms coming out of its ears). It was certainly too the same madness that carried Little Joe over into helping Jonathan make a crop. They starved themselves by not selling the seed grain—planting a crop that there was no market for out of that identical madness, or maybe frenzy to work, or ornery habit, or perhaps the dark fear of thinking as the other farmers thought, knotting idle around Ferber's Grain and Storage and thinking. Harvested the crop and sold it to the government, something the thinking farmers had never thought of—never thought that some wild-eyed biblical schemer in Washington would buy it to bury. And always Little Joe plunged right on figuring and running and investigating, and when he wasn't figuring and running and investigating—he was hiding.

Little Joe couldn't stand people. I remember one time clearly when we went to visit his family. Not that we ever had anything especially to say to our neighbors, but Father thought we should make something especially to say to them, that we should "contrive our piece of the world into something less of a wheated jungle." So on Sunday we went to see them and Joe was hiding. "He has been hiding ever since the dark night," Jonathan said. We all knew that he had been hiding before that. But that he had had particular reason to hide since the dark night was probably true. The "dark night" was the day we went underground, or the day Little Joe came out from underneath the rock.

We were all up in Charlie Peacock's tree house when we saw him come out from underneath the rock, but it wasn't until he passed close by us that we could tell it was Little Joe. "Where did you come from, Little Joe?" Gregory asked in a shout that is never so much a question with children as a challenge.

Little Joe swung his large head away from up at the tree and over to the rock as though checking certain that our point of vantage had not exposed his secret and that our question was only a challenge.

"Where did you come from, Little Joe?"

Little Joe took off into the swamp. We got down from the tree and followed him in. Little Joe had not taken off into the swamp in the manner of someone in flight but as though it were an old direction, a path to some other house or meeting-place of swamp-walkers, instead of a pathless ooze and suck, bayoneted with cattails and sword grass, circling without itself, endless because it began again without stopping after the river, which wasn't a river even here although it had channels that bled through the swamp with secret depths plumbed now by Gregory as he shot in head first and all the rest of us in after him except that we got tangled in razor brush and freed ourselves only in time to lift him out and set him on a bog. "There he goes," Gregory said, and following the turn of Gregory's head we saw through the reeds Little Joe's rear vanish down the hole he had come out of. When we got back to the hole Charlie Peacock went in first. Charlie Peacock came out again quick and said that it was so dark he couldn't see a damn thing and he wanted me to go in and then Eddie Markowitz and before they got to Gregory or Pete Nelson they said we shouldn't ought to go in without a light and before they got back to me again I said here goes the Crip and I went in.

It was much darker than Charlie Peacock said it was; that is, when you went in through a bush that hid the opening you made a quick double turn and even with that, without any doors or anything, you expected something more than absolute blackness. Then I saw a scratch of light, but surrounded by so much darkness I did not know for sure where I was, and yet it was already too late to turn back because after the first few steps I did not know which way was back and could only make toward the light that rose now and fell like some soft breathing flame, but it got all its quiet shock from the fact that every step in the now seeming floating world was a step that brought me that much nearer to Little Joe.

"Keep coming, Crip." It was Little Joe's voice, a low-pitched rasp.

"Okay, stop, Crip. You've gone far enough, Crip."

At once the light seemed to settle. It appeared to be about ten feet in front and then the face of Little Joe came into it.

"Maybe we've gone too far. That's what we've got to investigate. Be nonchalant, Crip."

Little Joe had other big words than nonchalant. He had fructify, vainglorious, persiflage, nonpareil, de trop and the Hanseatic League. He had more big words too, most of which he got from the commercials, but some he got from the Negro couple who were the cooks at the grange hall, Goldie and Gilmore; for example he had conjointly and copesetic.

"Are you here conjointly with others?" Little Joe's head cast no shadow nor did it appear to be attached to anything. It swayed in the light as though moved from above by strings that matched the darkness.

"I repeat, are you here conjointly with others? You'll have to answer that question."

"I'm conjointly here with others," I answered.

"You'll have to name names. Now whose idea was it to track me?"

A thumb and forefinger rose to the light and snuffed at it. Gasps of total darkness came and went.

"It wasn't nobody's idea," I said.

"I'll put that name down. Edward Markowitz."

"If you're going to put a name down put my name down."

"It doesn't make any difference. If you know him that makes you just as guilty."

There was a pause now, the light yellow, flickering Joe's mouth against his upper face.

"Do you think I'm being unfair?" he said.

"I think you're being nuts."

Little Joe moved the light so that it went over to the side of his face.

"We will have no more persiflage," he said, "or I will have to put out the light. I don't want any more redundancies and it's not me who's nuts. I never followed anybody down into a dark sewer."

"So it's a sewer, is it?"

"It's a kind of a sewer," Little Joe said. "But that's redundant. Will you or will you not answer the question before us?"

"I don't remember what the question is that is before us."

"Listen, my boy," Little Joe said finally, looking at me carefully now, "you don't have to remember the question because I am going to take care of you. Now come on over here and sit down."

I walked over beside the light and my knee touched something hard.

"Sit down there," Little Joe said.

I sat down on something cold.

"You wait," Little Joe said. "They'll be down and we'll find out what they're up to."

"I know what they're up to. They're not up to nothing."

"Wait till I get all the evidence and then make up your mind," Little Joe said. "You can know people all your life and not know what they're up to without knowing the evidence."

"Why do you want to know the evidence, Little Joe?"

"Because I want to have a lot of friends," Little Joe said. "And these people don't like me."

We stared out, both of us, through the yellow light that I could see now was a candle. The place had a smell like the kind of a smell you get when you put a fire out suddenly with water, more of a stench than a smell, and sharp.

"Are you going to make friends by giving the tree house boys a bad time, Little Joe?"

"They don't like me," Little Joe said. His words echoed back off some hard invisible wall.

"Why don't the boys in the tree house like you, Little Joe?"

"Well, for one thing—" Little Joe hesitated, his boy face suddenly aged and yellow in the unfair light. "For one thing I guess it's because I don't believe in known sayings."

"Well, I don't necessarily believe in known sayings myself," I said.

"Just name me one known saying you don't believe in," Little Joe said, confident.

I thought a while, even putting my hands against my head and thinking, but I couldn't think of one that wasn't perfect. I thought some more, testing many of them, but I couldn't find a hole in a single one of them. Then I even got to thinking about So Is Your Old Man and Yes We Have No Bananas which were almost known sayings at that time, and then I got to thinking what I was doing thinking at all when I didn't even know where I was except underground some place, and I got scared.

"See, you believe in all the known sayings," Little Joe said, touching me kind of clammy, and I must have moved.

"For example what known sayings don't you believe in?" I said suddenly, I guess to keep him from touching me.

"I hate them all," Little Joe said.

"For example," I said, as though saying something would keep him away, "do you hate Sink Or Swim, Paddle Your Own Canoe, Do Or Die, Survive Or Perish, Tom The Bootblack, Phil The Fiddler, From Canal Boy To President?"

"They're not known sayings," Little Joe said, patient again. "But I will tell you I hate them anyway— Hold it. I think the others are coming and I want you to do as you said you would."

"What did I say I would?"

"We must be very quiet," Little Joe said, hushed and overgentle.

They had evidently decided to come down all at once. You could hear them fumbling in the darkness. If not encouraged by leadership or sense of direction they shared a togetherness of ignorance, groping toward the yellow spume of light in the perfect blackness, seeming, as it had seemed to me, to be set against nothing and coming from nowhere; this joined now by the stench of the cave, sour and acrid, permeating, and finally by the voice of Little Joe.

"Which one is Paris France?"

They seemed not only to stop out there in the darkness but to bunch up like a herd of cows caught breaking into a corn field, their leader, or the one most in advance, or the one nearest the hired hand, belted by a pitchfork across the nose, the rest not retreating, quiet, puzzled, their legs and eyes abruptly frozen in movement, their bodies hanging awkward—like sometimes when a moving picture stops and you think the cameraman is going to run the film backwards.

"I repeat, which one is Paris France?"

"I guess that's me."

Little Joe shook his head, shadowless in the pallid light, amused and tolerant and still patient.

"You guess that's you. Don't you know? Do you use other names? What are they?"

"John Joplin."

"And what is your real name?"

"I guess John Joplin is my real name."

"Why do you use the foreign name of Paris France?"

"Because the kids started calling me that."

"Why did they start calling you that?"

"I guess because when we were standing around saying what we wanted to be when we grew up someone wanted to be a fireman and I wanted to go to Paris France."

"Why did you want to go to Paris France?"

"Because I had a fight with my mother."

"And do you expect us to believe that? Why, you must think we're vapid. Why did you have a fight with your mother?"

"Because she told me never to see you again. She said you were a creep and I said maybe you were a creep but I—"

"But you admit you had a fight with your mother?"

"Yes."

"Well, I don't think we have much respect for this witness. You may step back. Now will an Edward Markowitz step forward and be sure you don't slip in the four-hundred-foot hole. Now, Edward Markowitz, a man sitting here alongside of me who used to be one of you has made what you'd call a kind of statement. In this statement he named names and he named you. He said that you—"

"Wait a minute," I said. "Wait a minute. I nev—"

"That hole," Little Joe whispered over to me huskily. "That four-hundred-foot hole I was talking about ain't alongside them. It's right alongside you. I'd advise—"

"Wait a minute," I said, and looked out into the darkness where the others must be. "This four-hundred-foot hole he's been talking about, now he says it's over by me. He's just threatening us. I don't think it exists."

There was a mutter of voices from the invisible group and I felt encouraged. Then Little Joe said in Little Joe's voice, "If it doesn't exist then all of you take one step forward."

No one took the step forward, least of all me.

"Very well," Little Joe said. "Now that we have established the bravery I will tell you how smart you are. There may be four-hundred-foot holes four hundred feet deep. They may be here, they may be there. I don't know. I only know there is a certain way out where there are no holes and if you go along with me I will lead you to the light. Now if you would all repeat after me what I say, I would appreciate it very much. Little Joe is the Leader."

It seemed only two people repeated it after him—Pete Nelson was one, maybe Charlie Peacock, I wasn't sure or interested.

"Now, you can all do better than that," Little Joe said, friendly and very patient. "Now, if we try it again and get it right maybe we can get it over with and we won't have to spend our life down here. Now once again— Little Joe is the Leader."

"Little Joe is the Leader," they all said.

"I notice you didn't say it," Little Joe said, turning his head, the pale light yellow and faltering, catching only the highlights so that his face seemed an image thrown against nothing by a magic lantern using negatives.

I didn't answer anything and Little Joe went on without changing tone: "You're a very brave boy, still that's why you're on my team."

I still couldn't say anything.

"You were brave enough to inform on an Edward Markowitz."

"I didn't squeal on Eddie," I said. "And I'm not on your team."

"Then you would rather be at the bottom of a four-hundred-foot hole. Okay, if that is the way you choose to want it."

The yellow candle moved toward me followed by the face that was more a mask (not the gaudy kind you buy at the five-and-dime for Hallowe'en but colorless, self-made), that wavered and then came on again toward me.

"Don't push the Crip."

The face stopped and turned with the candle toward the invisible speaker. It was Eddie.

"Maybe I didn't hear you rightly," Little Joe said carefully into the darkness toward the voice. "But if I understood your meaning you want to wind up at the bottom of that hole yourself."

"I just said don't push a crip."

The yellow light was slowly put down again.

"Let me get this clear," Little Joe said with the old patience. "Did you get that out of a book? It's important to know where you got it. Not pushing a crip could be a good thing in most every instance. Now just let me know where you got it."

"None of your business," Eddie said.

"Oh," Little Joe said, pleased, the mask coming into a smile but the ends of the mouth still not turning up. "Oh, in that case I'm afraid I'll have to ask you to take one step forward." The voice was dead again and tired.

"I'm not taking any step anyplace."

"Very well, then. If you don't want to help the Crip, if you won't co-operate, then we'll have to finish this business."

The light and face came toward me and then almost at once there was a massed movement in the darkness. Little Joe stopped. "The four-hundred-foot hole," he said toward them, but the movement continued, gaining confidence now; and then almost gently in the weak light at the edge of the darkness the faces began to gather close to Little Joe.

"Very well," Little Joe said, threatened, without any movement of the face at all. "If that's the way you have to have it, if you think you can escape this darkness yourselves, if you don't think you need a light to show you the way, if you people think you can make it alone when it is only me who understands the darkness, all right then, let us see what you won't see."

Then Little Joe made a heavy pass with his bearlike arm toward the weak light and everything went black. You could sense now only the great underground stench and the solid silence that tensed us all.

"Yes. Maybe you don't need me at all to get out of the darkness. Maybe prayer will do it." The voice was confident and smooth now in the blackness. It had even lost its straining patience as though in pitting himself against God he would forego all that; as though he could perform finally within a situation where the two of them were equal. "You can pray or take a vote."

"You think maybe he has gone nuts?" It was the voice of Pete Nelson, low and intimate.

"No, it's Little Joe's own normal self," Paris France said.

"Anyway," and I think this was the voice of Gregory now, "I think maybe taking a vote is a good idea. We got to try finding our way out of here without getting killed and I think we should find out who is going to be the leader. If we don't have a leader some of us are bound never to get out of here."

"All right," I said, wanting to get moving. "When I call out your names you tell me who you want to be leader and Eddie will keep count."

"Before you vote," Little Joe's voice commanded from nowhere, "I want to warn you that no one knows how to get out of here except me. You followed me down and now your only chance to be saved is to stick with me."

"All right," I said. "No more speeches. Let's get the vote over with. Charlie Peacock, how do you vote?"

"I guess I vote for Little Joe. He's the only one who seems to know his way around down here."

And so did all the others, including, when it came my turn, myself. I guess we all reckoned there was no alternative now that we had played his game and gotten ourselves down here.

"All right," Little Joe said. "But if I am going to accept this candidature or whatever, I have got to have some concommitments as to what you people have been up to."

"I hope that's not a sequitur," Paris France said, topping Little Joe's word.

"It's a question," Little Joe said. "And I want an answer yes or no."

"But how can I give the answer if I don't know the question?"

"It's easy," Little Joe said. "Just say what I tell you to. Now try this: Little Joe is–"

But that was the end of his first empire. While Little Joe was being carried away by the sound of his own election Charlie Peacock had figured where the voice was coming from and snuck around in back of him and was twisting his arm up as though to break it if Little Joe didn't quit.

Little Joe quit and he led us out, in his pain, up to the real light. We sat Little Joe down in the middle of us beneath the tree house to have a careful look at him.

"I won the election fair and square," Little Joe said. "You didn't play it fair."

Little Joe lay curled up in front of us like some cornered thing, fearing to move as though movement might set off some chain of something which he was now unable to stop.

"Like something that crawls out alive, white, when you turn over a rotten log," Gregory said, reaching forward to touch Little Joe with his foot.

"Okay, okay, okay," Little Joe said. "But you never gave me a chance."

"What do you mean we never gave you a chance?" Eddie said.

"Never gave me a chance to help with the tree house or nothing."

"Maybe he's got a point," Paris France said. "You can't tell, maybe he's got a point."

"I don't think he ever had a point," Gregory said. "But we'll go up in the tree house and take a vote."

We were always going up in the tree house to vote on something. I don't think there was anything we didn't vote on in the tree house. We voted on who was going to carry the secrets down; we voted where to bury the old treasure and where to dig for the new, the rules for cheating at marbles and who was the shortest and the tallest and the fattest and the most likely to succeed in cutting off all his own hair.

"Me first," Little Joe said, unwinding and waddling over to the ladder.

"No, you last," Gregory said, pushing him to one side. Gregory went up first, then Eddie, then Paris France, Charlie Peacock, and me last, not because it was my position in the pecking order but because I had to pull the right leg after me, which made me slow. I got ready to go up, and Gregory hollered from way atop the tree, "Wait a minute–you make Little Joe come up first."

"He says you promised him he could go up last," I hollered back up.

"I changed my mind," Gregory's voice rang around the forest.

"He says that your decision–" I called and then paused to confer with Little Joe on one of his words. "He says your decision is arbitrary and should be put to a vote of the others."

There was a silence from above and Little Joe hollered up, "Hear this before you vote–you still don't know your way around down there. If you don't stick to your promise that you promised me maybe you never will."

The dead silence continued from way up in the tree. I looked up. The great pine, stripped of its branches and plumed with the thatched roof of the house, appeared palmlike, tropical, a stalk, naked and queer in the dark north.

"Okay," Gregory shouted down at last. "How do you vote?"

"I think I vote to put him on his honor and let him go last."

"Okay, that does it," Gregory shouted. "You better come up."

I started crawling up the pine-barked and poplar-runged ladder, making it slowly and pulling the bad leg after me. At the top the ladder began to vibrate and then thump, and if Paris France had not reached down and grabbed me I would have gone spinning down with the ladder.

Little Joe ran and jumped until it crashed, then he waddled back and solemnly, down to the last recognizable rung, destroyed our freedom with a great rock that seemed, as he lifted it over his antic body, larger than he was.

"Little Joe!" Charlie Peacock called, and then he called again, "Little Joe!"—each time the cry becoming more feeble because Little Joe had already gone, disappeared below again with all our secrets and treasures and maybe even rules and certainly all that we had that passed for confidence in our fellow Indians.

We all stood there teetering on the edge of our stalk-borne house raft in the now sunless sky almost one hundred feet above the soft black floor of the forest. We had carefully sheared off the branches so that the stumps would give no purchase to our enemies—the Moors and the Saracens, the Sioux, Blackfeet, and Crow.

We sailed on in the sky, seeming to have actual movement now, as though the sun westering not only brought the rawness of the night but also had left us without stability; cut off from the earth, we joined the movement of the beginning stars. As it grew darker, we shouted for a time, our voices skimming across the trees which with the blackness beneath us now seemed part of our new ocean, their big dark tops emerging and rolling softly like our raft.

At about midnight there was the noise of rough father voices beneath us, then the grunting and swearing of ladders being erected. We were informed that Little Joe had saved us, that we had invaded his tunnel and tried to force him into our house, but that in spite of this he had saved us. And four days later, which in our child's world could be four years, he still insisted he would save us again if the opportunity presented itself—and again and again and again. He would go on saving us, he said carefully across the desk-topped classroom silence to Charlie Peacock, until we were all dead.

(From The Western Review)

BROTHER QUINTILLIAN AND DICK THE CHEMIST

BY GEORGE P. ELLIOTT

BROTHER QUINTILLIAN JOSEPHUS at the age of thirty-five had achieved the station in life which he had desired from his earliest youth. From the days of his sad, timid, solitary boyhood in the streets of East Oakland, surrounded by dinginess and brutal fellows, the College of the Most Blessed St. Anselm had gleamed in his imagination as the green tranquility which only could requite his suffering years. St. Anselm's was a small college at the northeastern edge of the city, small and quiet and secluded among lawns and tall trees; he had seen it only three or four times when he was a boy with a very common name, Bob Johnson, for his family had had no car and he had not adventured about much on the streetcars by himself; but the green image of it glowed steadily in his mind like a vision of paradise. When he grew older he realized that he could find a place in St. Anselm's, but only if he became a professor there. So he had studied very hard, and he had found that he liked studying hard; he had joined the Congregation and had put in his years of teaching at dingy, brutal parochial schools in Stockton and Chico and South San Francisco. And now he was securely set, an Assistant Professor of Logic and Medieval History at St. Anselm's. But after two years of living in these most blessed grounds, teaching and disputing as he had long desired, he discovered that he would have to face after all a trouble long deferred, for there was nowhere in this life for him to go to avoid it any longer.

A mile or so above St. Anselm's, in the hills but still in Oakland, lived an atheist named Dick Carson. Every weekday morning Dick drove his old Dodge down to Emeryville where he worked as the chief research chemist for the Universal Metals Corporation. The final purpose of his researches was to increase the profits of Universal Metals. However, it's a stinking world as anyone can see, and Dick considered himself luckier than most to find only one thing he hated about his job. He lived in a new, modern house for which he had undertaken to pay $75 a month for fifteen years; it was so placed in a recess of a wooded mountainside that not another house, at least as yet, was visible from any of its windows. The house was designed to receive maximum benefit from the afternoon sun—Oakland is frequently overcast or foggy in the morning—and despite the surrounding trees it was both warm and bright on a good day. Dick had always wanted to be a scientist, and while he might have preferred it if he had been great he had settled down without much struggle to being good—"a sound man." He was an atheist because he saw no need for the hypothesis of a God at the basis of things in order to explain them; if he had seen the need he would have been perfectly willing to hypothesize the God, and he held no grudge against those who did. He could never have prayed to Him, however, and his acquaintance did not include many people who could. Dick was thirty-five too, and he too had a trouble; as he saw it, it had been pushed upon him by chance and there was nothing to be done but bear it: his wife of eleven years, whom he had loved, had been mashed to death in an automobile accident.

The doubt of Brother Quintillian could turn words into sounds and faces into vacant masks. For a long time he had not recognized what it was that was attacking him so, for it had not been subtle and intellectual as he had thought doubt would be; no, his doubt knew that he could syllogize it away if it came at him roundabout, so it jumped on him with bared teeth and tore at him through his senses. He would be standing in front of a classroomful of fresh and sullen faces, in the midst, say, of the Albigensian heresy in Languedoc or of a tight demonstration that some men are not all non-dogs, when suddenly he would be left standing there with not a notion in his head about what the next word was to be. "Dante's hatred for Boniface VIII was a result of many factors, chief among which was—" Chief among which was what? What was the next word to be and which of these tilted-up faces cared? He was not even tempted to be facetious and say something like "—the horns of dilemma on the papal bulls" as he had done once successfully in a seminar. He simply, for a few seconds, had no idea what any of his words stood for any longer and no idea what these faces were doing in front of him. Then he would catch himself and go on. His attacks had not been frequent, and he had attributed them to dizziness or nerves or eyestrain. They would upset him for a few hours, and then he would forget about them. But one day his doubt, weary of these impermanent sallies, assaulted him in his very fortress, where he was kneeling at Mass.

Dick was not sentimental, but he had loved his wife, loved her and needed her. She had fitted out their house with a taste that had become his own; she had persuaded him to go to parties and concerts and plays, where he had usually enjoyed himself; she had filled the house with a color and cheer which his rather saturnine turn of character had at once groused at and loved. The rugs and curtains were left, the bright chairs and the concerts and the wide acquaintance; but there was no cheer in any of it now she was dead. He stayed at home most of the time after her death, among the gay objects which with her absence became things only. Sometimes his friends, worried about him, would suggest that he ought to move out of this house which was full of associations for him, but he told them to shut up. He was not sentimental, and he knew that these objects of his were the things he liked best; to his taste they were functional and beautiful. To be sure, he did not like them now; but he thought that he would again, once he got out of his slump. She's dead and gone and that's an end to it; things are things, and it's morbid to go on talking about the whole mess; for Christ's sake can't a man be left to get over his own unhappiness by himself? He took many vitamin pills, and lost sleep.

It was a six o'clock Mass in late September, a cool morning after a mild night. He found himself in the pew behind old Brother Alphonsus, who spluttered and mumbled at his rosary. During the first part of the ritual he paid little attention to what was going on: it had happened so often before; his mood was sodden, the Eucharist exalted; like the seventy-seventh Hail Mary in a penance, it seemed one more salaam to boredom. The acolyte who was swinging the censer was taken with a fit of annoying sneezes from the incense. And by the time he had lifted his eyes to glance at the sneezing boy, the dreadful voiding had taken place. Father McElroy had become an old man in a silly costume, walking about, kneeling, bowing and bending and bringing his hands together before him, in a way that could not have been more inscrutable. As Brother Quintillian looked, he saw the celebrant like a chef turn over some pages of a book, repeat as it were the recipe aloud in his silly cook's language, look into the tabernacle as it were into a little oven, then step aside to wait till the crackers should be ready to eat. He was so astonished that anyone should do these things that he did not even find it ludicrous; he even forgot to rise and sit and kneel and rise with the others about him. Not until the bell tinkled did he come to himself, and then he was so horrified at what he had done that he sat back in the pew in a cold tremble. Both at the same time he felt that he could not have desecrated the Eucharist more profoundly had he blasphemed aloud at the moment of transubstantiation, and that it would be silly even in a ballet to dance around pretending to cook that flavorless, packaged fragment of God. When the rest of the community left, he stayed behind, as it were in prayer. He was too weak to rise. He was wondering what he should do, for he thought that surely he was falling into a state of damnation.

For the psychosomatic theory of illness Dick had a physical chemist's scorn. When a high correlation between isolable personality traits and specific pathological symptoms could be demonstrated on a statistically sound basis, he was quite willing to admit that there was some connection between the two; what connection, he refused to say. Himself, he leaned towards the endocrine view—that both symptoms and traits derived from some malfunction of the ductless glands. This unhappiness of his could hardly be called a character trait; yet he had plenty of symptoms beyond those called for by his grief, bad sleep and bad dreams, sour stomach, irascibility, constipation, lethargy. Vitamin-complex tablets didn't do it, and his doctor could discover no infection in him, and four days in bed resting didn't do it. He was driven back upon his endocrines, and in particular he suspected his pituitary gland, the controller. But what it was secreting, which of its many chemicals (sixteen, was it?) was doing the damage, science could not yet tell him; there was nothing to be done. He could not bear to do nothing, so he fell back upon the remedy his mother had thought appropriate to any ill, diet. Sometimes he thought he benefited from cutting out all alcohol and fats, sometimes from eating only vegetables and milk, sometimes from a very high protein diet; but the only permanent benefit he got from the dieting was the discovery that he was allergic to okra. Meanwhile, his sleeping was troubled by the memory of the newspaper photograph of his wife's body half sprawled out of the car in which she had been killed, and his waking was troubled by the irrational thought that if only he had gone with her on that ride instead of going to a movie he might have saved her.

The day on which Brother Quintillian was praying in the chapel despite classes and meals, Dick was putting in his eight hours analyzing an aluminum alloy made by a competitor of Universal Metals. At five o'clock when Brother Quintillian emerged, half staggering, Dick was buying yoghurt, wheat germ and canned glutenburger at a health food store.

Both of them were five feet ten inches tall, weighed about one hundred and fifty pounds, had ordinary brown hair, flecked blue eyes, and rather fair complexion, and both of them were wondering how to get through the night.

Some of the brothers would be in the common room listening to the radio, reading the paper, talking. Some would be out strolling, or pottering in some favorite part of the garden. Some younger ones would be playing handball or working out in the gym. He was afraid that if he went directly to his room from the chapel, he would be thought aloof and proud. He would have preferred to take a walk in the mellow air, nodding to whomever he met and meditating on the flowers, but his knees would not support him on such a venture. He went to the common room. It took all his strength for him to open the heavy door in a natural way and to step inside the room confidently, unhesitantly. There were four other brothers in the room. When he entered, they glanced at him. The two who were talking fell silent, and the one next the radio turned it down. He was sure that they were ashamed of him, embarrassed for him, even revolted by him; for he thought that by some little gesture, some mumbled word, he must have let them glimpse this morning at Mass his full impiety.

"Good afternoon, brother," said Brother John to him. "Would you like to see the sporting page?"

Brother John's voice seemed altered a little, somewhat subdued, somewhat strained; he normally called Brother Quintillian by his nickname, Quin; he doted on baseball. Why then, Brother Quintillian wondered, did he behave like this? Surely he was being ironical in his offer? Surely he was being charitable to this leper?

"No, thank you," said Brother Quintillian. He sank into a chair. "I think I will just rest here a while."

He unbuttoned his collar in back, and pulled his cassock up so that he could cross his legs.

"You look tired," said Brother Alphonsus, a strong old man.

"It's nothing, nothing. I'll rest a while."

He was sorry he had not gone to his room to rest. He was making them very uncomfortable.

"It's Friday," said Brother Alphonsus.

"Yes, we're having fresh fish," said Brother Adrian.

"Do you know what kind?" asked Brother John.

"Halibut," said Brother Adrian. "I saw them unloading it."

"Do you like halibut?" asked Brother John.

None of the others answered, so Brother Quintillian knew that the question had been addressed to him. But he kept his eyes closed. His knees ached from the hours and hours of kneeling, and though he had not eaten or drunk all day he did not feel hungry. He was very tired, and he was sorry for the others, who were having to be nice to him. He would try to meet their charity by lightening them of the burden of courtesy, by pretending to doze.

"No," said Brother Gilbert from across the room, "he is not at all fond of halibut."

"What does he like?" said Brother John eagerly.

"How does he like it prepared?" asked Brother Adrian.

"Well," said Brother Gilbert, who was the epicure of the community, "he prefers a bouillabaisse, as I remember."

"Oh, Gilbert, we'll never be able to get that for him by dinnertime," said Brother John. "What can we do for him?"

"No, I suppose not," said Brother Gilbert. "He likes finnan haddie."

"Can you prepare it?" asked Brother John.

"He has fasted since last night," said Brother Adrian. "We must be careful."

"If I had some," said Brother Gilbert, "I could prepare a mild sauce for it. And toast."

"Alphonse, you drive," said Brother John. "Go down right away to Spenger's and get a pound of finnan haddie. Anything else, Gilbert?"

"A jar of capers. But are you sure he wants to eat?"

"I'll go," said Brother Alphonsus, and left.

"He has not eaten for nearly twenty-four hours," said Brother Adrian. "He has been praying all day."

"A great humiliation," said Brother John.

They fell silent.

Brother Quintillian felt no hunger, least of all for finnan haddie. He wished only to be left alone. But he did not want to reject their kindness, so he said nothing.

"We should leave him to sleep a little," said Brother John.

"Yes," said Brother Adrian. "Gil, turn off the radio and come along."

"I must phone my sister before dinner," said Brother Gilbert.

"How is she getting along?" asked Brother Adrian.

"Very well. She's out of the cast now and her ribs are quite mended."

"I'm glad to hear that. Wasn't there a woman killed in that accident?"

"Yes, in the same car, a friend of hers."

"What was her name?"

"Sylvia Carson."

"Pity."

"A great humiliation," said Brother John mostly to himself as they went out the door.

Like a sea anemone after the tidepool falls still, he slowly began to unfold. Sylvia Carson, Sylvia Carson. The name had been floating around during the past month, since the accident. He had some other association to it. He spent several minutes uncovering his recollection—that good-looking fellow he'd seen at so many concerts and recitals, a chemist, to whose house he had gone a few months before with a mutual friend. He had never met the wife, Sylvia. She had not been a lover of music. Duane? Dan? Duke? Dick, that was it, Dick Carson. Poor fellow, to have his wife killed like that. He was probably not a believer; he would need friends now. Poor man.

Brother Quintillian made his way circuitously to the refrigerator where he drank a glass of milk and put an apple in his pocket, went to his room to change into his black suit and select an album of records, and slipped out the side door. He did not feel weak any longer, and though he was sorry to disappoint the brothers who were getting and preparing the finnan haddie for him, he could not have eaten it. He felt he should go immediately.

It took him an hour to find Dick's place. The road was all uphill, and he got himself lost. His sore legs hardly obeyed him.

As he turned a corner among pines, he saw the little house there below him. He sat on the bank to rest a bit and eat the apple, so that he would not be trembling with fatigue when he came to the door, and looked curiously at the house. There was a built-in ladder by the carport, for the use of anyone who wanted to sunbathe on the flat roof. The windows went from floor to ceiling; the wall that he could see was nearly solid with window. He was looking at the northern, back side of the house; he could see directly into the two bedrooms, one of which was tidy and perfect, the other rumpled and used. The only chair he could see was a piece of yellow canvas artfully slung upon an iron frame, an angel-wing chair. The floor of the house was a slab of concrete only a few inches higher than the ground. The aim of all this, Brother Quintillian had read, was to be functional and to promote indoor-outdoor living. Brother Quintillian was an indoors man himself; he enjoyed the outdoors once in a while, on a beautiful day like this or in the well-ordered gardens of St. Anselm's; but the notion of mixing the two, of making little of the distinction between them, astonished him. He had no theory about this indoor-outdoor business except that it was very sophisticated; savages, he was sure, would never think of doing it; nature is man's enemy, and only a sophisticate would doubt it. He saw Dick come into the white, mechanized kitchen, take pans off the wall and spoons from a drawer, and open a can. He threw away his apple core, picked up the album he had laid beside him on the bank, and went down the road to this solitary house.

He saw Dick glance up at him and scowl; his heart sank within him. But Brother Quintillian made a great point of maintaining an outward appearance of confidence and good manners. He went directly to the kitchen door, smiling, and nodded to Dick. With elaborate reluctance Dick wiped his hands and opened the door.

"I am Brother Quintillian. You may not remember me."

"I remember you."

Brother Quintillian had intended to say something consoling to Dick, but this tone of his clearly made it impossible.

"I brought some records which I hoped you would find interesting."

"Okay. Go in front and sit down. I'll be along when I'm through eating."

Manners required Brother Quintillian to say something about how he hoped he wasn't intruding. But it was clear that he was intruding and that Dick if asked would say that he was; he felt it more important to stay than to be polite. "Thank you, I will," he said, and went into the living room.

Not living room—living area. Dick was cooking in the kitchen area of the same room, on the other side of a partial wall. Behind a full-length green hanging, as Brother Quintillian saw through an opening in it, was one of the sleeping areas. The other sleeping area, he remembered having seen, had four walls and a door, and the bathroom of course did too—though the outer wall of the bathroom was a pane of frosted glass. Brother Quintillian took his seat on an odd but comfortable wooden chair, glad for a few minutes of freedom in which to look about him. There was not even an atavistic fireplace in the room, just areas of white wall. There were three low bookshelves and a narrow one that reached to the ceiling. On the walls hung three abstract paintings and a primitive mask with corn husks for hair. In the center of the room stood a glass table on iron legs, low, large, free-form (that is to say, kidney-shaped); on the wall in the darkest corner, just above the telephone, to his distress he saw an exquisite icon.

"Will you have something to eat?" Dick said around the corner, still in a churly voice.

"No, no thanks."

"It's not much of a dinner, but you're welcome."

"No, no, you just go ahead. I'll be happy to wait."

And he was happy to wait, for in trying to understand what view of things could produce this amazing house and what effect living in it would have on a man's soul, he quite forgot his own concern. It was not that his doubt had been trivial, or his experience that morning superficial; quite the contrary. But he had exhausted for the time his capacity for spontaneous remorse, so that wonder at this house quite made him feel happy, allowing him to forget what he could hardly bear to remember, his own great sin.

He heard Dick serving himself up his meal, the spoon angry in the saucepan. How dreadful, thought Brother Quintillian, to have no God to submit to. How angry he must be with nothing to do but blame chance, idiot chance. How afraid. And then Brother Quintillian did something that a man of his delicacy, his scruples, could not have done in his situation without the strongest prompting, and he felt almost scandalized at himself for doing it: he tiptoed to the record player, adjusted it without Dick's permission or knowledge, and started playing the records he had brought. The records contained an ordinary of the Ambrosian Mass chanted by monks in a twelfth-century monastery. Technically the records were excellent, and the machine was superb. The thin voices, sepulchral and echoing and very pure, seemed to Brother Quintillian in some way not entirely foreign to this angular, stark house.

When the first side was played, Dick appeared at the end of the dividing wall, plate in hand, and stood listening attentively. He tossed his forelock back with a sweeping motion of the head; his body was not so slouched over as it had been. His fair eyes, dulled when Brother Quintillian had come in, were bright and quick.

"Hey," said Dick between bites, "that's terrific singing. That's an Ambrosian ordinary, isn't it?"

"Yes, yes, in what is believed to be its purest form."

Brother Quintillian stuttered a little in his pleasure.

"You get that quaver?" said Dick. "Lord, what technique."

"Yes, indeed. One has to write to Europe for the album."

"I think I'll get it. How much they stick you?"

"I'm ashamed to say. Three and a half dollars a record. I can get the address for you if you like."

"Sure, do that. Let's cut it till I'm through eating. I want to really listen."

"Certainly, certainly."

Brother Quintillian stopped the machine.

"Hey, brother," Dick called from back of his wall again, "tell me something about those records. That's the best singing I've heard in months."

Brother Quintillian went to the end of the cooking area. Dick was sitting at a leaf that dropped from the wall.

"Well, I've done a little work in the modes of the chants. I'm no expert, nothing like one, you understand, just an amateur.—Pardon me, what a convenient kitchen you have here. I've never seen one more compact. They're usually so crowded."

"It's all right. It doesn't make the glutenburger taste any better."

"Ah." There was a brief silence. "Would you tell me, what is glutenburger?"

"Ersatz meat. It's all right with enough ketchup. Have some."

"Just a bite."

"Here's a fork. Isn't it poor?"

"Not very good. Why do you eat it?"

"Some sort of nutritional trouble. The doctors haven't been able to isolate it. I thought I'd experiment around with diet."

"Any luck?" asked Brother Quintillian smiling.

"None. If a man hasn't got an appetite he might as well eat health food. Brother, you're sure you've had dinner?"

"No, thank you, no dinner. I fasted today."

"Is that so?" said Dick looking at him with interest. "Nothing to eat at all?"

"When I decided to come up to see you—it's quite a climb—I drank a glass of milk and ate an apple."

"Is that so? I haven't tried fasting yet. Just one day?"

"Usually. It depends."

"Do you find it does you good?"

"I think it does. I think so very sincerely. I believe I shall do it more often from now on."

"Is that so?" Dick was through with his meal. "I think I'll try it myself."

"Pardon me, but I am not sure you understand. It's not just doing without food."

"I know about fasting," said Dick rather heavily. "I think I'll try it all the same. Maybe it'll help me sleep. I sleep on something hard, you know."

"Indeed?"

But Dick was annoyed with himself for all these confidences he was making.

"Let's go listen to those records."

In the passageway there was some confusion because neither of these fastidious men wanted to touch the other and neither wanted to go first. Finally Brother Quintillian, mumbling apologetically, went guestlike ahead. He started to seat himself, but Dick told him to go put on the records.

They listened for forty-five minutes with complete attention. They did not speak, but looked at each other only once or twice, at some particularly impressive passage.

When it was over, Brother Quintillian turned the machine off, and Dick leaned back in his chair shaking his head slowly.

"What musicianship," he said several times. "What musicianship."

"You liked it?" asked Brother Quintillian eagerly. "I am delighted."

"Perfection of technique. Is this the only recording they've made?"

"I'm afraid it is."

"What a pity it's all locked up in there."

"Maybe someday . . . ," Brother Quintillian said spreading his hands. "The monks were directed by Burckhardt, of course."

"Never heard of him."

"Oscar Burckhardt. He had a theory of phrasing, which he developed from an annotated manuscript he found in Yugoslavia. He instructed this monastery in his method; they found it very difficult because it was so different from their own tradition. This is the result."

"A sound scholar," said Dick. " A damned sound man. The greatest pre-Baroque music I ever heard."

"Doesn't it suggest the arches of some of the Lombardy Romanesque cathedrals? The same austere intensity?"

"No," said Dick brusquely. "I don't have anything to do with cathedrals."

"Just the lines," said Brother Quintillian fluttering his hands.

An uncomfortable silence settled upon them.

I'll keep him at arm's length, thought Dick to himself. He's trying to creep up on me with these cathedrals and Masses. He's a pleasant enough guy, but he can take a hint. I wonder why he came up to see me. Well, maybe I can learn something from him.

"Pardon me," said Brother Quintillian, "perhaps I had better go now. I really came just to play the records for you."

"Stick around," said Dick. "You've only been here an hour or so."

"We must have another musical evening soon."

"Sure, I've got a honey of a recording of Monteverdi. Setting of a sestina by Petrarch. What form! It makes those lieder-writers look sick, for getting the most out of the words."

"I believe you," said Brother Quintillian. "I look forward to hearing it. Tell me, that icon over there . . . ?"

"Sylvia's. She got it in Kodiak on a trip she took before the war. Sentimental, nineteenth-century stuff. Let's play chess."

"Oh yes. Still, it has its own charm.—Chess? Oh dear, I'm not very good at it."

They set up the board and began an earnest game, the awkwardness between them gradually dissipating. In the midst of contemplating which of three weak moves it would be best for him to make, Dick spoke in a musing voice, not raising his head.

"What do you know about the history of fasting?"

"You mean in the Church?"

"No."

"It's mentioned frequently in the Old Testament."

"Anything else?"

"It is usually connected with purification."

"I guess I'll take your bishop," said Dick.

"You oblige me to take your knight," said Brother Quintillian.

"Now what?—There's often something to these old customs."

"Wisdom of the folk?"

"A sound physiochemical basis, like the use of bread-mold poultices generations before the discovery of penicillin. Of course, there's a lot of crap mixed up with it too. Superstition and that sort of stuff."

"As there is with science."

"For instance?" asked Dick still in a brooding voice.

"Some of the mental healers."

"All of them. There's no experimental basis for their theories. They're about as scientific as a Christian Science practitioner or a piece of the true Cross."

"Dianetics," said Brother Quintillian.

"It's a shame."

"Pardon me, if you take that pawn, I'll be able to capture your queen in two moves."

"Thanks. I'll take it back if you don't mind."

"Not at all. It would be a pity to spoil a good game with a trivial error."

"A trivial error but I lose my queen," said Dick, and lapsed into silence.

After the game, Brother Quintillian stood up energetically, thanked Dick for his hospitality, took up his records, and said goodbye.

"Wait a minute," said Dick, "I'll run you down the hill."

"I won't hear of it," said Brother Quintillian. "It's only a few minutes' walk."

"You haven't eaten today. Your blood sugar level is low. It wouldn't be good for you."

"No, please, I beg you. It's a lovely night out."

"All the more reason for me to go out into it. I'm a safe driver."

"I had no thought . . . Thank you very much."

As they were winding slowly down the hill toward St. Anselm's, Dick spoke.

"You know, I'm enjoying this drive more than any I've taken for a long time."

"Why, how extraordinary. Why? What do you mean?"

"I'm not in a hurry," said Dick with uncalled-for energy. "I'm under no pressure. Sometimes I've thought if I could just sit at home and never have to go out, I'd be all right."

"Have you ever tested your theory, just stayed home for a while?"

"Yes."

"Were you all right?"

"No. I could hardly wait to get back in my car again."

"I understand," said Brother Quintillian. "I understand very well."

At St. Anselm's, Dick parked and turned off the motor and the lights.

"Remember that three-voice Kyrie towards the end?"

"Like this?" said Brother Quintillian and hummed a few notes. "In unison?"

"Yes. I never heard anything so pure in my life."

"True, true."

For a few moments in the dark car side by side, each was freed from his trouble, silently joined with the other in the memory of those thin and disciplined voices which celebrated by the very renunciation of overtone and separateness, by a perfect weakness, their fearful mortality.

"Good night," they said to each other in the dark, "goodbye."

He drove back to his house feeling more nearly at peace with himself than he had felt for some time. As he was walking from the carport towards the front door, a sighing of wind in the trees drew his attention upward. It was a cloudless night, rare for Oakland; the stars were brightly shining. He could remember the names of only a few of them, of only, he discovered by counting, fifteen of them. He sighed as he thought of the great pleasure it had given him to study astronomy in college. What's the point of all that studying if you forget most of it? What use is it? Just a game. Still, it had been a great pleasure, learning, and it still was. Not the keenest pleasure he had known, but the most enduring. He turned off the lights in the main room, and prepared for bed. On the stand beside the bed lay the current issue of a scientific journal; it contained a symposium on Einstein's unified field theory. He had read all the articles once, and some he intended to read again; but though he picked it up, he decided against reading it now. He turned off the light and lay on his back thinking.

The library lights were still burning, and from the student dormitories drifted radio music. He wanted to preserve intact the equanimity he had gained so recently and so tenuously; therefore he would have to avoid any stray student or some brother tardily walking in the garden at his offices. He got to his room safely enough, locked the door and did not turn on the light. There were duties he knew he should be attending to, community duties, the daily duties of every brother, the duties of a sinner. But he could not have performed any routine task well, or profitably to himself, and he did not feel full of sin at this moment but rather full of wonder and joy. A holy wonder at the mysterious ways of God that had brought him thus to a deeper love for God by means of doubt and humiliation; joy in the thought of God's mercy and God's perfection. He undressed and lay on his bed naked to God. His heart beat fast, his breath labored, and tears filled his eyes. There was pressed from his deepest feeling a prayer of thanksgiving.

The theory that would reconcile the great contradiction in physics, that would include in itself all the known data, that would harmonize in a few utter symbols all inferior theories—that he must try to understand. He knew it would be the crown of years of hard work, and he knew he might never achieve his high goal. But he remembered the labor he had performed to grasp the quantum theory in a seminar he had taken and the final reward of it; and he knew, lying on his bed, that for him there could be no other full satisfaction in his life but to set out on that vague and perhaps unattainable and perhaps illusory quest: for an understanding and an explanation of the limit of things. To be sure, he knew that even if he should attain this comprehension he would not be able to hold it long, that the arduous studies by which he would approach his goal would be too much for him to hold all at once in his mind, that the conclusion based on these studies would slip from him quickly. Quickly, but not completely; for though he would be able to reproduce the theory no better than he could reproduce the quantum theory, still he knew that once he had grasped it he would feel a security and solidity that nothing could take from him, and that even if he failed finally to grasp it he yet would feel that he had been engaged in the highest enterprise of all.

The prayer that issued in a tumultuous whisper from his mouth was extravagant and ungrammatical at times, but true; it was his own and it meant his thanksgiving. The words were not, like the Hail Mary, accurately placed and polished by centuries of use; but neither were they, like the beads he had told in the chapel that day, words strung on a cord of fear. In half an hour he was empty, empty and weary. He was ready to sleep, but the bed was too soft. How could gratitude to God survive such luxury as a warm, soft bed?

Even with a board between the mattress and the springs, the bed was not hard enough. He did not quite see how lying on a hard surface could promote sound sleep; there was some physiochemical basis to it, no doubt, possibly connected with the tonus of the striated muscles. But he was not interested in speculating on it now; he was sleepy, and content that he had made up his mind at last about his life, about his high and private quest. He spread out a blanket on the floor, on the side of the bed away from the window; stretched himself out on it, without a pillow; and covered himself with another blanket. His feet stuck out, but he didn't care.

In his high and narrow cell, with the window-blind pulled tight, on the concrete floor, he rolled himself up in a single blanket and lay on his side, glad of the cold and hardness, as happy as he would be.

(*From The Paris Review*)

THE HUNDREDTH CENTENNIAL

BY MAC HYMAN

THEY piled into the truck and started on the thirteen miles over the hard rutted dirt roads to the highway. The high sideboards with the straw still in between the cracks banged wildly from side to side, jerking back and forth the two girls who sat on the boxes at the end of the truck, holding to the sides with one hand and onto the skirts of their prim pink satin dresses with the other. They finally reached the highway and stopped, the steam hissing up in the top of the radiator; they waited, resting, while the clean-shaven man behind the wheel craned his neck this way and that inside the clean starched collar, then shifted into first, jolted up over the hump in the highway and made the long laborious turn toward town, the tin on the hood rattling ominously, the sideboards beginning to sway rhythmically again.

The occupants in the back of the truck began shifting their weights for the new sensation over the paved roads. The two girls in their pink dresses, looking almost like twins, straightened themselves and their skirts, and Polly Ann, the younger of the two, reached back and put her hand on the top of the head of the six-year-old Maddie Claude to keep her from bouncing, giving the child a hunched squat look but not helping much otherwise as the truck still jolted and her legs still bounced up and down, the heels of her shoes clicking sharply on the bottom. Seth stood at the front of the truck, his straw Panama hat sitting cockwise on his head, not holding on or balancing himself but chewing nonchalantly on a matchstick, his legs in the pinstripe pants weaving back and forth almost imperceptibly, his body motionlesss, like a bird on a limb in a high wind. Jonny stood beside him, a small edition of himself coming up to about his shoulders, watching Seth and trying himself not to hold on but finally letting one hand steal out to the wabbling sideboards and the other to the brim of his own straw hat. The hat was too big for him; it came down over his hair and formed a line running just above the eyebrows and the top of his ears so that he seemed to be staring at you out of a deep hole, and no matter how much he tightened the muscles in his forehead, the wind kept catching under the brim so that he finally had no other choice than to reach up and shamefully hold onto it.

They headed on down the highway, the truck settling down to a steady rattle and hissing, the dirt in the bottom bouncing slightly from the small jolts in the road. Tom Hamilton gripped onto the vibrating wheel, wrapping his big knuckled fingers all the way around it, his lean gaunt face staring ahead statuesquely like an unbearded Abraham Lincoln; only the lower portion of his face moved chewing on his tobacco. He held intently to the wheel as if trying to prove to himself that he actually had control over the truck when it was moving while his wife Mamie sat huddled up next to him, her manly hands with the blunt nails resting on the baby's stomach. Her round, boneless looking face stared blankly ahead as if she were already in town pricing the food at the store. She sat silently leaving a large gap between herself and the short squat man at her side, Albert, her husband's brother, who always smelled of tobacco and whiskey and breathed in a wheezing sound and looked far more like her than he did his own brother; he sat there now wheezing and humming to himself and looking around at the fields and at the road and at the front of the truck, his small blue eyes darting from side to side. They joggled along the road and rose up slightly with the rolls in the pavement, the three of them and the baby all lifting up suddenly with the same expressions on their faces, holding the same positions, rising up into the air and down again as if they had never moved, the way a juggler can throw balls in the air and have them suspended in the same formation—they hit, rose up, came down, bounced a few more times never moving, staring straight ahead.

They had just strained up one hill and started down it, seeing Callville in the distance, when the Model A came into sight. It was about a half a mile ahead of them at the time and they could see the black heads inside of it, its high top, the right rear wheel wabbling frantically on a loose axle. They gained on it, the truck coming down the hill and getting some speed behind it. Tom Hamilton let his foot down slowly, giving the motor a different sound but with no immediate change in speed; his brogan shoe mashed it to the floorboard and his jaw moved faster, slowed up, moved faster again; his wife held the baby up and juggled her and Albert twisted in his seat, his eye on the wabbling wheel, and quit humming for a few seconds. They gained slowly, the Model A looking motionless in front of them as if it were sitting there and shaking all over like a wet dog. Seth moved his mouth, flipping the matchstick over to the other side of his lips so that somehow his hat seemed to be cocked even more than before; Jonny began chewing on a straw as if it were gum, holding on to the sideboards with both hands now. Tom Hamilton pressed his foot hard against the accelerator; he then twisted the wheel with great deliberation, moving his shoulders as if it were a manly struggle, and held it there waiting for the truck to respond. Finally it jerked over and headed for the center line, the steering wheel bumping and knocking now. He turned it back and leveled out on the lefthand side of the road, pulling out some fifty feet behind the Model A, settling down for the long trip around it.

None of them looked at it as they gained but Albert who leaned over staring at the wabbling wheel; they looked all around it but not at it. They came within twenty feet and then ten and then almost upon it, and then Tom Hamilton let go the wheel with his right hand and reached forward touching the horn wire that dangled out below the dash to the charge, letting out a blare from the horn that could be heard even above the noises of the truck; then he put both hands back on the wheel again, his jaw moving rapidly. All of them kept their eyes on a point far down the road as if the car did not exist; they saw it as they went by only out of the corners of their eyes, seeing the closely huddled seven or eight Negroes' white eyeballs as the Model A pulled far over to the right. They passed it and got in front with Seth and Jonny staring straight ahead, and Polly Ann and Margaret peering intently over the top of it at something way off in the distance as it came into view behind them.

They came into Callville a few minutes later. They came over the railroad crossing on the south of town where the truck rumbled from side to side, the large sideboards banging and flapping powerfully like the wings of a huge bird. The girls and their boxes bounced around and the small girl on the floor went up and down and sideways while Polly Ann kept her hand pressed down on the top of her head; Seth's legs joggled up and down like two piston rods while his body remained motionless and Jonny's hat jumped from side to side; the three of them in the front seat moved together as if they were jointed, left and right, then rose up and came down again. The truck hissed to a stop; Tom Hamilton shoved it in first again to get it on across the railroad.

They made it on up the small incline that led into the middle of town and past the Confederate monument where the soldier on top stood poised with his rifle ready to charge North at the given signal—they were just passing around the monument when they began to notice the decorations and the difference in the uptown section. They saw strung between lamp posts entwining ribbons of red and white, going from post to post and across the streets; they saw drapes over the doors, signs in windows, red and white placards, Confederate and American flags in front of the stores and a big streamer across the street in front of the stoplight saying: "Hundredth Centennial."

They looked around the streets as they went through. The streamers went down the street toward the railroad, on the stores on either side, and up the other street. Seth took the match stem out of his mouth and looked from side to side just by shifting his eyes; Jonny moved up next to him, turning his head around looking at all the decorations. "Hey, what is it?" he asked.

Seth put the match back in his mouth, clamped his teeth on it and nodded at the sign by the stoplight.

"What?" Jonny asked.

He nodded at the sign, "The hundredth centnal."

"Yeah? What's that?"

Seth flicked his eyes at him then away. He finally cleared his throat and turned his back, picking at his teeth with the match stem. Jonny looked up and down the street, then stepped back to where Polly Ann and Margaret sat and pointed to the sign. "The hundredth centnal," he said. "It looks like they done decorated up for my birthday, dont it?"

Polly Ann looked at him and said, "Huh!"

"Well, hits the same day, aint it? Today's my birthday, aint it? I'm sixteen today and they done decorated for it!"

"What's the hundredth centnal?" Margaret asked.

Nobody answered; they looked up and down the street as the truck turned at the corner, and Jonny went back to the front where Seth was and said, "The hundredth centnal is on the same day as my birthday."

"Yeah," Seth said.

"The very same day."

"Yeah."

They parked on Smoky Road in a lot in front of the feedstore where there were no parking meters, across the street from the red, corrugated roof depot. They got out and stretched and patted their clothes right and brushed the dust off the smaller girl who stood staring at the train just coming in across the street, watching while the steam hissed and the black smoke puffed up in great explosive bursts; they fussed over her while Albert went over to the feedstore and began talking with an old man in overalls, soon arguing loudly; Tom Hamilton carefully rolled a cigarette out of the little white sack as Mamie talked at him, going over the list of groceries she had to get; he listened while he packed the cigarette with his blunt fingers and licked it moistly and put it in his mouth and lit it, the paper on the end flaming up and burning down half an inch before it reached the tobacco. He heard her out and then fumbled in his back pocket for the little greasy purse which he clicked open and counted out for her six rolled up dollar bills and a fifty cent piece while the others slowly gathered around and watched so that he finally pulled out three quarters and handed one each to Jonny, Margaret, and Polly Ann, hesitated a moment and then pulled a dime from somewhere in the bottom of it for the six-year-old Maddie Claude, then snapped it shut quickly, glancing uneasily at Seth who stood apart from the little group staring at something down the street as if he were intent on watching it.

They stood around the truck after that only so long as propriety demanded, then drifted off in different directions, Seth first, strolling off slowly, then moving faster with his steel taps clicking sharply on the pavement. Jonny hesitated; he looked first at his mother and then turned to Polly Ann who was also looking at him as if she were ready to say something. He said quickly, "I think I'll go with Seth today." They stared at each other for a second and she said, "You're not going to go with us down to. . .?" but let it trail off as she looked away from him, and he turned his head too so that neither of them was looking at the other any more; he then turned suddenly and started after Seth, twisting his head this way and that at the ribbons and the drapes over the doorways.

And in a few minutes, Polly Ann and Margaret left too, walking fast through the crowd, huddled over talking excitedly as if over some deep secret; and then Mamie, holding Maddie Claude by the right hand and holding the baby with the other, while Tom Hamilton went over and sat down on the steps of the feedstore and listened to Albert and old man Biggers argue; he sat there a minute or two and got up and left, going down Smoky Road to where some men sat on a bench in front of a hardware store—they moved over and made room for him.

It was about ten o'clock when they all parted at the truck; they would not meet again there until late that night. Seth, with Jonny following along, headed up past the ten-cent store and the picture show to the pool room where he sat at one of the chairs on the side watching two men shoot snooker on the front table; Jonny sat next to him, blinking his eyes trying to get used to the cool remote darkness after the bright April sunlight outside. The pool room was not crowded yet; the tables in the back were racked up with the lights off. Seth lounged in the chair watching the game; he crossed his legs and lit a cigarette as Jonny watched him out of the corner of his eye. Jonny blinked his eyes again, glanced at Seth and then lounged down in his seat too and crossed his legs, watching the smoke rising up under the buzzing blue neon lights that came down across the table, the roof of his mouth drawing up in distaste as he watched the fat man with the white shirt take a cigar out of his mouth, the ends of it wet and limp, and turn up a mug of beer he had on the counter. He eyed Seth a few more times and finally leaned over and said casually and rather harshly, "Give me a cigarette, will you, Seth?"

Seth didn't answer him at first; he was dragging on his own, his eyes squenched up. Jonny turned back to watch the game again but could feel Seth shifting his eyes at him. He jumped slightly when he heard Seth say, "Give you what?" He couldn't think of anything to say.

"What?" he said.

"Give you a cigarette?"

"Yeah, come on Seth. I want to try one."

Seth didn't say anything for a moment and he held his breath. Then Seth finally reached down into his pocket and pulled out the pack; Jonny, his eyes still toward the table, took one out and put it between his lips, holding it right in the center of his lips with them puckered out, and handed the pack back.

He took another deep breath and said, "How about a match?" and waited while Seth slowly fished it out and handed it to him. Jonny lit the cigarette and blew the smoke out without inhaling. He held it between his front two fingers both fingers stiff, dragging on it and blowing the smoke out in great gushes, his eyes watering and stinging, staring at the red balls on the table.

Polly Ann and Margaret were at the bus station. They sat at the white counter and ordered Cokes from the fat girl in the white dress. They sipped at them, huddled over together while Polly Ann kept glancing at herself in the mirror just behind the counter. They darted their eyes this way and that at the people coming in, the country people in their clean khakis and blue jeans and overalls; they turned around to watch the bus unload, giggling together at the large colored woman with all the bundles who almost tripped off. They watched, turned and whispered to each other as Polly Ann, glancing at the mirror, pulled her shoulders back making her breasts rise a little and point more under the pink satin front, glancing at times at the fat girl and back at herself again. She then turned to Margaret who was talking to her and lowered her eyes several times, noticing the lines she was forming; she would look at her year older sister, then back at herself again—then, seemingly satisfied, at whatever or whomever Margaret was talking about at the time. They turned their eyes from the door and concentrated on something on the counter as two boys about their own ages whom they knew came in; neither of them looked up, giving the boys a chance to speak to them without their seeming willing; they huddled and concentrated until the two boys went out the door again without speaking, and then they looked up at the same time without any kind of conscious signal and watched the people indifferently, a little irritated with each other somehow. Polly Ann turned all the way around on the stool and watched the two boys going across the street. She said, "There goes Tim and that other boy. They're the stuck-uppidest things."

"Where?"

"Over yonder," Polly Ann said.

"Oh, is that them? That aint them, is it?"

"I think so," Polly Ann said.

"Well, I'm glad they didn't see us," Margaret said. "They are the stuck-uppidest things . . ."

They were just finishing up their Cokes and ready to leave when the north bound bus came in. They each began sipping more slowly waiting to see who would get off, discussing what they were going to get Jonny for his birthday, trying to decide between the green top that Margaret wanted to buy and the cigarette lighter that Polly Ann insisted on. "What would he want with that?" Margaret said. "He don't even smoke."

"Well, he might someday. He's sixteen now, aint he?"

"Well," Margaret said, "I just dont see the sense in it when he dont even smoke, and we dont have the money for it nohow."

They argued the point, not looking at each other but at the bus outside the door, watching the blond headed woman who was getting off, seeing the long, red-colored fingernails and rings as she reached out taking the driver's helping hand. They talked and watched her as she walked primly on the very high heels, clicking toward the door of the station, the muscles in her hips moving like a well-oiled machine under the tight fitting skirt. She came in, her eyes looking a little blank, her blond hair seeming somehow wrong against her complexion. Polly Ann dug at a piece of ice in the bottom of her glass, turning her back as the woman sat down at the counter a seat away from her and said to the waitress who was also watching her, "Bring me a Coke, will you, honey, and put a little bit of lemon in it."

She clicked her purse open, got out a handerchief and leaned over to look in the mirror, straightening her lipstick; then took out a cigarette and lit it. Polly Ann watched the fat girl contemptuously as she suddenly became bashful and confused when the woman asked her what all the decorations around town were for.

"They're going to have the hundredth centnal, or something like that," the fat girl said, blushing.

"What is it, honey, some kind of fair?"

"Well, something like that, I guess."

A man sitting on the other side of her, a grey headed man with a grey suit who had been watching her, said, "I dont think nobody knows what it is, but they are going to celebrate it all right." The woman turned and looked at him and the man laughed, his voice unnatural, his laugh strained, his face turning a little red; Polly Ann could see his finger moving nervously over the sandwich he was eating. From the color of his face she could tell that he was from the country, despite the grey suit he was wearing.

"Where you from?" he asked, the smile becoming a little frozen on his face, twisting slightly on the seat.

"Jacksonville," she said, not even looking at him now.

"Where you headed?"

For a moment it seemed as if she wasn't even going to answer him. Then she said shortly, "The other direction." Some people snickered and the man turned redder in the face, looking confused and nervous, then turned back and took a large bite out of his sandwich. In a minute he left, leaving the sandwich half-eaten, going sheepishly out of the station.

They waited until she had finished her Coke and watched her walk over to the ticket window and ask about what time the other buses were going out; they got up then to leave, Margaret going for the door and Polly Ann stopping and suddenly boldly staring at the woman, up and down, as she went past. Then she followed Margaret to the door and out and on down the street, holding her shoulders back with her breasts pushing out, her hips moving slightly. "Wasn't that man disgusting, though," she said. "I'll bet he was sixty years old."

"Ugh," Margaret said. "Did you see how her hair looked?"

"She had it blondeened, I bet," Polly Ann said. "I think I'll have mine done like that."

"Oh, my goodness," Margaret said, looking at her.

"Well, she aint no bigger than I am without those high heels, is she?" Polly Ann said suddenly. But then she laughed and Margaret did too, and it suddenly seemed very funny to both of them so that they put their arms in between each other's, huddling together down the street, giggling mysteriously every time they looked at each other until they reached the corner where Polly Ann stopped giggling except when Margaret started it up again.

They looked in the reflections of the windows, Margaret studying the displays, Polly Ann touching at the back of her hair as she glanced at herself.

The town gradually became more crowded as the people came in. They parked their pick-up and two-ton trucks on the street by the railroad; old cars stopped and people climbed out like midgets at a circus; there were wagons and mules and cut down Model T's, and by noon the streets were filled with Negroes and whites in overalls and khakis, women with children and bundles, men standing around in little groups on the corners talking about crops and the weather and prices and all the decorations around town. Jonny, still in the pool room, ate a hot dog for dinner sitting in the chair next to the table where Seth leaned over shooting, the cigarette smoke curling up around his eyes, holding his cue with grace and ease, chalking the end of it after each shot. Jonny watched proudly as Seth ran up thirty-three points at one time, and then he finished up his hot dog and licked the mustard off his fingers and got in a game of eight-ball with the boy who racked the balls up. He sank only two balls but learned to powder and chalk the cue without all the awkwardness that he had noted somewhat contemptuously in the other beginners.

Albert ate dinner by himself at a little restaurant near the railway station and kidded the waitress who giggled at him; he drank three beers and left with a man to go to the ball park where they were going to have some ceremonies and speeches. He rode out with the man and was disappointed in the fact that no more than thirty people were there, and the speakers on the platforms became self-conscious and ended up by kidding each other over the loud speakers, making private jokes so that nobody else laughed much. Albert finally got tired of it and walked back to town and back to the restaurant to drink some more beer and talk with the waitress some more; he was just starting on his second one when the woman came in.

She came in behind him so that he could not see her at first, but from the perfume he almost knew what she was like without looking. He sucked in his breath sharply, his nostrils contracting, and turned to see her short, well-formed, small body and the blond hair and the red fingernails as she slid herself onto the stool right down from him, the sharp line of the indentation of her bloomers making a little ridge in the silkish dress just below her buttocks. He breathed shortly for a few moments, shifting his eyes at her. He grinned broadly suddenly and moved down next to her, saying, "You're a stranger here, I bet. What's the chances of buying a stranger a good cold brew." He held a good-natured smile on his face, his eyes twinkling, as she looked him over. He stood there grinning; she stared at him coldly then angrily, then contemptuously, and finally, when he did not wilt, cordially, and said, "Well, I might at that, being as you offered."

"Sho," Albert said. "Besides, we're having our hundredth centnal today. And besides that my nephew's having a birthday—going to have to do something for that boy. Good boy, sixteen today."

"Well, I'll have one to your nephew then," she said smiling. "I remember when I was sixteen."

"Well, sir, I wish to God I could," Albert said. "Honey, bring the lady here a good cool brew . . ."

At about four o'clock that afternoon, the man from the radio station came uptown. He parked his truck with the man inside who controlled the output down near the picture show, then got out and started stringing out the wires leading from it, testing it for the program that was supposed to begin at four-thirty. He worked busily getting everything set up, moving among the silently forming bunch of staring faces with an apologetic smile frozen on his face. He begged pardons and excused himself, smiling from one to the other, the short bow tie bobbing up and down on his Adam's apple as he tested saying, "One, two, three, four . . . Do you hear it. Charlie?"

The people formed a little half circle around the busy man in the middle, staring at him. Old man Biggers stood watching, chewing violently on a wad of tobacco, asking every once in a while, "What's that fer, there?" Tom Hamilton came up from the bench where he was sitting and stood next to him and they watched the goings-on. In a little while Mamie came out of the grocery store holding the baby and the groceries in her arms with Maddie Claude tagging along; she came and watched a minute, then took the groceries back to the truck before coming to see the movie that she always went to on Saturday. She came back just as the man was beginning the program, standing by her husband and blankly watching the tangle of wires around the truck. "I wonder where Jonny went off to," she said. "I thought I'd take him to the show being as it's his birthday and all, you know."

"He's off with Seth somewheres," Tom Hamilton said not looking at her.

"And usually he's deviling me to death to go," she said.

Tom Hamilton nodded his head, not answering her but watching the man in the middle. Mamie looked around vaguely for Jonny, finally said again, "Well, I wonder where they went?"

Tom Hamilton looked at her; he leaned over and spat and wiped his mouth off on the sleeve of his shirt. "Well, there aint no sense in waiting around here on him," he said. "Maybe he dont want to go nohow."

After that, he didn't say anything else to her. He got interested in the announcer's answer when he began clicking the microphone and Mr. Biggers asked, "What's that fer, there?" Mamie finally turned and headed for the box office and paid her money, looking back over her shoulder for Jonny before disappearing into the darkness where already the horses thundered and the shots were ringing out.

At four-thirty, just as Mamie went into the movie, the announcer got a nod from the man in the truck. His face became suddenly animated with a wide grin; his voice rang out loudly and enthusiastically, his little bow tie jumping up and down on his throat. He talked, nodded, smiled and bobbed around, waving his arms exclaiming on the crowd that had gathered on this, the Hundredth Centennial of Callville. He described the decorations and the crowds and told about the street dance they were going to have that night with Roy Bolton and his boys playing right here in the middle of town. Then he began his interviewing, looking around mischievously, and tried to get a large woman with a bundle of groceries in her arms to say just a few words, only she tightened her lips and moved back and started on up the street, as he described her departure with a great many forced chuckles in his voice.

Seth and Jonny came out of the pool room and stood around the edge of the group, Seth's head coming up above the others, Jonny secretly standing on his toes. Tom Hamilton took out the little sack and began to roll a cigarette and Mr. Biggers stared at the tangle of wires around the truck, his jaw moving rapidly. The announcer had cornered a lanky boy who looked at him stupidly, grinning, shaking his head from side to side. The announcer said, "Won't you just tell us your name?" The boy smiled broadly at the announcer, showing an ungodly amount of teeth. "Just your name. Won't you just tell us your *name*?" He was leaned over holding the microphone in front of the boy's lips and the boy still looked at him grinning, both of them staring at each other as the boy's lips started to move and stopped, as the announcer leaned over bobbing his head up and down like a mother with a daughter who had forgotten her nursery rhyme, trying to force the words out of the grinning face. Then he jerked backed the microphone and began talking into it, his face assuming a hideous smile that barely exposed his teeth. "Well," he said, "that young man didn't seem to care to talk over the radio. But there are lots of other folks around today. Yessir, you folks at home by your radios . . . You, sir, how about telling us your name . . ." This to a tall hard-looking man in overalls. "Won't you even tell us your name? . . . Well, maybe this gentleman . . . ha! ha! ha! . . . Well, I guess he was in pretty much of a hurry; he just kept right on going. Yessir, you folks at home . . ."

The crowd watched him impassively as he went on like this for some fifteen minutes without getting anybody to say a word, his laugh by this time becoming a forced gurgle that he seemed to push up out of his stomach, his face knotted into a smile so tightly that sometimes his lips would begin jerking involuntarily. They stood and watched as he cornered one man who for some reason kept grunting at him, and one other who didn't say anything but did at least start to, only to get strangled at the time and begin coughing and keep coughing until the announcer had to pull back the microphone to say a few words himself to keep the program going; he waited, moving from one foot to the other while the man gasped and strangled and hacked, holding the microphone over when he thought he had stopped, then having to jerk it back again, saying once or twice, "Well, he really did get strangled, didn't he?" He waited another minute while the man heaved and choked, said again, "Well, he really did get strangled, didn't he?" and tried to laugh again. He managed to wait this one out hopefully though until the man finally stopped, then held the microphone over to his lips only to get the sounds of the man hacking, clearing his throat, spitting, and then blowing his nose loudly, after which he went on down the street like the others.

Albert and the woman whose name he had learned was Clarene came out of the restaurant and saw the crowd and started for it, Albert walking bouncily, smiling and talking and pointing to things along the way as she walked beside him in her short steps, the heels of her shoes clicking loudly and the muscles in her body moving rhythmically. They stopped and stood on the edge of the crowd, smelling like a mixture of perfume and beer, as the people moved back slightly to look at them. She looked vaguely at the truck and the announcer and said brightly, "Oh, they're having a radio progum," slurring over her words and ending them with a slight hiccup, after which she raised one hand to her mouth daintily.

The announcer was trying to use up the rest of his time now, seriously describing with dead-pan face the different decorations around the stores, and trying to get eloquent once or twice, saying, "It's too bad that some of our fathers and grandfathers and great-grandfathers are not here today to witness this tribute to the hundredth anniversary of our town. Yes, we miss them and wish they were here, but we know that they are out yonder somewhere watching us today—and we wish you folks at home listening in were here too . . ."

They stood listening, Albert looking around smiling from one to the other, his hand straight down by his side so that when Clarene moved it brushed up against the silky smoothness of her bottom. Clarene listened to the announcer's eloquence and reached in her purse and got out a handkerchief and dabbed at her eyes which were beginning to smart, mumbling, "Yes, they are off somewheres, seeing us. I remember when I was sixteen."

Seth saw her over the crowd of heads and his eyes stopped suddenly and he clamped his teeth down on the match, staring at her, then turned to Flip who had come out of the pool room with them and who had just seen her too, and they nodded their heads at each other. Flip shook his head sidewise unbelievingly and a light hissing came out of his teeth.

"Aint that your uncle with her?"

Seth nodded, staring at them. "Je-sus!"

"Man," Flip said. "Lordy, lawd!"

"Je-sus!" Seth hissed.

"What is it?" Jonny asked standing on his toes. "What is it?"

The crowd was just breaking up when Polly Ann and Margaret came out of the ten-cent store. The announcer had wound up the broadcast five minutes before time actually so that they had to fill in the rest of it with music; he was now helping to load up the truck, moving listlessly, his eyes rather blank, taking deep heaving breaths every once in a while as some of the crowd still stood there and watched him silently, jaws moving up and down on wads of tobacco and chewing gum. Polly Ann and Margaret saw the crowd and wondered about it but neither of them mentioned it as they were arguing at the time; neither one looked at the other. "You go on and get what you want," Polly Ann said. "But I aint going to put nothing in it. He dont care nothing about a green top no more."

"Well, he sho dont care anything about a cigarette lighter."

"Well, that's what I'm going to get. I dont care what you say. He's sixteen now and dont want no green top."

"Do you know how much those things cost? I think you are losing your mind or something. The cheapest one you found yet was that one at the drugstore and that cost a dollar and a half! And you got fifty cents and I got thirty . . . I dont see how you expect to get it and I dont see what he would want with one anyhow. Honest to goodness Polly Ann sometimes you act like you crazy. I dont see why Jonny would even want one anyhow. I . . ."

"There's lots of things you dont see," Polly Ann replied bitterly, and headed on up the street, not even looking back to see if she were following.

Seth and Flip and Jonny had followed along behind Albert and Clarene, getting glimpses of her from time to time through the crowd of Negroes and whites that now crowded the streets, seeing her small body twitching below the curvature of her back they had followed them down to Red's Place on Smoky Road where they had gone inside out of sight, and Seth and Flip stood outside talking about it and hesitating, Flip saying, "Hell, let's go on in."

But Seth hesitated while Jonny leaned up against the wall waiting, his hands in his pockets. Seth bit the matchstick and thought, saying, "I kind of hate to cut in," and Flip said, "Hell, you dont cut in on one like that. You take turns. He's your uncle, aint he?" They finally decided and went into the place that had a wood cracked floor and little blue lights and a gaudy juke organ that changed colors from pink to green as the music blared out; they went back to the booth where they saw Albert who not only invited them but seemed very happy to see them, moving over so that Jonny could sit next to Clarene, saying, "You slide in here, Jonny boy. We're going to celebrate your birthday."

"Oh, is this him?" asked Clarene. She smiled and put her hand on his arm. "I remember when I was sixteen," she said and lifted the bottle with one finger stuck out, taking a great gulp of it.

They stayed in Red's Place until nearly eight o'clock and when they came out, the festivities were blaring. It had developed in a very peculiar way. At first, it seemed as if the whole thing was going to be a flop. Roy Bolton and his boys had not shown up and the juke organ that they had put on the platform of the decorated truck did not work over the loud speaker, and when they did get it to working, the records wabbled so that it didn't even sound like music. Then while they were trying to repair that, one of the men from the Chamber of Commerce tried to entertain the crowd with a long joke, only the microphone went dead in the middle of it, and finally when he did get to tell the joke, he was so angry that nobody laughed much. They had sprinkled sawdust along the street but this did not work too well either as it only filled up the holes in the pavement. People milled around in little groups talking and looking on; high school students standing around became rather contemptuous; the country people talked of the same things they usually talked about, the Negroes hung about on the corners greeting one another in their elaborately polite manners. It wasn't until Roy Bolton and his boys showed up that things started moving at all, and this was not because of the band but because of a man who fell off the truck trying to manage a keg of beer and broke his leg. The screaming siren of the ambulance did something to the crowd, and then somebody set off a string of firecrackers and Roy Bolton and his boys started playing, and within about fifteen minutes, what seemed at first a dismal evening developed into a melee that was worthy of this, the hundredth anniversary of Callville.

So that when Seth and Albert and Jonny and Clarene left Red's Place, it was like leaving a comfortable, cozy place into a mass of confusion. Somebody was setting off another string of firecrackers which exploded rapidly and loudly, the smoke and the smell of burnt powder drifting down the street. Mr. Biggers gave a whoop and began dancing with a woman next to the truck and then somebody set off the first skyrocket; it went screaming into the air with the fire out behind it along with moans from the crowd and then exploded with a noise that made everybody gasp. Albert laughed and pointed and gave a whoop himself, and Clarene grabbed onto Jonny's arm. The band swung out on "Rocky Bottom on Saturday Night" and the street became more crowded with people as they started to dance—men in overalls dancing stiffbacked with their wives, younger people bouncing around self-consciously, and one high school boy who held his head up high and his buttocks poked out, doing intricate steps with a good many twists and turns and dips; Mr. Biggers finally got up on the truck and did a buck dance all by himself, his brogan shoes banging up and down; they crowded in the street in an incongruous mass of farmers and storekeepers and clerks and women in country gingham with hard-knuckled hands and town women in prim dresses with soft diamonded hands; Roy Bolton sang, his voice cracking and yodeling, and the bass fiddle player straddled his instrument as if riding a horse, beating on the side of it, while children screamed and swarmed around the truck. The storekeepers that were still open came to the doors and watched, and the Negroes pointed and clapped each other on the back and finally got up a little dance of their own down on the corner; somebody else set off some firecrackers and the women squealed; the smoke floated down the street and another bunch went off. Mr. Travis, the bank president, donated two more kegs of beer, and watched, smiling to himself as he sat fat-stomached behind the wheel of his Buick as they opened it; Albert danced with Clarene, springing lightly and laughing, and then Seth broke in and danced with her, his hat still sitting cockwise on his head—she broke away from him finally and went over to get Jonny, taking him by the arm saying, "We're just about the same size, aint we?"

Jonny followed her out, trying to swagger but only succeeding in looking stiff all over as he started to dance. She showed him how to hold her, saying, "I couldn't dance neither when I was sixteen. No, honey, like this. What's the matter, you never held a girl before? That's right. That's right. Oh, honey, you do learn fast!"

He moved around in circles with her while she led him, pushing up against him as if somebody were tickling her in the back. Jonny tried to follow, stumbling, glancing around while Albert and Flip and Seth yelled at him. Albert waved his arms around in the air and shouted, "Yessir, that's my present! That's what I'm going to get for you. By God, I remember my first time!" He cupped his hands around his mouth and called, "Go to it, Jonny boy. You the best they is!" He kept yelling and taking on until Flip finally looked sourly at him and made a remark about him trying to hog everything.

Albert made so much noise that people began looking at Jonny, and then Polly Ann, who was up near the truck saw him. She and Margaret were standing there with two boys, and Polly Ann's eyes lighted up and she punched Margaret viciously in the side, saying, "Look at Jonny. What did I tell you? What did I tell you?" Margaret looked at him, her lips coming together, and said lamely, "Oh, well, you aint got the money nohow," then turned back to her partner; Polly Ann stared another minute, then walked off by herself, leaving the group of them alone.

Jonny kept dancing until Flip got disgusted with it and went out and broke in on them, taking Clarene in his arms rightly and whispering in her ear until she shoved away from him, saying loudly, "You keep away from me, you bastard!" and left him standing there. Albert laughed and Flip turned red. She went back and got Jonny again, and Flip turned, cursing her, and headed up the street away from the group. He started for the drugstore when he saw the pink satin dress of Polly Ann going through the door alone; he hurried along, went in and sat on a stool watching her and running his eyes up and down her as she fingered the cigarette lighter and asked the girl behind the counter how much it was. She looked a little angry when the girl said, "Aint it marked on the side?"

She turned it over. "Oh, yeah, I just didn't think it would be that much."

Flip edged over to her, glancing at it, saying, "How much?"

She looked at him coolly, but he was looking at the lighter and not at her. She said, "A dollar and a half."

"That's a right nice one all right. I think I'll get me one." He smiled at her. "You're too young to be smoking anyhow."

"Huh!"

"You are, I bet. I bet you dont even know how."

"That's how much you know."

They both looked at the box; he reached over to hold it, touching her hand so that at first she gave a jump; then, her eyes shifting, left her finger next to his as he wrapped it around hers. He said, "Yessir, if I didn't think you was too young, I would just buy it for you myself."

"I dont even know you," she said, still looking at the box.

"If we dance some, you'll get to know me. That is, if you aint too young."

"I aint too young," she said.

She stood in the door and waited for him, looking uneasily up and down the street; he came out in a minute sticking the package in his pocket. He led her toward the crowd, saying vulgarly, "We dont have to dance long, do we? There are other things to do, aint there?" giving her arm a squeeze, as she walked along, glancing up and down the street excitedly.

Jonny felt that he must be drunk. In his hand now he held the paper cup that had beer from the keg in it and whiskey that Clarene had poured into it; his head whirled and his face felt numb and he decided that now he was actually for the first time really and truly drunk. He would be dancing and then without knowing it, they would have stopped dancing and he would be standing with Albert on one side and Clarene on the other, talking and laughing, with Albert clapping him on the back. Everything in front of him was confused; firecrackers kept exploding and he looked up once to see another skyrocket just above his head; he never heard the sound of it—it seemed that it had just floated up there silently by itself. They were standing there and then he was going across the street again and he and Clarene were standing next to the truck with a paper cup in her hand pulling a bottle out of her purse again; then they were dancing and he could feel her body jerking convulsively every once in a while from the hiccups. He was drinking again with it going down smoother than before, and then he was dancing, floating, doing steps that he had never thought possible before. Then they were back at the truck and somebody had put a cigarette between his lips but it wouldn't stay in because his lips were so numb; it fell out to the ground and then she was holding it in his mouth for him saying,

"I'll light it for you, baby. Here you go, baby."

And after that they were on another street which he didn't recognize even though he knew every street in town, and Seth was sitting on the curbing. Nobody was around, and he couldn't figure out what Seth was doing just sitting there, and then he remembered Albert.

"No, you just wait a minute." It was Clarene standing close to him, holding his arms. They were up against a wall and she was kissing him. "Albert will be back in a minute. He had to go see the man." She was leaning up against him; he felt something stirring in him; then she was saying, "Wait, honey. Wait. Albert will be back in a minute. You're a little devil, aren't you? Oh, wait, wait just a minute."

Then Albert appeared from somewhere and they went up the long dark steps that creaked under his feet. Somebody was holding him saying, "No, on down the hall," and then the next thing he knew he was sitting in a chair asleep, and Albert was rubbing a wet rag over his face, saying, "Is that the way a man should act? Boys sho have changed since I was a boy."

Then all of a sudden, except for being dizzy, he was sober. He knew he was sober even though he didn't know how he got over to the door, but he knew immediately what was behind the door. He gave a quick shove against Albert and fell against a chair trying to get around it, going for the hall. But then he was back at the other door again and Albert was laughing and Seth was holding him by the arm grinning at him, and then the door opened and Clarene's head stuck out; she said, "Come on now, honey. Now." And as he went into the darkened room, he felt her bare arms around his neck, her small bare body grinding painfully against him. He never knew how it was they got to the bed.

It was all over about two o'clock that morning, and the Hamiltons headed back for the truck from the different sections of town. The town was quiet now; the big truck with the platform on it had moved off and the ropes had been taken down; the crowds had gone home leaving the scattered mess, the beer-soaked sawdust in the middle of the street, many paper cups, pieces of fireworks. Candy and bottles and pieces of ice cream cones littered the gutters and the sidewalks; the breeze came along from somewhere and picked up a newspaper and skidded it along the pavement like a small white dog running across the street. The lights burned dimly on the corners and from somewhere came the sound of a car shifting into second. Seth's iron taps clicked loudly on the sidewalk as they headed back for the truck which sat by itself now. Tom Hamilton was in the front seat, his hands on the wheel, looking around as if he were driving; Mamie sat next to him still holding the baby in her arms, her head falling down sideways and jerking back up again; in the back of the truck Margaret sat on one of the boxes with her head leaned up against the boards, her neck looking out of place and uncomfortable, her legs stretched out before her as she slept. Polly Ann sat hunched over on the box on the other side, her eyes wide open and knees together, staring at the corner light as she waited, holding the small package in her hands with her fingers clasped around it. She leaned forward listening, her lips tight together. She and Tom Hamilton both turned their heads hearing the steps coming closer, clicking on the pavement like somebody hitting a nail with a hammer; the noise echoed up and down the windblown and beer-soaked streets like small sharp cracks from a rifle. Tom Hamilton quit chewing a second and twisted his head around while the steps got louder, watching the corner as the sound reached a peak and the three forms turned the corner, looming up black and shadowy against the light. Seth was in front and Jonny followed along behind, his shoulders hunched over, his hands in his pockets, having to stretch to keep up with the pace that Seth was setting. Albert rolled along something like a bear, his hair messed up, looking at the sidewalk, walking like a man who has long since given up all attempt to move of his own accord but just keeps going by habit.

They got to the truck and Seth reached up and put his hands on the boards and slung himself in and took his stand at the head of it; Albert went around to the side of the front door and opened it, causing Mamie to jerk awake suddenly, and move over next to her husband, saying, "My lands, we been waiting . . ." but not bother to finish, only blinking her eyes again and letting her head nod back over. Albert got in, first having to pick up the lifeless form of Maddie Claude and drop her in his lap like a sack; he gave a deep sigh and then reached out and put his hand on the door and with what seemed like the absolutely final act that he could perform, hesitating a second to muster all his strength, slammed it shut with a loud clanging sound. Tom Hamilton hit the starter saying, "We done bout give yall out . . ." but Albert said nothing; he leaned back breathing heavily, resting, as if he did not yet have strength enough to close his eyes and sleep.

They drove off then up the main street where only two cars were left; they turned and went down the sawdust-covered street moving aside to avoid one bottle broken in the middle of it; they went past the place where the platform truck had been, its tire marks now showing in the sawdust; they turned and headed out of town again under the ripped banner hanging down at the stoplight so that it read: "HUNDR-" with the rest of the sign hanging down so that it couldn't be seen. They passed the monument where a man was sleeping and bumped over the railroad, going down the dark highway as the breeze, fresh and clean and cool, blew in whirls around the truck, the stars overhead bright and motionless. They settled down then for the ride back in the quietness, the motor sounding quiet somehow, the frogs and crickets setting up a chatter in the woods along the way. They drove past branchy places where the mist settled ghostily, Seth standing at the head of the truck letting the wind beat him in the face, Albert sitting in dry-eyed exhaustion; the wind whirled in the back blowing up some of the trash on the floor, getting some in Polly Ann's eye so that she gave a little cry and put her finger in it. Jonny looked at her and moved back beside her. He said roughly, "Well, dont rub it then."

She snatched her head around at him angrily, almost crying. "Well, who asked you about it anyhow? Who asked you about it?"

"Well I dont care then. Who cares anyhow?" Jonny answered, turning his head aside from her. They didn't say anything else to each other until they had reached the place where they turned off; at that time Polly Ann abruptly and rudely shoved the little package at him and said, "Here!"

He stared at her, not making any move to take it. "What's that?"

"It's your present."

"What is it?"

"Open it and see," she said angrily. "You can open it as good as I can."

He opened it sullenly, begrudgingly. When he took it out and looked at it, his face flushed somehow and he said quietly, "What makes you think I smoke?"

"If you dont want it, just throw it away then," she said to him. "Just throw it away."

"What would I want with a cigarette lighter?" he accused angrily. "Just because you run around smoking dont mean everybody . . ." Then he looked at her face and said, "Well, I didn't ask you to get it, did I? I didn't ask you to get it!"

Then she yelled, almost hysterically, her small hands clasped in her lap, leaning forward and staring at him with her eyes wild looking. "I dont care whether you want it or not! Throw it away! Throw it away then!"

"Well, you needn't yell at me," he shouted furiously, getting on his knees in the bottom of the truck. "I didn't ask you to get it, did I?"

"Throw it away! Throw it away!"

"What do I want . . ."

"Throw it away!"

She grabbed for it then, and both of them tussled over it trying to hold on to it; her voice broke out in a high wailing furious sob as she snatched it toward her, throwing her body from side to side. Jonny held on too, jerking at it, his voice cracking almost effeminately as he cried out in anger and tried to hold on to the package and jab his elbow in her stomach all at the same time. They snatched and jerked and screamed, their voices rising up in unreal chatter like squirrels; then they both at the same time began cursing each other, using words that neither had used before. She fell off the box then to the bottom of the truck and Jonny got his elbow in her breast and bored it in until she gave a stifled, pitiful cry. He pulled at the package and she jerked herself to her knees and snatched it and threw it so that it sailed over the side of the truck and into the bushes along the edge of the road; then she sat on the box, sobbing, staring at him and saying wildly, "There! There!" and he kept drawing back his fist at her as if to hit her, saying through clenched teeth, "You shut up now, goddamn you. Goddamn your soul!"

It was all over then. Seth had turned and looked at them with his eyes blank, showing neither approval nor disapproval; Margaret woke up and opened her eyes and stared as if she couldn't move, her feet still spread out before her; she watched them on the floor beside her, watched them get back up and Jonny go up to the front of the truck again, saying nothing as if she were looking at a dream.

Her eyes focused dully on Polly Ann's back for a moment after it was over; then she went back to sleep again.

They finally got to the house and got out, one by one, creaking, the truck sitting there making clicking noises in the motor as if it had not stopped yet. They passed into the house in stunned exhaustion; lights were turned on, then off again. The car settled down and quit clicking and the hounds stretched back out on the porch again to sleep. There was only the sound of the wind in the top of the pine trees, rustling lightly, mysteriously, godlike, like far off faint voices. Down in the woods somewhere a killdee began to cry, clear and lovely, piercing and deadly.

(From The New Yorker)

THE RESTING PLACE

BY OLIVER LA FARGE

THE POSSIBILITY that Dr. Hillebrand was developing kleptomania caused a good deal of pleasure among his younger colleagues—that is, the entire personnel of the Department of Anthropology, including its director, Walter Klibben. It was not that anybody really disliked the old boy. That would have been hard to do, for he was coöperative and gentle, and his humor was mild; he was perhaps the greatest living authority on Southwestern archeology, and broadly learned in the general science of anthropology; and he was a man who delighted in the success of others.

Dr. Hillebrand was the last surviving member of a group of men who had made the Department of Anthropology famous in the earlier part of the twentieth century. His ideas were old-fashioned; to Walter Klibben, who at forty was very much the young comer, and to the men he had gathered about him, Dr. Hillebrand's presence, clothed with authority, was as incongruous as that of a small, mild brontosaurus would be in a modern farmyard.

On the other hand, no one living had a finer archeological technique. Added to this was a curious intuition, which caused him to dig in unexpected places and come up with striking finds—the kind of thing that delights donors and trustees, such as the largest unbroken Mesa Verde black-on-white jar known up to that time, the famous Biltabito Cache of turquoise and shell objects, discovered two years before and not yet on exhibition, and, only the previous year, the mural decorations at Painted Mask Ruin. The mural, of which as yet only a small part had been uncovered, compared favorably with the murals found at Awatovi and Kawaika-a by the Peabody Museum, but was several centuries older. Moreover, in the part already exposed there was an identifiable katchina mask, unique and conclusive evidence that the katchina cult dated back to long before the white man came. This meant, Dr. Klibben foresaw gloomily, that once again all available funds for publication would be tied up by the old coot's material.

The trustees loved him. Several years ago, he had reached the age of retirement and they had waived the usual limitation in his case. He was curator of the museum, a position only slightly less important than that of director, and he occupied the Kleinman Chair in American Archeology. This was an endowed position paying several thousand a year more than Klibben's own professorship.

Dr. Hillebrand's occupancy of these positions, on top of his near monopoly of publication money, was the rub. He blocked everything. If only the old relic would become emeritus, the younger men could move up. Klibben had it all worked out. There would be the Kleinman Chair for himself, and McDonnell could accede to his professorship. He would leave Steinberg an associate, but make him curator. Thus, Steinberg and McDonnell would have it in mind that the curatorship always might be transferred to McDonnell as the man with senior status, which would keep them both on their toes. At least one assistant professor could, in due course, be made an associate, and young George Franklin, Klibben's own prized student, could be promoted from instructor to assistant. It all fitted together and reinforced his own position. Then, given free access to funds for monographs and papers . . .

But Dr. Hillebrand showed no signs of retiring. It was not that he needed the money from his two positions; he was a bachelor and something of an ascetic, and much of his salary he put into his own expeditions. He loved to teach, he said—and his students liked him. He loved his museum; in fact, he was daffy about it, pottering around in it until late at night. Well, let him retire, and he could still teach a course or two if he wanted; he could still potter, but Klibben could run his Department as he wished, as it ought to be run.

Since there seemed no hope that the old man would give out physically in the near future, Klibben had begun looking for symptoms of mental failure. There was, for instance, the illogical way in which Dr. Hillebrand often decided just where to run a trench or dig a posthole. As Steinberg once remarked, it was as if he were guided by a ouija board. Unfortunately, this eccentricity produced splendid results.

Then, sometimes Hillebrand would say to his students, "Now, let us imagine—" and proceed to indulge in surprising reconstructions of the daily life and religion of the ancient cliff dwellers, going far beyond the available evidence. The director had put Franklin onto that, because the young man had worked on Hopi and Zuñi ceremonial. Franklin reported that the old boy always made it clear that these reconstructions were not science, and, further, Franklin said that they were remarkably shrewd and had given him some helpful new insights into aspects of modern Indians' religion.

The possibility of kleptomania was something else again. The evidence—insufficient so far—concerned the rich Biltabito Cache, which Dr. Hillebrand himself was enumerating, cataloguing, and describing, mostly evenings, when the museum was closed. He was the only one who knew exactly how many objects had been in the find, but it did look as if some of it might now be missing. There was also what the night watchman thought he had seen. And then there was that one turquoise bead—but no proof it had come from that source, of course—that McDonnell had found on the floor near the cast of the Quiriguá stela, just inside the entrance to the museum.

The thefts—if there had been any—had taken place in April and early May, when everyone was thinking of the end of the college year and the summer's field trips. A short time later, and quite by accident, Klibben learned from an associate professor of ornithology that old Hillebrand had obtained from him a number of feathers, which he said he wanted for repairing his collection of katchina dolls. Among them were parrot and macaw feathers, and the fluffy feathers from the breast of an eagle.

Klibben's field was not the American Southwest, but any American anthropologist would have been able to draw an obvious conclusion; turquoise, shell, and feathers of those sorts were components of ritual offerings among the modern Hopis and Zuñis, and possibly their ancestors, among whose remains Dr. Hillebrand had carried on his lifework. Dr. Klibben began to suspect—or hope—that the old man was succumbing to a mental weakness far more serious than would be evidenced by the mere stealing of a few bits of turquoise and shell.

The Director made tactful inquiries at the genetics field laboratory to see if the old man had been seeking corn pollen, another component of the ritual offerings, and found that there the question of the evolution of *Zea maiz* in the Southwest was related to the larger and much vexed question of the origin and domestication of that important New World plant, so interesting to archeologists, botanists, and geneticists. Dr. Hillebrand had been collecting specimens of ancient corn from archeological sites for a long time—ears, cobs, and grains extending over two millenniums or more, and other parts of the plant, including some fragments of tassels. It was, Klibben thought, the kind of niggling little detail you would expect to find Hillebrand spending good time on. Dr. Hillebrand had been turning his specimens over to the plant and heredity boys, who were delighted to have them. They, in turn, had followed this up by obtaining—for comparison—seed of modern Pueblo Indian, Navajo, and Hopi corn, and planting it. It was natural enough, then, that from time to time Dr. Hillebrand should take specimens of seed and pollen home to study on his own. It might be clear as day to Klibben that the old boy had gone gaga to the point of making ritual offerings to the gods of the cliff dwellings; he still had nothing that would convince a strongly pro-Hillebrand board of trustees.

Even so, the situation was hopeful. Klibben suggested to the night watchman that, out of concern for Professor Hillebrand's health, he keep a special eye on the Professor's afterhours activities in the museum. Come June, he would arrange for Franklin—with his Southwestern interests, Franklin was the logical choice—to go along on Hillebrand's expedition and see what he could see.

Franklin took the assignment willingly, by no means unaware of the possible advantages to himself should the old man be retired. The archeologist accepted the addition of the young man to his staff with equanimity. He remarked that Franklin's knowledge of Pueblo daily life would be helpful in interpreting what might be uncovered, while a better grounding in Southwestern prehistory would add depth to the young man's ethnographic perceptions.

Right after commencement, they set out for the Navajo country of Arizona, accompanied by two undergraduate and four graduate students.

At Farmington, in New Mexico, they picked up the university's truck and station wagon, and Hillebrand's own field car, a Model A Ford as archaic as its owner. In view of the man's income, Franklin thought, his hanging on to the thing was one more oddity, an item that could be added to many others to help prove Klibben's case. At Farmington, too, they took on a cook and general helper. Dr. Hillebrand's work was generously financed, quite apart from what went into it from his own earnings.

The party bounced over the horrifying road past the Four Corners and around the north end of Beautiful Mountain, into the Chinlee Valley, then southward and westward until, after having taken a day and a half to drive about two hundred miles, they reached the cliffs against which stood Painted Mask Ruin. The principal aim of the current summer's work was to excavate the decorated kiva in detail, test another kiva, and make further, standard excavations in the ruin as a whole.

By the end of a week, the work was going nicely. Dr. Hillebrand put Franklin, as the senior scientist under him, in charge of the work in the painted kiva. Franklin knew perfectly well that he was deficient in the required techniques; he would, in fact, be dependent upon his first assistant, Philip Fleming, who was just short of his Ph.D. Fleming had worked in that kiva the previous season, had spent three earlier seasons with Dr. Hillebrand, and was regarded by him as the most promising of the many who had worked under him. There was real affection between the two men.

Two of the other graduate students were well qualified to run a simple dig for themselves. One was put in charge of the untouched second kiva, the other of a trench cutting into the general mass of the ruin from the north. Franklin felt uncomfortably supernumerary, but he recognized that that was an advantage in pursuing his main purpose of keeping a close watch on the expedition's director.

After supper on the evening of the eighth day, Dr. Hillebrand announced rather shyly that he would be gone for about four days, "to follow an old custom you all know about." The younger men smiled. Franklin kept a blank face to cover his quickened interest.

This was a famous, or notorious, eccentricity of the old man's, and one in which Drs. Klibben, McDonnell, and the rest put great hope. Every year, early in the season, Dr. Hillebrand went alone to a ruin he had excavated early in his career. There was some uncertainty as to just where the ruin was; it was believed to be one known to the Navajos as Tsekaiye Kin. No one knew what he did there. He said he found the surroundings and the solitude invaluable for thinking out the task in hand. It was usually not long after his return from it that he would announce his decision to dig in such-and-such a spot, and proceed to uncover the painted kiva, or the Kettle Cave fetishes, or the Kin Hatsosi blanket, or some other notable find.

If Franklin could slip away in the station wagon and follow the old man, he might get just the information he wanted. So far, Dr. Hillebrand's activities on the expedition had evidenced nothing but his great competence. If the old man ever performed mad antique rites with stolen specimens, it would be at his secret place of meditation. Perhaps he got up and danced to the ancient gods. One might be able to sneak a photo . . .

Dr. Hillebrand said, "I shan't be gone long. Meantime, of course, Dr. Franklin will be in charge." He turned directly to his junior. "George, there are several things on which you must keep a close watch. If you will look at these diagrams—and you, too, Phil . . ."

Franklin and Fleming sat down beside him. Dr. Hillebrand expounded. Whether the ancient devil had done it intentionally or not, Franklin saw that he was neatly hooked. In the face of the delicacy and the probable outcome of the next few days' work, he could not possibly make an excuse for absenting himself when the head of the expedition was also absent.

Dr. Hillebrand took off early the next morning in his throbbing Model A. He carried with him a Spartan minimum of food and bedding. It was good to be alone once more in the long-loved reaches of the Navajo country. The car drove well. He still used it because, short of a jeep, nothing newer had the clearance to take him where he wanted to go.

He drove slowly, for he was at the age when knowledge and skill must replace strength, and getting stuck would be serious. When he was fifty, he reflected, he would have reached T'iiz Hatsosi

Canyon from this year's camp in under four hours; when he was thirty, if it had been possible to travel this country in a car, he would have made even greater speed, and as like as not ended by getting lost. He reached the open farming area outside the place where T'iiz Hatsosi sliced into the great mesa to the south. There were nearly twice as many hogans to be seen as when he had first come here; several of them were square and equipped with windows, and by some of them cars were parked. Everything was changing, but these were good people still, although not as genial and hospitable as their grandparents had been when he first packed in.

He entered the narrow mouth of T'iiz Hatsosi Canyon in the late afternoon, and by the exercise of consummate skill drove some four miles up it. At that point, it was somewhat wider than elsewhere, slightly under two hundred feet across at the bottom. The heavy grazing that had so damaged all the Navajos' land had had some effect here. There was less grass than there used to be—but then, he reflected, he had no horses to graze—and the bed of the wash was more deeply eroded, and here and there sharp gullies led into it from the sides.

Still, the cottonwoods grew between the occasional stream and the high, warmly golden-buff cliffs. Except at noon, there was shade, and the quality of privacy, almost of secrecy, remained. In the west wall was the wide strip of white rocks from which the little ruin took its name, Tsekaiye Kin, leading the eye to the long ledge above which the cliff arched like a scallop shell, and upon which stood the ancient habitations. The lip of the ledge was about twenty feet above the level of the canyon, and approachable by a talus slope that was not too hard to negotiate. Some small evergreens grew at the corners of the ledge. From the ground, the settlement did not seem as if it had been empty for centuries, but rather as if its occupants at the moment happened not to be visible. The small black rectangles of doorways and three tiny squares of windows made him feel, as they had done over forty years ago, as if the little settlement were watching him.

South of the far end of the ledge, and at the level of the canyon floor, was the spring. Water seeped richly through a crack in the rock a few feet above the ground and flowed down over rock to form a pool at the base. The wet golden-brown stone glistened; small water growths clung to crevices. In the pool itself, there was cress, and around it moss and grass rich enough to make a few feet of turf.

Here Dr. Hillebrand deposited his bedroll and his food. He estimated that he had better than two hours of daylight left. He cut himself a supply of firewood. Then he took a package out of his coffeepot. The package was wrapped in an old piece of buckskin. With this in hand, he climbed up the slope to the ruin.

The sense of peace had begun once he was out of sight of the camp at Painted Mask Ruin. It had grown when he entered T'iiz Hatsosi Canyon; it had become stronger when he stepped out of the car and glimpsed through the cottonwoods his little village, with its fourteen rooms. By the spring, it had become stronger yet, and mixed with a nostalgia of past times that was sweetly painful, like a memory of an old and good lost love. These feelings were set aside as he addressed himself to the task of climbing, which was not entirely simple; then they returned fourfold when he was in the ruin. Here he had worked alone, a green young man with a shiny new Doctor's degree, a boy-man not unlike young Fleming. Here he had discovered what it was to like to step into a room that still had its roof intact, and see the marks of the smoke from the household fire, the loom ties still in place in the ceiling and floor, the broken cooking pot still in the corner.

He paid his respects to that chamber—Room 4-B; stood in the small, open, central area; then went to the roofless, irregular oval of the kiva. All by himself he had dug it out.

Could Dr. Franklin have been there then, spying unseen, he would have been most happy. From under a stone that appeared firmly embedded in the clay flooring Dr. Hillebrand took an ancient, crude stone pipe fitted with a recent willow stem. He filled it with tobacco, performed curious motions as he lit it, and puffed smoke in the six directions. Then he climbed out of the kiva on the inner side, and went behind the double row of habitations, to the darker area under the convex curve of the wall at the back of the cave, the floor of which was a mixture of earth and rubbish. Two smallish, rounded stones about three feet apart inconspicuously marked a place. Sitting by it on a convenient ledge of rock, he puffed at the pipe again; then he opened the buckskin package and proceeded to make an offering of ancient turquoise beads, white and red shell, black stone, feathers and down, and corn pollen.

Sitting back comfortably, he said, "Well, here I am again."

The answer did not come from the ground, in which the bones of the speaker reposed, but from a point in space, as if he were sitting opposite Dr. Hillebrand. "Welcome, old friend. Thank you for the gifts; their smell is pleasing to us all."

"I don't know whether I can bring you any more," the archeologist said. "I can buy new things, of course, but getting the old ones is becoming difficult. They are watching me."

"It is not necessary," the voice answered. "We are rich in the spirits of things such as these, and our grandchildren on earth still offer them to us. It has been rather for your benefit that I have had you bringing them, and I think that that training has served its purpose."

"You relieve me." Then, with a note of anxiety, "That doesn't mean that I have to stop visiting you?"

"Not at all. And, by the way, there is a very handsome jar with a quantity of beans of an early variety in it where you are digging now. It was left behind by accident when the people before the ones who built the painted kiva moved out. It belonged to a woman called Bluebird Tailfeather. Her small child ran off and was lost just as they were moving, and by the time she found him, the war chief was impatient. However, we can come back to that later. I can see that you have something on your mind."

"I'm lonely," Dr. Hillebrand said simply. "My real friends are all gone. There are a lot of people I get on nicely with, but no one left I love—that is, above the ground—and you are the only one below the ground I seem to be able to reach. I—I'd like to take your remains back with me, and then we could talk nights."

"I would not like that."

"Then of course I won't."

"I was sure of that. Your country is strange to me, and travelling back and forth would be a lot of effort. What I saw that time I visited you was alien to me; it would be to you, too, I think. It won't be long, I believe, before I am relieved of attachment to my bones entirely, but if you moved them now, it would be annoying. You take that burial you carried home ten years ago—old Rabbit Stick. He says you treat him well and have given him the smell of ceremonial jewels whenever you could, but sometimes he arrives quite worn out from his journey."

"Rabbit Stick," Dr. Hillebrand mused. "I wondered if there were not someone there. He has never spoken to me."

"He couldn't. He was just an ordinary Reed Clan man. But he is grateful to you for the offerings, because they have given him the strength he needed. As you know, I can speak with you because I was the Sun's Forehead, and there was the good luck that you were thinking and feeling in the right way when you approached me. But tell me, don't the young men who learn from you keep you company?"

"Yes. There is one now who is like a son to me. But then they have learned, and they go away. The men in between, who have become chiefs, you might say, in my Department, have no use for me. They want to make me emeritus—that is, put me on a pension, take over my authority and my rewards, and set me where I could give advice and they could ignore it. They have new ways, and they despise mine. So now they are watching me. They have sent a young man out this time just to watch me. They call him a student of the ways of your grandchildren; he spent six weeks at Zuñi once, and when even he could see that the people didn't like him, he went and put in the rest of the summer at Oraibi."

"New Oraibi or Old Oraibi?" the Sun's Forehead asked.

"New Oraibi."

The chief snorted.

"So, having also read some books, he thinks he is an ethnographer, only he calls himself a cultural anthropologist. And he is out here to try to find proof that my mind is failing." He smiled. "They'd certainly think so if they saw me sitting here talking to empty air."

The Sun's Forehead chuckled.

"They certainly would. They wouldn't be able to hear me, you know." Then his voice became serious again. "That always happens, I think. It happened to me. They wanted to do things differently, when I had at last come to the point at which an Old Man talked to me. I reached it in old age—not young, as you did. They could not take my title, but they wanted to handle my duties for me, bring me enough food to live on, hear my advice and not listen to it. Struggling against them became wearying and distasteful, so finally I decided to go under. At the age I had reached—about your age—it is easy to do."

"And now you say that you are about to be detached from your bones entirely? You are reaching the next stage?"

"Let us say that I begin to hope. Our life is beautiful, but for a hundred years or so now I have been longing for the next, and I begin to hope."

"How does it happen? Or is it wrong for me to know?"

"You may know. You are good, and you keep your secrets, as our wise men always did. You will see a man who has become young, handsome, and full of light. When we dance, he dances with great beauty; his singing is beautiful, and you feel as if it were creating life. Then one time when the katchinas themselves are dancing before us—not masks, you understand, the katchinas themselves—you can't find him among the watchers. Then you seem to recognize him, there among the sacred people, dancing like them. Then you think that the next time our grandchildren on earth put on the masks and dance, that one, whom you knew as a spirit striving to purify himself, who used to tell you about his days on the earth, will be there. With his own eyes he will see our grandchildren and bless them." The chief's voice trailed off, as though the longing for what he was describing deprived him of words.

"To see the katchinas themselves dancing," Dr. Hillebrand mused. "Not the masks, but what the masks stand for . . . That would keep me happy for centuries. But then, I could not join your people. I was never initiated. I'd be plain silly trying to dance with them. It's not for me."

"For over forty years I have been initiating you," the Sun's Forehead said. "As for dancing—you will no longer be in that old body. You will not be dancing with those fragile, rheumatic bones. There is room for you in our country. Why don't you come over? Just lie down in that crevice back there and make up your mind."

"You know," Dr. Hillebrand said, "I think I will."

Both the Kleinman Professor of American Archeology and the spirit who once had been the Sun's Forehead for the settlements in the neighborhood of T'iiz Hatsosi were thoroughly unworldly. It had not occurred to either of them that within six days after Dr. Hillebrand had left camp Dr. George Franklin would organize a search for him, and that four days later his body would be found where he had died of, apparently, heart failure. Above all, it had not occurred to them that his body would be taken home and buried with proper pomp in the appropriate cemetery. (But Philip Fleming, close to tears, resolutely overlooked the scattering of turquoise and shell in the rubbish between the crevice and the kiva.)

Dr. Hillebrand found himself among people as alien to him as they had been to the Sun's Forehead. They seemed to be gaunt from the total lack of offerings, and the means by which they should purify and advance themselves to where they could leave this life for the next, which he believed to be the final one, were confused. He realized that his spirit was burdened with much dross, and that it would be a long time before he could gather the strength to attempt a journey to the country of his friend.

His portrait, in academic gown and hood, was painted posthumously and hung in the entrance of the museum, to one side of the stela from Quiriguá and facing the reproduction of the famous Painted Kiva mural. Dr. Klibben adroitly handled the promotions and emoluments that fell under his control. Philip Fleming won his Ph.D. with honor, and was promptly offered a splendid position at Harvard. Moved by he know not what drive, and following one or two other actions he had performed to his own surprise, Fleming went to Dr. Hillebrand's grave, for a gesture of respect and thanks.

It had seemed to him inappropriate to bring any flowers. Instead, as he sat by the grave, with small motions of his hands he sprinkled over it some bits of turquoise and shell he had held out from a necklace he had unearthed, and followed them with a pinch of pollen given him by a Navajo. Suddenly his face registered utter astonishment; then careful listening.

The following season, Fleming returned to Painted Mask Ruin by agreement with Dr. Klibben, who was delighted to get his Department entirely out of Southwestern archeology. There he ran a trench that led right into a magnificent polychrome pot containing a store of beans of high botanical interest.

Within a few years, he stopped visiting the grave, but he was sentimentalist enough to make a pilgrimage all alone to Tsekaiye Kin at the beginning of each field season. It was jokingly said among his confreres that there he communed with the spirit of old Hillebrand. Certainly he seemed to have inherited that legendary figure's gift for making spectacular finds.

(From Partisan Review)

THE MAGIC BARREL

BY BERNARD MALAMUD

NOT LONG AGO there lived in uptown New York, in a small, almost meager room, though crowded with books, Leo Finkle, a rabbinical student in the Yeshivah University. Finkle, after six years of study, was to be ordained in June and had been advised by an acquaintance that he might find it easier to win himself a congregation if he were married. Since he had no present prospects of marriage, after two tormented days of turning it over in his mind, he called in Pinye Salzman, a marriage broker, whose two-line advertisement he had read in the *Forward*.

The matchmaker appeared one night out of the dark fourth-floor hallway of the graystone rooming house, grasping a black, strapped portfolio that had been worn thin with use. Salzman, who had been long in the business, was of slight but dignified build, wearing an old hat and an overcoat too short and tight for him. He smelled frankly of fish, which he loved to eat, and although he was missing a few teeth, his presence was not displeasing, because of an amiable manner curiously contrasted by mournful eyes. His voice, his lips, his wisp of beard, his bony fingers were animated, but give him a moment of repose and his mild blue eyes soon revealed a depth of sadness, a characteristic that put Leo a little at ease although the situation, for him, was inherently tense.

He at once informed Salzman why he had asked him to come, explaining that his home was in Cleveland, and that but for his parents, who had married comparatively late in life, he was alone in the world. He had for six years devoted himself entirely to his studies, as a result of which, quite understandably, he had found himself without time for a social life and the company of young women. Therefore he thought it the better part of trial and error—of embarrassing fumbling—to call in an experienced person to advise him in these matters. He remarked in passing that the function of the marriage broker was ancient and honorable, highly approved in the Jewish community, because it made practical the necessary without hindering joy. Moreover, his own parents had been brought together by a matchmaker. They had made, if not a financially profitable marriage—since neither had possessed any worldly goods to speak of—at least a successful one in the sense of their everlasting devotion to one another. Salzman listened in embarrassed surprise, sensing a sort of apology. Later, however, he experienced a glow of pride in his work, an emotion that had left him years ago, and he heartily approved of Finkle.

The two men went to their business. Leo had led Salzman to the only clear place in the room, a table near a window that overlooked the lamp-lit city. He seated himself at the matchmaker's side but facing him, attempting by an act of will to suppress the unpleasant tickle in his throat. Salzman eagerly unstrapped his portfolio and removed a loose rubber band from a thin packet of much handled cards. As he flipped through them, a gesture and sound that physically hurt Leo, the student pretended not to see and gazed steadfastly out the window. Although it was still February, winter was on its last legs, signs of which he had for the first time in years begun to notice. He now observed the round white moon, moving high in the sky through a cloud menagerie, and watched with half-open mouth as it penetrated a huge hen, and dropped out of her like an egg laying itself. Salzman, though pretending through eyeglasses he had just slipped on to be engaged in scanning the writing on the cards, stole occasional glances at the young man's distinguished face, noting with pleasure the long, severe scholar's nose, brown eyes heavy with learning, sensitive yet ascetic lips, and a certain almost hollow quality of the dark cheeks. He gazed around at shelves upon shelves of books and let out a soft but happy sigh.

When Leo's eyes fell upon the cards, he counted six spread out in Salzman's hand.

"So few?" he said in disappointment.

"You wouldn't believe me how much cards I got in my office,"

Salzman replied. "The drawers are already filled to the top, so I keep them now in a barrel, but is every girl good for a new rabbi?"

Leo blushed at this, regretting all he had revealed of himself in a curriculum vitae he had sent to Salzman. He had thought it best to acquaint him with his strict standards and specifications, but in having done so now felt he had told the marriage broker more than was absolutely necessary.

He hesitantly inquired, "Do you keep photographs of your clients on file?"

"First comes family, amount of dowry, also what kind promises," Salzman replied, unbuttoning his tight coat and settling himself in the chair. "After comes pictures, rabbi."

"Call me Mr. Finkle. I'm not a rabbi yet."

Salzman said he would, but instead called him doctor, which he changed to rabbi when Leo was not listening too attentively.

Salzman adjusted his horn-rimmed spectacles, gently cleared his throat and read in an eager voice the contents of the top card:

"Sophie P. Twenty-four years. Widow for one year. No children. Educated high school and two years college. Father promises eight thousand dollars. Has wonderful wholesale business. Also real estate. On the mother's side comes teachers, also one actor. Well known on Second Avenue."

Leo gazed up in surprise. "Did you say a widow?"

"A widow don't mean spoiled, rabbi. She lived with her husband maybe four months. He was a sick boy, she made a mistake to marry him."

"Marrying a widow has never entered my mind."

"This is because you have no experience. A widow, specially if she is young and healthy like this girl, is a wonderful person to marry. She will be thankful to you the rest of her life. Believe me, if I was looking now for a bride, I would marry a widow."

Leo reflected, then shook his head.

Salzman hunched his shoulders in an almost imperceptible gesture of disappointment. He placed the card down on the wooden table and began to read another:

"Lily H. High school teacher. Regular. Not a substitute. Has savings and new Dodge car. Lived in Paris one year. Father is successful dentist thirty-five years. Interested in professional man. Well Americanized family. Wonderful opportunity.

"I know her personally," said Salzman. "I wish you could see this girl. She is a doll. Also very intelligent. All day you could talk to her about books and theyater and what not. She also knows current events."

"I don't believe you mentioned her age?"

"Her age?" Salzman said, raising his brows in surprise. "Her age is thirty-two years."

Leo said after a while, "I'm afraid that seems a little too old."

Salzman let out a laugh. "So how old are you, rabbi?"

"Twenty-seven."

"So what is the difference, tell me, between twenty-seven and thirty-two? My own wife is seven years older than me. So what did I suffer?—Nothing. If Rothschild's a daughter wants to marry you, would you say on account her age, no?"

"Yes," Leo said dryly.

Salzman shook off the no in the yes. "Five years don't mean a thing. I give you my word that when you will live with her for one week you will forget her age. What does it mean five years—that she lived more and knows more than somebody who is younger? On this girl, God bless her, years are not wasted. Each one that it comes makes better the bargain."

"What subject does she teach in high school?"

"Languages. If you heard the way she reads French, you will think it is music. I am in the business twenty-five years, and I recommend her with my whole heart. Believe me, I know what I'm talking, rabbi."

"What's on the next card?" Leo said abruptly.

Salzman reluctantly turned up the third card:

"Ruth K. Nineteen years. Honor student. Father offers thirteen thousand dollars cash to the right bridegroom. He is a medical doctor. Stomach specialist with marvelous practice. Brother-in-law owns own garment business. Particular people."

Salzman looked up as if he had read his trump card.

"Did you say nineteen?" Leo asked with interest.

"On the dot."

"Is she attractive?" He blushed. "Pretty?"

Salzman kissed his fingertips. "A little doll. On this I give you my word. Let me call the father tonight and you will see what means pretty."

But Leo was troubled. "You're sure she's that young?"

"This I am positive. The father will show you the birth certificate."

"Are you positive there isn't something wrong with her?" Leo insisted.

"Who says there is wrong?"

"I don't understand why an American girl her age should go to a marriage broker."

A smile spread over Salzman's face.

"So for the same reason you went, she comes."

Leo flushed. "I am pressed for time."

Salzman, realizing he had been tactless, quickly explained. "The father came, not her. He wants she should have the best, so he looks around himself. When we will locate the right boy he will introduce him and encourage. This makes a better marriage than if a young girl without experience takes for herself. I don't have to tell you this."

"But don't you think this young girl believes in love?" Leo spoke uneasily.

Salzman was about to guffaw but caught himself and said soberly, "Love comes with the right person, not before."

Leo parted dry lips but did not speak. Noticing that Salzman had snatched a quick glance at the next card, he cleverly asked, "How is her health?"

"Perfect," Salzman said, breathing with difficulty. "Of course, she is a little lame on her right foot from an auto accident that it happened to her when she was twelve years, but nobody notices on account she is so brilliant and also beautiful."

Leo got up heavily and went to the window. He felt curiously bitter and upbraided himself for having called in the marriage broker. Finally, he shook his head.

"Why not?" Salzman persisted, the pitch of his voice rising.

"Because I hate stomach specialists."

"So what do you care what is his business? After you marry her, do you need him? Who says he must come every Friday night to your house?"

Ashamed of the way the talk was going, Leo dismissed Salzman, who went home with melancholy eyes.

Though he had felt only relief at the marriage broker's departure,

Leo was in low spirits the next day. He explained it as arising from Salzman's failure to produce a suitable bride for him. He did not care for his type of clientele. But when Leo found himself hesitating over whether to seek out another matchmaker, one more polished than Pinye, he wondered if it could be—his protestations to the contrary, and although he honored his father and mother—that he did not, in essence, care for the matchmaking institution. This thought he quickly put out of mind yet found himself still upset. All day he ran around in a fog—missed an important appointment, forgot to give out his laundry, walked out of a Broadway cafeteria without paying and had to run back with the ticket in his hand; had even not recognized his landlady in the street when she passed with a friend and courteously called out, "A good evening to you, Doctor Finkle." By nightfall, however, he had regained sufficient calm to sink his nose into a book and there found peace from his thoughts.

Almost at once there came a knock on the door. Before Leo could say enter, Salzman, commercial cupid, was standing in the room. His face was gray and meager, his expression hungry, and he looked as if he would expire on his feet. Yet the marriage broker managed, by some trick of the muscles, to display a broad smile.

"So good evening. I am invited?"

Leo nodded, disturbed to see him again, yet unwilling to ask him to leave.

Beaming still, Salzman laid his portfolio on the table. "Rabbi, I got for you tonight good news."

"I've asked you not to call me rabbi. I'm still a student."

"Your worries are finished. I have for you a first-class bride."

"Leave me in peace concerning this subject." Leo pretended lack of interest.

"The world will dance at your wedding."

"Please, Mr. Salzman, no more."

"But first must come back my strength," Salzman said weakly. He fumbled with the portfolio straps and took out of the leather case an oily paper bag, from which he extracted a hard seeded roll and a small smoked whitefish. With one motion of his hand he stripped the fish out of its skin and began ravenously to chew. "All day in a rush," he muttered.

Leo watched him eat.

"A sliced tomato you have maybe?" Salzman hesitantly inquired.

"No."

The marriage broker shut his eyes and ate. When he had finished he carefully cleaned up the crumbs and rolled up the remains of the fish in the paper bag. His spectacled eyes roamed the room until he discovered, amid some piles of books, a one-burner gas stove. Lifting his hat he humbly asked, "A glass tea you got, rabbi?"

Conscience-stricken, Leo rose and brewed the tea. He served it with a chunk of lemon and two cubes of lump sugar, delighting Salzman.

After he had drunk his tea, Salzman's strength and good spirits were restored.

"So tell me, rabbi," he said amiably, "you considered any more the three clients I mentioned yesterday?"

"There was no need to consider."

"Why not?"

"None of them suits me."

"What, then, suits you?"

Leo let it pass because he could give only a confused answer.

Without waiting for a reply, Salzman asked, "You remember this girl I talked to you—the high school teacher?"

"Age thirty-two?"

But, surprisingly, Salzman's face lit in a smile. "Age twenty-nine."

Leo shot him a look. "Reduced from thirty-two?"

"A mistake," Salzman avowed. "I talked today with the dentist. He took me to his safety deposit box and showed me the birth certificate. She was twenty-nine years last August. They made her a party in the mountains where she went for her vacation. When her father spoke to me the first time I forgot to write the age and I told you thirty-two, but now I remember this was a different client, a widow."

"The same one you told me about? I thought she was twenty-four?"

"A different. Am I responsible that the world is filled with widows?"

"No, but I'm not interested in them, nor for that matter, in schoolteachers."

Salzman passionately pulled his clasped hands to his breast. Looking at the ceiling he exclaimed, "Jewish children, what can I say to somebody that he is not interested in high school teachers? So what then you are interested?"

Leo flushed but controlled himself.

"In who else you will be interested," Salzman went on, "if you not interested in this fine girl that she speaks four languages and has personally in the bank ten thousand dollars? Also her father guarantees further twelve thousand. Also she has a new car, wonderful clothes, talks on all subjects, and she will give you a first-class home and children. How near do we come in our life to paradise?"

"If she's so wonderful, why wasn't she married ten years ago?"

"Why?" said Salzman with a heavy laugh. "—Why? Because she is *partikler*. This is why. She wants only the *best*."

Leo was silent, amused at how he had trapped himself. But Salzman had aroused his interest in Lily H., and he began seriously to consider calling on her. When the marriage broker observed how intently Leo's mind was at work on the facts he had supplied, he felt positive they would soon come to an agreement.

Late Saturday afternoon, conscious of Salzman, Leo Finkle walked with Lily Hirschorn along Riverside Drive. He walked briskly and erectly, wearing with distinction the black fedora he had that morning taken with trepidation out of the dusty hatbox on his closet shelf, and the heavy black Saturday coat he had thoroughly whisked clean. Leo also owned a walking stick, a present from a distant relative, but had decided not to use it. Lily, petite and not unpretty, had on something signifying the approach of spring. She was *au courant*, animatedly, with all subjects, and he weighed her words and found her surprisingly sound—score another for Salzman, whom he uneasily sensed to be somewhere around, hiding perhaps high in a tree along the street, flashing the lady signals; or perhaps a cloven-hoofed Pan, piping nuptial ditties as he danced his invisible way before them, strewing wild buds on the walk and purple summer grapes in their path, symbolizing fruit of a union, of which there was yet none.

Lily startled Leo by remarking, "I was thinking of Mr. Salzman, a curious figure, wouldn't you say?"

Not certain what to answer, he nodded.

She bravely went on, blushing, "I for one am grateful for his introducing us. Aren't you?"

He courteously replied, "I am."

"I mean," she said with a little laugh—and it was all in good taste, or at least gave the effect of being not in bad—"do you mind that we came together so?"

He was not afraid of her honesty, recognizing that she meant to set the relationship aright, and understanding that it took a certain amount of experience in life, and courage, to want to do it quite that way. One had to have some sort of past to make that kind of beginning.

He said that he did not mind. Salzman's function was traditional and honorable—valuable for what it might achieve, which, he pointed out, was frequently nothing.

Lily agreed with a sigh. They walked on for a while and she said after a long silence, again with a nervous laugh, "Would you mind if I asked you something a little bit personal? Frankly, I find the subject fascinating." Although Leo shrugged, she went on half embarrassedly, "How was it that you came to your calling? I mean was it a sudden passionate inspiration?"

Leo, after a time, slowly replied, "I was always interested in the Law."

"You saw revealed in it the presence of the Highest?"

He nodded and changed the subject. "I understand you spent a little time in Paris, Miss Hirschorn?"

"Oh, did Mr. Salzman tell you, Rabbi Finkle?" Leo winced but she went on, "It was ages and ages ago and almost forgotten. I remember I had to return for my sister's wedding."

But Lily would not be put off. "When," she asked in a trembly voice, "did you become enamored of God?"

He stared at her. Then it came to him that she was talking not about Leo Finkle, but a total stranger, some mystical figure, perhaps even passionate prophet that Salzman had conjured up for her—no relation to the living or dead. Leo trembled with rage and weakness. The trickster had obviously sold her a bill of goods, just as he had him, who'd expected to become acquainted with a young lady of twenty-nine, only to behold, the moment he laid eyes upon her strained and anxious face, a woman past thirty-five and aging very rapidly. Only his self-control, he thought, had kept him this long in her presence.

"I am not," he said gravely, "a talented religious person," and in seeking words to go on, found himself possessed by fear and shame. "I think," he said in a strained manner, "that I came to God not because I loved Him, but because I did not."

This confession he spoke harshly because its unexpectedness shook him.

Lily wilted. Leo saw a profusion of loaves of bread sailing like ducks high over his head, not unlike the loaves by which he had counted himself to sleep last night. Mercifully, then, it snowed, which he would not put past Salzman's machinations.

He was infuriated with the marriage broker and swore he would throw him out of the room the moment he reappeared. But Salzman did not come that night, and when Leo's anger had subsided, an unaccountable despair grew in its place. At first he thought this was caused by his disappointment in Lily, but before long it became evident that he had involved himself with Salzman without a true knowledge of his own intent. He gradually realized—with an emptiness that seized him with six hands—that he had called in the broker to find him a bride because he was incapable of doing it himself. This terrifying insight he had derived as a result of his meeting and conversation with Lily Hirschorn. Her probing questions had somehow irritated him into revealing—to himself more than her—the true nature of his relationship with God, and from that it had come upon him, with shocking force, that apart from his parents, he had never loved anyone. Or perhaps it went the other way, that he did not love God so well as he might, because he had not loved man. It seemed to Leo that his whole life stood starkly revealed and he saw himself, for the first time, as he truly was—unloved and loveless. This bitter but somehow not fully unexpected revelation brought him to a point of panic controlled only by extraordinary effort. He covered his face with his hands and wept.

The week that followed was the worst of his life. He did not eat, and lost weight. His beard darkened and grew ragged. He stopped attending lectures and seminars and almost never opened a book. He seriously considered leaving the Yeshivah, although he was deeply troubled at the thought of the loss of all his years of study—saw them like pages from a book strewn over the city—and at the devastating effect of this decision upon his parents. But he had lived without knowledge of himself, and never in the Five Books and all the Commentaries—mea culpa—had the truth been revealed to him. He did not know where to turn, and in all this desolating loneliness there was no *to whom,* although he often thought of Lily but not once could bring himself to go downstairs and make the call. He became touchy and irritable, especially with his landlady, who asked him all manner of questions; on the other hand, sensing his own disagreeableness, he waylaid her on the stairs and apologized abjectly, until, mortified, she ran from him. Out of this, however, he drew the consolation that he was yet a Jew and that a Jew suffered. But gradually, as the long and terrible week drew to a close, he regained his composure and some idea of purpose in life: to go on as planned. Although he was imperfect, the ideal was not. As for his quest of a bride, the thought of continuing afflicted him with anxiety and heartburn, yet perhaps with this new knowledge of himself he would be more successful than in the past. Perhaps love would now come to him and a bride to that love. And for this sanctified seeking who needed a Salzman?

The marriage broker, a skeleton with haunted eyes, returned that very night. He looked, withal, the picture of frustrated expectancy—as if he had steadfastly waited the week at Miss Lily Hirschorn's side for a telephone call that never came.

Casually coughing, Salzman came immediately to the point: "So how did you like her?"

Leo's anger rose and he could not refrain from chiding the matchmaker: "Why did you lie to me, Salzman?"

Salzman's pale face went dead white, as if the world had snowed on him.

"Did you not state that she was twenty-nine?" Leo insisted.

"I give you my word—"

"She was thirty-five. *At least* thirty-five."

"Of this I would not be too sure. Her father told me—"

"Never mind. The worst of it was that you lied to her."

"How did I lie to her, tell me?"

"You told her things about me that weren't true. You made me out to be more, consequently less than I am. She had in mind a totally different person, a sort of semi-mystical Wonder Rabbi."

"All I said, you was a religious man."

"I can imagine."

Salzman sighed. "This is my weakness that I have," he confessed. "My wife says to me I shouldn't be a salesman, but when I have two fine people that they would be wonderful to be married, I am so happy that I talk too much." He smiled wanly. "This is why Salzman is a poor man."

Leo's anger went. "Well, Salzman, I'm afraid that's all."

The marriage broker fastened hungry eyes on him.

"You don't want any more a bride?"

"I do," said Leo, "but I have decided to seek her in a different way. I am no longer interested in an arranged marriage. To be frank, I now admit the necessity of premarital love. That is, I want to be in love with the one I marry."

"Love?" said Salzman, astounded. After a moment he said, "For us, our love is our life, not for the ladies. In the ghetto they—"

"I know, I know," said Leo. "I've thought of it often. Love, I have said to myself, should be a by-product of living and worship rather than its own end. Yet for myself I find it necessary to establish the level of my need and to fulfill it."

Salzman shrugged but answered, "Listen, rabbi, if you want love, this I can find for you also. I have such beautiful clients that you will love them the minute your eyes will see them."

Leo smiled unhappily. "I'm afraid you don't understand."

But Salzman hastily unstrapped his portfolio and withdrew a manila packet from it.

"Pictures," he said, quickly laying the envelope on the table.

Leo called after him to take the pictures away, but as if on the wings of the wind, Salzman had disappeared.

March came. Leo had returned to his regular routine. Although he felt not quite himself yet—lacked energy—he was making plans for a more active social life. Of course it would cost something, but he was an expert in cutting corners; and when there were no corners left he could make circles rounder. All the while Salzman's pictures had lain on the table, gathering dust. Occasionally as Leo sat studying, or enjoying a cup of tea, his eyes fell on the manila envelope, but he never opened it.

The days went by and no social life to speak of developed with a member of the opposite sex—it was difficult, given the circumstances of his situation. One morning Leo toiled up the stairs to his room and stared out the window at the city. Although the day was bright his view of it was dark. For some time he watched the people in the street below hurrying along and then turned with a heavy heart to his little room. On the table was the packet. With a sudden relentless gesture he tore it open. For a half-hour he stood there, in a state of excitement, examining the photographs of the ladies Salzman had included. Finally, with a deep sigh he put them down. There were six, of varying degrees of attractiveness, but look at them long enough and they all became Lily Hirschorn: all past their prime, all starved behind bright smiles, not a true personality in the lot. Life, despite their anguished struggles and frantic yoohooings, had passed them by; they were photographs in a briefcase that stank of fish. After a while, however, as Leo attempted to return the pictures into the envelope, he found another in it, a small snapshot of the type taken by a machine for a quarter. He gazed at it a moment and let out a cry.

Her face deeply moved him. Why, he could at first not say. It gave him the impression of youth—all spring flowers, yet age—a sense of having been used to the bone, wasted; this all came from the eyes, which were hauntingly familiar, yet absolutely strange. He had a strong impression that he had met her before, but try as he might he could not place her, although he could almost recall her name, as if he had read it written in her own handwriting. No, this couldn't be; he would have remembered her. It was not, he affirmed, that she had an extraordinary beauty—no, although her face was attractive enough; it was that *something* about her moved him. Feature for feature, even some of the ladies of the photographs could do better; but she leaped forth to the heart—had lived, or wanted to—more than just wanted, perhaps regretted it—had somehow deeply suffered: it could be seen in the depths of those reluctant eyes, and from the way the light enclosed and shone from her, and within her, opening whole realms of possibility: this was her own. Her he desired. His head ached and eyes narrowed with the intensity of his gazing, then, as if a black fog had blown up in the mind, he experienced fear of her and was aware that he had received an impression, somehow, of filth. He shuddered, saying softly, it is thus with us all. Leo brewed some tea in a small pot and sat sipping it, without sugar, to calm himself. But before he had finished drinking, again with excitement he examined the face and found it good: good for him. Only such a one could truly understand Leo Finkle and help him to seek whatever he was seeking. How she had come to be among the discards in Salzman's barrel he could never guess, but he knew he must urgently go find her.

Leo rushed downstairs, grabbed up the Bronx telephone book, and searched for Salzman's home address. He was not listed, nor was his office. Neither was he in the Manhattan book. But Leo remembered having written down the address on a slip of paper after he had read Salzman's advertisement in the "personals" column of the *Forward.* He ran up to his room and tore through his papers, without luck. It was exasperating. Just when he needed the matchmaker he was nowhere to be found. Fortunately Leo remembered to look in his wallet. There on a card he found his name written and a Bronx address. No phone number was listed, which, Leo now recalled, was the reason he had originally communicated with Salzman by letter. He got on his coat, put a hat on over his skull cap and hurried to the subway station. All the way to the far end of the Bronx he sat on the edge of the seat. He was more than once tempted to take out the picture and see if the girl's face was as he remembered it, but he refrained, allowing the snapshot to remain in his inside coat pocket, content to have her so close. When the train pulled into the station he was waiting at the door and bolted out. He quickly located the street Salzman had advertised.

The building he sought was less than a block from the subway, but it was not an office building, nor even a loft, nor a store in which one could rent office space. It was an old and grimy tenement. Leo found Salzman's name in pencil on a soiled tag under the bell and climbed three dark flights to his apartment. When he knocked, the door was opened by a thin, asthmatic, gray-haired woman, in felt slippers.

"Yes?" she said, expecting nothing. She listened without listening. He could have sworn he had seen her somewhere before but knew it was illusion.

"Salzman—does he live here? Pinye Salzman," he said, "the matchmaker?"

She stared at him a long time. "Of course."

He felt embarrassed. "Is he in?"

"No." Her mouth was open, but she offered nothing more.

"This is urgent. Can you tell me where his office is?"

"In the air." She pointed upward.

"You mean he has no office?" Leo said.

"In his socks."

He peered into the apartment. It was sunless and dingy, one large room divided by a half-open curtain, beyond which he could see a sagging metal bed. The near side of the room was crowded with rickety chairs, old bureaus, a three-legged table, racks of cooking utensils, and all the apparatus of a kitchen. But there was no sign of Salzman or his magic barrel, probably also a figment of his imagination. An odor of frying fish made Leo weak to the knees.

"Where is he?" he insisted. "I've got to see your husband."

At length she answered, "So who knows where he is? Every time he thinks a new thought he runs to a different place. Go home, he will find you."

"Tell him Leo Finkle."

She gave no sign that she had heard.

He went downstairs, deeply depressed.

But Salzman, breathless, stood waiting at his door.

Leo was overjoyed and astounded. "How did you get here before me?"

"I rushed."

"Come inside."

They entered. Leo fixed tea and a sardine sandwich for Salzman. As they were drinking he reached behind him for the packet of pictures and handed them to the marriage broker.

Salzman put down his glass and said expectantly, "You found maybe somebody you like?"

"Not among these."

The marriage broker turned sad eyes away.

"Here's the one I like." Leo held forth the snapshot.

Salzman slipped on his glasses and took the picture into his trembling hand. He turned ghastly and let out a miserable groan.

"What's the matter?" cried Leo.

"Excuse me. Was an accident this picture. She is not for you."

Salzman frantically shoved the manila packet into his portfolio. He thrust the snapshot into his pocket and fled down the stairs.

Leo, after momentary paralysis, gave chase and cornered the marriage broker in the vestibule. The landlady made hysterical outcries but neither of them listened.

"Give me back the picture, Salzman."

"No." The pain in his eyes was terrible.

"Tell me who she is then."

"This I can't tell you. Excuse me."

He made to depart, but Leo, forgetting himself, seized the matchmaker by his tight coat and shook him frenziedly.

"Please," sighed Salzman. *"Please."*

Leo ashamedly let him go. "Tell me who she is," he begged. "It's very important for me to know."

"She is not for you. She is a wild one—wild, without shame. This is not a bride for a rabbi."

"What do you mean wild?"

"Like an animal. Like a dog. For her to be poor was a sin. This is why she is dead now."

"In God's name, what do you mean?"

"Her I can't introduce to you," Salzman cried.

"Why are you so excited?"

"Why he asks," Salzman said, bursting into tears. "This is my baby, my Stella, she should burn in hell."

Leo hurried up to bed and hid under the covers. Under the covers he thought his whole life through. Although he soon fell asleep he could not sleep her out of his mind. He woke, beating his breast. Though he prayed to be rid of her, his prayers went unanswered. Through days of torment he struggled endlessly not to love her; fearing success, he escaped it. He then concluded to convert her to goodness, himself to God. The idea alternately nauseated and exalted him.

He perhaps did not know that he had come to a final decision until he encountered Salzman in a Broadway cafeteria. He was sitting alone at a rear table, sucking the bony remains of a fish. The marriage broker appeared haggard, and transparent to the point of vanishing.

Salzman looked up at first without recognizing him. Leo had grown a pointed beard and his eyes were weighted with wisdom.

"Salzman," he said, "love has at last come to my heart."

"Who can love from a picture?" mocked the marriage broker.

"It is not impossible."

"If you can love her, then you can love anybody. Let me show you some new clients that they just sent me their photographs. One is a little doll."

"Just her I want," Leo murmured.

"Don't be a fool, doctor. Don't bother with her."

"Put me in touch with her, Salzman," Leo said humbly. "Perhaps I can do her a service."

Salzman had stopped chewing, and Leo understood with emotion that it was now arranged.

Leaving the cafeteria, he was, however, afflicted by a tormenting suspicion that Salzman had planned it all to happen this way.

Leo was informed by letter that she would meet him on a certain corner, and she was there one spring night, waiting under a street lamp. He appeared, carrying a small bouquet of violets and rosebuds, Stella stood by the lamppost, smoking. She wore white with red shoes, which fitted his expectations, although in a troubled moment he had imagined the dress red, and only the shoes white. She waited uneasily and shyly. From afar he saw that her eyes—clearly her father's—were filled with desperate innocence. He pictured, in hers, his own redemption. Violins and lit candles revolved in the sky. Leo ran forward with the flowers outthrust.

Around the corner, Salzman, leaning against a wall, chanted prayers for the dead.

(From Fantasy and Science Fiction)

DEAD CENTER

BY JUDITH MERRIL

THEY GAVE HIM sweet ices, and kissed him all round, and the Important People who had come to dinner all smiled in a special way as his mother took him from the living room and led him down the hall to his own bedroom.

"Great kid you got there," they said to Jock, his father, and "Serious little bugger, isn't he?" Jock didn't say anything, but Toby knew he would be grinning, looking pleased and embarrassed. Then their voices changed, and that meant they had begun to talk about the important events for which the important people had come.

In his own room, Toby wriggled his toes between crisp sheets, and breathed in the powder-and-perfume smell of his mother as she bent over him for a last hurried goodnight kiss. There was no use asking for a story tonight. Toby lay still and waited while she closed the door behind her and went off to the party, click-tap, tip-clack, hurrying on her high silver heels. She had heard the voices change back there too, and she didn't want to miss anything. Toby got up and opened his door just a crack, and set himself down in back of it, and listened.

In the big square living room, against the abstract patterns of gray and vermilion and chartreuse, the men and women moved in easy patterns of familiar acts. Coffee, brandy, cigarette, cigar. Find your partner, choose your seat. Jock sprawled with perfect relaxed contentment on the low couch with the deep red corduroy cover. Tim O'Heyer balanced nervously on the edge of the same couch, wreathed in cigar smoke, small and dark and alert. Gordon

Kimberly dwarfed the big easy chair with the bulking importance of him. Ben Stein, shaggy and rumpled as ever, was running a hand through his hair till it too stood on end. He was leaning against a window frame, one hand on the back of the straight chair in which his wife Sue sat, erect and neat and proper and chic, dressed in smart black that set off perfectly her precise blond beauty. Mrs. Kimberly, just enough overstuffed so that her pearls gave the appearance of *actually* choking her, was the only stranger to the house. She was standing near the doorway, politely admiring Toby's personal art gallery, as Allie Madero valiantly strove to explain each minor masterpiece.

Ruth Kruger stood still a moment, surveying her room and her guests. Eight of them, herself included, and all Very Important People. In the familiar comfort of her own living room, the idea made her giggle. Allie and Mrs. Kimberly both turned to her, questioning. She laughed and shrugged, helpless to explain, and they all went across the room to join the others.

"Guts," O'Heyer said through the cloud of smoke. "How do you do it, Jock? Walk out of a setup like this into . . . God knows what?"

"Luck," Jock corrected him. "A setup like this helps. I'm the world's pampered darling and I know it."

"Faith is what he means," Ben put in. "He just gets by believing that last year's luck is going to hold up. So it does."

"Depends on what you mean by *luck*. If you think of it as a vector sum composed of predictive powers and personal ability and accurate information and . . ."

"Charm and nerve and . . ."

"Guts," Tim said again, interrupting the interrupter.

"All right, all of them," Ben agreed. "*Luck* is as good a word as any to cover the combination."

"We're all lucky people." That was Allie, drifting into range, with Ruth behind him. "We just happened to get born at the right time with the right dream. Any one of us, fifty years ago, would have been called wild-eyed visiona—"

"Any one of us," Kimberly said heavily, "fifty years ago, would have had a different dream—in time with the times."

Jock smiled, and let them talk, not joining in much. He listened to philosophy and compliments and speculations and comments, and lay sprawled across the comfortable couch in his own living room, with his wife's hand under his own, consciously letting his mind play back and forth between the two lives he lived: this, here . . . and the perfect mathematic bleakness of the metal beast that would be his home in three days' time.

He squeezed his wife's hand, and she turned and looked at him, and there was no doubt a man could have about what the world held in store.

When they had all gone, Jock walked down the hall and picked up the little boy asleep on the floor, and put him back into his bed. Toby woke up long enough to grab his father's hand and ask earnestly, out of the point in the conversation where sleep had overcome him:

"Daddy, if the universe hasn't got any ends to it, how can you tell where you are?"

"Me?" Jock asked. "I'm right next to the middle of it."

"How do you *know?*"

His father tapped him lightly on the chest.

"Because that's where the middle is." Jock smiled and stood up. "Go to sleep, champ. Good night."

And Toby slept, while the universe revolved in all its mystery about the small center Jock Kruger had assigned to it.

"Scared?" she asked, much later, in the spaceless silence of their bedroom.

He had to think about it before he could answer. "I guess not. I guess I think I ought to be, but I'm not. I don't think I'd do it at all if I wasn't *sure.*" He was almost asleep, when the thought hit him, and he jerked awake and saw she was sure enough lying wide-eyed and sleepless beside him. *"Baby!"* he said, and it was almost an accusation. "Baby, *you're* not scared, are you?"

"Not if you're not," she said. But they never could lie to each other.

Toby sat on the platform, next to his grandmother. They were in the second row, right in back of his mother and father, so it was all right for him to wriggle a little bit, or whisper. They couldn't hear much of the speeches back there, and what they did hear mostly didn't make sense to Toby. But every now and then Grandma would grab his hand tight all of a sudden, and he understood what the whole thing was about: it was because Daddy was going away again.

His grandma's hand was very white, with little red and tan dots in it, and big blue veins that stood out higher than the wrinkles in her skin, whenever she grabbed at his hand. Later, walking over to the towering skyscraping rocket, he held his mother's hand; it was smooth and cool and tan, all one color, and she didn't grasp at him the way Grandma did. Later still, his father's two hands, picking him up to kiss, were bigger and darker tan than his mother's, not so smooth, and the fingers were stronger, but so strong it hurt sometimes.

They took him up in an elevator, and showed him all around the inside of the rocket, where Daddy would sit, and where all the food was stored, for emergency, they said, and the radio and everything. Then it was time to say goodbye.

Daddy was laughing at first, and Toby tried to laugh, too, but he didn't really want Daddy to go away. Daddy kissed him, and he felt like crying because it was scratchy against Daddy's cheek, and the strong fingers were hurting him now. Then Daddy stopped laughing and looked at him very seriously. "You take care of your mother, now," Daddy told him. "You're a big boy this time."

"Okay," Toby said. Last time Daddy went away in a rocket, he was not-quite-four, and they teased him with the poem in the book that said, *James James Morrison Morrison Weatherby George Dupree, Took great care of his mother, though he was only three. . . .* So Toby didn't much like Daddy saying that now, because he knew they didn't really mean it.

"Okay," he said, and then because he was angry, he said, "Only she's supposed to take care of me, isn't she?"

Daddy and Mommy both laughed, and so did the two men who were standing there waiting for Daddy to get done saying goodbye to him. He wriggled, and Daddy put him down.

"I'll bring you a piece of the moon, son," Daddy said, and Toby said, "All right, fine." He reached for his mother's hand, but he found himself hanging onto Grandma instead, because Mommy and Daddy were kissing each other, and both of them had forgotten all about him.

He thought they were never going to get done kissing.

Ruth Kruger stood in the glass control booth with her son on one side of her, and Gordon Kimberly breathing heavily on the other side. *Something's wrong,* she thought, *this time something's wrong.* And then, swiftly, *I mustn't think that way!*

Jealous? she taunted herself. Do you *want* something to be wrong, just because this one isn't all yours, because Argent did some of it?

But if anything is wrong, she prayed, let it be now, right away, so he can't go. If anything's wrong let it be in the firing gear or the . . . what? Even now, it was too late. The beast was too big and too delicate and too precise. If something went wrong, even now, it was too late. It was . . .

You didn't finish that thought. Not if you were Ruth Kruger, and your husband was Jock Kruger, and nobody knew but the two of you how much of the courage that had gone twice round the moon, and was about to land on it, was yours. When a man knows his wife's faith is *unshakeable,* he can't help coming back. (But: "Baby! *You're* not scared, are you?")

Twice around the moon, and they called him Jumping Jock. There was never a doubt in anyone's mind who'd pilot the KIM-VII, the bulky beautiful beast out there today. Kruger and Kimberly, O'Heyer and Stein. It was a combo. It won every time. *Every* time. Nothing to doubt. No room for doubt.

"Minus five . . ." someone said into a mike, and there was perfect quiet all around. "Four . . . three . . ."

(But he held me too tight, and he laughed too loud. . . .)

". . . two . . . one . . ."

(Only because he thought *I* was scared, she answered herself.)

". . . Mar—"

You didn't even hear the whole word, because the thunder-drumming roar of the beast itself split your ears.

Ringing quiet came down and she caught up Toby, held him tight, tight. . . .

"Perfect!" Gordon Kimberly sighed. "*Per*fect!"

So if anything *was* wrong, it hadn't showed up yet.

She put Toby down, then took his hand. "Come on," she said. "I'll buy you an ice-cream soda." He grinned at her. He'd been looking very strange all day, but now he looked real again. His hair had got messed up when she grabbed him.

"We're having cocktails for the press in the conference room," Kimberly said. "I think we could find something Toby would like."

"Wel-l-l-l . . ." She didn't want a cocktail, and she didn't want to talk to the press. "I think maybe we'll beg off this time. . . ."

"I think there might be some disappointment—" the man started; then Tim O'Heyer came dashing up.

"Come on, babe," he said. "Your old man told me to take personal charge while he was gone." He leered. On him it looked cute. She laughed. Then she looked down at Toby. "What would you rather, Tobe? Want to go out by ourselves, or go to the party?"

"I don't care," he said.

Tim took the boy's hand. "What we were thinking of was having a kind of party here, and then I think they're going to bring some dinner in, and anybody who wants to can stay up till your Daddy gets to the moon. That'll be pretty late. I guess you wouldn't want to stay up late like that, would you?"

Somebody else talking to Toby like that would be all wrong, but Tim was a friend, Toby's friend too. Ruth still didn't want to go to the party, but she remembered now that there had been plans for something like that all along, and since Toby was beginning to look eager, and it *was* important to keep the press on their side . . .

"You win, O'Heyer," she said. "Will somebody please send out for an ice-cream soda? Cherry syrup, I think it is this week . . ." She looked inquiringly at her son. ". . . and . . . *strawberry* ice cream?"

Tim shuddered. Toby nodded. Ruth smiled, and they all went in to the party.

"Well, young man!" Toby thought the redheaded man in the brown suit was probably what they called a reporter, but he wasn't sure. "How about it? You going along next time?"

"I don't know," Toby said politely. "I guess not."

"Don't you want to be a famous flier like your Daddy?" a strange woman in an evening gown asked him.

"I don't know," he muttered, and looked around for his mother, but he couldn't see her.

They kept asking him questions like that, about whether he wanted to go to the moon. Daddy said he was too little. You'd think all these people would know that much.

Jock Kruger came up swiftly out of dizzying darkness into isolation and clarity. As soon as he could move his head, before he fully remembered why, he began checking the dials and meters and flashing lights on the banked panel in front of him. He was fully aware of the ship, of its needs and strains and motion, before he came to complete consciousness of himself, his weightless body, his purpose, or his memories.

But he was aware of himself as a part of the ship before he remembered his name, so that by the time he knew he had a face and hands and innards, these parts were already occupied with feeding the beast's human brain a carefully prepared stimulant out of a nippled flask fastened in front of his head.

He pressed a button under his index finger in the arm rest of the couch that held him strapped to safety.

"Hi," he said. "Is anybody up besides me?"

He pressed the button under his middle finger and waited.

Not for long.

"Thank God!" a voice crackled out of the loudspeaker. "You really conked out this time, Jock. Nothing wrong?"

"Not so I'd know it. You want . . . How long was I out?"

"Twenty-three minutes, eighteen seconds, takeoff to reception. Yeah. Give us a log reading."

Methodically, in order, he read off the pointers and numbers on the control panel, the colors and codes and swinging needles and quiet ones that told him how each muscle and nerve and vital organ of the great beast was taking the trip. He did it slowly and with total concentration. Then, when he was all done, there was nothing else to do except sit back and start wondering about that big blackout.

It shouldn't have happened. It never happened before. There was nothing in the compendium of information he'd just sent back to Earth to account for it.

A different ship, different . . . different men. Two and a half years different. Years of easy living and . . . growing old? Too old for this game?

Twenty-three minutes!

Last time it was under ten. The first time maybe 90 seconds more. It didn't matter, of course, not at takeoff. There was nothing for him to do then. Nothing now. Nothing for four more hours. He was there to put the beast back down on . . .

He grinned, and felt like Jock Kruger again. Identity returned complete. *This* time he was there to put the beast down where no man or beast had ever been before. This time they were going to the moon.

Ruth Kruger sipped at a cocktail and murmured responses to the admiring, the curious, the envious, the hopeful, and the hate-full ones who spoke to her. She was waiting for something, and after an unmeasurable stretch of time Allie Madero brought it to her.

First a big smile seeking her out across the room, so she knew it had come. Then a low-voiced confirmation.

"Wasn't it . . . an awfully long time?" she asked. She hadn't been watching the clock, on purpose, but she was sure it was longer than it should have been.

Allie stopped smiling. "Twenty-three," she said.

Ruth gasped. "What . . . ?"

"*You* figure it. I can't."

"There's nothing in the ship. I mean nothing was changed that would account for it." She shook her head slowly. This time she didn't know the ship well enough to talk like that. There *could* be something. Oh, *Jock!* "I don't know," she said. "Too many people worked on that thing. I . . ."

"Mrs. Kruger!" It was the redheaded reporter, the obnoxious one. "We just got the report on the blackout. I'd like a statement from you, if you don't mind, as designer of the ship—"

"I am not the designer of this ship," she said coldly.

"You worked on the design, didn't you?"

"Yes."

"Well, then, to the best of your knowledge . . . ?"

"To the best of my knowledge, there is no change in design to account for Mr. Kruger's prolonged unconsciousness. Had there been any such prognosis, the press would have been informed."

"Mrs. Kruger, I'd like to ask you whether you feel that the innovations made by Mr. Argent could—"

"Aw, lay off, will you?" Allie broke in, trying to be casual and kidding about it; but behind her own flaming cheeks, Ruth was aware of her friend's matching anger. "How much do you want to milk this for, anyhow? So the guy conked out an extra ten minutes. If you want somebody to crucify for it, why don't you pick on one of us who doesn't happen to be married to him?" She turned to Ruth before the man could answer. "Where's Toby? He's probably about ready to bust from cookies and carbonation."

"He's in the lounge," the reporter put in. "Or he was a few minutes—"

Ruth and Allie started off without waiting for the rest. The redhead had been talking to the kid. No telling how many of them were on top of him now.

"I thought Tim was with him," Ruth said hastily, then she thought of something, and turned back long enough to say: "For the record, Mr. . . . uh . . . I know of no criticism that can be made of any of the work done by Mr. Argent." Then she went to find her son.

There was nothing to do and nothing to see except the instrument meters and dials to check and log and check and log again. Radio stations all around Earth were beamed on him. He could have kibitzed his way to the moon, but he didn't want to. He was thinking.

Thinking back, and forward, and right in this moment. Thinking of the instant's stiffness of Ruth's body when she said she wasn't scared, and the rambling big house on the hill, and Toby politely agreeing when he offered to bring him back a piece of the moon.

Thinking of Toby growing up some day, and how little he really knew about his son, and what would they do, Toby and Ruth, if anything . . .

He'd never thought that way before. He'd never thought anything except to know he'd come back, because he couldn't stay away. It was always that simple. He couldn't stay away now, either. That hadn't changed. But as he sat there, silent and useless for the time, it occurred to him that he'd left something out of his calculations. *Luck,* they'd been talking about. Yes, he'd had luck. But—what was it Sue had said about a vector sum?—there was more to figure in than your own reflexes and the beast's strength. There was the *outside.* Space . . . environment . . . God . . . destiny. What difference does it make what name you give it?

He couldn't *stay* away . . . but maybe he could be *kept* away.

He'd never thought that way before.

"You tired, honey?"

"No," he said. "I'm just sick of this party. I want to go home."

"It'll be over pretty soon, Tobe. I think as long as we stayed this long, we better wait for . . . for the end of the party."

"It's a silly party. You said you'd buy me an ice-cream soda."

"I did, darling," she said patiently. "At least, if I didn't *buy* it, I got it for you. You had it, didn't you?"

"Yes, but you *said* we'd go *out* and have one."

"Look. Why don't you just put your head down on my lap and . . ."

"I'm no *baby!* Anyhow I'm not tired."

"All right. We'll go pretty soon. You just sit here on the couch, and you don't have to talk to anybody if you don't feel like it. I'll tell you what. I'll go find you a magazine or a book or something to look at, and—"

"I don't *want* a magazine. I want my own book with the pirates in it."

"You just stay put a minute, so I can find you. I'll bring you something."

She got up and went out to the other part of the building where the officers were, and collected an assortment of leaflets and folders with shiny bright pictures of mail rockets and freight transports and jets and visionary moon rocket designs, and took them back to the little lounge where she'd left him.

She looked at the clock on the way. Twenty-seven more minutes. There was *no* reason to believe that anything was wrong.

They were falling now. A man's body is not equipped to sense direction *toward* or *from, up* or *down,* without the help of landmarks or gravity. But the body of the beast was designed to know such things; and Kruger, at the nerve center, knew everything the beast knew.

Ship is extension of self, and self is—extension or limitation?—of ship. If Jock Kruger is the center of the universe—remember the late night after the party, and picking Toby off the floor?—then ship is extension of self, and the man is the brain of the beast. But if ship *is* universe—certainly continuum; that's universe, isn't it?—then the weakling man-thing in the couch is a limiting condition of the universe. A human brake. He was there to make it stop when it didn't "want" to.

Suppose it wouldn't stop? Suppose it had decided to be a self-determined, free-willed universe?

Jock grinned, and started setting controls. His time was coming.

It was measurable in minutes, and then in seconds . . . *now!*

His hand reached for the firing lever (but *what* was she scared of?), groped, and touched, hesitated, clasped, and pulled.

Grown-up parties at home were fun. But other places, like this one, they were silly. Toby half woke up on the way home, enough to realize his Uncle Tim was driving them, and they weren't in their own car. He was sitting on the front seat next to his mother, with his head against her side, and her arm around him. He tried to come all the way awake, to listen to what they were saying, but they weren't talking, so he started to go back to sleep.

Then Uncle Tim said, "For God's sake, Ruth, he's safe, and whatever happened certainly wasn't *your* fault. He's got enough supplies to hold out till . . ."

"Shh!" his mother said sharply, and then, whispering, "I know."

Now he remembered.

"Mommy . . ."

"Yes, hon?"

"Did Daddy go to the moon all right?"

"Y . . . yes, dear."

Her voice was funny.

"Where is it?"

"Where's what?"

"The moon."

"Oh. We can't see it now, darling. It's around the other side of the earth."

"Well, when is he going to come *back?*"

Silence.

*"Mom*my . . . *when?"*

"As soon as . . . just as soon as he can, darling. Now go to sleep."

And now the moon was up, high in the sky, a gilded football dangling from Somebody's black serge lapel. When she was a little girl, she used to say she loved the man in the moon, and now the man in the moon loved her too, but if she was a little girl still, somebody would tuck her into bed, and pat her head and tell her to go to sleep, and she would sleep as easy, breathe as soft, as Toby did. . . .

But she wasn't a little girl, she was all grown up, and she married the man, the man in the moon, and sleep could come and sleep could go, but sleep could never stay with her while the moonwash swept the window panes.

She stood at the open window and wrote a letter in her mind and sent it up the path of light to the man in the moon. It said:

"Dear Jock: Tim says it wasn't my fault, and I can't explain it even to him. I'm sorry, darling. Please to stay alive till we can get to you. Faithfully yours, Cassandra."

The glasses and ashes and litter and spilled drinks had all been cleared away. The table top gleamed in polished stripes of light and dark, where the light came through the louvered plastic of the wall. The big chairs were empty, waiting, and at each place, arranged with the precision of a formal dinner-setting, was the inevitable pad of yellow paper, two freshly-sharpened pencils, a small neat pile of typed white sheets of paper, a small glass ashtray and a shining empty water glass. Down the center of the table, spaced for comfort, three crystal pitchers of ice and water stood in perfect alignment.

Ruth was the first one there. She stood in front of a chair, fingering the little stack of paper on which someone (Allie? She'd have had to be up early to get it done so quickly) had tabulated the details of yesterday's events. "To refresh your memory," was how they always put it.

She poured a glass of water, and guiltily replaced the pitcher on the exact spot where it had been; lit a cigarette, and stared with dismay at the burnt match marring the cleanliness of the little ashtray; pulled her chair in beneath her and winced at the screech of the wooden leg across the floor.

Get it over with! She picked up the typed pages, and glanced at them. Two at the bottom were headed "Recommendations of U.S. Rocket Corps to Facilitate Construction of KIM-VIII." That could wait. The three top sheets she'd better get through while she was still alone.

She read slowly and carefully, trying to memorize each sentence, so that when the time came to talk, she could think of what had happened this way, from outside, instead of remembering how it had been for *her*.

There was nothing in the report that she didn't already know.

Jock Kruger had set out in the KIM-VII at 5:39 P.M., C.S.T., just at sunset. First report after recovery from blackout came at 6:02 plus. First log readings gave no reason to anticipate any difficulty. Subsequent reports and radioed log readings were, for Kruger, unusually terse and formal, and surprisingly infrequent; but earth-to-ship contact at twenty-minute intervals had been acknowledged. No reason to believe Kruger was having trouble at any time during the trip.

At 11:54, an attempt to call the ship went unanswered for 56 seconds. The radioman here described Kruger's voice as "irritable" when the reply finally came, but all he said was, "Sorry. I was firing the first brake." Then a string of figures, and a quick log reading—everything just what you'd expect.

Earth acknowledged, and waited.

Eighteen seconds later:

"Second brake." More figures. Again, everything as it should be. But twenty seconds after that call was completed:

"This is Kruger. Anything wrong with the dope I gave you?"

"Earth to Kruger. Everything okay in our book. Trouble?"

"Track me, boy. I'm off."

"You want a course correction?"

"I can figure it quicker here. I'll keep talking as I go. Stop me if I'm wrong by your book." More figures, and Kruger's calculations coincided perfectly with the swift work done at the base. Both sides came to the same conclusion, and both sides knew what it meant. The man in the beast fired once more, and once again, and made a landing.

There was no reason to believe that either ship or pilot had been hurt. There was no way of finding out. By the best calculations, they were five degrees of arc around onto the dark side. And there was no possibility at all, after that second corrective firing that Kruger had enough fuel left to take off again. The last thing Earth had heard, before the edge of the moon cut off Kruger's radio, was:

"Sorry, boys. I guess I fouled up this time. Looks like you'll have to come and . . ."

One by one, they filled the seats: Gordon Kimberly at one end, and the Colonel at the other; Tim O'Heyer to one side of Kimberly, and Ruth at the other; Allie, with her pad and pencil poised, alongside Tim; the Colonel's aide next down the line, with his little silent stenotype in front of him; the Steins across from him, next to Ruth. With a minimum of formality, Kimberly opened the meeting and introduced Colonel Swenson.

The Colonel cleared his throat. "I'd like to make something clear," he said. "Right from the start, I want to make this clear. I'm here to help. Not to get in the way. My presence does not indicate any—*criticism* on the part of the Armed Services. We are entirely satisfied with the work you people have been doing." He cleared his throat again, and Kimberly put in:

"You saw our plans, I believe, Colonel. Everything was checked and approved by your outfit ahead of time."

"Exactly. We had no criticism then, and we have none now. The rocket program is what's important. Getting Kruger back is important, not just for ordinary humanitarian reasons—pardon me, Mrs. Kruger, if I'm too blunt—but for the sake of the whole program. Public opinion, for one thing. That's your line, isn't it, Mr. O'Heyer? And then, *we have to find out what happened!*

"I came down here today to offer any help we can give you on the relief ship, and to make a suggestion to facilitate matters."

He paused deliberately this time.

"Go ahead, Colonel," Tim said. "We're listening."

"Briefly, the proposal is that you all accept temporary commissions while the project is going on. Part of that report in front of you embodies the details of the plan. I hope you'll find it acceptable. You all know there is a great deal of—necessary, I'm afraid—*red tape,* you'd call it, and 'going through channels,' and such in the Services. It makes cooperation between civilian and military groups difficult. If we can all get together as one outfit 'for the duration,' so to speak . . ."

This time nobody jumped into the silence. The Colonel cleared his throat once more.

"Perhaps you'd best read the full report before we discuss it any further. I brought the matter up now just to—to let you know the *attitude* with which we are submitting the proposal to you . . ."

"Thank you, Colonel." O'Heyer saved him. "I've already had a chance to look at the report. Don't know that anyone else has, except of course Miss Madero. But I personally, at least, appreciate your attitude. And I think I can speak for Mr. Kimberly too. . . ."

He looked sideways at his boss; Gordon nodded.

"What I'd like to suggest now," O'Heyer went on, "since I've seen the report already, and I believe everyone else would like to have a chance to bone up some—perhaps you'd like to have a first-hand look at some of our plant, Colonel? I could take you around a bit. . . . ?"

"Thank you. I would like to." The officer stood up, his gold Rocket Corps uniform blazing in the louvered light. "If I may say so, Mr. O'Heyer, you seem remarkably sensible, for a—well, a *publicity* man."

"That's all right, Colonel." Tim laughed easily. "I don't even think it's a dirty word. You seem like an all-right guy yourself—for an *officer,* that is."

They all laughed then, and Tim led the blaze of glory out of the room while the rest of them settled down to studying the R.C. proposals. When they had all finished, Kimberly spoke slowly, voicing the general reaction:

"I hate to admit it, but it makes sense."

"They're being pretty decent about it, aren't they?" Ben said. "Putting it to us as a proposal instead of pulling a lot of weight."

He nodded. "I've had a little contact with this man Swenson before. He's a good man to work with. It . . . makes sense, that's all."

"On paper, anyhow," Sue put in.

"Well, Ruth . . ." the big man turned to her, waiting. "You haven't said anything."

"I . . . it seems all right to me," she said, and added: "Frankly, Gordon, I don't know that I ought to speak at all. I'm not quite sure why I'm here."

Allie looked up sharply, questioning, from her notes; Sue pushed back her chair and half-stood. "My God, you're not going to back out on us now?"

"I . . . look, you all know I didn't do any of the real work on the last one. It was Andy Argent's job, and a good one. I've got Toby to think about, and . . ."

"Kid, we *need* you," Sue protested. "Argent can't do this one; this is going to be another Three, only more so. Unmanned, remote-control stuff, and no returning atmosphere-landing problems. This is up your alley. It's . . ." She sank back; there was nothing else to say.

"That's true, Ruth." Tim had come back in during the last outburst. Now he sat down. "Speed is what counts, gal. That's why we're letting the gold braid in on the job—we are, aren't we?" Kimberly nodded; Tim went on: "With you on the job, we've got a working team. With somebody new—well, you know what a ruckus we had until Sue got used to Argent's blueprints, and how Ben's pencil notes used to drive Andy wild. And we can't even use him this time. It's not his field. He did do a good job, but we'd have to start in with somebody new all over again . . ." He broke off, and looked at Kimberly.

"I hope you'll decide to work with us, Ruth," he said simply.

"If . . . obviously, if it's the best way to get it done *quick,* I will," she said. "Twenty-eight hours a day if you like."

Tim grinned. "I guess we can let the braid back in now . . . ?" He got up and went to the door.

Another Three, only more so . . . Sue's words danced in her mind while the Colonel and the Colonel's aide marched in, and took their places while voices murmured politely, exchanging good will.

Another Three—the first ship she had designed for Kimberly. The ship that made her rich and famous, but that was nothing, because it was the ship that brought Jock to her, that made him write the letter, that made her meet him, that led to the Five and Six and now . . .

"I've got some ideas for a manned ship," he'd written. "If we could get together to discuss it some time . . ."

". . . pleasure to know you'll be working with us, Mrs. Kruger." She shook her head sharply, and located in time and place.

"Thank you, Colonel. I want to do what I can, of course. . . ."

James James Morrison's mother put on a golden gown . . .

Toby knew the whole thing, almost, by heart. The little boy in the poem *told* his mother not to *go down to the end of the town,* wherever that was, unless she took him along. And she said she wouldn't, but she put on that golden gown and went, and thought she'd be back in time for tea. Only she wasn't. She never came back at all. *Last seen wandering vaguely . . . King John said he was sorry* . . .

Who's King John? And what time is tea?

Toby sat quietly beside his mother on the front seat of the car, and looked obliquely at the golden uniform she wore, and could not find a way to ask the questions in his mind.

Where was James James's *father?* Why did James James have to be the one to keep his mother from going down to the end of the town?

"Are you in the Army now, Mommy?" he asked.

"Well . . . sort of. But not for long, darling. Just till Daddy comes home."

"When is Daddy coming home?"

"Soon. Soon, I hope. Not too long."

She didn't sound right. Her voice had a cracking sound like Grandma's, and other old ladies. She didn't look right, either, in that golden-gown uniform. When she kissed him goodbye in front of the school, she didn't *feel* right. She didn't even *smell* the same as she used to.

" 'Bye, boy. See you tonight," she said—the same words she always said, but they sounded different.

" 'Bye." He walked up the driveway and up the front steps and down the corridor and into the pretty-painted room where his teacher was waiting. Miss Callahan was nice. Today she was *too* nice. The other kids teased him, and called him teacher's pet. At lunch time he went back in the room before anybody else did, and made pictures all over the floor with colored chalk. It was the worst thing he could think of to do. Miss Callahan made him wash it all up, and she wasn't nice any more for the rest of the afternoon.

When he went out front after school, he couldn't see the car anywhere. It was true then. His mother had put on that golden gown, and now she was gone. Then he saw Grandma waving to him out of *her* car, and he remembered Mommy had said Grandma would come and get him. He got in the car, and she grabbed at him like she always did. He pulled away.

"Is Daddy home yet?" he asked.

Grandma started the car. "Not yet," she said, and she was crying. He didn't dare ask about Mommy after that, but she wasn't home when they got there. It was a long time after that till dinner was ready.

She came home for dinner, though.

"You have to allow for the human factor. . . ."

Nobody had said it to her, of course. Nobody would. She wondered how much tougher it made the job for everybody, having her around. She wondered how she'd stay sane, if she didn't have the job to do.

Thank God Toby was in school now! She couldn't do it, if it meant leaving him with someone else all day—even his grandmother. As it was, having the old lady in the house so much was nerve-racking.

I ought to ask her if she'd like to sleep here for a while, Ruth thought, and shivered. Dinner time was enough.

Anyhow, Toby liked having her there, and that's what counted.

I'll have to go in and see his teacher. Tomorrow, she thought. I've got to make time for it tomorrow. Let her know . . . but of course she knew. Jock Kruger's family's affairs were hardly private. Just the same, I better talk to her. . . .

Ruth got out of bed and stood at the window, waiting for the moon. Another ten minutes, fifteen, twenty maybe, and it would edge over the hills on the other side of town. The white hands on the clock said 2:40. She had to get some sleep. She couldn't stand here waiting for the moon. Get to sleep now, before it comes up. That's better. . . .

Oh, *Jock!*

". . . the human factor . . ." They didn't know. She wanted to go tell them all, find somebody right away, and shout it. *"It's not his fault. I did it!"*

"You're *not scared, are you, baby?"*

Oh, no! No, no! Don't be silly. Who, me? Just stiff and trembling. The cold, you know . . . ?

Stop that!

She stood at the window, waiting for the moon, the man, the man in the moon.

Human factor . . . well, there wouldn't be a human factor in this one. If she went out to the field on takeoff day and told KIM-VIII she was scared, it wouldn't matter at all.

Thank God I can do something, at least!

Abruptly, she closed the blind, so she wouldn't know when it came, and pulled out the envelope she'd brought home; switched on the bed light, and unfolded the first blueprints.

It was all familiar. Just small changes here and there. Otherwise, it was the Three all over again—the first unmanned ship to be landed successfully on the moon surface. The only important difference was that this one had to have some fancy gadgetry on the landing mech. Stein had given her the orbit calcs today. The rest of the job was hers and Sue's: design and production. Between them, they could do it. What they needed was a goldberg that would take the thing once around low enough to contact Jock, if . . . to contact him, that's all. Then back again, prepared for him to take over the landing by remote, according to instructions, if he wanted to. If he could. If his radio was working. If . . .

Twice around, and then down where they figured he was, if he hadn't tried to bring it down himself.

It was complicated, but only quantitatively. Nothing basically new, or untried. And no *human* factors to be allowed for, once it was off the ground.

She fell asleep, finally, with the light still on, and the blind drawn, and the blueprints spread out on the floor next to the bed.

Every day, she drove him to school, dressed in her golden gown. And every afternoon, he waited, telling himself she was sure to come home.

That was a very silly little poem, and he wasn't three, he was six now.

But it was a long time since Daddy went away.

"I'd rather not," she said stiffly.

"I'm sorry, Ruth. I know—well, I *don't* know, but I can imagine how you feel. I hate to ask it, but if you can do it at all . . . just be there and look confident, and . . . *you* know."

Look confident! I couldn't do it for Jock, she thought; why should I do it for *them?* But of course that was silly. They didn't know her the way Jock did. They couldn't read her smiles, or sense a barely present stiffness, or know anything except what she chose to show on the front of her face.

"Look confident? What difference does it make, Tim? If the thing works, they'll all know soon enough. If . . ."

She stopped.

"All right, I'll be blunt. If it *doesn't* work, it's going to make a hell of a difference what the public feeling was at the time it went off. If we have to try again. If—damn it, you want it straight, all right! If we can't save Jock, we're not going to give up the whole thing! We're not going to let space travel wait another half century while the psychological effects wear off. *And Jock wouldn't want us to!* Don't forget that. It was his dream, too. It was yours, once upon a time. If . . ."

"All *right!*" She was startled by her voice. She was screaming, or almost.

"All right," she said bitterly, more quietly. "If you think I'll be holding up progress for fifty years by not dragging Toby along to a launching, I'll come."

"Oh, Ruth, I'm sorry. No, it's not that important. And I had no business talking that way. But listen, babe, you used to understand this—the way I feel, the way Jock fel—feels. Even a guy like Kimberly. You used to feel it too. Look: the single item of you showing your face at the takeoff doesn't amount to much. Neither does one ounce of fuel. But either one could be the little bit that makes the difference. Kid, we got to put *everything* we've got behind it this time."

"All right," she said again. "I told you I'd come."

"You do understand, don't you?" he pleaded.

"I don't know, Tim. I'm not sure I do. But you're right. I would have, once. Maybe—I don't know. It's different for a woman, I guess. But I'll come. Don't worry about it."

She turned and started out.

"Thanks, Ruth. And I *am* sorry. Uh—want me to come and pick you up?"

She nodded. "Thanks." She was glad she wouldn't have to drive.

He kept waiting for a chance to ask her. He couldn't do it in the house before they left, because right after she told him where they were going, she went to get dressed in her golden uniform, and he had to stay with Grandma all the time.

Then Mr. O'Heyer came with the car, and he couldn't ask because, even though he sat up front with Mommy, Mr. O'Heyer was there too.

When they got to the launching field, there were people around all the time. Once he tried to get her off by himself, but all she did was think he had to go to the bathroom. Then, bit by bit, he didn't *have* to ask, because he could tell from the way they were all talking, and the way the cameras were all pointed at her all the time, like they had been at Daddy the other time.

Then there was the speeches part again, and this time *she* got up and talked, so that settled it.

He was glad he hadn't asked. They probably all thought he knew. Maybe they'd even told him, and he'd forgotten, like he sometimes did. "Mommy," he listened to himself in his mind, "Mommy, are you going to the moon too?" Wouldn't that sound silly!

She'd come back for him, he told himself. The other times, when Daddy went some place—like when they first came here to live, and Daddy went first, then Mommy, and then they came back to get him, and some other time, he didn't remember just what—but when Daddy went away, Mommy always went to stay with him, and then they *always* came to get him too.

It wasn't any different from Mommy going back to be with Daddy at a party or something, instead of staying in his room to talk to him when she put him to bed. It didn't feel any worse than that, he told himself.

Only he didn't believe himself.

She never did tell me! I wouldn't of forgotten that! She should *of told me!*

She did not want to make a speech. Nobody had warned her that she would be called upon to make a speech. It was bad enough trying to answer reporters coherently. She stood up and went forward to the microphone dutifully, and shook hands with the President of the United States, and tried to look confident. She opened her mouth and nothing came out.

"Thank you," she said finally, though she didn't know just what for. "You've all been very kind." She turned to the mike, and spoke directly into it. "I feel that a good deal of honor is being accorded me today which is not rightfully mine. We gave ourselves a two-month limit to complete a job, and the fact that it was finished inside of six weeks instead . . ."

She had to stop because everybody was cheering, and they wouldn't have heard her.

". . . that fact is not something for which the designer of a ship can be thanked. The credit is due to all the people at Kimberly who worked so hard, and to the Rocket Corps personnel who helped so much. I think . . ."

This time she paused to find the right words. It had suddenly become very important to level with the crowd, to tell them what she honestly felt.

"I think it is I who should be doing the thanking. I happen to be a designer of rockets, but much more importantly, to me, I am Jock Kruger's wife. So I want to thank everyone who helped . . ."

Grandma's hand tightened around his, and then pulled away to get a handkerchief, because she was crying. Right up here on the platform! Then he realized what Mommy had just said. She said that being Jock Kruger's wife was more important to her than anything else.

It was funny that Grandma should feel bad about that. Everybody else seemed to think it was a right thing to say, the way they were yelling and clapping and shouting. It occurred to Toby with a small shock of surprise that maybe Grandma sometimes felt bad about things the same way he did.

He was sort of sorry he wouldn't have much chance to find out more about that.

She broke away from the reporters and V.I.P.'s, and went and got Toby, and asked him did he want to look inside the rocket before it left.

He nodded. He was certainly being quiet today. Poor kid—he must be pretty mixed up about the whole thing by now.

She tried to figure out what was going on inside the small brown head, but all she could think of was how *much* like Jock he looked today.

She took him up the elevator inside the rocket. There wasn't much room to move around, of course, but they'd rigged it so that all the big shots who were there could have a look. She was a little startled to see the President and her mother-in-law come up together in the next elevator, but between trying to answer Toby's questions, and trying to brush off reporters, she didn't have much time to be concerned about such oddities.

She had never seen Toby so intent on anything. He wanted to know *everything*. Where's this, and what's that for? And where are you going to sit, Mommy?

"I'm not, hon. You know that. There isn't room in this rocket for . . ."

"Mrs. Kruger, pardon me, but . . ."

"Just a minute, *please*."

"Oh, I'm sorry."

"What was it you wanted to know now, Tobe?" There were too many people; there was too much talk. She felt slightly dizzy. "Look, hon, I want to go on down." It was hard to talk. She saw Mrs. Kruger on the ramp, and called her, and left Toby with her. Down at the bottom, she saw Sue Stein, and asked her if she'd go take over with Toby and try to answer his questions.

"Sure. Feeling rocky, kid?"

"Kind of." She tried to smile.

"You better go lie down. Maybe Allie can get something for you. I saw her over there. . . ." She waved a vague hand. "You look like hell, kid. Better lie down." Then she rushed off.

He got away from Grandma when Sue Stein came and said Mother wanted her to show him everything. Then he said he was tired and got away from *her*. He could find his Grandma all right, he said.

He'd found the spot he wanted. He could just about wriggle into it, he thought.

The loudspeaker crackled over her head. Five minutes now.

The other women who'd been fixing their hair and brightening their lipstick snapped their bags shut and took a last look and ran out, to find places where they could see everything. Ruth stretched out on the couch and closed her eyes. Five minutes now, by herself, to get used to the idea that the job was done.

She had done everything she could do, including coming here today. There was nothing further she could do. From now on, or in five minutes' time, it was out of anyone's hands, but—Whose? And Jock's, of course. Once the relief rocket got there, it was up to him.

If it got there.

If he was there for it to get to.

The way they had worked it, there was a chance at least they'd know the answer in an hour's time. If the rocket made its orbit once, and only once, it would mean he was alive and well and in control of his own ship, with the radio working, and . . .

And if it made a second orbit, there was still hope. It *might* mean nothing worse than that that his radio was out. But that way they would have to wait . . .

God! It could take months, if the calculations as to where he'd come down were not quite right. If . . . *if* a million little things that would make it harder to get the fuel from one rocket to the other.

But if they only saw one orbit . . .

For the first time, she let herself, forced herself to consider the possibility that Jock was dead. That he would not come back.

He's not dead, she thought. I'd know it if he was. Like I knew something was wrong last time. Like I'd know it now if . . .

"Sixty seconds before zero," said the speaker.

But there is! She sat bolt upright, not tired or dizzy any more. Now she had faced it, she didn't feel confused. There was something . . . something dreadfully *wrong*. . . .

She ran out, and as she came on to the open field, the speaker was saying, "Fifty-one."

She ran to the edge of the crowd, and couldn't get through, and had to run, keep running, around the edges, to find the aisle between the cords.

Stop it! she screamed, but not out loud, because she had to use all her breath for running.

And while she ran, she tried to think.

"Minus forty-seven."

She couldn't make them stop without a reason. They'd think she was hysterical . . .

". . . forty-five . . ."

Maybe she was, at that. Coolly, her mind considered the idea and rejected it. No; there was a problem that hadn't been solved, a question she hadn't answered.

But *what* problem? What . . .

"Minus forty."

She dashed down between the ropes, toward the control booth. The guard stepped forward, then recognized her, and stepped back. The corridor between the packed crowds went on forever.

"Minus thirty-nine . . . eight . . . thirty-seven."

She stopped outside the door of Control, and tried to think, think, *think!* What *was* it? What could she tell them? How could she convince them? *She knew,* but they'd want to know what, why . . .

You just didn't change plans at a moment like this.

But if they fired the rocket before she figured it out, before she remembered the problem, and then found an answer, it was as good as murdering Jock. They could never get another one up quickly enough if anything went wrong this time.

She pushed open the door.

"Stop!" she said. "Listen, you've got to stop. Wait! There's something . . ."

Tim O'Heyer came and took her arm, and smiled and said something. Something soothing.

"Minus nineteen," somebody said into a microphone, quietly.

She kept trying to explain, and Tim kept talking at her, and when she tried to pull away she realized the hand on her arm wasn't just there to comfort her. He was keeping her from making trouble. He . . .

Oh, God! If there was just some way to make them understand! If she could only remember *what* was wrong . . .

"Minus three . . . two . . ."

It was no use.

She stopped fighting, caught her breath, stood still and saw Tim's approving smile, as the word and the flare went off together:

"Mark!"

Then, in a dead calm, she looked around and saw Sue.

"Where's Toby?" she asked.

She was looking in the reserved grandstand seats for Mrs. Kruger, when she heard the crowd sigh, and looked up and saw it happening.

The crash fire did not damage the inside of the rocket at all. The cause of the crash was self-evident, as soon as they found Toby Kruger's body wedged into the empty space between the outer hull of the third stage, and the inner hull of the second.

The headlines were not as bad as might have been expected. Whether it was the tired and unholy calm on Ruth Kruger's face that restrained them, or Tim O'Heyer's emergency-reserve supply of Irish whisky that convinced them, the newsmen took it easy on the story. All America couldn't attend the funeral, but a representative hundred thousand citizens mobbed the streets when the boy was buried; the other hundred and eighty million saw the ceremonies more intimately on their TV sets.

Nobody who heard the quiet words spoken over the fresh grave—a historic piece of poetry to which the author, O'Heyer, could never sign his name—nobody who heard that simple speech remained entirely unmoved. Just where or when or with whom the movement started is still not known; probably it began spontaneously in a thousand different homes during the brief ceremony; maybe O'Heyer had something to do with that part of it, too. Whichever way, the money started coming in, by wire, twenty minutes afterwards; and by the end of the week "Bring Jock Back" was denting more paychecks than the numbers racket and the nylon industry combined.

The KIM-IX was finished in a month. They didn't have Ruth Kruger to design this time, but they didn't need her: the KIM-VIII plans were still good. O'Heyer managed to keep the sleeping-pill story down to a tiny back-page notice in most of the papers, and the funeral was not televised.

Later, they brought back the perfectly preserved, emaciated body of Jock Kruger, and laid him to rest next to his wife and son. He had been a good pilot and an ingenious man. The moon couldn't kill him; it took starvation to do that.

They made an international shrine of the house, and the garden where the three graves lay.

Now they are talking of making an interplanetary shrine of the lonely rocket on the wrong side of the moon.

(From *The University of Kansas City Review*)

PORTRAIT OF MY SON AS A YOUNG MAN

BY ELIZABETH H. MIDDLETON

IT WAS three o'clock on a hot, sultry morning and in her cubicle of a room on the ground floor of Gannon's Hotel old Sarah Gannon lay awake. Perspiration soaked her ancient cotton nightgown. Her hands ached from clenching them. Overhead she could hear Dave pacing up and down, and she saw him as clearly as if he were in the room, the furrows folded deep in his forehead and one hand unconsciously ruffling his hair. Old Gannon used to do that, too, when he wrestled with a thing; in him decision came fast and action followed after. But in Dave there had to be this agony of deliberation, duty, and longing battling. When he wanted a thing, he wanted it as badly as ever old Gannon had, and to give it up for whatever reason came hard, this time harder than ever, for not only duty reached out to hold him, but love. With the fierce possessiveness of the young, Kathryn had cried out, "I *will* not let him go!"

Dave had his father's brawny build, heavy set and firmly planted, and his father's eyes that looked afar to all the length and breadth of the world. When he was five he asked, "How big is the ocean?" At ten he yearned for the sky. But when he was fifteen, without losing the distant vision, he discovered a new world close at hand—a world of earth and wood and stream—and he said, "I shall be a naturalist and travel all over the world."

He began to read and study. "Did you know that in Outer Mongolia they serve sheep's eyes to distinguished visitors?" But it was not adventure that drew him, nor any honors that might be given;

it was the great soul of earth, the deep and turning earth with its far-flung secret places. He was old Gannon's son.

Hers as well. He had her silences and stubborn clinging to duty and obligation. He did a man's work at the hotel and need never be reminded. Once, when she was ill, he gave up a trip into the north woods on which his heart was set. "There are things to be done here," he said, his eyes as bleak as rain. And he stayed and did them. He was a good boy, old for his years—a steady boy—but he was still old Gannon's son.

She drew herself up on the edge of the bed and swung thin legs to the floor. Why was a child given to you at all, when from the womb's secret unity this later cleavage must come? Tired she was, and worn and old, but somehow she must find strength for this one service she still owed her son.

The seeds of this day were planted long ago; they lay in the mysteries of gene and chromosome, and in the ways of men. But the more immediate and tangible cause had appeared only two weeks ago when, at the close of the day, Sarah saw a station wagon jeep drive up to the hotel. It was packed to the last inch with neatly stowed gear and on top of it, firmly lashed, were fishing poles, paddles, and a collapsible yellow rubber life raft. A man climbed out and stood at the bottom step. He was small and hard, brown and dry like a mummy, with eyes of an intense bright blue and bleached hair that fell across his forehead. He was neither young nor old, but ageless.

"Good afternoon," said he, with a hint of a flourish. "I am—ah—Professor Ridge, and I am looking for a room. Have you one available?"

She could see he was not like others who stopped at this hotel. "I have one, but you wouldn't like it. Try the Inn. It's two blocks up the street, turn right."

He smiled and bowed. "I beg your pardon, madam, but I doubt if I would care for the Inn. This is the sort of place I am looking for."

She warmed slightly. "Traveling men like it, summer people don't. It's plain but clean. I'll show you the room."

It was on third, under the eaves, and it had a slit of a window overlooking the service entrance where all day trucks and milk wagons rattled. The sun beat down on the low sloping roof.

"This will do very well," the Professor said.

"It's hot and it's noisy," she told him frankly. "I'm afraid you'll have trouble sleeping."

He assured her that such would not be the case. "I can sleep anywhere and I have, in my time: in the woods, in railroad stations, in a cave with bats, once on a pile of straw in a jail—not, let me explain, as prisoner, but as guest; it was in Colombia and I was visiting the *jefe,* a friend of mine who doubled as police chief."

Within old Sarah something woke and turned. "You travel?"

"Indeed I do. I am a botanist. In my profession it is easy to combine business with—ah—inclination. I am a field man."

"You're not married?"

He laughed. "My dear madam, *I* am a free man."

A free man! That too was what old Gannon had said to her so long ago, but he had married, yes, and he had loved his Sarah, too, in his hearty, roistering way; yet he remained a free man. The world was very wide and beautiful and he heard its call, and he went away one day and hadn't yet come back. She heard from him sometimes, a postal from Panama, a brass from Bangkok, an embroidery from China, and once, when he was very drunk, a cable in which he called her his love, his heart's delight, his darling.

The Professor said, "I shall want the room for two weeks. I have it in mind to try a bit of fishing before I set off again. One thing more: with *flora* I am at home anywhere, with *fauna* I am not unacquainted, but *pisces*—I admit to total ignorance. Is there someone you could recommend, some reliable person I might hire to teach me the mysteries of rod and reel? Preferably a silent fellow, for in my experience I have found it generally true that he who speaks least makes the best companion."

"In that case," Sarah said, "you'll want my son Dave. If there's nothing else, I'll go down."

She found Dave in the kitchen helping Kathryn who was so fair, who had the bright eyes of the Norwegian people and their sunny hair, who moved as gracefully as the willow. He had never before looked at any of the girls who came and went in Sarah's kitchen, but Kathryn he had noticed from the first day. Sarah told him about the Professor.

"I'll take him to the Flowage," he said. "Anyone can catch a muskie there." He bent to kiss the hair in Kathryn's neck that lay coiled against the flesh like a golden spring. "How do you like my girl?"

"I like her fine," old Sarah said, but pity stirred her. Would the years bring to Kathryn the emptiness and the waiting? "He'll be here two weeks."

Each day the two men set out very early, taking a lunch, and stayed away until evening. When they came back they were not the same as when they had gone out in the morning. Peace lay upon them. Even though they seldom spoke during the long hours of the day, in silence they were not apart. Sarah could see how it was with them, and so could Kathryn. "I'm afraid," she said.

"What are you afraid of?" Sarah said, knowing the answer.

"I don't know. Of him, I guess, the Professor. When he and Dave are together . . . I feel left out."

"He'll soon be gone."

"Not soon enough," Kathryn said.

And she was right. Old Sarah knew it in a woman's way that leaps beyond fact and reason to come face to face with truth.

"I know what will happen," Kathryn said. "They get along so well he'll want Dave to go with him—and you know where he's going, don't you?"

Sarah knew all about it. The Professor was going to El Salvador to collect for some university. He might be gone a year, or two—or five. What was time to him, or money either, so long as he had enough to live? And such a man could live on next to nothing because he did not value those things that other men valued, but only freedom. He drove in his jeep when he felt like it, ate when he was hungry, slept wherever he happened to be. If he came to a lake and wanted to explore for water plants, he simply blew up the rubber life raft and paddled away. When night came he could sleep in the jeep or roll up on the ground in a sleeping bag. Food was merely something to satisfy hunger and he did not care how it was cooked, or whether it was steak or beans.

"As for Dave . . ." Kathryn stopped, choking. "You mustn't let him go. Don't *let* him!" She flung herself against old Sarah, weeping. "Oh, I love him."

"That I know," old Sarah said.

"Then we'll stick together. We'll keep him here with us."

Bitter wisdom knew better. Sarah said, "What has loving got to do with keeping a man?"

Kathryn pushed away. "I love him, I tell you, and I won't let him go."

A few days later Dave came to them and told them what they already knew. "He wants me to be his assistant. He'll teach me what I need to know. What do you think?" He spoke as if this were a week-end jaunt to Chicago or Minneapolis, but the light in his eyes betrayed him. Kathryn cried out and ran to hold him, but old Sarah turned gruffly aside. "Make up your own mind."

At least she had been spared that question when old Gannon went away. He did not come and ask permission to be free. Not he! In the sunset he came to her and laid himself upon the bed folding his hands on his stomach. He stared far into the ceiling and beyond it in that way he had when he was very drunk, and, speaking softly, told her what he was about to do. "Sarah, old girl, you're a fine, good woman, a faithful hard-working woman who does her duty, and now I am going to leave you. How can I stay? There are seas and deserts and mountains. What is a woman to me now? If I stay with you I shall hate you, but if I go I shall love you to the end of my days. There's no help for it, old girl. A man has to be what the Lord made him, a man must be free." She had not cried, nor spoken against it, and in the morning, more sober than any judge, he kissed her and went his way.

But Dave was not old Gannon even though he was his son, and in him conscience snared and fought that wild impulse to be free. Day after day he waged the battle, grim and silent. He took the Professor to the Flowage by day, and at night helped Kathryn in the kitchen, kissing the golden spring as before but not knowing that he did it.

Old Sarah could not sleep these nights. Often she rose at two or three to scrub a floor on hands and knees, or set a batch of biscuits, or wash a tub of clothes. And in these lonely hours old Gannon's face rose up before her with that distant hunger in it, and Dave's face rose beside it and the hunger was the same, the hunger of all men who set their eyes to the horizon.

Now she could not delay any longer. In the morning the Professor would be gone. What is a mother but a brood hen who raises her young only to cast them forth upon the world? She climbed the stairs.

He opened at her knock, startled, and let her in.

"You'd better pack," she said. "He leaves at six."

His face closed in. His mouth drew thin. "Who says I'm going?"

She opened dresser drawers. "You want me to help?"

He pulled her back. "I tell you, I'm not going. You need me, and Kathryn . . ." He turned his face away. "I don't want to go. It was all a crazy notion."

"I can get along all right without you," she said.

"Are you trying to get rid of me?"

"I've done my duty, I've raised you. Now I don't need you any more." She went back to the dresser and this time he let her take out his shirts and socks and underwear and pile them on the bed.

"You're old," he smiled, speaking with brutal tenderness. "You can't go on working much longer. This place is too much. You need a man here."

But she refused to listen. Already she could see him going down the same dusty road old Gannon had traveled before him, the long road, the empty road, and she cried out, "I don't need help from anyone. Why don't you go and make your own place in the world like others do? You're a man aren't you?" Then, gently, "I'll get you a suitcase that was your father's, and there's a shirt needs ironing. You'll want to take it with you."

In the lobby Kathryn stared with burning eyes. "Where have you been? What have you been doing?" But she knew, oh! she knew. She raised a hand to her face as if Sarah had struck her.

"I'm getting a suitcase."

Kathryn spread her arms, barring the way. "You *want* him to go. You *want* him to leave me."

"You can't chain a man," old Sarah said.

"*I* can, and I *will*," Kathryn said.

Sarah shook her head. "You are young. You do not understand. You think if you can hold him, he's yours. But I tell you, you never can be sure of any man till you let him go. Maybe he'll come back and maybe he won't, but if he does then you can be sure."

They faced each other in the dim light like enemies, the oldest enemies of all, the mother who tears her body in pain to give life to a child, and the girl who fights to hold a lover. It was Kathryn who looked away first and pushed aside and ran upstairs.

When Sarah went back to the room she found them together;

Kathryn was weeping and Dave stroked her fair hair. She put the suitcase on the bed. "I brought your things."

"He's not going," Kathryn said, in triumph, through her tears. "We're going to stay here and get married and run this place so you can take it easy."

Dave did not speak. He did not look at his mother.

She stood quietly and folded her hands and drew herself up. What did these two know of love? "I don't want your pity," she said. "And I won't have you taking everything away from me, either. This is *my* hotel. Old Gannon left it with me and all these years I've taken good care of it. I've scrubbed the floors and stoked the fires and painted the walls. I've waited on the guests and cooked for them and made their beds. It's mine! Do you think I'll let anyone, even you, Dave, take it away from me? I've raised you the best I knew how. I don't owe you anything. Now you've got a chance to do something on your own, not hanging on to me. Take it." Kathryn gave a little cry, and Sarah turned on her. "Think I'm hard on him, don't you? Well, I am." She faced back to Dave. "Go with the Professor. Get a taste of what it is to be a man. When I can be proud of you, then you can come back—not before. That's all I've got to say."

As she talked he watched her, and she saw the light come up in his eyes, bright like the sun. She turned away. "Help him pack," she said to Kathryn and went out, stumbling on the stairs.

Later she stood behind the plate glass window in the lobby and watched him ride away down the long, dusty road. She had done what she had set herself to do, and there was no more strength in her. On the steps Kathryn wept. How can the young be expected to see victory in defeat? But Dave, for all he was old Gannon's son, was a good boy, a steady boy, and when he had climbed his mountain and seen his sea he would remember where his heart lay.

And old Gannon? The world is wide and very beautiful and the years are long, but in the end, pray God! at evening, the wanderer turns his face toward home.

(From Shenandoah)

THE PROFESSOR AND THE POET

BY MARVIN MUDRICK

QUINCY TAYLOR was a New Englander, a Yale Ph.D. (winner in 1940 of the Jonathan Pratt Peabody Award for his dissertation on Emerson), Professor of English and Chairman of the Department for four years at a small but dignified California college, and not yet forty. The town he lived in was, like most coastal California towns, a resort, but dignified. The city elders held off heavy industry, kept the beaches clear of hot-dog stands, and, to supplement the gatherings of the "old" Californians (those who had come before the earthquake of '25), welcomed into their Spanish-tile-and-eucalyptus suburbs the families of retired Eastern plumbing manufacturers. The sober newspaper ("All the news without fear or favor") reported in tastefully brief items the police-court antics of the Mexican inhabitants of the lower end of town, found no space at all for accounts of local damage in the latest earthquake or drunk-and-disorderly charges against members of the old families, publicized the college ("Dr. Floyd Gudge, Professor of Practical Arts, is attending a Conference of Western States Practical Arts Teachers on improved methods of sharpening kitchen cutlery . . ."), and featured a drama-music-literature-art section on Sunday. A symphony orchestra visited three times a year, and, as in many California towns, there was a thriving community theater.

Taylor and the town got on well together. As an Easterner, he was qualified to patronize the rawness of California. He subscribed to *The New Yorker,* the *New York Times,* and the *Saturday Review*

("Otherwise I'd never know what's going on in the *civilized* world"). As a graceful speaker, he could preside over classrooms, auditoriums, theater audiences, and monthly meetings of the Department or the Country Club or the Community Theater Group with authority and satisfaction.

California attracts and rewards people with a flair. Taylor, with his ascetic figure, his politely sardonic smile, his agile step and platform manner, had a flair. At the college, students took "Taylor courses." To freshmen he brought Shakespeare. "In this scene I recall Katharine Cornell as Juliet, in a black cape that revealed a scarlet lining when she flung it open against the bare white backdrop." His Modern Poetry course was a sharing of the fabulous past. "I asked Robert Frost exactly what he meant by . . ." and "In those days Edna Millay looked . . . ." Every year, at the beginning of the fall semester, he opened the College Poetry Readings with a performance of *The Waste Land.* Students, faculty, and townspeople filled the chairs and sat cross-legged on the floor of the Women's Clubroom watching as his hands gestured, his bright actor's eyes moved over them, his voice intoned: "Un*re*al City . . . ." His special knowledge was, of course, 19th-century American literature. To his advanced class, he lectured with a manner of brilliant, mobile impromptu from meticulously handwritten notes; a former student, son of a prominent local merchant and now playing bit parts on television, had written of Taylor in a college-days reminiscence for the local paper: "When he spoke of *Moby Dick,* or *Hiawatha,* or the *Divinity School Address,* one felt that the slender man behind the desk had gradually risen several inches off the floor, suspended in his own severe exaltation." Taylor kept two copies, one at home and one in his desk at the college.

For the local theater group, he delighted capacity audiences and the local drama critic by playing the college professor, the witty old codger, the dreamy intellectual in ten-year-old Broadway hits, with his own postures or a set of carefully learned ones. Two or three times a year he was given fifteen minutes over the local radio station (owned by the newspaper): he read poetry, or spoke of Emerson, Whittier, and Longfellow. He belonged to a liberal church of New England ancestry; once a year, at the request of the respectful pastor, he ascended black-robed, stern-eyed, and straight-faced to the pulpit, to deliver a "lay sermon" on the necessity of righteousness or the decay of gentility.

His tastes, he often said, were conservative. From *The New Yorker* he neatly scissored out stories which parodied highbrow techniques, and, from the *Times* and the *Saturday Review,* articles which assailed what Taylor called "the brand-new criticism." He handed them around among his colleagues for their sharply observed amusement, and then took them home to paste the scraps of paper into a large scrapbook of other people's follies.

Still, he enjoyed celebrities, even avant-garde poets, in person. Sean O'Shaughnessy, founder of the new Orgiastic School of British poetry, sketched with Shelleyesque curls by Augustus John and praised by Miss Sitwell, had been only a rather distasteful name to him; but when he read in the *Times* that O'Shaughnessy was touring the country for lecture fees and would shortly be in California, he hastened to notify the Committee on Lectures and Drama. Telegrams were exchanged; and soon the *Press-Gazette* informed its readers that Sean O'Shaughnessy, celebrated young poet, would on a certain date be reading from his own poetry in the college auditorium.

So far, so good. Taylor read of O'Shaughnessy's arrival in Los Angeles to fulfill an engagement at one of the universities there. The first cloud appeared in the form of a phone call from the chairman of the Committee on Lectures and Drama. This gentleman had received troubling news from the metropolis. The poet, it seemed, drank; he refused to stop drinking; he had read his poems drunk; and he had hurled a glass of water, glass and all, at a face—it turned out to belong to a Professor Emeritus of Education—which he afterwards said looked too offensively stupid to be endured. Would the college please send somebody at once to pick up and pack off the poet?

Taylor volunteered to go. He was himself an almost invulnerable drinker, and he felt confident. He kissed his wife, told her he would be back the following afternoon, said a curt goodbye to his wife's son by her first marriage (the eight-year-old was overjoyed: Mama would let him come into bed with her in the morning while Quin, who forbade the practice, was gone), and set off by auto for Los Angeles.

Finding O'Shaughnessy was a job. Taylor had the name of his

hotel, but he had not been there for more than twenty-four hours. Nobody at the university knew where he was, and it was implied that at this point nobody cared to know. Taylor called a few literary lights of his acquaintance in the city, but none had seen him. Finally, the chairman of the University's English Department, phoned at his home for possible clues, recalled the name of a downtown bar that O'Shaughnessy had mentioned with special approval in the course of his reading.

He was there, seated on a bar stool, drinking, staring up at the television image high in a corner of the room. Taylor recognized him from a recent photo in the *Times,* very different from the Shelleyesque sketch. In person he was less prepossessing still. He was rather dumpy, even fat; his features had a potato-like grossness; his very coarse dark hair lay tangled on his head and brow; his clothes had obviously been worn for an indefinite period through all kinds of personal weather. Taylor paused to let his momentary distaste pass away, then walked over and took an adjacent stool.

He ordered a drink. O'Shaughnessy kept staring upward. "Mr. O'Shaughnessy," said Taylor, "I have come to claim you." O'Shaughnessy did not turn his head. "Think of all the money they make," he said. "First the movies, now this thing. Do you know anybody who could get me a job writing for them?" "I do know a script writer in town," said Taylor. O'Shaughnessy turned around; his eyes were small and dull. "What college are *you* from?" Taylor told him. "Could you take me to see this writer?" Taylor said he could. They left after Taylor had phoned the writer, mentioned the famous name, and made an engagement.

The writer was a round bald Englishman in a pink stucco cottage in North Hollywood. He was delighted to see the poet (whom Taylor had meanwhile persuaded to wash up and put on a less grimy jacket at the hotel), and he served the best Scotch. He talked about poets. He knew the British expatriates, at least well enough to tell amusing anecdotes about them. "Read the comics and trust in the Primate," said O'Shaughnessy. When he became rhetorical, his voice developed an impressive baritone richness. The writer was disconcerted: he was High Church himself. O'Shaughnessy wanted to know about Hollywood. The writer had anecdotes; so did Taylor, who knew a number of minor Hollywood actors. "How do you meet the people who do the hiring?" asked O'Shaughnessy. Well, it was hard to break in and hard to stay in; luck had a lot to do with it; writing a successful play or novel helped; may I get you another drink? By two in the morning Taylor had managed to coax O'Shaughnessy to bed in his hotel and to fall asleep himself in a nearby room pondering and shaping the play he would write, a sort of variation on *Candida* . . .

Taylor found the ride back home exhilarating. He had not been able to prevent the poet's leisurely tour of bars in the vicinity, and they had not started till late in the afternoon; but O'Shaughnessy was comparatively rested, he brightened himself now and then with a draught from a bottle, and he told stories of London celebrities, of Osbert and Cyril and Uncle Tom the Deacon. Taylor took detailed mental notes. "O'Shaughnessy was saying it's common gossip in London . . ." He was still taking notes when they arrived at his home. He had O'Shaughnessy to himself that night for a late dinner Emily prepared, and for talk and drinks afterward. O'Shaughnessy was working on a close schedule, to make as much money, he explained, in as short a time as possible: tomorrow afternoon's reading at the college, the midnight Pullman to San Francisco for a reading there the following day. While Emily asked O'Shaughnessy about his family, Taylor phoned Gil Ross (Secretary of the Community Theater Group; old local family) and Alec Stillman (former Chairman of the Department; Yale Ph.D., 1931), tempted them with a few tidbits, and invited them to an after-dinner party on the following evening in honor of the poet, a farewell party. He rejoined Emily and O'Shaughnessy, who were talking about the wife and children left at home in London.

Morning at the college was pleasant. O'Shaughnessy was still safely in bed, and Emily had promised to keep him in the house until Taylor returned to pick him up for the reading. In the parking lot, he met one of his young instructors and mentioned casually that O'Shaughnessy was staying with him during the unfortunately brief visit. "Delightful fellow, no pretensions whatever," he said. At the office, Miss Brainerd responded with appropriate respect to the same information. Taylor, long convinced that his secretary adored him, treated her always with special blandness: she was, as a matter of fact, hopelessly in love with a dapper Associate Professor of Sociology, who drove a convertible, wore sports clothes and dark glasses with corrected lenses, and taught his predominantly female students crime and punishment in the fall semester and marriage and the family in the spring; but Miss Brainerd regarded Taylor's complacence as kindness, and they got on well together. His mail, already on his desk, was agreeable: a complimentary copy of a new anthology of American literature, a letter from a Columbia graduate student asking for a job ("You are aware, I am sure," Taylor would answer, "that at this time uncertainty as to future enrollments . . ."). He reminded his classes of the event in the afternoon, and urbanely commanded them to attend. Between classes, he dropped in on Alec Stillman and told him more about O'Shaughnessy. Stillman, whom Taylor had succeeded as chairman, was a large solemn man; but he belonged to the same church, and they both attended the local Yale Club dinners—"oases in the Great Western Desert," Taylor had once remarked as toastmaster (laughter and applause).

The *Press-Gazette* had been notified while Taylor was at the office and when he got home the newspaper's human-interest reporter was sitting with Emily and O'Shaughnessy. The reporter was a large, self-assured middle-aged woman, whose self-assurance had grown out of a round of musical evenings at the homes of the best families ("Last evening Mrs. Malvina Trinkle threw open her lovely home in the foothills to a small gathering of friends and music-lovers, who were privileged to hear a concert by . . .") and catch-in-the-throat stories about children at school and at play ("Could you, if you were asked just like that, name all the forty-eight states? AND the territories? Little Billy Myers could, and did . . ."). Emily and O'Shaughnessy had apparently been drinking together: the glasses, the water, and the well-started bottle were still there. After the flurry of politenesses, Taylor listened. "Who are your favorite poets, Mr. O'Shaughnessy?" the reporter asked. "Shakespeare and Yeats, the poets of skin, blood, and lubricity." "Do you have any hobbies?" "Drinking." "What poem of your own is your favorite?" "They are all superb; but the best is my latest, 'The Impotent Centaur'." "What is your ambition as a poet?" "To make a mint of money." "What do you think of our little city?" "I have seen very little of your little city, but it seems a hideous little picture postcard of a city."

She left finally, baffled, with her information. Taylor was annoyed: he did not like his wife to be drinking in the afternoon, though he knew she often did while he was gone and her son was at school; she got drunk and maudlin, and at last cataleptic, very easily. She was now maudlin, telling O'Shaughnessy how mean her first husband had been to her, how big and empty Texas was with a mean no-account husband, how kind and polite Quin had been to her when she first knew him in Austin, where he'd been teaching then. Taylor told her to tidy herself up before the boy came home, and left with O'Shaughnessy to drive to the college.

O'Shaughnessy had—Taylor the amateur actor recognized—the actor's sense for audience. He was charming. He was creaseless and soiled, his doughy little figure barely dominated the lectern, but his voice was a wonderful, almost human instrument. He held and unified the crowd of students, faculty, and townspeople; he made them laugh with the confidence of being proximate to greatness. "When I was younger and the war was on, I went where all poets go when they're naughty—the BBC. I did my bit by playing Hamlet for the boys." He read poems by Yeats, Stephens, and Joyce, all in the same apocalyptic incantatory tone: "Great English poets, all Irish." He read from "Anna Livia Plurabelle." He read, in conclusion, a group of his own poems: "Ruddy Wedding," "The White Thighs of the Drover," "Umbilicus," "The Hair of the Grass," "The Impotent Centaur." Afterwards, there was prolonged applause, and many people gathered round to shake his hand, speak to him for a moment, collect his autograph. Taylor saw Gill Ross, red-faced with enthusiasm, press through to O'Shaughnessy's side, say something to him and shake his hand. Ross caught sight of Taylor and hurried over. "A great man!" he cried. "If we could only get him to play Hamlet for *us!*"

A great man; and given the opportunity to make his impression because Taylor had so tactfully kept him in hand. Taylor felt a comfortable gratification, an expansive altruism. He was not envious of O'Shaughnessy: there were poets and there were the interpreters of poets, and he was content to be one of these—interpreter, friend, and unobtrusive supervisor of poets. Even Emily failed to dent his euphoria when she served dinner in sulky alcoholic silence and retired to the kitchen with her son. O'Shaughnessy had been pleased by the response to the reading and, drinking his Scotch and water while Taylor ate, talked exuberantly about new ideas for poems, about a verse-play commissioned by the BBC, about a poem he had begun just the other day in Los Angeles. He showed a piece of yellow paper covered with minute handwriting. Taylor knew that he had to have it. "Is that your only copy?" No, there was a second draft. "Might I have it as a memento?" "For the bed and the liquor," said O'Shaughnessy, handing it over. Taylor folded the paper and put it casually into his pocket.

By the time the Rosses arrived, Emily had made herself moderately presentable, and she even chatted for a moment with Jenny Ross. Gill Ross was cheerful with everyone, he introduced his wife to O'Shaughnessy and continued his congratulations of the afternoon. The Stillmans came, Isabel Stillman tall and frostily English-looking but with a gracious smile for the poet. For the first time O'Shaughnessy seemed somewhat uneasy; he sat down with finality on the sofa and went back to his drink, which he had carried from the dining room. Emily, relapsed into sullenness, brought in a snack tray, set it on the sideboard, and took to the sofa also. Taylor made the drinks and passed them around.

Polite provocation of O'Shaughnessy had no effect. They drank. They turned to theater talk: first about the new English playwrights (no response); then about the "serious" Broadway hits, which the Rosses had seen on a recent trip to New York; then about the Community Theater's most recent production, in which Taylor had played the leading role. Isabel Stillman remarked on the finished quality of Quin's performance. Taylor, at Ross's insistence, did amusing imitations of the pansy director at work, the leading lady in a temper, the ex-Broadway ancient who enjoyed dressing down his juniors. The Rosses had taken minor parts, and both were animated about the pleasures of realizing oneself in stagecraft, of "belonging to a whole." Taylor played a tape recording he had made of one of the scenes in rehearsal, his whimsical-philosopher scene; more reminiscence and compliments, except from Emily and O'Shaughnessy.

Ross, emboldened by all the talk, asked O'Shaughnessy about his acting on the BBC, and was answered in monosyllables, mostly indistinct. "There's nothing like that over here," said Ross, "nothing at all." "The English tolerate at least a token display of culture," said Taylor. "We have heard fine reports about the Third Program," said Stillman. "It's a dirty, dead and rotten country," said O'Shaughnessy; "no cash, no corpuscles, all starched front and scraggy behind." Isabel Stillman began to look professionally British, and Jenny Ross's social smile lost some of its voltage. Taylor said that perhaps with the infusion of new blood from Ireland England could be saved. Emily, who had been drinking without comment, looked up long enough to say that Quin, damn him, thought he could always smooth things over. "Thank you, my dear," said Taylor, who felt like Congreve in a constellation of lively drinking company. Emily added, "Smooth as a baby's ass."

They played charades. The Stillmans did *The Importance of Being Earnest,* the Rosses *You Can't Take It With You,* and Taylor (Emily refused) *The Way of the World.* O'Shaughnessy stood up, pounded his chest with both fists, rolled with hunched shoulders and bowed arms to the window, and jumped to hang by his hands from the ledge above it: he swung there for a moment, grunting experimentally at various pitches. "Tarzan," he announced at last in a creditably anthropoid voice, "and the Apes," leaped at a nearby cord, and brought down a large Venetian blind and himself with his own dull thump and a reverberating clatter of thin metal. He crawled on all fours to the middle of the room, turned a neat circle on his hands so that each quarter might observe the seat of his trousers, rose, brushed off his hands lightly on the shiny seat, and returned to the sofa.

Emily was almost inert beside him; even Taylor felt unusually warm and good-humored. O'Shaughnessy seemed now to be settling into a portentous sulk, and the others, relaxed and rosy, Emily with damp drowsy eyes, watched him in furtive compassion. "My wife and kids left back there, that hole of a flat, so I can earn a miserable bit for them over here, all alone, all of us." Tears started in his eyes. Suddenly his head was in Emily's lap and he was sobbing noisily; Emily sat bolt upright wide-eyed, then scandalized as a hand rose from the crumpled body and fitted itself to the jut of her bodice, then crying, "Quin, make him stop!" Taylor was himself surprised at the depth of his sympathy: "Don't be silly," he said sharply, "he's just lonely." "Quin!" she cried helplessly. "Let him alone," came the sad muffled voice from below, "yield to the voice of the womb, be the huge engrossing earth-mother." The spectators stared, trying to collect themselves into a suitable attitude. Emily pushed the hand down. "Let me tell you something about my husband," she said with heavy deliberateness, "he's no man out of bed or in." "Emily has her own notions of virility," said Taylor, "which are I am sure of no interest to anyone else."

O'Shaughnessy bethought himself of something, stirred, rose, moved irresolutely toward the hall unbuttoning himself, did not manage to avoid a slight mishap on the living-room carpet, but kept going. Jenny Ross was propelled out of her chair shrieking: she ran past him into the bedroom, emerged holding her husband's coat and violently putting on her own, and pulled Ross toward the door. A remote hostess-bell apparently began ringing in Emily's brain; she got up and tried vaguely to intercept them: "Must you go, Jenny?" she asked. "Get away from me!" Jenny screamed, and dragged her husband with her out into the night. Isabel Stillman had decided to be superciliously amused, but Stillman was shocked into a goggle-eyed sobriety; after an exchange of courtesies with Emily and with Taylor, who was savoring his own imperturbable courtliness to the very door, they departed.

O'Shaughnessy had come back and sat down to somebody's unfinished drink. "I'm going to bed," said Emily. "I'll join you after I take our guest to the train," said Taylor amiably. "You can go to hell,"she said, leaving.

There was very little time, and Taylor brought in the volumes of O'Shaughnessy's poems he had bought earlier in the day. O'Shaughnessy autographed all of them: To Emily and Quin, With love, From Sean. The volumes would grace, carelessly, a table in the living room and his desk in the Department office. "Everything passes, art remains," said Taylor, driving O'Shaughnessy to the station. "We don't have to worry, do we," said O'Shaughnessy, "as long as we have people like you on our side." "Thank you," said Taylor, feeling moisture in his eyes. "Where will I get my liquor in San Francisco?" said O'Shaughnessy.

When Taylor returned to the house, he lingered for several minutes over the books, reading each inscription closely, observing the peculiarities of the handwriting, the bold initial T, the imperial S of the signature. He went into the bedroom at last. Emily was asleep and snoring. About to take off his suitcoat, he remembered. He took the piece of yellow paper out of his pocket and read carefully, in the doorway by the dim hall light, as much of the tiny scrawl as he could decipher. He replaced it reverently in the pocket and hung up the coat. He undressed and slipped into bed beside her. He thought of the poet at bay, and began to weep.

(*From The Hudson Review*)

YORE

BY HOWARD NEMEROV

OVER THE LAVISH *Forgeterie* of the Beauldvoir Hotel rose the bone-china moon, rubbing all things to a hard beauty that looked permanent. Tomorrow would be the war, and everywhere in the hotel people accordingly rose and fell in value; meanwhile here was the moon swinging over the lovely gardens and the pool.

Alone at a marble-topped table, Mr. Luc le Mesurier bent his ancient head, baldness tipped in moonlight, toward the small ivory radio which murmuringly kept him company; from time to time he drew out of his coat-tail and consulted his memorandum book, a thin, tall volume bound in calfskin. Here with a gold pencil he made a note now and again, or placed a mark against the name of some acquaintance, or crossed off a name entirely; then with a slight contortion and a sigh he would turn to slip the book back into the tail of his coat, but always a remark made by the radio could cause him to get it out again almost at once.

Mr. Luc le Mesurier was a lean, elegant old gentleman, whose subtly gleaming black and white clothes fitted him like a second skin; when he arose, as he now did to welcome his expected companions, the tails of his coat curled slightly but deftly up and back as though they belonged to his own muscular arrangements. The dark tan of his face left off at the brow, for on bright days at the Beauldvoir Beach he was accustomed to wear, besides a black loincloth, a skullcap against the sun, and for this reason he looked, as he bowed and nodded, like an old priest or haloed saint.

After turning off the radio he drew out a chair for Madame Mastaba, who with care placed her enormous backside between its arms and pressed down. The black sequins of her dress writhed with moonlight as, emplaced, she shook herself into comfort. Mr. Aiken Drum, the American millionaire, sat beside her and opposite to the place which Mr. le Mesurier now resumed. Mr. Aiken Drum was a large shaggy man with a full head of grey hair, rather unkempt. In this company Mr. le Mesurier resembled a whangee cane placed on exhibition beside a knobkerry stick and a pillow—an exhibition, perhaps, in a black museum, of instruments employed in the commission of long-forgotten crimes.

"It is hard to believe," said Mr. Aiken Drum, "but it has happened at last."

"It was bound to come sooner or later," said Mr. le Mesurier. "I suppose none of you knows where Great Coco is? This is something the announcer has neglected to inform us of so far."

"It will be very quickly over," averred Madame Mastaba. "Atom bombs, hydrogen bombs, very quickly over."

"No, no, this will not be very quickly over," said Mr. Aiken Drum somberly enough yet with a certain tone of pride. "It will be a long, bitter struggle. At least," he added, "we have seen my daughter married before it began."

Felicia Drum had been wed that very afternoon to Sir Layamon Brute, Marquess of Yore; the Bishop of Norfolk had been flown in to preside. It was now in the interval between the service and the wedding supper that the three elderly friends had gathered in the *Forgeterie,* at a table beside the pool.

"She does not love him, poor thing," said Madame Mastaba. "A great shame."

"Well, no," replied Mr. Drum. "But she is a good girl, is Felicia, and knows that first things come first."

"He will perish in this war," said Mr. le Mesurier.

"Well," said Mr. Drum, spreading wide his hands, "that of course can't be helped." He snuffled slightly, and brushed the end of his nose with delicacy on the back of his wrist. "They will be down in a few minutes. Let us be cheerful."

A waiter now took their orders. Mr. le Mesurier had been drinking a wine which he persuaded the others to try, a very fine wine expressed from seaweed, tasting something like iodine, dry, reddish-brown and puckering. As an afterthought, he instructed the waiter to find out where in the world was Great Coco.

"It will doubtless be an island," he said, "for the announcer speaks of 'the airbase *on* Great Coco.' "

"Who would have thought," said Madame Mastaba, "we should have lived to see the day when we had to feel responsible for an airbase on Great Coco?"

"But reality is always improbable," observed Mr. le Mesurier.

Great Coco, the waiter told them, was in the Bay of Bengal.

"I am scarcely any the wiser for that," said Madame Mastaba.

Mr. le Mesurier suddenly snapped on the radio again. After a silent moment they heard a chorus of young voices repeating the Hail Mary over and over again with the swaying emphasis of a roller coaster which takes a deep breath at the top of its initial climb, then rushes downward.

"No news as yet," said Mr. le Mesurier, turning the radio off.

"But that is more frightening than anything I have heard so far," said Madame Mastaba. "During the First World War I was at the School of the Sacred Heart in Grenoble."

"I really cannot understand," said Mr. Aiken Drum, "why man cannot learn to live at peace with his fellow-man."

"It is possibly because, my dear," returned Madame Mastaba, "man living at peace with his fellow-man would use considerably less oil than he will have to use under the present circumstances."

"My dear Andrea," said Mr. Aiken Drum in a dignified manner, "I did not want this war to happen."

With a slight wiggling motion Mr. le Mesurier now reached around to his coat-tail and drew forth his memorandum book.

"I was reflecting before you came," he said, "on where in the world one might go next. Doubtless everything will be destroyed in a few weeks, or the hotels will have no food and the servants will have been conscripted. Tananarive, possibly? But there will of course be an airbase there as well. Mukalla? Porto Alegre? Toby Lustig has a small inn at Misurata, but will it still be there? And will any sort of transport be available? On the other hand—Kristiansund? Or a farm near Stornoway? Ireland may be neutral; a visit with Salvadi at Castlebar? I fear life will not be made easy for the traveler."

"I shall go to my cousin at Denderah," said Madame Mastaba.

"No one ever bothers with the Upper Nile."

"And I return to the States tomorrow," said Mr. Drum. "Not exotic, but quite safe if one stays far from the cities. You are both invited. It is the children I am worried about."

"They will be evacuated, poor things, in droves," said Madame Mastaba.

"It was my children I meant," said Mr. Drum. "Felicia and Layamon."

"She will go to Yore, I suppose," said Mr. le Mesurier, "and he to join his squadron."

"But they are coming in now," said Madame Mastaba, raising her massive white head and peering toward the entrance.

Over the black water of the pool, moon-whitened in rippled streaks, an orchestra hidden in an island grove began to play The Wedding March. Felicia Drum advanced on the arm of her new husband the Marquess of Yore, the pair of them preceded by a small headwaiter who continually turned toward them to bow as he directed their path to the table. The girl, though she had put aside her white veil, still wore the wedding dress of white satin and a white cap of the same material. She looked pale and sullen, but charming. Sir Layamon Brute wore the somewhat Germanic-looking grey dress uniform of the Royal Air Force, with embroidered silver wings on the breast, three equal stripes of a Wing Commander on each sleeve, and upon his head the dully gleaming helmet with its high, horsehair crest, under which his thin, ruddy, pleasant face with its small red moustache did not appear especially adequate. A saber in scabbard swung at his side. Amid applause from the many guests at the tables beside the pool the bridal couple were seated with their elders just as the March came to an end.

"Exactly like a chamber pot," said Sir Layamon of his helmet, which he took off now and placed in the center of the table.

"It does form a strange costume for an aviator," observed Madame Mastaba. "I thought they wore something more *sportif.*"

"I am afraid," said Mr. Aiken Drum, "that this war will not be much of a wedding present for you two." He shook his head seriously, and Felicia, who at seventeen remained very uncertain about the great world, considered for a moment the idea that her father had really arranged the war with the object of giving her pleasure, and that he now rather regretted having gone to all that trouble. Under the fleeting influence of this notion she smiled brightly at him, to show appreciation.

"It can't be helped, sir," said Sir Layamon quietly. "Felicia will stay with Mother at Yore. I shall pack off to my Group as soon as we get back." He looked tenderly at his bride. "Not much of a show for you, my dear," he said.

Felicia looked back with an appearance of equal tenderness and leaned over to whisper something in his ear. What she whispered was, "You know what you can do with your stiff upper lip," but the others, unable to hear, interpreted the Marquess's sudden rigidity of expression as pleased surprise. After a moment he whispered back in her ear, pushing aside with his nose her brown hair, "I shall die in this war. You won't be troubled with me for very long." To which Felicia replied aloud, and with a slight smile, "We can't help that, can we?" It seemed to her that she was being unnecessarily cruel, but apart from having been both annoyed and fatigued by the long ceremony, she felt quite bewildered about the nature of the feelings that would henceforth, it seemed, be officially demanded of her. She had seen in the *Tatler* pictures of Yore, towering and ancient amid great trees, and it seemed to her that in order to live up to such a possession she would have to be somewhat haughty, inscrutable, full of cold, cryptic sentences and surprised at nothing, like a great lady in the movies. It was also true that she did not love her husband, but this was only because she did not know from any personal experience what love was, and also perhaps because he failed to frighten her, even when wearing the helmet with the horsehair crest.

A waiter brought more wine, the delicious, bitter wine from seaweed. Mr. le Mesurier turned on the radio again, and now an announcer was describing in a tense, professionally anxious voice the preparations for reprisal that were going on all over the world: the battleships and carriers getting up steam at Guam and Pearl and Scapa Flow; the huge aircraft engines beginning to turn on the runways at Reykjavik and Disco and Yell and distant Thule; vast uneasy populations beginning to move through the Balkans, through Turkey, through India; the air of the world laced with radio messages; the President of the United States would speak to the Congress.

"The King of Thule," said Madame Mastaba. "We used to sing

that song at school. There was a golden cup, a silver cup?"

"This is the century of dreams come true, is it not?" Mr. le Mesurier with doubtful relevance observed.

London and Paris, the announcer said, were under attack from the air. There was no news from these places, there was radio silence from these places.

"What a strange phrase," said Felicia, "as though *radio silence* were more golden than other kinds."

"It is a technical term," said the Marquess.

"A technical term," said Mr. le Mesurier, "meaning silence."

"But look," said Mr. Aiken Drum, suddenly reaching out and turning off the radio, "the floor show is about to begin."

"Now there is radio silence indeed," said Madame Mastaba.

Across the water the orchestra had begun to play once again, a brilliant fanfare followed by a dreamy, muted tune.

"It can hardly be a *floor* show," said Felicia, "unless the performers walk on water, which I understand is not done even in the century of dreams come true."

"My dear girl," her father replied, "you do not know everything about the world as yet."

While he spoke the music became louder, and gradually the depths of the pool beside them began to glow increasingly with light. Soon the reflexions of the moon, and the black surface itself, disappeared from view and were replaced by a softly brilliant fairyland of coral castles and coral foliage underwater. Small, brightly striped fish swam slowly about, and there was even the submerged hull of a ship, with broken masts and tattered rigging, half-sunken in sand covered with waving green moss. It was altogether a beautiful and strange sight, which Felicia had certainly not been expecting, and it made her feel for a moment privileged to mystery.

"It is a floor show of the ocean floor," said Madame Mastaba. "They have it only here, at the Beauldvoir, I have seen it many times. It is very beautiful."

Now through the softly radiant water, from the doorway of a distant castle, came swimming a dozen mermaids, naked and white as pearls. They moved effortlessly forward with sinuous twistings of their tails, and soon formed into a circle, around which they swam for some minutes.

"How do they stay under so long?" asked Felicia.

"They are said to be perfectly real mermaids," Madame Mastaba replied, "imported from the Seychelles Islands. Only here do they have them. Nowhere else in the world."

"At the Beauldvoir you know you are getting the real thing, expensive as it is," said Mr. Aiken Drum.

"All the same," Mr. le Mesurier said, "I am inclined to think they are not real. Rather, the legs of those girls have been slipped into the hinder skins, the tails, you understand, of very large fish —glued there, you know."

"Ugh," said Felicia.

"But how, in that case, do they stay under for so long?" asked the Marquess. "Unless of course it is a trick," he added, anxious not to appear naive.

"Ah," said Mr. le Mesurier, "that I cannot tell you."

"I will tell you," said Madame Mastaba with a certain emphasis. "It is because they are real mermaids, imported." She frowned at Mr. Luc le Mesurier. "You men," she said disdainfully.

"But there are no such things as mermaids," said Felicia petulantly, feeling nevertheless as though she were betraying her whole sex for nothing more than a cheap rationalistic idea picked up at school.

"There are these mermaids," replied Madame Mastaba.

"There are more things in heaven and earth, Horatio, than are dreamt of in your philosophy," said Mr. Aiken Drum.

"Horatio?" inquired Madame Mastaba.

At this moment the music left off, and a galleon-like ship, manned in statuesque poses by a crew of perhaps a dozen men, moved slowly from behind the orchestra's island into the center of the pool; the spectators could see for an instant the outstretched hands of a number of waiters, porters and bellhops who must have given it a strong push. This ship came to a stop on the still water, its paper sails billowed out as though with a stiff breeze. One could see it wholly, down to the keel, seeming to hang in a medium scarcely existing, so clear and smooth the water; and down below the mermaids slowly swam about.

Now in the silence there broke forth the sound of a number of pianos dispersed around the place, a loud, confused rumbling and tinkling and clanging; and a blond young man climbed to the high poop of the vessel, placed one hand over his heart and, in the crook of the elbow thus formed, the golden crown he had been wearing. So poised, he began half to sing and half to declaim a long recitative interwoven with passages of balladry, to which the pianos formed a remote and intermittently allusive background. Because of those pianos and becausee of the fact that the young man did not sing extraordinarily well—he looked stupid, unhappy and rather helpless despite his breastplate, crown, scepter and golden hair—the group at the table did not easily distinguish at first what he was singing about; Felicia thought possibly he sung in German or some other foreign tongue. Presently, however, she got used to it, and it became clear that he was a prince "from an island beyond the foam" and that his wicked stepmother had prevailed with the king his father to have him exiled. Not only this, but because of his father's power no other nation would give him refuge, and in all the wide world he had only this ship for home, to sail the seas with till he died. His song was very lonely and sad even though he did not sing well, and presently the mermaids themselves rose to the surface and poked their heads through to listen. ("Ah," said the Marquess with satisfaction, as though he had been holding his own breath. "They are real nevertheless," said Madame Mastaba.)

And now there came through the clear water from the coral castle in the distance a new mermaid. This one wore, like the young prince, a crown, and she too rose to the surface to hear his song. Upon seeing this creature the young man became more passionate in his declamation; nowhere in the world, on land or at sea, was there woman half so beautiful as she. He stretched forth his scepter, and in a burst of exalted and flourishing song declared that she alone must be his bride. The pianos rumbled loudly at this.

"He is quite Wagnerian, with his bare knees," said Mr. le Mesurier.

The mermaid princess now made her reply, singing in a voice cool and steady as a night wind off the water. She was indeed a beautiful woman, or mermaid, with very white skin and with long, black hair which even though wet curled in reptilian folds about her breasts and back. She would be his bride, she sang, but she could never leave the sea which was her home. She pitied his exile, but alas, they were doomed, the two of them, to eternal separation by the elements they breathed.

The young prince, hearing this, declared, still singing, that if he could not have her to wife the world held nothing more to please him—an exile and alone, condemned to sail forever across the seven seas. To have her love what might he better do than die, so be he died in her white arms? All this he sang in a voice which was evidently becoming somewhat distressed with fatigue.

The mermaid princess sternly yet perhaps a little coyly forbade him the death he so eloquently sought; while she sang she provocatively waved those white arms, making her breasts move just below the surface of the water. The hero, with an artificial vehemence and ferocity very convincing, insisted. She again imperiously denied. This went on, in the form of a duet, for some time.

"It is a little boring, *tout ce* Papageno-Papagena," said Madame Mastaba, "but the spectacle is brilliant."

Felicia agreed. Charmed at first, she had very quickly become bored as the two lovers passed this theme back and forth between them, while the pianos went on like stones bouncing down a hill. The whole scene rapidly began to seem ridiculous, not least because the labored healthy earnestness of the young man contrasted so unfavorably with the cool, queenly demeanor and effortless voice of the mermaid. Because she was bored, Felicia paid, finally, not much heed to the course of all these antics, and was in fact lighting a cigarette at just the moment when—with a theatrical scream of loving anguish and a somewhat awkward splash—the young prince cast away scepter and crown and leapt into the water, into the embrace of his mermaid sweetheart. And she? What did she do? Felicia was quite in time to see that she, her long white arms fixed firmly around her lover's middle, her silver tail flashing in one powerful turn and dive, dragged him away below. The audience, leaning over the edge of the pool, had a clear view of his silent writhings, kicking and strugglings, accompanied by chains of bubbles from the air in his clothing and one final chain of bubbles from the air in his lungs; after this—it had taken over a minute—he lay still at the entrance of the coral castle, until presently a cortege of mermaids swam down and carried him away, while on distant pianos empty octaves bounded angrily up and down their deserted, echoing stairwells. Then all was over, and the underwater light began to fade. It was oddly noticeable that scepter and crown, made of some light materials, still floated on the surface; but soon all was dark on the water, dark and opaque and resuming the reflexion of the moonlight.

"So you see," said Madame Mastaba, laughing, to the Marquess, "the mermaids were real, after all."

Felicia saw that her husband had got very red in the face. So he had not been expecting it either, she thought, and made herself smile as at some remote and secret thought.

"How did you like it, my dear?" inquired Mr. le Mesurier, putting his bony old hand upon hers. Felicia turned the smile in his direction.

"I thought it was quite sweet, really," she said, "but maybe just a little too long."

Mr. Aiken Drum coughed.

"It is doubtless on account of the expense," he said. "They prolong it deliberately, to make the most of the materials."

"I find it," said Mr. le Mesurier, "an ominously romantic conception. That is, after all, not the kind of world we live in today. It is more like—like this Valkyrie's headpiece," he added, indicating the Marquess's helmet with the horsehair crest.

"Ah, but there will always be romance," said Madame Mastaba profoundly sighing. "No matter what they do to the poor world, there will be romance."

"It is hard to believe," said Mr. Aiken Drum, "it is hard to believe that we are at war once again. Reality is harsh, after this fairyland." He gestured broadly toward the dark pool beside them.

"It cannot go on forever," said Mr. le Mesurier. "Before we know it we shall meet again, perhaps here in this very place."

"We are old," said Madame Mastaba. "The world may never again be as we know it. But there will be romance for the young, will there not, Felicia?"

But Felicia had not heard. She sat very straight, with the smile of a great lady playing distantly upon her face, and was caught in a vision, wherein she saw her husband and herself, he wearing the helmet that lay there on the table, flying alone in the silent aircraft, high in the dark night, back to the stone towers and the stately trees of Yore. In her mind's eye, then, she saw herself walking endlessly through silent corridors hung with portraits, and down the sweeping curve of a grand staircase, all in the silence. The silence continued, it seemed for years.

"What are you thinking, my dear?" asked the Marquess. Abruptly Felicia came to the surface of her dream.

"I was thinking," she said with a laugh both grand and gay, "that if there's anything in the world I love, it's reality."

And though the Marquess seemed confused for a moment, the elders laughed indulgently. Then they all had more of the bitter wine from seaweed.

(From *The Kenyon Review*)

A CIRCLE IN THE FIRE

BY FLANNERY O'CONNOR

SOMETIMES the last line of trees was a solid grey blue wall a little darker than the sky but this afternoon it was almost black and behind it the sky was a livid glaring white. "You know that woman that had that baby in that iron lung?" Mrs. Pritchard said. She and the child's mother were underneath the window the child was looking down from. Mrs. Pritchard was leaning against the chimney, her arms folded on a shelf of stomach, one foot crossed and the toe pointed into the ground. She was a large woman with a small pointed face and steady ferreting eyes. Mrs. Cope was the opposite, very small and trim, with a large round face and black eyes that seemed to be enlarging all the time behind her thick glasses as if she were continually being astonished. She was squatting down pulling grass out of the border beds around the house. Both of them had on sunhats that had once been identical but Mrs. Pritchard's was faded and out of shape while Mrs. Cope's was still stiff and bright green.

"I read about her," she said.

"She was a Pritchard that married a Brookins and so's kin to me—about my seventh or eighth cousin by marriage."

"Well, well," Mrs. Cope muttered and threw a large clump of nut grass behind her. She worked at the weeds and nut grass as if they were an evil sent directly by the devil to destroy the place.

"Beinst she was kin to us, we gone to see the body," Mrs. Pritchard said. "Seen the little baby too."

Mrs. Cope didn't say anything. She was used to these calamitous stories; she said they wore her to a frazzle. Mrs. Pritchard would go thirty miles for the satisfaction of seeing someone laid away. Mrs. Cope always changed the subject to something cheerful but the child had observed that this only put Mrs. Pritchard in a bad humor.

The child thought the blank sky looked as if it were pushing against the fortress fall, trying to break through. The trees across the near field were a patchwork of grey and yellow greens. Mrs. Cope was always worrying about fires in her woods. When the nights were very windy, she would say to the child, "Oh Lord, do pray there won't be any fires, it's so windy," and the child would grunt from behind her book or not answer at all because she heard it so often. In the evenings in the summer when they sat on the porch, Mrs. Cope would say to the child who was reading fast to catch the last light, "Get up and look at the sunset, it's gorgeous. You ought to get up and look at it," and the child would scowl and not answer or glare up once across the lawn and two front pastures to the grey blue sentinel line of trees and then begin to read again with no change of expression, sometimes muttering for meanness, "It looks like a fire. You better get up and smell around and see if the woods ain't on fire."

"She had her arm around it in the coffin," Mrs. Pritchard went on, but her voice was drowned out by the sound of the tractor that the Negro, Culver, was driving up the road from the barn. The wagon was attached and another Negro was sitting in the back, bouncing, his feet jogging about a foot from the ground. The one on the tractor drove it past the gate that led into the field on the left.

Mrs. Cope turned her head and saw that he had not gone through the gate because he was too lazy to get off and open it. He was going the long way around at her expense. "Tell him to stop and come here!" she shouted.

Mrs. Pritchard heaved herself from the chimney and waved her arm in a fierce circle but he pretended not to hear. She stalked to the edge of the lawn and screamed, "Get off, I toljer! She wants you!"

He got off and started toward the chimney, pushing his head and shoulders forward at each step to give the appearance of hurrying. His head was thrust up to the top in a white cloth hat striated with different shades of sweat. The brim was down and hid all but the lower parts of his reddish eyes.

Mrs. Cope was on her knees, pointing the trowel into the ground, "Why aren't you going through the gate there?" she asked and waited, her eyes shut and her mouth stretched flat as if she were prepared for any ridiculous answer.

"Got to raise the blade on the mower if we do," he said and his gaze bore just to the left of her. Her Negroes were as destructive and impersonal as the nut grass.

Her eyes, as she opened them, looked as if they would keep on enlarging until they turned her wrongsideout. "Raise it," she said and pointed across the road with the trowel.

He moved off.

"It's nothing to them," she said. "They don't have to pay for the gas. It's nothing to anybody but the one with the responsibility. I thank the Lord all these things don't come at once. They'd destroy me."

"Yeah, they would," Mrs. Pritchard shouted against the sound of the tractor. He opened the gate and raised the blade and drove through and down into the field; the noise diminished as the wagon disappeared. "I don't see myself how she had it *in* it," she went on in her normal voice.

Mrs. Cope was bent over, digging fiercely at the nut grass again. "We have a lot to be thankful for," she said. "Every day you should say a prayer of thanksgiving. Do you do that?"

"Yes'm," Mrs. Pritchard said. "See she was in it four months before she even got thataway. Look like to me if I was in one of them, I would leave off . . . how you reckon they. . . ."

"Every day I say a prayer of thanksgiving," Mrs. Cope said. "Think of all we have. Lord," she said and sighed, "we have everything," and she looked around at her rich pastures and hills that were heavy with timber and shook her head as if it all might be a burden she was trying to shake off her back.

Mrs. Pritchard studied the woods. "All I got is four abscess teeth," she remarked.

"Well, be thankful you don't have five," Mrs. Cope snapped and threw back a clump of grass. "We might all be destroyed by a hurricane. I can always find something to be thankful for."

Mrs. Pritchard took up a hoe resting against the side of the house and struck lightly at a weed that had come up between two bricks in the chimney. "Yeah?" she said, her voice a little more nasal than usual with contempt.

"Why, think of all those poor Europeans," Mrs. Cope went on, "that they put in boxcars like cattle and rode them to Siberia. Lord," she said, "we ought to spend half our time on our knees."

"I know if I was in an iron lung there would be some things I wouldn't do," Mrs. Pritchard said, scratching her bare ankle with the end of the hoe.

"Even that poor woman had plenty to be thankful for," Mrs. Cope said.

"She could be thankful she wasn't dead."

"Certainly," Mrs. Cope said, and then she pointed the trowel up at Mrs. Pritchard and said, "I have the best kept place in the county and do you know why? Because I work. I've had to work to save this place and work to keep it." She emphasized each word with the trowel. "I don't let anything get ahead of me and I'm not always looking for trouble. I take it as it comes."

"If it all come at oncet sometime," Mrs. Pritchard began.

"It doesn't all come at once," Mrs. Cope said sharply.

The child could see over to where the dirt road joined the highway. She saw a pick-up truck stop at the gate and let off three boys who started walking up the pink dirt road. They walked single-file, the middle one bent to the side carrying a black pig-shaped valise.

"Well, if it ever did," Mrs. Pritchard said, "it wouldn't be nothing you could do but fling your hands."

Mrs. Cope didn't even answer this. Mrs. Pritchard folded her arms and gazed down the road as if she could easily enough see all these fine hills flattened to nothing. She saw the three boys who had almost reached the front walk by now. "Lookit yonder," she said. "Who you reckon they are?"

Mrs. Cope leaned back and supported herself with one hand behind her and looked. The three came toward them but as if they were going to walk on through the side of the house. The one with the suitcase was in front now. Finally about four feet from her, he stopped and set it down. The three boys looked something alike except that the middle-sized one wore silver-rimmed spectacles and carried the suitcase. One of his eyes had a slight cast to it so that his gaze seemed to be coming from two directions at once as if it had them surrounded. He had on a sweat shirt with a faded destroyer printed on it but his chest was so hollow that the destroyer was broken in the middle and seemed on the point of going under. His hair was stuck to his forehead with sweat. He looked to be about thirteen. All three boys had white penetrating stares. "I don't reckon you remember me, Mrs. Cope," he said.

"Your face is certainly familiar," she said, scrutinizing him, "now let's see. . . ."

"My daddy used to work here," he hinted.

"Boyd?" she said. "Your father was Mr. Boyd and you're J. C.?"

"Nome, I'm Powell, the secont one, only I've growed some since then and my daddy he's daid now. Done died."

"Dead. Well I declare," Mrs. Cope said as if death were always an unusual thing. "What was Mr. Boyd's trouble?"

One of Powell's eyes seemed to be making a circle of the place, examining the house and the white water tower behind it and chicken houses and the pastures that rolled away on either side until they met the first line of woods. The other eye looked at her. "Died in Florda," he said and began kicking the valise.

"Well, I declare," she murmured. After a second she said, "And how is your mother?"

"Mah'd again." He kept watching his foot kick the suitcase. The other two boys stared at her impatiently.

"And where do you all live now?" she asked.

"Atlanta," he said. "You know, out to one of them developments."

"Well, I see," she said, "I see." After a second she said it again. Finally she asked, "And who are these other boys?" and smiled at them.

"Garfield Smith him, and W. T. Harper him," he said nodding his head backward first in the direction of the large boy and then the small one.

"How do you boys do?" Mrs. Cope said. "This is Mrs. Pritchard. Mr. and Mrs. Pritchard work here now."

They ignored Mrs. Pritchard who watched them with steady beady eyes. The three seemed to hang there, waiting, watching Mrs. Cope.

"Well, well," she said, glancing at the suitcase, "it's nice of you to stop and see me. I think that was real sweet of you."

Powell's stare seemed to pinch her like a pair of tongs. "Come back to see how you was doing," he said hoarsely.

"Listen here," the smallest boy said, "all the time we been knowing him he's been telling us about this here place. Said it was everything here. Said it was horses here. Said he had the best time of his entire life right here on this here place. Talks about it all the time."

"Never shuts his trap about his place," the big boy grunted, drawing his arm across his nose as if to muffle his words.

"Always talking about them horses he rid here," the small one continued, "and said he would let us ride them too. Said it was one name Gene."

Mrs. Cope was always afraid someone would get hurt on her place and sue her for everything she had. "They aren't shod," she said quickly. "There was one named Gene but he's dead now but I'm afraid you boys can't ride the horses because they aren't shod and they're in the pasture and I'm afraid you might get hurt. They're dangerous," she said, speaking very fast.

The large boy sat down on the ground with a noise of disgust and began to finger rocks out of his tennis shoe. The small one darted looks here and there and Powell fixed her with his stare and didn't say anything.

After a minute the little boy said, "Say, lady, you know what he said one time? He said when he died he wanted to come here!"

For a second Mrs. Cope looked blank; then she blushed; then a peculiar look of pain came over her face as she realized that these children were hungry. They were staring because they were hungry! She almost gasped in their faces, and then she asked them quickly if they would have something to eat. They said they would but their expressions, composed and unsatisfied, didn't lighten any. They looked as if they were used to being hungry.

The child upstairs had grown red in the face with excitement. She was kneeling down by the window so that only her eyes and forehead showed over the sill. Mrs. Cope told the boys to come around on the other side of the house where the lawn chairs were and she led the way and Mrs. Pritchard followed. The child moved from the right bedroom across the hall and over into the left bedroom and looked down on the other side of the house where there were three white lawn chairs and a red hammock strung between two hazelnut trees. She was a pale fat girl of twelve with a frowning squint and a large mouth full of silver bands. She knelt down at the window.

The three boys came around the corner of the house and the large one threw himself into the hammock and lit a stub of cigaret. The small boy tumbled down on the grass next to the black suitcase and rested his head on it and Powell sat down on the edge of one of the chairs and looked as if he were trying to enclose the whole place in one encircling stare. The child heard her mother and Mrs. Pritchard in a muted conference in the kitchen. She got up and went out into the hall and leaned over the banisters.

Mrs. Cope's and Mrs. Pritchard's legs were facing each other in the back hall. "Those poor children are hungry," Mrs. Cope said in a dead voice.

"You seen that suitcase?" Mrs. Pritchard asked. "What if they intend to spend the night with you?"

Mrs. Cope gave a slight shriek. "I can't have three boys in here with only me and Sally Virginia," she said. "I'm sure they'll go when I feed them."

"I only know they got a suitcase," Mrs. Pritchard said.

The child hurried back to the window. The large boy was stretched out in the hammock with his wrists crossed under his head and the cigaret stub in the center of his mouth. He spit it out in an arc just as Mrs. Cope came around the corner of the house with a plate of crackers. She stopped instantly as if a snake had been slung in her path. "Ashfield!" she said, "please pick that up. I'm afraid of fires."

"Gawfield!" the little boy shouted indignantly, "Gawfield!"

The large boy raised himself without a word and lumbered for the butt. He picked it up and put it in his pocket and stood with his back to her, examining a tattooed heart on his forearm. Mrs. Pritchard came up holding three Coca-Colas by the necks in one hand and gave one to each of them.

"I remember everything about this place," Powell said, looking down the opening of his bottle.

"Where did you all go when you left here?" Mrs. Cope asked and put the plate of crackers on the arm of his chair.

He looked at it but didn't take one. He said, "I remember it was one name Gene and it was one name George. We gone to Florda and my daddy he, you know, died, and then we gone to my sister's and then my mother she, you know, mah'd, and we been there ever since."

"There are some crackers," Mrs. Cope said and sat down in the chair across from him.

"He don't like it in Atlanta," the little boy said, sitting up and reaching indifferently for a cracker. "He ain't ever satisfied with where he's at except this place here. Lemme tell you what he'll do, lady. We'll be playing ball, see, on this here place in this development we got to play ball on, see, and he'll quit playing and say, 'Goddam, it was a horse down there name Gene and if I had him here I'd bust this concrete to hell riding him!' "

"I'm sure Powell doesn't use words like that, do you Powell?" Mrs. Cope said.

"No, mam," Powell said. His head was turned completely to the side as if he were listening for the horses in the field.

"I don't like them kind of crackers," the little boy said and returned his to the plate and got up.

Mrs. Cope shifted in her chair. "So you boys live in one of those nice new developments," she said.

"The only way you can tell your own is by smell," the small boy volunteered. "They're four stories high and there's ten of them, one behind the other. Let's go see them horses," he said.

Powell turned his pinching stare on Mrs. Cope. "We thought we would just spend the night in your barn," he said. "My uncle brought us this far on his pick-up truck and he's going to stop for us again in the morning."

There was a moment in which she didn't say a thing and the child in the window thought: she's going to fly out of that chair and hit the tree.

"Well, I'm afraid you can't do that," she said, getting up suddenly. "The barn's full of hay and I'm afraid of fire from your cigarets."

"We won't smoke," he said.

"I'm afraid you can't spend the night there just the same," she repeated as if she were talking politely to a gangster.

"Well we can camp out in the woods then," the little boy said.

"We brought our own blankets anyways. That's what we got in thatere suitcase. Come on."

"In the woods!" she said, "Oh no! The woods are very dry now, I can't have people smoking in my woods. You'll have to camp out in the field, in this field here next to the house, where there aren't any trees."

"Where she can keep her eye on you," the child said under her breath.

"Her woods," the large boy muttered and got out of the hammock.

"We'll sleep in the field," Powell said but not particularly as if he were talking to her. "This afternoon I'm going to show them about this place." The other two were already walking away and he got up and bounded after them and the two women sat with the black suitcase between them.

"Not no thank-you, not no nothing," Mrs. Pritchard remarked.

"They only played with what we gave them to eat," Mrs. Cope said in a hurt voice.

"Maybe they don't like soft drinks," Mrs. Pritchard muttered.

"They certainly *looked* hungry," Mrs. Cope said.

About sunset they appeared out of the woods, dirty and sweating, and came to the back porch and asked for water. They did not ask for food but Mrs. Cope could tell that they wanted it. "All I have is some cold guinea," she said. "Would you boys like some guinea and some sandwiches?"

"I wouldn't eat nothing bald-headed like a guinea," the little boy said. "I would eat a chicken or a turkey but not no guinea."

"Dog wouldn't eat one of them," the large boy said. He had taken off his shirt and stuck it in the back of his trousers like a tail. Mrs. Cope carefully avoided looking at him. The little boy had a cut on his arm.

"You boys haven't been riding the horses when I asked you not to, have you?" she asked suspiciously and they all said, "No mam!" at once in loud enthusiastic voices like the Amens that are said in country churches.

She went into the house and made them sandwiches and, while she did it, she held a conversation with them from inside the kitchen, asking where they went to school and what their fathers did and how many brothers and sisters they had. They answered in short explosive sentences, pushing each other's shoulders and doubling up with laughter as if the questions had meanings that she didn't know about. "And does you mother work, Powell?" she called.

"She ast you does your mother work!" the little boy yelled. "His mind's affected by them horses he only looked at," he said. "His mother she works at a factory and leaves him home to mind the rest of them only he don't mind them much. Lemme tell you, lady, one time he locked his little brother in a box and set it on fire."

"I'm sure Powell wouldn't do a thing like that," she said, coming out with the plate of sandwiches and setting it down on the step. They emptied the plate at once and she picked it up and stood holding it, looking at the sun which was going down in front of them, almost on top of the tree line. It was swollen and flame-colored and hung in a net of ragged cloud as if it might burn through any second and fall into the woods. From the upstairs window the child saw her shiver and catch both arms to her sides. "We have so much to be thankful for," she said suddenly in a mournful marvelling tone. "Do you boys thank God every night for all He's done for you? Do you thank Him for everything?"

This put an instant hush over them. They bit into the sandwiches as if they had lost all taste for food.

"Do you?" she persisted.

They were as silent as thieves hiding. They chewed without a sound.

"Well, I know I do," she said at length and turned and went back in the house and the child watched their shoulders drop. The large one stretched his legs out as if he were releasing himself from a trap. The sun burned so fast that it seemed to be trying to set everything in sight on fire. The white water tower was glazed pink and the grass was an unnatural green as if it were turning to glass. The child suddenly stuck her head far out the window and said, "Uggggrhhh," in a loud voice, crossing her eyes and hanging her tongue out as far as possible as if she were going to vomit.

The large boy looked up and stared at her. "Jesus," he growled, "another woman."

She dropped back from the window and stood with her back against the wall, squinting fiercely as if she had been slapped in the face and couldn't see who had done it. As soon as they left the steps, she came down into the kitchen where Mrs. Cope was washing the dishes. "If I had that big boy down I'd beat the daylight out of him," she said.

"You keep away from those boys," Mrs. Cope said, turning sharply. "Ladies don't beat the daylight out of people. You keep out of their way. They'll be gone in the morning."

But in the morning they were not gone.

When she went out on the porch after breakfast, they were standing around the back door, kicking the steps. They were smelling the bacon she had had for her breakfast. "Why, boys!" she said, "I thought you were going to meet your uncle." They had the same look of hardened hunger that had pained her yesterday but today she felt faintly provoked.

The big boy turned his back at once and the small one squatted down and began to scratch in the sand. "We ain't, though," Powell said.

The big boy turned his head just enough to take in a small section of her and said, "We ain't bothering nothing of yours."

He couldn't see the way her eyes enlarged but he could take note of the significant silence. After a minute she said in an altered voice, "Would you boys care for some breakfast?"

"We got plenty of our own food," the big boy said. "We don't want nothing of yours."

She kept her eyes on Powell. His thin white face seemed to confront but not actually to see her. "You boys know that I'm glad to have you," she said, "but I expect you to behave. I expect you to act like gentlemen."

They stood there, each looking in a different direction, as if they were waiting for her to leave. "After all," she said in a suddenly high voice, "this is my place."

The big boy made some ambiguous noise and they turned and walked off toward the barn, leaving her there with a shocked look as if she had had a searchlight thrown on her in the middle of the night.

In a little while Mrs. Pritchard came over and stood in the kitchen door with her cheek against the edge of it. "I reckon you know they rode them horses all yesterday afternoon," she said. "Stole a bridle out of the saddle room and rode bareback, because Hollis seen them. He runnum out the barn at nine o'clock last night and then he runnum out at ten and they was smoking both times and then he runnum out the milk room this morning and there was milk all over their mouths like they had been drinking out the cans."

"I cannot have this," Mrs. Cope said and stood at the sink with both fists knotted at her sides. "I cannot have this," and her expression was the same as when she tore at the nut grass.

"There ain't a thing you can do about it," Mrs. Pritchard said. "What I expect is you'll have them for a week or so until school begins. They just figure to have themselves a vacation in the country and there ain't nothing you can do but fold your hands."

"I do not fold my hands," Mrs. Cope said. "Tell Mr. Pritchard to put the horses up in the stalls."

"He's already did that. You take a boy thirteen year old is equal in meanness to a man twicet his age. It's no telling what he'll think up to do. You never know where he'll strike next. This morning Hollis seen them behind the bull pen and that big one ast if it wasn't some place they could wash at and Hollis said no it wasn't and that you didn't want no boys dropping cigaret butts in your woods and he said, 'She don't own them woods,' and Hollis said, 'She does too,' and that there little one he said, 'Man, Gawd owns them woods and her too,' and that there one with the glasses said, 'I reckon she owns the sky over this place too,' and that there littlest one says, 'Owns the sky and can't no airplane go over here without she says so,' and then the big one says, 'I never seen a place with so many damn women on it, how do you stand it here?' and Hollis said he had done had enough of their big talk by then and he turned and walked off without giving no reply one way or the other."

"I'm going out there and tell those boys they can get a ride away from here on the milk truck," Mrs. Cope said and she went out the back door, leaving Mrs. Pritchard and the child together in the kitchen.

"Listen," the child said. "I could handle them quicker than that."

"Yeah?" Mrs. Pritchard murmured, giving her a long leering

look, "how'd you handle them?"

The child gripped both hands together and made a contorted face as if she were strangling someone.

"They'd handle you," Mrs. Pritchard said with satisfaction.

The child retired to the upstairs window to get out of her way and looked down where her mother was walking off from the three boys who were squatting under the water tower, eating something out of a cracker box. She heard her come in the kitchen door and say, "They say they'll go on the milk truck, and no wonder they aren't hungry—the have that suitcase half full of food."

"Likely stole every bit of it too," Mrs. Pritchard said.

When the milk truck came, the three boys were nowhere in sight, but as soon as it left without them their three faces appeared, looking out of the opening in the top of the calf barn. "Can you beat this?" Mrs. Cope said, standing at one of the upstairs windows with her hands at her hips. "It's not that I wouldn't be glad to have them—it's their attitude."

"You never like nobody's attitude," the child said. "I'll go tell them they got five minutes to leave here in."

"You are not to go anywhere near those boys, do you hear me?" Mrs. Cope said.

"Why?" the child asked.

"I'm going out there and give them a piece of my mind," Mrs. Cope said.

The child took over the position in the window and in a few minutes she saw the stiff green hat catching the glint of the sun as her mother crossed the road toward the calf barn. The three faces immediately disappeared from the opening, and in a second the large boy dashed across the lot, followed an instant later by the other two. Mrs. Pritchard came out and the two women started for the grove of trees the boys had vanished into. Presently the two sunhats disappeared in the woods and the three boys came out at the left side of it and ambled across the field and into another patch of woods. By the time Mrs. Cope and Mrs. Pritchard reached the field, it was empty and there was nothing for them to do but come home again.

Mrs. Cope had not been inside long before Mrs. Pritchard came running toward the house, shouting something. "They've let out the bull!" she hollered, "let out the bull!" And in a second she was followed by the bull himself, ambling, black and leisurely, with four geese hissing at his heels. He was not mean until hurried and it took Mr. Pritchard and the two Negroes a half hour to ease him back to his pen. While the men were engaged in this, the boys let the oil out of the three tractors and then disappeared again into the woods.

Two blue veins had come out on either side of Mrs. Cope's forehead and Mrs. Pritchard observed them with satisfaction. "Like I toljer," she said, "there ain't a thing you can do about it."

Mrs. Cope ate her dinner hastily, not conscious that she had her sunhat on. Every time she heard a noise, she jumped up. Mrs. Pritchard came over immediately after dinner and said, "Well, you want to know where they are now?" and smiled in an omniscient rewarded way.

"I want to know at once," Mrs. Cope said, coming to an almost military attention.

"Down to the road, throwing rocks at your mailbox," Mrs. Pritchard said, leaning comfortably in the door. "Done already about knocked it off its stand."

"Get in the car," Mrs. Cope said.

The child got in too and the three of them drove down the road to the gate. The boys were sitting on the embankment on the other side of the highway, aiming rocks across the road at the mailbox. Mrs. Cope stopped the car almost directly beneath them and looked up out of her window. The three of them stared at her as if they had never seen her before, the large boy with a sullen glare, the small one glint-eyed and unsmiling, and Powell with his two-sided glassed gaze hanging vacantly over the crippled destroyer on his shirt.

"Powell," she said, "I'm sure your mother would be ashamed of you," and she stopped and waited for this to make its effect. His face seemed to twist slightly but he continued to look through her at nothing in particular.

"Now I've put up with this as long as I can," she said. "I've tried to be nice to you boys. Haven't I been nice to you boys?"

They might have been three statues except that the big one, barely opening his mouth, said, "We're not even on your side the road, lady."

"There ain't a thing you can do about it," Mrs. Pritchard hissed loudly. The child was sitting on the back seat close to the side. She had a furious outraged look on her face but she kept her head drawn back from the window so that they couldn't see her.

Mrs. Cope spoke slowly, emphasizing every word. "I think I have been very nice to you boys. I've fed you twice. Now I'm going into town and if you're still here when I come back, I'll call the sheriff," and with this, she drove off. The child, turning quickly so that she could see out the back window, observed that they had not moved; they had not even turned their heads.

"You done angered them now," Mrs. Pritchard said, "and it ain't any telling what they'll do."

"They'll be gone when we get back," Mrs. Cope said.

Mrs. Pritchard could not stand an anticlimax. She required the taste of blood from time to time to keep her equilibrium. When they returned from town, the boys were not on the embankment and she said, "I would rather to see them than not to see them. When you see them you know what they're doing."

"Ridiculous," Mrs. Cope muttered. "I've scared them and they've gone and now we can forget them."

"I ain't forgetting them," Mrs. Pritchard said. "I wouldn't be none surprised if they didn't have a gun in that there suitcase."

Mrs. Cope prided herself on the way she handled the type of mind that Mrs. Pritchard had. When Mrs. Pritchard saw signs and omens, she exposed them calmly for the figments of imagination that they were, but this afternoon her nerves were taut and she said, "Now I've had about enough of this. Those boys are gone and that's that."

"Well, we'll wait and see," Mrs. Pritchard said.

Everything was quiet for the rest of the afternoon but at supper time, Mrs. Pritchard came over to say that she had heard a high vicious laugh pierce out of the bushes near the hog pen. It was an evil laugh, full of calculated meanness, and she had heard it come three times, herself, distinctly.

"I haven't heard a thing," Mrs. Cope said.

"I look for them to strike just after dark," Mrs. Pritchard said.

That night Mrs. Cope and the child sat on the porch until nearly ten o'clock and nothing happened. The only sounds came from tree frogs and from one whippoorwill who called faster and faster from the same spot of darkness as if he had forgotten what the danger was but remembered the warning. "They've gone," Mrs. Cope said, "poor things," and she began to tell the child how much they had to be thankful for, for she said they might have had to live in a development themselves or they might have been Negroes or they might have been in iron lungs or they might have been Europeans ridden in boxcars like cattle, and she began a litany of her blessings, in a stricken voice, that the child, straining her attention for a sudden shriek in the dark, didn't listen to.

There was no sign of them the next morning either. The fortress line of trees was a hard granite blue, the wind had risen overnight and the sun had come up a pale gold. The season was changing. Even a small change in the weather made Mrs. Cope thankful, but when the seasons changed she seemed almost frightened at her good fortune in escaping whatever it was that pursued her. As she sometimes did when one thing was finished and another about to begin, she turned her attention to the child, who had put on a pair of overalls over her dress and had pulled a man's old felt hat down as far as it would go on her head and was arming herself with two pistols in a decorated holster that she had fastened around her waist. The hat was very tight and seemed to be squeezing the redness into her face. It came down almost to the tops of her glasses. Mrs. Cope watched her with a tragic look. "Why do you have to look like an idiot?" she asked. "Suppose company were to come? When are you going to grow up? What's going to become of you? I look at you and I want to cry! Sometimes you look like you might belong to Mrs. Pritchard!"

"Leave me be," the child said in a high irritated voice. "Leave me be. Just leave me be. I ain't you," and she went off to the woods as if she were stalking out an enemy, her head thrust forward and each hand gripped on a gun.

Mrs. Pritchard came over, sour-humored, because she didn't have anything calamitous to report. "I got the misery in my face today," she said, holding on to what she could salvage. "Theseyer teeth. They each one feel like an individual boil."

The child crashed through the woods, making the fallen leaves sound ominous under her feet. The sun had risen a little and was only a white hole like an opening for the wind to escape through in a sky a little darker than itself, and the tops of the trees were black against the glare. "I'm going to get you," she said. "I'm going to get you one by one and beat you black and blue. Line up. LINE UP!" she said and waved one of the pistols at a cluster of long bare-trunked pines, four times her height, as she passed them. She kept moving, muttering and growling to herself and occasionally hitting out with one of the guns at a branch that got in her way. From time to time she stopped to remove the thorn vine that caught at her shirt and she would say, "Leave me be, I told you. Leave me be," and give it a crack with the pistol and then stalk on.

Presently she sat down on a stump to cool off but she planted both feet carefully and firmly on the ground. She lifted them and put them down several times, grinding them fiercely into the dirt as if she were crushing something under her heels. Suddenly she heard a laugh.

She sat up, prickle-skinned. It came again. She heard the sound of splashing and she stood up, uncertain which way to run. She was not far from where this patch of woods ended and the back pasture began. She eased toward the pasture, careful not to make a sound, and coming suddenly to the edge of it, she saw the three boys, not twenty feet away, washing in the cow trough. Their clothes were piled against the black valise out of reach of the water that flowed over the side of the tank. The large boy was standing up and the small one was trying to climb onto his shoulders. Powell was sitting down looking straight ahead through glasses that were splashed with water. He was not paying any attention to the other two. The trees must have looked like green waterfalls through his wet glasses. The child stood partly hidden behind a pine trunk, the side of her face pressed into the bark.

"I wish I lived here!" the little boy shouted, balancing with his knees clutched around the big one's head.

"I'm goddam glad I don't," the big boy panted, and jumped up to dislodge him.

Powell sat without moving, without seeming to know that the other two were behind him, and looked straight ahead like a ghost sprung upright in his coffin. "If this place was not here anymore," he said, "you would never have to think of it again."

"Listen," the big boy said, sitting down quietly in the water with the little one still moored to his shoulders, "it don't belong to nobody."

"It's ours," the little boy said.

The child behind the tree did not move.

Powell jumped out of the trough and began to run. He ran all the way around the field as if something were after him and as he passed the tank coming back, the other two jumped out and raced with him, the sun glinting on their long wet bodies. The big one ran the fastest and was the leader. They dashed around the field twice and finally dropped down by their clothes and lay there with their ribs moving up and down. After a while, the big one said hoarsely, "Do you know what I would do with this place if I had the chance?"

"No, what?" the little boy said and sat up to give him his full attention.

"I'd build a big parking lot on it, or something," he muttered.

They began to dress. The sun made two white spots on Powell's glasses and blotted out his eyes. "I know what let's do," he said. He took something small from his pocket and showed it to them. For almost a minute they sat looking at what he had in his hand. Then without any more discussion, Powell picked up the suitcase and they got up and moved past the child and entered the woods not ten feet from where she was standing, slightly away from the tree now, with the imprint of the bark embossed red and white on the side of her face.

She watched with a dazed stare as they stopped and collected all the matches they had between them and began to set the brush on fire. They began to whoop and holler and beat their hands over their mouths and in a few seconds there was a narrow line of fire widening between her and them. While she stared, it reached up from the brush, snatching and biting at the lowest branches of the trees. The wind carried rags of it higher and the boys disappeared shrieking behind it.

She turned and tried to run across the field but her legs were too heavy and she stood there, weighted down with some new unplaced misery that she had never felt before. But finally she began to run.

Mrs. Cope and Mrs. Pritchard were in the field behind the

barn when Mrs. Cope saw smoke rising from the woods across the pasture. She shrieked and Mrs. Pritchard pointed up the road to where the child came loping heavily, screaming, "Mama, Mama, they're going to build a parking lot here!"

Mrs. Cope began to scream for the Negroes while Mrs. Pritchard, charged now, ran down the road shouting. Mr. Pritchard came out of the open end of the barn and the two Negroes stopped filling the manure spreader in the lot and started toward Mrs. Cope with their shovels. "Hurry, hurry!" she shouted, "start throwing dirt on it!" They passed her almost without looking at her and headed off slowly across the field toward the smoke. She ran after them a little way, charging them like a fierce dog, shrilling, "Hurry, hurry, don't you see it! Don't you see it!"

"It'll be there when we git there," Culver said and they thrust their shoulders forward a little and went on at the same pace.

The child came to a stop beside her mother and stared up at her face as if she had never seen it before. It was the face of the new misery she felt, but on her mother it looked old and it looked as if it might have belonged to anybody, a Negro or a European or to Powell himself. The child turned her head quickly, and past the Negroes' ambling figures she could see the grey column of smoke rising and widening unchecked inside the granite line of trees. She stood taut, listening, and could just catch in the distance a few wild high shrieks of joy as if the prophets were dancing in the fiery furnace, in the circle the angel had cleared for them. "I known a man oncet that his wife was poisoned by a child she had adopted out of pure kindness," she said.

(From The New Yorker)

TIP ON A DEAD JOCKEY

BY IRWIN SHAW

LLOYD BARBER was lying on his bed reading *France-Soir* when the phone rang. It was only two o'clock in the afternoon, but it was raining for the fifth consecutive day and he had no place to go anyway. He was reading about the relative standing of the teams in the Rugby leagues. He never went to Rugby games and he had no interest at all in the relative standings of Lille and Pau and Bordeaux, but he had finished everything else in the paper. It was cold in the small, dark room, because there was no heat provided between ten in the morning and six in the evening, and he lay on the lumpy double bed, his shoes off, covered with his overcoat.

He picked up the phone, and the man at the desk downstairs said, "There is a lady waiting for you here, M. Barber."

Barber squinted at himself in the mirror above the bureau across from the bed. He wished he was better-looking. "Did she give her name?" he asked.

"No, Monsieur. Should I demand it?"

"Never mind," Barber said. "I'll be right down."

He hung up the phone and put on his shoes. He always put the left one on first, for luck. He buttoned his collar and pulled his tie into place, noticing that it was frayed at the knot. He got into his jacket and patted his pockets to see if he had cigarettes. He had no cigarettes. He shrugged, and left the light on vindictively, because the manager was being unpleasant about the bill, and went downstairs.

Maureen Richardson was sitting in the little room off the lobby, in one of those age-colored plush chairs that fourth-rate Parisian hotels furnish their clientele to discourage excessive conviviality on the ground floor. None of the lamps was lit, and a dark, dead, greenish light filtered in through the dusty curtains from the rainy street outside. Maureen had been a young, pretty girl with bright, credulous blue eyes when Barber first met her, during the war, just before she married Jimmy Richardson. But she had had two children since then and Richardson hadn't done so well, and now she was wearing a worn cloth coat that was soaked, and her complexion had gone, and in the greenish lobby light she seemed bone-colored and her eyes were pale.

"Hello, Beauty," Barber said. Richardson always called her that, and while it had amused his friends in the squadron, he had loyally stuck to it, and finally everyone had picked it up.

Maureen turned around quickly, almost as though he had frightened her. "Lloyd," she said. "I'm so glad I found you in."

They shook hands, and Barber asked if she wanted to go someplace for a coffee.

"I'd rather not," Maureen said. "I left the kids with a friend for lunch and I promised I'd collect them at two-thirty and I don't have much time."

"Sure," Barber said. "How's Jimmy?"

"Oh, Lloyd . . ." Maureen pulled at her fingers, and Barber noticed that they were reddened and the nails were uneven. "Have you seen him?"

"What?" Barber peered through the gloom at her, puzzled. "What do you mean?"

"Have you seen him?" Maureen persisted. Her voice was thin and frightened.

"Not for a month or so," Barber said. "Why?" He asked it, but he almost knew why.

"He's gone, Lloyd," Maureen said. "He's been gone thirty-two days. I don't know what I'm going to do."

"Where did he go?" Barber asked.

"I don't know." Maureen took out a pack of cigarettes and lit one. She was too distracted to offer the pack to Barber. "He didn't tell me." She smoked the cigarette avidly but absently. "I'm so worried. I thought maybe he'd said something to you—or that you'd bumped into him."

"No," Barber said carefully. "He didn't say anything."

"It's the queerest thing. We've been married nearly ten years and he never did anything like this before," Maureen said, trying to control her voice. "He just came to me one night and he said he'd got leave of absence from his job for a month and that he'd be back inside of thirty days and he'd tell me all about it when he got back, and he begged me not to ask any questions."

"And you didn't ask any questions?"

"He was acting so strangely," Maureen said. "I'd never seen him like that before. All hopped up. Excited. You might even say happy, except that he kept going in all night to look at the kids. And he's never given me anything to worry about in the— the girl department," Maureen said primly. "Not like some of the other boys we know. And if there was one thing about Jimmy, it was that you could trust him. So I helped him pack."

"What did he take?"

"Just one Valpak," Maureen said. "With light clothes. As though he was going off on a summer vacation. He even took a tennis racket."

"A tennis racket." Barber nodded, as though it were the most natural thing in the world for husbands to take tennis rackets along when disappearing. "Did you hear from him at all?"

"No," Maureen said. "He told me he wouldn't write. Did you ever hear of anything like that?" Even in her anguish, she permitted herself a tone of wifely grievance. "I knew we shouldn't have come to Europe. It's different for you. You're not married and you were always kind of wild anyway, not like Jimmy—"

"Did you call his office?" Barber asked, interrupting. He didn't want to hear how wild people thought he was, or how unmarried.

"I had a friend call," Maureen said. "It would look too fishy— his wife calling to ask where he was."

"What did they say?"

"They said that they had expected him two days ago but he hadn't come in yet."

Barber took one of Maureen's cigarettes and lit it. It was the first one in four hours and it tasted wonderful. He had a little selfish twinge of gratitude that Maureen had come to his hotel.

"Lloyd, do you know anything?" Maureen asked, worn and shabby in her damp, thin coat in the foggy green light.

Barber hesitated. "No," he said. "But I'll put in a couple of calls and I'll telephone you tomorrow."

They both stood up. Maureen pulled on gloves over her reddened hands. The gloves were worn and greenish black. Looking at them, Barber suddenly remembered how neat and shining Maureen had been when they first met, in Louisiana, so many years before, and how healthy and well-dressed he and Jimmy and the others had been in their lieutenants' uniforms with the new wings on their breasts.

"Listen, Beauty," Barber said. "How are you fixed for dough?"

"I didn't come over for that," Maureen said firmly.

Barber took out his wallet and peered judiciously into it. It wasn't necessary. He knew exactly what was there. He took out a five-thousand-franc note. "Here," he said, handing it to her. "Try this on for size."

Maureen made a motion as though to give it back to him. "I really don't think I should . . ." she began.

"Sh-h-h, Beauty," Barber said. "There isn't an American girl in Paris who couldn't use five *mille* on a day like this."

Maureen sighed and put the bill in her pocketbook. "I feel terrible about taking your money, Lloyd."

Barber kissed her forehead. "In memory of the wild blue yonder," he said, pocketing the wallet, with its remaining fifteen thousand francs, which, as far as he knew, would have to last him for the rest of his life. "Jimmy'll give it back to me."

"Do you think he's all right?" Maureen asked, standing close to him.

"Of course," Lloyd said lightly and falsely. "There's nothing to worry about. I'll call you tomorrow. He'll probably be there, answering the phone, getting sore at me for sucking around his wife when he's out of town."

"I bet." Maureen smiled miserably. She went through the cavelike murk of the lobby, out into the rainy street, on her way to pick up the two children, who had been sent out to lunch at the home of a friend.

Barber went to his room and picked up the phone and waited for the old man downstairs to plug in. There were two suitcases standing open on the floor, with shirts piled in them, because there wasn't enough drawer space in the tiny bureau supplied by the hotel. On top of the bureau there were: a bill, marked overdue, from a tailor; a letter from his ex-wife, in New York, saying she had found an Army pistol of his in the bottom of a trunk and asking him what he wanted her to do with it, because she was afraid of the Sullivan Law; a letter from his mother, telling him to stop being a damn fool and come home and get a regular job; a letter from a woman in whom he was not interested, inviting him to come and stay with her in her villa near Eze, where it was beautiful and warm, she said, and where she needed a man around the house; a letter from a boy who had flown as his waist-gunner during the war and who insisted that Barber had saved his life when he was hit in the stomach over Palermo, and who, surprisingly, had written a book since then. Now he sent long, rather literary letters at least once a month to Barber. He was an odd, intense boy, who had been an excitable gunner, and he was constantly examining himself to find out whether he and the people he loved, among whom he rather embarrassingly included Barber, mostly because of the eight minutes over Palermo, were living up to their promise. "Our generation is in danger," the boy had typed in the letter on the bureau, "the danger of diminution. We have had our adventures too early. Our love has turned to affection, our hate to distaste, our despair to melancholy, our passion to preference. We have settled for the life of obedient dwarfs in a small but fatal sideshow."

The letter had depressed Barber and he hadn't answered it. You got enough of that sort of thing from the French. He wished the ex-waist-gunner would stop writing him, or at least write on different subjects. Barber hadn't answered his ex-wife, either, because he had come to Europe to try to forget her. He hadn't answered his mother, because he was afraid she was right. And he hadn't gone down to Eze, because no matter how broke he was, he wasn't selling that particular commodity yet.

Stuck into the mirror above the bureau was a photograph of himself and Jimmy Richardson, taken on the beach at Deauville the summer before. The Richardsons had taken a cottage there, and Barber had spent a couple of weekends with them. Jimmy Richardson was another one who had attached himself to Barber during the war. Somehow, Barber was always being presented with the devotion of people whose devotion he didn't want. "People hang on to you," a girl who was angry at him once told him, "because you're an automatic hypocrite. As soon as somebody comes into the room, you become gay and confident."

Jimmy and he had been in bathing trunks when the picture was snapped, and Barber was tall and blessed with a blond, California kind of good looks next to Jimmy, who seemed like a fat, incompetent infant, standing there with the sunny sea behind him.

Barber peered at the photograph. Jimmy didn't look like the sort of man who would ever be missing from anywhere for thirty-two days. As for himself, Barber thought wryly, he looked automatically gay and confident.

He leaned over and took the picture down and threw it into a drawer. Then, holding the phone loosely, he stared around him with distaste. In the glare of the unshaded lamp, the dark woodwork looked gloomy and termite-ridden, and the bed, with its mottled velours spread, the color of spoiled pears, looked as though it had been wallowed on by countless hundreds of obscenely shaped men and women who had rented the room for an hour at a time. For a second, he was piercingly homesick for all the rooms of all the Hotel Statlers he had slept in and all the roomettes on trains between New York and Chicago, and St. Louis and Los Angeles.

There was a whistling, staticlike sound in the phone, and he shook himself and gave the number of the George V. When he got the George V, he asked for M. Smith, M. Bert Smith. After a while, the girl said M. Smith was no longer at the hotel. Barber asked hurriedly, before the girl could cut him off, whether M. Smith was expected to return shortly or if he had left a forwarding address. No, the girl said after a long wait, he was not expected to return and there was no forwarding address.

Barber hung up. He was not surprised about Bert Smith. He was a man who wandered mysteriously from hotel to hotel, and he might have used a half-dozen names besides Smith since Barber had spoken to him last.

With a conscious effort, Barber tried not to think about Jimmy Richardson or his wife, who was called, as a friendly squadron joke, Beauty, or about Jimmy Richardson's two small sons.

Scowling, Barber went over to the window. The winter rain of Paris was seeping down into the narrow street, blurring it with the unproductive malice of city rain, chipping colorlessly at the buildings opposite, making it impossible to imagine what they had looked like when they were new. A workman was unloading cases of wine from a truck, looking persecuted by the weather, the Paris sound of clinking bottles muted and made hollow and mournful by the flow of gray water from the skies and from window ledges and signs and rolled awnings. It was not a day for a husband to be missing, for a friend to be missing. It was not a day to be alone or to have only fifteen thousand francs in your pocket or to be in a narrow hotel room where the heat was off from ten in the morning till six at night. It was not a day to be without a job or cigarettes or lunch. It was not a day on which to examine yourself and realize that no matter how many excuses you gave yourself, you were going to wind up knowing that, finally, you were responsible.

Barber shook himself again. There was no sense in just staying in the room all day. If he was going to do any good, he would have to find Bert Smith. He looked at his watch. It was nearly two-thirty. He tried to remember all the places he had ever seen Bert Smith at two-thirty in the afternoon. The fancy restaurant near the Rond-Point, where the movie people and the French newspaper owners and the rich tourists ate; the bistro on the Boulevard Latour-Maubourg, on the Left Bank; the restaurants at Auteuil and Longchamp and St. Cloud. Barber looked at the newspaper. They were running at Auteuil today.

If he was not at the races and if he was still in Paris, Bert Smith was likely to be in one art gallery or another in the middle of the afternoon. Bert Smith was an art lover, or at least he bought pictures, shrewdly and knowingly. Since Smith lived in hotel rooms, which were unlikely places for a collection, it was probable that he bought paintings on speculation or as an agent or, when they were important ones that the government did not wish to have leave the country, to be smuggled out of France.

Barber had also seen Smith late in the afternoons in the steam room at Claridge's, a small, round man with surprisingly well-shaped legs, sitting in the vapor, wrapped in a sheet, growing pinker and pinker, smiling luxuriously in the steam, sweating off the fat that he had accumulated in many years of eating in the best restaurants in Europe.

He had also seen Smith several times around six o'clock in the evening in the barbershop at the George V getting shaved, and after that in the bar upstairs, and in the bar at the Relais Plaza and the English bar downstairs at the Plaza-Athénée. And late at night he had seen him at various night clubs—Carrère's, L'Eléphant Blanc, La Rose Rouge . . .

Barber thought unhappily of the last fifteen thousand francs in his wallet. It was going to be a long, wet, hard, expensive day. He put on his hat and coat and went out. It was still raining, and he hailed a taxi and gave the driver the address of the restaurant near the Rond-Point.

It had started about two months before, in the stand at Auteuil just before the sixth race. The day was misty and there weren't many spectators, and Barber had not been doing very well, but he had got a tip on the sixth race, on an eight-to-one shot. He put five thousand down on the nose and climbed high up in the stand to get a good view of the race.

There was only one other spectator near him in the stand, a small, round man wearing an expensive-looking velours hat, and carrying a pair of binoculars and a rolled umbrella, like an Englishman. He smiled at Barber and nodded. As Barber smiled back politely, he realized that he had seen the man many times before, or his brother, or a half-dozen other men who looked like him, in restaurants and in bars and on the street, usually with tall girls who might have been lower-class mannequins or upper-class tarts.

The man with the umbrella moved over to him along the damp concrete row of seats. He had little, dapper feet and a bright necktie, and he had a well-cared-for, international kind of face, with large, pretty, dark eyes, fringed by thick black lashes. He had what Barber had come to call an import-export face. It was a face that was at the same time bland, cynical, self-assured, sensual, hopeless, and daring, and its owner might be Turkish or Hungarian or Greek or he might have been born in Basra. It was a face you might see in Paris or Rome or Brussels or Tangier, always in the best places, always doing business. It was a face, you felt somehow, that was occasionally of interest to the police.

"Good afternoon," the man said, in English, tipping his hat. "Are you having a lucky day?" He had an accent, but it was difficult to place it. It was as though as a child he had gone to school everywhere and had had ten nurses of ten different nationalities.

"Not bad," Barber said carefully.

"Which do you like in this one?" The man pointed with his umbrella at the track, where the horses were gingerly going up to the distant starting line on the muddied grass.

"Number Three," Barber said.

"Number Three." The man shrugged, as though he pitied Barber but was restrained by his good breeding from saying so. "How is the movie business these days?" the man asked.

"The movie business went home a month ago," Barber said, slightly surprised that the man knew anything about it. An American company had been making a picture about the war, and Barber had had four lucky, well-paid months as a technical expert, buckling leading men into parachutes and explaining the difference between a P-47 and a B-25 to the director.

"And the blond star?" the man asked, taking his glasses away from his eyes. "With the exquisite behind?"

"Also home."

The man moved his eyebrows and shook his head gently, indicating his regret that his new acquaintance and the city of Paris were now deprived of the exquisite behind. "Well," he said, "at least it leaves you free in the afternoon to come to the races." He peered out across the track through the glasses. "There they go."

No. 3 led all the way until the stretch. In the stretch, he was passed rapidly by four other horses.

"Every race in this country," Barber said as the horses crossed the finish line, "is a hundred metres too long." He took out his tickets and tore them once and dropped them on the wet concrete.

He watched with surprise as the man with the umbrella took out some tickets and tore them up, too. They were on No. 3, and Barber could see that they were big ones. The man with the umbrella dropped the tickets with a resigned, half-amused expression on his face, as though all his life he had been used to tearing up things that had suddenly become of no value.

"Are you staying for the last race?" the man with the umbrella asked as they started to descend through the empty stand.

"I don't think so," Barber said. "This day has been glorious enough already."

"Why don't you stay?" the man said. "I may have something."

Barber thought for a moment, listening to their footsteps on the concrete.

"I have a car," the man said. "I could give you a lift into town, Mr. Barber."

"Oh," Barber said, surprised, "you know my name."

"Of course," the man said, smiling. "Why don't you wait for me at the bar? I have to go and cash some tickets."

"I thought you lost," Barber said suspiciously.

"On Number Three," the man said. From another pocket he took out some more tickets and waved them gently. "But there is always the insurance. One must always think of the insurance," he said. "Will I see you at the bar?"

"O.K.," Barber said, not because he hoped for anything in the way of information on the next race from the man with the umbrella but because of the ride home. "I'll be there. Oh—by the way, what's your name?"

"Smith," the man said. "Bert Smith."

Barber went to the bar and ordered a coffee, then changed it to a brandy, because coffee wasn't enough after a race like that. He stood there, hunched over the bar, reflecting sourly that he was one of the category of people who never think of the insurance. Smith, he thought, Bert Smith. More insurance. On how many other names, Barber wondered, had the man lost before he picked that one?

Smith came to the bar softly, on his dapper feet, smiling, and laid a hand lightly on Barber's arm. "Mr. Barber," he said, "there is a rumor for the seventh race. Number Six."

"I never win on Number Six," Barber said.

"It is a lovely little rumor," Smith said. "At present, a twenty-two-to-one rumor."

Barber looked at the man doubtfully. He wondered briefly what there was in it for Smith. "What the hell," he said, moving toward the seller's window. "What have I got to lose?"

He put five thousand francs on No. 6 and superstitiously remained at the bar during the race, drinking brandy. No. 6 won, all out, by half a length, and, although the odds had dropped somewhat, paid eighteen to one.

Barber walked through the damp twilight, across the discarded newspapers and the scarred grass, with its farmlike smell, patting his inside pocket with the ninety thousand francs in a comforting bulge there, pleased with the little man trotting beside him.

Bert Smith had a Citroën, and he drove swiftly and well and objectionably, cutting in on other cars and swinging wide into the outside lane to gain advantage at lights.

"Do you bet often on the races, Mr. Barber?" he was saying as they passed a traffic policeman, forlorn in his white cape on the gleaming street.

"Too often," Barber said, enjoying the warmth of the car and the effects of the last brandy and the bulge in his pocket.

"You like to gamble?"

"Who doesn't?"

"There are many who do not like to gamble," Smith said, nearly scraping a truck. "I pity them."

"Pity them?" Barber looked over at Smith, a little surprised at the word. "Why?"

"Because," Smith said softly, smiling, "in this age there comes a time when everyone finds that he is forced to gamble—and not only for money, and not only at the seller's window. And when that time comes, and you are not in the habit, and it does not amuse you, you are most likely to lose."

They rode in silence for a while. From time to time, Barber peered across at the soft, self-assured face above the wheel, lit by the dashboard glow. I would like to get a look at his passport, Barber thought—at all the passports he's carried for the last twenty years.

"For example," Smith said, "during the war . . ."

"Yes?"

"When you were in your plane," Smith said, "on a mission. Weren't there times when you had to decide suddenly to try something, to depend on your luck for one split second, and if you hesitated, if you balked at the act of gambling—sssszt!" Smith took one hand from the wheel and made a gliding, falling motion, with his thumb down. He smiled across at Barber. "I suppose you are one of the young men who were nearly killed a dozen times," he said.

"I suppose so," Barber said.

"I prefer that in Americans," Smith said. "It makes them more like Europeans."

"How did you know I was in the war?" Barber said. For the first time, he began to wonder if it was only a coincidence that

Smith had been near him in the stand before the sixth race.

Smith chuckled. "You have been in Paris how long?" he said. "A year and a half?"

"Sixteen months," Barber said, wondering how the man knew *that.*

"Nothing very mysterious about it," Smith said. "People talk at bars, at dinner parties. One girl tells another girl. Paris is a small city. Where shall I drop you?"

Barber looked out the window to see where they were. "Not far from here," he said. "My hotel is just off the Avenue Victor Hugo. You can't get in there with a car."

"Oh, yes," Smith said, as though he knew about all hotels. "If it doesn't seem too inquisitive," he said, "do you intend to stay long in Europe?"

"It depends."

"On what?"

"On luck." Barber grinned.

"Did you have a good job in America?" Smith asked, keeping his eyes on the traffic ahead of him.

"In thirty years, working ten hours a day, I would have been the third biggest man in the company," Barber said.

Smith smiled. "Calamitous," he said. "Have you found more interesting things to do here?"

"Occasionally," Barber said, beginning to be conscious that he was being quizzed.

"After a war it is difficult to remain interested," Smith said. "While it is on, a war is absolutely boring. But then when it over, you discover peace is even more boring. It is the worst result of wars. Do you still fly?"

"Once in a while."

Smith nodded. "Do you maintain your license?"

"Yes."

"Yes, that's wise," Smith said.

He pulled the car sharply in to the curb and stopped, and Barber got out.

"Here you are," Smith said. He put out his hand, smiling, and Barber shook it. Smith's hand was softly fleshed, but there was a feeling of stone beneath it.

"Thanks for everything," Barber said.

"Thank you, Mr. Barber, for your company," Smith said. He

held Barber's hand for a moment, looking across the seat at him. "This has been very pleasant," he said. "I hope we can see each other again soon. Maybe we are lucky for each other."

"Sure," Barber said, grinning. "I'm always at home to people who can pick eighteen-to-one shots."

Smith smiled, relinquishing Barber's hand. "Maybe one of these days we'll have something even better than an eighteen-to-one shot," he said.

He waved a little and Barber closed the car door. Smith spurted out into the traffic, nearly causing two *quatre chevaux* to pile up behind him.

It had taken two weeks for Smith to declare himself. From the beginning, Barber had known that something was coming, but he had waited patiently curious and amused, lunching with Smith in the fine restaurants Smith patronized, going to galleries with him and listening to Smith on the subject of the Impressionists, going out to the race tracks with him and winning more often than not on the information Smith picked up from tight-lipped men around the paddocks. Barber pretended to enjoy the little, clever man more than he actually did, and Smith, on his part, Barber knew, was pretending to like *him* more than he actually did. It was kind of veiled and cynical wooing, in which neither party had yet committed himself. Only, unlike more ordinary wooings, Barber for the first two weeks was not sure in just which direction his desirability, as far as Smith was concerned, might lie.

Then, late one night, after a large dinner and a desultory tour of the night clubs, during which Smith had seemed unusually silent and abstracted, they were standing in front of Smith's hotel and he made his move. It was a cold night, and the street deserted except for a prostitute with a dog, who looked at them without hope as she passed them on the way to the Champs-Elysées.

"Are you going to be in your hotel tomorrow morning, Lloyd?" Smith asked.

"Yes," Barber said. "Why?"

"Why?" Smith repeated absently, staring after the chilled-looking girl and her poodle walking despairingly down the empty, dark street. "Why?" He chuckled irrelevantly. "I have something I would like to show you," he said.

"I'll be in all morning," Barber said.

"Tell me, my friend," Smith said, touching Barber's sleeve lightly with his gloved hand. "Do you have any idea why I have been calling you so often for the last two weeks, and buying you so many good meals and so much good whiskey?"

"Because I am charming and interesting and full of fun," Barber said, grinning. "And because you want something from me."

Smith chuckled, louder this time, and caressed Barber's sleeve. "You are not absolutely stupid, my friend, are you?"

"Not absolutely," said Barber.

"Tell me, my friend," Smith said, almost in a whisper. "How would you like to make twenty-five thousand dollars?"

"What?" Barber asked, certain that he had not heard correctly.

"Sh-h-h," Smith said. He smiled, suddenly gay. "Think about it. I'll see you in the morning. Thank you for walking me home." He dropped Barber's arm and started into the hotel.

"Smith!" Barber called.

"Sh-h-h." Smith put his finger playfully to his mouth. "Sleep well. See you in the morning."

Barber watched him go through the glass revolving doors into the huge, brightly lit, empty lobby of the hotel. Barber took a step toward the doors to follow him in, then stopped and shrugged and put his collar up, and walked slowly in the direction of his own hotel. I've waited this long, he thought, I can wait till morning.

Barber was still in bed the next morning when the door opened and Smith came in. The room was dark, with the curtains drawn, and Barber was lying there, half asleep, thinking drowsily, Twenty-five thousand, twenty-five thousand. He opened his eyes when he heard the door open. There was a short, bulky silhouette framed in the doorway against the pallid light of the corridor.

"Who's that?" Barber asked, without sitting up.

"Lloyd. I'm so sorry," Smith said. "Go back to sleep. I'll see you later."

Barber sat up abruptly. "Smith," he said. "Come in."

"I don't want to disturb—"

"Come in, come in." Barber got out of bed and, barefooted, went over to the window and threw back the curtains. He looked out at the street. "By God, what do you know?" he said, shivering and closing the window. "The sun is shining. Shut the door."

Smith closed the door. He was wearing a loose gray tweed overcoat, very British, and a soft Italian felt hat, and he was carrying a large manila envelope. He looked newly bathed and shaved, and wide awake.

Barber, blinking in the sudden sunshine, put on a robe and a pair of moccasins and lit a cigarette. "Excuse me," he said. "I want to wash." He went behind the screen that separated the washbasin and the bidet from the rest of the room. As he washed, scrubbing his face and soaking his hair with cold water, he heard Smith go over to the window. Smith was humming, in a soft, true, melodious tenor voice, a passage from an opera that Barber knew he had heard but could not remember. Aside from everything else, Barber thought, combing his hair roughly, I bet the son of a bitch is cultured.

Feeling fresher and less at a disadvantage with his teeth washed and his hair combed, Barber stepped out from behind the screen.

"Paris," Smith said, at the window, looking out. "What a satisfactory city. What a farce." He turned around, smiling. "Ah," he said, "how lucky you are. You can afford to put water on your head." He touched his thin, well-brushed hair sadly. "Every time I wash my hair, it falls like the leaves. How old did you say you are?"

"Thirty," Barber said, knowing that Smith remembered it.

"What an age." Smith sighed. "The wonderful moment of balance. Old enough to know what you want, still young enough to be ready for anything." He came back and sat down and propped the manila envelope on the floor next to the chair. "Anything." He looked up at Barber, almost coquetishly. "You recall our conversation, I trust," he said.

"I recall a man said something about twenty-five thousand dollars," Barber said.

"Ah—you do remember," Smith said gaily. "Well?"

"Well what?"

"Well, do you want to make it?"

"I'm listening," Barber said.

Smith rubbed his soft hands together gently in front of his face, his fingers rigid, making a slight, dry, sliding sound. "A little proposition has come up," he said. "An interesting little proposition."

"What do I have to do for my twenty-five thousand dollars?" Barber asked.

"What do you have to do for your twenty-five thousand dollars?" Smith repeated softly. "You have to do a little flying. You have flown for considerably less, from time to time, haven't you?" He chuckled.

"I sure have," Barber said. "What else do I have to do?"

"Nothing else," Smith said, sounding surprised. "Just fly. Are you still interested?"

"Go on," said Barber.

"A friend of mine has just bought a brand-new single-engine plane. A Navion. A perfect, pleasant, comfortable, one-hundred-per-cent dependable aircraft," Smith said, describing the perfect little plane with pleasure in its newness and its dependability. "He himself does not fly, of course. He needs a private pilot, who will be on tap at all times."

"For how long?" Barber asked, watching Smith closely.

"For thirty days. Not more." Smith smiled up at him. "The pay is not bad, is it?"

"I can't tell yet," Barber said. "Go on. Where does he want to fly to?"

"He happens to be an Egyptian," Smith said, a little deprecatingly, as though being an Egyptian were a slight private misfortune, which one did not mention except among friends, and then in lowered tones. "He is a wealthy Egyptian who likes to travel. Especially back and forth to France. To the South of France. He is in love with the South of France. He goes there at every opportunity."

"Yes?"

"He would like to make two round trips from Egypt to the vicinity of Cannes within the next month," Smith said, peering steadily at Barber, "in his private new plane. Then, on the third trip, he will find that he is in a hurry and he will take the commercial plane and his pilot will follow two days later, alone."

"Alone?" Barber asked, trying to keep all the facts straight.

"Alone, that is," Smith said, "except for a small box."

"Ah," Barber said, grinning. "Finally the small box."

"Finally." Smith smiled up at him delightedly. "It has already been calculated. The small box will weigh two hundred and fifty pounds. A comfortable margin of safety for this particular aircraft for each leg of the journey."

"And what will there be in the small two-hundred-and-fifty-pound box?" Barber asked, cool and relieved now that he saw what was being offered to him.

"Is it absolutely necessary to know?"

"What do I tell the customs people when they ask me what's in the box?" Barber said. " 'Go ask Bert Smith'?"

"You have nothing to do with customs people," Smith said. "I assure you. When you take off from the airport in Cairo, the box is not on board. And when you land at the airport at Cannes, the box is not on board. Isn't that enough?"

Barber took a last pull at his cigarette and doused it. He peered thoughtfully at Smith, sitting easily on the straight-backed chair in the rumpled room, looking too neat and too well dressed for such a place at such an hour. Drugs, Barber thought, and he can stuff them . . .

"No, Bertie boy," Barber said roughly. "It is not enough. Come on. Tell."

Smith sighed. "Are you interested up to now?"

"I am interested up to now," Barber said.

"All right," Smith said regretfully. "This is how it will be done. You will have established a pattern. You will have been in and out of the Cairo airport several times. Your papers always impeccable. They will know you. You will have become a part of the legitimate routine of the field. Then, on the trip when you will be taking off alone, everything will still be perfectly legitimate. You will have only a small bag with you of your personal effects. Your flight plan will show that your destination is Cannes and that you will come down at Malta and Rome for refueling only. You will take off from Cairo. You will go off course by only a few miles. Some distance from the coast, you will be over the desert. You will come down on an old R.A.F. landing strip that hasn't been used since 1943. There will be several men there. . . . Are you listening?"

"I'm listening." Barber had walked to the window and was standing there, looking out at the sunny street below, his back to Smith.

"They will put the box on board. The whole thing will not take more than ten minutes," Smith said. "At Malta, nobody will ask you anything, because you will be in transit and you will not leave the plane and you will stay only long enough to refuel. The same thing at Rome. You will arrive over the south coast of France in the evening, before the moon is up. Once more," Smith said, speaking as though he was savoring his words, "you will be just a little off course. You will fly low over the hills between Cannes and Grasse. At a certain point, you will see an arrangement of lights. You will throttle down, open the door, and push the box out, from a height of a hundred feet. Then you will close the door and turn toward the sea and land at the Cannes airport. Your papers will be perfectly in order. There will have been no deviations from your flight plan. You will have nothing to declare. You will walk away from the airplane once and for all, and we will pay you the twenty-five thousand dollars I have spoken of. Isn't it lovely?"

"Lovely," Barber said. "It's just a delicious little old plan, Bertie boy." He turned away from the window. "Now tell me what will be in the box."

Smith chuckled delightedly, as though what he was going to say was too funny to keep to himself. "Money," he said. "Just money."

"How much money?"

"Two hundred and fifty pounds of money," Smith said, his eyes crinkled with amusement. "Two hundred and fifty pounds of tightly packed English notes in a nice, strong, lightweight metal box. Five-pound notes."

At that moment, it occurred to Barber that he was speaking to a lunatic. But Smith was sitting there, matter-of-fact and healthy, obviously a man who had never for a minute in all his life had a single doubt about his sanity.

"When would I get paid?" Barber asked.

"When the box was delivered," Smith said.

"Bertie boy . . ." Barber shook his head reprovingly.

Smith chuckled. "I have warned myself that you were not stupid," he said. "All right. We will deposit twelve thousand five hundred dollars in your name in a Swiss bank before you start for the first time to Egypt."

"You'll trust me for that?"

Fleetingly the smile left Smith's face. "We'll trust you for that," he said. Then the smile reappeared. "And immediately after the delivery is made, we will deposit the rest. A lovely deal. Hard currency. No income tax. You will be a rich man. Semi-rich." He chuckled at his joke. "Just for a little plane ride. Just to help an Egyptian who is fond of the South of France and who is naturally a little disturbed by the insecurity of his own country."

"When will I meet this Egyptian?" Barber asked.

"When you go to the airfield to take off for your first flight," Smith said. "He'll be there. Don't you worry. He'll be there. Do you hesitate?" he asked anxiously.

"I'm thinking," Barber said.

"It's not as though you were involved in your own country," Smith said piously. "I wouldn't ask a man to do that, a man who had fought for his country in the war. It isn't even as though it had anything to do with the English, for whom it is possible you have a certain affection. But the Egyptians . . ." He shrugged and bent over and picked up the manila envelope and opened it. "I have all the maps here," he said, "if you would like to study them. The route is all marked out, but, of course, it would be finally in your hands, since it would be you who was doing the flying."

Barber took the thick packet of maps. He opened one at random. All it showed was the sea approaches to Malta and the location of the landing strips there. Barber thought of twenty-five thousand dollars and the map shook a little in his hands.

"It is ridiculously easy," Smith said, watching Barber intently. "Foolproof."

Barber put the map down. "If it's so easy, what are you paying twenty-five thousand bucks for?" he said.

Smith laughed. "I admit," he said, "there may be certain little risks. It is improbable, but one never knows. We pay you for the improbability, if you want to put it that way." He shrugged. "After all, after a whole war you must be somewhat hardened to risks."

"When do you have to know?" Barber asked.

"Tonight," Smith said. "If you say no, naturally we have to make other plans. And my Egyptian friend is impatient."

"Who is we?" Barber asked.

"Naturally," Smith said, "I have certain colleagues."

"Who are they?"

Smith made a small regretful gesture. "I am terribly sorry," he said, "but I cannot tell you."

"I'll call you tonight," said Barber.

"Good." Smith stood up and buttoned his coat and carefully put the soft Italian felt hat on his head, at a conservative angle. He played gently and appreciatively with the brim. "This afternoon, I will be at the track. Maybe you would like to join me there."

"Where're they running today?"

"Auteuil," Smith said. "Jumping today."

"Have you heard anything?"

"Perhaps," Smith said. "There is a mare who is doing the jumps for the first time. I have spoken to the jockey and I have been told the mare has responded in training, but I'll hear more at three o'clock."

"I'll be there."

"Good," Smith said enthusiastically. "Although it is against my interests, of course, to make you too rich in advance." He chuckled. "However, for the sake of friendship . . . Should I leave the maps?"

"Yes," said Barber.

"Until three o'clock," Smith said as Barber opened the door. They shook hands, and Smith went out into the corridor, a rich, tweedy, perfumed figure in the impoverished light of the pallid hotel lamps.

Barber locked the door behind him and picked up the packet of maps and spread them on the bed, over the rumpled sheets and blankets. He hadn't looked at aerial maps for a long time. Northern Egypt. The Mediterranean. The island of Malta. Sicily and the Italian coast. The Gulf of Genoa. The Alpes-Maritimes. He stared at the maps. The Mediterranean looked very wide. He didn't like to fly over open water in a single-engined plane. In fact, he didn't like to fly. Since the war, he had flown as little as possible. He hadn't made any explanations to himself, but when he had had to travel, he had gone by car or train or boat whenever he could.

Twenty-five thousand dollars, he thought.

He folded the maps neatly and put them back into the envelope. At this point, the maps weren't going to help.

He lay down on the bed again, propped against the pillows with his hands clasped behind his head. Open water, he thought. Five times. Even that wouldn't be too bad. But what about the Egyptians? He had been in Cairo briefly during the war. He remembered that at night the policemen walked in pairs, carrying carbines. He didn't like places where the policemen carried carbines. And Egyptian prisons . . .

He moved uneasily on the bed.

Who knew how many people were in on a scheme like this? And it would only take one to cook you. One dissatisfied servant or accomplice, one greedy or timid partner . . . He closed his eyes and almost saw the fat, dark uniformed men with their carbines walking up to the shiny, new little plane.

Or suppose you blew a tire or crumpled a wheel on the landing strip? Who knew what the strip was like, abandoned in the desert since 1943?

Twenty-five thousand dollars.

Or you would think you were making it. The box would be on the seat beside you and the coast of Egypt would be falling off behind you and the sea stretching blue below and ahead and the engine running like a watch—and then the first sign of the patrol. The shimmering dot growing into . . . What did the Egyptian Air Force fly? Spitfires, left over from the war, he supposed. Coming up swiftly, going twice as fast as you, signalling you to turn around . . . He lit a cigarette. Two hundred and fifty pounds. Say the box alone—it would have to be plenty tough—weighed a hundred and fifty pounds. How much did a five-pound note weigh? Would there be a thousand to a pound? Five thousand multiplied by a hundred, with the pound at two-eighty. Close to a million and a half dollars.

His mouth felt dry, and he got up and drank two glasses of water. Then he made himself sit down on the chair, keeping his hands still. If there was an accident, if for any reason you failed to come through with it . . . If the money was lost, but you were saved. Smith didn't look like a murderer, although who knew what murderers looked like these days? And who knew what other people he was involved with? My colleagues, as Smith called them, who would then be your colleagues. The wealthy Egyptian, the several men at the old R.A.F. landing strip in the desert, the people who were to set out the lights in the certain arrangement in the hills behind Cannes— How many others, sliding across frontiers, going secretly and illegally from one country to another with guns and gold in their suitcases, the survivors of war, prison, denunciation— How many others whom you didn't know, whom you would see briefly in the glare of the African sun, as a running figure on a dark French hillside, whom you couldn't judge or assess and on whom your life depended, who were risking prison, deportation, police bullets for their share of a box full of money . . .

He jumped up and put on his clothes and went out, locking the door. He didn't want to sit in the cold, disordered room, staring at the maps.

He walked around the city aimlessly for the rest of the morning, looking blindly into shopwindows and thinking of the things he would buy if he had money. Turning away from a window, he saw a policeman watching him incuriously. Barber looked speculatively at the policeman, who was small, with a mean face and a thin mustache. Looking at the policeman, Barber remembered some of the stories about what they did to suspects when they questioned them in the back rooms of the local prefectures. An American passport wouldn't do much good if they picked you up with five hundred thousand English pounds under your arm.

This is the first time in my life, Barber thought curiously, walking slowly on the crowded street, that I have contemplated moving over to the other side of the law. He was surprised that he was considering it so calmly. He wondered why that was. Perhaps the movies and the newspapers, he thought. You get so familiar with crime it becomes humanized and accessible. You don't think about it, but then, suddenly, when it enters your life, you realize that subconsciously you have been accepting the idea of crime as an almost normal accompaniment of everyday life. Policemen must know that, he thought, all at once seeing things from the other side. They must look at all the shut, ordinary faces going past them and they must know how close to theft, murder, and defaulting everyone is, and it must drive them crazy. They must want to arrest everybody.

While Barber was watching the horses move in their stiff-legged, trembling walk around the paddock before the sixth race, he felt a light tap on his shoulder.

"Bertie boy," he said, without turning around.

"I'm sorry I'm late," Smith said, coming up to the paddock rail beside Barber. "Were you afraid I wouldn't come?"

"What's the word from the jock?" Barber asked.

Smith looked around him suspiciously. Then he smiled. "The

jockey is confident," Smith said. "He is betting himself."

"Which one is it?"

"Number Five."

Barber looked at No. 5. It was a light-boned chestnut mare with a delicate, gentle head. Her tail and mane were braided, and she walked alertly but not too nervously, well-mannered and with a glistening coat. Her jockey was a man of about forty, with a long, scooped French nose. He was an ugly man, and when he opened his mouth, you saw that most of his front teeth were missing. He wore a maroon cap, with his ears tucked in, and a white silk shirt dotted with maroon stars.

Barber, looking at him, thought, It's too bad such ugly men get to ride such beautiful animals.

"O.K., Bertie boy," he said. "Lead me to the window."

Barber bet ten thousand francs on the nose. The odds were a comfortable seven to one. Smith bet twenty-five thousand francs. They walked side by side to the stands and climbed up together as the horses came out on the track. The crowd was small and there were only a few other spectators that high up.

"Well, Lloyd?" Smith said. "Did you look at the maps?"

"I looked at the maps," Barber said.

"What did you think?"

"They're very nice maps."

Smith looked at him sharply. Then he decided to chuckle. "You want to make me fish, eh?" he said. "You know what I mean. Did you decide?"

"I . . ." Barber began, staring down at the cantering horses. He took a deep breath. "I'll tell you after the race," he said.

"Lloyd!" The voice came from below, to the right, and Barber turned in that direction. Toiling up the steps was Jimmy Richardson. He had always been rather round and baby-plump, and Parisian food had done nothing to slim him down, and he was panting, his coat flapping open, disclosing a checkered vest, as he hurried toward Barber.

"How are you?" he said breathlessly as he reached their level. He clapped Barber on the back. "I saw you up here and I thought maybe you had something for this race. I can't figure this one and they've been murdering me all day. I'm lousy on the jumps."

"Hello, Jimmy," Barber said. "Mr. Richardson. Mr. Smith."

"Pleased to meet you," Richardson said. "How do you spell it?" He laughed loudly at his joke. "Say, really, Lloyd, do you know anything? Maureen'll murder me if I go home and tell her I went into the hole for the afternoon."

Barber looked across at Smith, who was watching Richardson benignly. "Well," he said, "Bertie boy, here, thinks he heard something."

"Bertie boy," Richardson said, "please . . ."

Smith smiled thinly. "Number Five looks very good," he said. "But you'd better hurry. They're going to start in a minute."

"Number Five," Richardson said. "Roger. I'll be right back." He went galloping down the steps, his coat flying behind him.

"He's a trusting soul, isn't he?" Smith said.

"He was an only child," Barber said, "and he never got over it."

Smith smiled politely. "Where do you know him from?"

"He was in my squadron."

"In your squadron." Smith nodded, looking after Richardson's hurrying, diminishing figure on the way to the seller's window. "Pilot?"

"Uh-huh."

"Good?"

Barber shrugged. "Better ones got killed and worse ones won every medal in the collection."

"What is he doing in Paris?"

"He works for a drug company," Barber said.

The bell rang and the horses raced toward the first jump.

"Your friend was too late, I'm afraid," Smith said, putting his binoculars to his eyes.

"Yep," Barber said, watching the bunched horses.

No. 5 fell on the fourth jump. She went over with two other horses, and suddenly she was down and rolling. The pack passed around her. The fourth jump was far off down the track, and it was hard to see what, exactly, was happening until, a moment later, the mare struggled to her feet and cantered after the pack, her reins broken and trailing. Then Barber saw that the jockey was lying there motionless, crumpled up clumsily on his face, with his head turned in under his shoulder.

"We've lost our money," Smith said calmly. He took his binoculars from his eyes and pulled out his tickets and tore them and dropped them.

"May I have those, please?" Barber reached over for the binoculars. Smith lifted the strap over his head, and Barber trained the glasses on the distant jump where the jockey was lying. Two men were running out to him and turning him over.

Barber adjusted the binoculars, and the figures of the two men working on the motionless figure in the maroon-starred shirt came out of the blur into focus. Even in the glasses, there was something terribly urgent and despairing in the fovements of the distant men. They picked the jockey up between them and started running clumsily off with him.

"Damn it!" It was Richardson, who had climbed up beside them again. "The window closed just as I—"

"Do not complain, Mr. Richardson," Smith said. "We fell at the fourth jump."

Richardson grinned. "That's the first bit of luck I had all day."

Down below, in front of the stands, the riderless mare was swerving and trotting off down the track to avoid a groom who was trying to grab the torn reins.

Barber kept the glasses on the two men who were carrying the jockey. Suddenly, they put him down on the grass, and one of the men bent down and put his ear against the white silk racing shirt. After a while, he stood up. Then the two men started to carry the jockey again, only now they walked slowly, as though there was no sense in hurrying.

Barber gave the glasses back to Smith. "I'm going home," he said. "I've had enough of the sport for one day."

Smith glanced at him sharply. He put the glasses to his eyes and stared at the men carrying the jockey. Then he put the glasses into their case and hung the case by its strap over his shoulder. "They kill at least one a year," he said in a low voice. "It is to be expected in a sport like this. I'll take you home."

"Say," Richardson said. "Is that fellow dead?"

"He was getting too old," Smith said. "He kept at it too long."

"Holy man!" Richardson said, staring down the track. "And I was sore because I came too late to bet on him. That was some tip." He made a babyish grimace. "A tip on a dead jock."

Barber started down toward the exit.

"I'll come with you," Richardson said. "This isn't my lucky day."

The three men went down under the stands without speaking. People were standing in little groups, and there was a queer rising, hissing sound of whispering all over the place, now that the news was spreading.

When they reached the car, Barber got into the back, allowing Richardson to sit next to Smith, on the front seat. He wanted to be at least that much alone for the time being.

Smith drove slowly and in silence. Even Richardson spoke only once. "What a way to get it," he said as they drove between the bare, high trees. "In a lousy, three-hundred-thousand-franc claiming race."

Barber sat in the corner, his eyes half closed, not looking out. He kept remembering the second time the two men had picked up the jockey. Smith's selection for the afternoon, Barber thought. He closed his eyes altogether and saw the maps spread out on the bed in his room. The Mediterranean. The wide reaches of open water. He remembered the smell of burning. The worst smell. The smell of your dreams during the war. The smell of hot metal, smoldering rubber. Smith's tip.

"Here we are," Smith was saying.

Barber opened his eyes. They were stopped at the corner of the dead-end street down which was the entrance to his hotel. He got out.

"Wait a minute, Bertie boy," Barber said. "I have something I want to give you."

Smith looked at him inquiringly. "Can't it wait, Lloyd?" he asked.

"No. I'll just be a minute." Barber went into his hotel and up to his room. The maps were folded in a pile on the bureau, except for one, which was lying open beside the others. The approaches to Malta. He folded it quickly and put all the maps into the manila envelope and went back to the car. Smith was standing beside the car, smoking, nervously holding on to his hat, because a wind had come up and dead leaves were skittering along the pavement.

"Here you are, Bertie boy," Barber said, holding out the envelope.

Smith didn't take it. "You're sure you know what you're doing?" he said.

"I'm sure."

Smith still didn't take the maps. "I'm in no hurry," he said softly. "Why don't you hold on to them another day?"

"Thanks, no."

Smith looked at him silently for a moment. The fluorescent street lamps had just gone on, hard white-blue light, and Smith's smooth face looked powdery in the shadows under his expensive hat, and his pretty eyes were dark and flat under the curled lashes.

"Just because a jockey falls at a jump—" Smith began.

"Take them," Barber said, "or I'll throw them in the gutter."

Smith shrugged. He put out his hand and took the envelope. "You'll never have a chance like this again," he said, running his finger caressingly over the envelope edge.

"Good night, Jimmy." Barber leaned over the car and spoke to Richardson, who was sitting there watching them, puzzled. "Give my love to Maureen."

"Say, Lloyd," Richardson said, starting to get out. "I thought maybe we could have a couple of drinks. Maureen doesn't expect me home for another hour yet and I thought maybe we could cut up some old touches and—"

"Sorry," Barber said, because he wanted, more than anything else, to be alone. "I have a date. Some other time."

Smith turned and looked thoughtfully at Richardson. "He always has a date, your friend," Smith said. "He's a very popular boy. I feel like a drink myself, Mr. Richardson. I would be honored if you'd join me."

"Well," Richardson said uncertainly, "I live way down near the Hôtel de Ville and—"

"It's on my way," Smith said, smiling warmly.

Richardson settled back in his seat, and Smith started to get into the car. He stopped and looked up at Barber. "I made a mistake about you, didn't I, Lloyd?" he said contemptuously.

"Yes," Barber said. "I'm getting too old. I don't want to keep at it too long."

Smith chuckled and got into the car. They didn't shake hands. He slammed the door, and Barber watched him pull sharply away from the curb, making a taxi-driver behind him jam on his brakes to avoid hitting him.

Barber watched the big black car weave swiftly down the street, under the hard white-blue lights. Then he went back to the hotel and up to his room and lay down, because an afternoon at the races always exhausted him.

An hour later, he got up. He splashed cold water on his face to wake himself, but even so he felt listless and empty. He wasn't hungry and he wasn't thirsty and he kept thinking about the dead jockey in his soiled silks. There was no one he wanted to see. He put on his coat and went out, hating the room as he closed the door behind him.

He walked slowly toward the Etoile. It was a raw night and a fog was moving in from the river, and the streets were almost empty, because everybody was inside eating dinner. He didn't look at any of the lighted windows, because he wasn't going to buy anything for a long time. He passed several movie houses, neon in the drifting fog. In the movies, he thought, the hero would have been on his way to Africa by now. He would nearly be caught several times in Egypt, and he would fight his way out of a trap on the desert, killing several dark men just in time on the airstrip. And he would develop engine trouble over the Mediterranean and just pull out, with the water lapping at the wing tips, and he would undoubtedly crash, without doing too much damage to himself, probably just a photogenic cut on the forehead, and would drag the box out just in time. And he would turn out to be a Treasury agent or a member of British Intelligence and he would never doubt his luck and his nerve would never fail him and he would not end the picture with only a few thousand francs in his pocket. Or, if it was an artistic picture, there would be a heavy ground mist over the hills and the plane would drone on and on, desperate and lost, and then, finally, with the fuel tanks empty, the hero would crash in flames. Battered and staggering as he was, he would try to get the box out, but he wouldn't be able to move it, and finally the flames would drive him back and he would stand against a tree, laughing crazily, his face blackened with smoke, watching the plane and the money burn, to show the vanity of human aspiration and greed.

Barber grinned bleakly, rehearsing the scenarios in front of the giant posters outside the theatres. The movies do it better, he thought. They have their adventures happen to adventurers. He turned off the Champs-Elysées, walking slowly and aimlessly, trying to decide whether to eat now or have a drink first. Almost automatically, he walked toward the Plaza-Athénée. In the two weeks that he had been wooed by Smith, they had met in the English bar of the Plaza-Athénée almost every evening.

He went into the hotel and downstairs to the English bar. As he came into the room, he saw, in the corner, Smith and Jimmy Richardson.

Barber smiled. Bertie boy, he thought, are you whatever wasting your time. He stood at the bar and ordered a whiskey.

". . . fifty missions," he heard Richardson say. Richardson had a loud, empty voice that carried anywhere. "Africa, Sicily, Italy, Yugo—"

Then Smith saw him. He nodded coolly, with no hint of invitation. Richardson swivelled in his chair then, too. He smiled uncomfortably at Barber, getting red in the face, like a man who has been caught by a friend with his friend's girl.

Barber waved to them. For a moment, he wondered if he ought to go over and sit down and try to get Richardson out of there. He watched the two men, trying to figure out what they thought of each other. Or, more accurately, what Smith thought of Richardson. You didn't have to speculate about Jimmy. If you bought Jimmy a drink, he was your friend for life. For all that he had been through—war and marriage and being a father and living in a foreign country—it had still never occurred to Jimmy that people might not like him or might try to do him harm. When you were enjoying Jimmy, you called it trustfulness. When he was boring you, you called it stupidity.

Barber watched Smith's face carefully. By now, he knew Smith well enough to be able to tell a great deal of what was going on behind the pretty eyes and the pale, powdered face. Right now, Barber could tell that Smith was bored and that he wanted to get away from Jimmy Richardson.

Barber turned back to his drink, smiling to himself. It took Bertie boy just about an hour, he thought, an hour of looking at that good-natured empty face, an hour of listening to that booming, vacant voice, to decide that this was no man to fly a small box of five-pound notes from Cairo to Cannes.

Barber finished his drink quickly and went out of the bar before Smith and Richardson got up from the table. He had nothing to do for the evening, but he didn't want to get stuck with Jimmy and Maureen Richardson for dinner.

And now it was almost two months later and nobody had heard from Jimmy Richardson for thirty-two days.

In the whole afternoon of searching, Barber had not come upon any trace of Bert Smith. He had not been at the restaurants or the track or the art galleries, the barbershop, the steam bath, the bars. And no one had seen him for weeks.

It was nearly eight o'clock when Barber arrived at the English bar of the Plaza-Athénée. He was wet from walking in the day's rain, and tired, and his shoes were soggy, and he felt a cold coming on. He looked around the room, but it was almost empty. Indulging himself, thinking unhappily of all the taxi fares he had paid that day, he ordered a whiskey.

Barber sipped his whiskey in the quiet room, thinking circularly, I should have said something. But what could I have said? And Jimmy wouldn't have listened. But I should have said something. *The omens are bad, Jimmy, go on home. . . . I saw a plane crashing at the fourth jump, I saw a corpse being carried across dead grass by Egyptians, Jimmy, I saw silks and maps stained by blood.*

I had to be so damned superior, Barber thought bitterly. I had to be so damned sure that Jimmy Richardson was too stupid to be offered that much money. I had to be so damned sure that Bert Smith was too clever to hire him.

He hadn't said any of the things he should have said, and it had all wound up with a frantic, husbandless, penniless girl pleading for help that could only be too late now. Penniless. Jimmy Richardson had been too stupid even to get any of the money in advance.

He remembered what Jimmy and Maureen had looked like, smiling and embarrassed and youthfully important, standing next to Colonel Sumners, the Group Commander, at their wedding in Shreveport. He remembered Jimmy's plane just off his wing over Sicily; he remembered Jimmy's face when he landed at Foggia with an engine on fire; he remembered Jimmy's voice singing drunkenly in a bar in Naples; he remembered Jimmy the day after he arrived in Paris, saying, "Kid, this is the town for me, I got Europe in my blood."

He finished his drink and paid and went upstairs slowly. He went into a phone booth and called his hotel to see if there were any messages for him.

"Mme. Richardson has been calling you all day," the old man at the switchboard said. "Ever since four o'clock. She wanted you to call her back."

"All right," Barber said. "Thank you." He started to hang up.

"Wait a minute, wait a minute," the old man said irritably. "She called an hour ago to say she was going out. She said that if you came in before nine o'clock, she would like you to join her at the bar of the Hotel Bellman."

"Thanks, Henri," Barber said. "If she happens to call again, tell her I'm on my way." He went out of the hotel. The Bellman was nearby, and he walked toward it slowly, even though it was still raining. He was in no hurry to see Maureen Richardson.

When he reached the Bellman, he hesitated before going in, feeling too tired for this, wishing Maureen could be put off at least until the next day. He sighed, and pushed the door open.

The bar was a small one, but it was crowded with large, well-dressed men who were taking their time over drinks before going out to dinner. Then he saw Maureen. She was sitting in a corner, half turned away from the room, her shabby, thin coat thrown back over her chair. She was sitting alone and there was a bottle of champagne in a bucket in a stand beside her.

Barber went over to her, irritated by the sight of the champagne. Is that what she's doing with my five thousand francs, he thought, annoyed. Women are going crazy, too, these days.

He leaned over and kissed the top of her head. She jumped nervously, then smiled when she saw who it was. "Oh, Lloyd," she said, in a funny kind of whisper. She jumped up and kissed him, holding him hard against her. There was a big smell of champagne on her breath and he wondered if she was drunk. "Lloyd, Lloyd . . ." she said. She pushed him away a little, holding on to both his hands. Her eyes were smeary with tears and her mouth kept trembling.

"I came as soon as I got your message," Lloyd said, trying to sound practical, afraid Maureen was going to break down in front of all the people in the bar. She kept standing there, her mouth working, her hands gripping his avidly. He looked down, embarrassed, at her hands. They were still reddened and the nails were still uneven, but there was an enormous ring glittering, white and blue, on her finger. It hadn't been there when she came to his hotel, and he knew he had never seen her with a ring like that before. He looked up, almost frightened, thinking, What the hell has she started? What has she got herself into?

Then he saw Jimmy. Jimmy was making his way among the tables toward him. He was smiling broadly and he had lost some weight and he was dark brown and he looked as though he had just come from a month's vacation on a southern beach.

"Hi, kid," Jimmy said, his voice booming across the tables, across the barroom murmur of conversation. "I was just calling you again."

"He came home," Maureen said. "He came home at four o'clock this afternoon, Lloyd." She sank suddenly into her chair. Whatever else had happened that afternoon, it was plain that she had had access to a bottle. She sat in her chair, still holding on to one of Barber's hands, looking up, with a shimmering, half-dazed expression on her face, at her husband.

Jimmy clapped Barber on the back and shook his hand fiercely. "Lloyd," he said. "Good old Lloyd. *Garçon!*" he shouted, his voice reverberating through the whole room. "Another glass. Take your coat off. Sit down. Sit down."

Lloyd took his coat off and sat down slowly.

"Welcome home," he said quietly. He blew his nose. The cold had arrived.

"First," Jimmy said, "I have something for you." Ceremoniously he dug his hand into his pocket and brought out a roll of ten-thousand-franc notes. The roll was three inches thick. He took off one of the notes. "Maureen told me," he said seriously. "You were a damn good friend, Lloyd. Have you got change of ten?"

"I don't think so," Barber said. "No."

"Garçon," Jimmy said to the waiter, who was putting down a third glass, "get me two fives for this, please." When he spoke French, Jimmy had an accent that made even Americans wince.

Jimmy filled the three glasses carefully. He lifted his glass and clinked it first against Barber's and then against Maureen's. Maureen kept looking at him as though she had just seen him for the first time and never hoped to see anything as wonderful again in her whole life.

"To crime," Jimmy said. He winked. He made a complicated face when he winked, like a baby who has trouble with a movement of such subtlety and has to use the whole side of its face and its forehead to effect it.

Maureen giggled.

They drank. It was very good champagne.

"You're having dinner with us," Jimmy said. "Just the three of us. The victory dinner. Just Beauty and me and you, because if it hadn't been for you . . ." Suddenly solemn, he put his hand on Barber's shoulder.

"Yes," said Barber. His feet were icy and his trousers hung soddenly around his wet socks and he had to blow his nose again.

"Did Beauty show you her ring?" Jimmy asked.

"Yes," Barber said.

"She's only had it since six o'clock," Jimmy said.

Maureen held her hand up and stared at her ring. She giggled again.

"I know a place," Jimmy said, "where you can get pheasant and the best bottle of wine in Paris and . . ."

The waiter came back and gave Jimmy the two five-thousand-franc notes. Dimly, Barber wondered how much they weighed.

"If ever you're in a hole," Jimmy said, giving him one of the notes, "you know where to come, don't you?"

"Yes," Barber said. He put the note in his pocket.

He started to sneeze then, and ten minutes later he said he was sorry but he didn't think he could last the evening with a cold like that. Both Jimmy and Maureen tried to get him to stay, but he could tell that they were going to be happier without him.

He finished a second glass of champagne, and said he'd keep in touch, and went out of the bar, feeling his toes squish in his wet shoes. He was hungry and he was very fond of pheasant and actually the cold wasn't so bad, even if his nose kept running all the time. But he knew he couldn't bear to sit between Maureen and Jimmy Richardson all night and watch the way they kept looking at each other.

He walked back to his hotel, because he was through with taxis, and went up and sat on the edge of his bed in his room, in the dark, without taking his coat off. I better get out of here, he thought, rubbing the wet off the end of his nose with the back of his hand. This continent is not for me.

(From Harper's Magazine)

MAIDEN IN A TOWER

BY WALLACE STEGNER

THE HIGHWAY entering Salt Lake City from the west curves around the southern end of Great Salt Lake past Black Rock and its ratty beaches, swings north away from the spouting smoke of the smelter towns, veers toward the onion-shaped domes of the Saltair Pavilion, and straightens out eastward again on the speedway. Ahead, across the white flats, the city and its mountains are a mirage, or a mural: metropolitan towers, then houses and trees and channeled streets, and then the mountain wall.

Driving into that, Kimball Harris began to feel like the newsreel diver whom the reversed projector sucks feet first out of his splash. Perhaps fatigue from the hard day and a half across the desert explained both the miragelike look of the city and his own sense that he was being run backward toward the beginning of the reel. But the feeling grew as he bored townward along the straight road, the same road out which, as a high-school boy, he had driven much too fast in a stripped-down Ford bug with screaming companions in the rumble seat. They must have driven back, too, but he remembered only the going out. To see the city head-on, like this, was strange to him.

Middle-aged, rather tired, but alert with the odd notion that he was returning both through distance and through time, he passed the airport and the fair grounds and slowed for the first streets of the city.

Twenty-five years had made little difference. The city had spread some, and he was surprised, after the desert, by the green luxuriance of the trees, but the streets were still a half-mile wide, and water still ran in the gutters. It was a really a good town, clean, with a freshness about it that revived him. Circling the Brigham Young monument, he nodded gravely to the figure with the outstretched hand, and like a native returning he went through the light and turned around the button in the middle of the block and came back to park before the Utah Hotel, careful to park well out from the curb so as not to block the flowing gutter. They gave you a ticket for that. It tickled him that he had remembered.

The doorman collared his bag, a bellhop climbed in to take the car around to the garage. Still running pleasantly backward into the reel, he went into the unchanged lobby and registered, and was carried up the unchanged elevators to the kind of room he remembered, such a room as they used to take when they held fraternity parties in the hotel, back in Prohibition times. During those years he had been on a diet for ulcers, and couldn't drink, but he had retired religiously with the boys, gargled raw Green River redeye, and spit it out again in the washbowl, only for the pleasure of lawbreaking and of carrying a distinguished breath back to the ballroom and the girls.

He shook his head, touched for a moment with his giddy and forgotten youth.

Later, fresh from the shower, with a towel around him, he picked up the telephone book, so dinky and provincial-seeming after the ponderous San Francisco directory that he caught himself feeling protective about it. But when he found the Merrill Funeral Parlors in the yellow pages he sat thinking, struck by the address. 363 East South Temple. On the Avenues side, just below Fourth East. He tried to visualize that once-familiar street but it was all gone except for a general picture of tall stone and brick houses with high porches and lawns overtaken by plantain weeds. One, the one Holly had lived in, had a three-story stone tower.

That tower! With all the Jazz Age Bohemians crawling in and out. Havelock Ellis, Freud, Mencken, *The Memoirs of Fanny Hill, Love's Coming of Age, The Well of Loneliness,* Harry Kemp, Frank Harris. My Lord.

He was flooded with delighted recollection, they were all before him: reed-necked aesthetes, provincial cognoscenti, sad sexy yokels, lovers burning with a hard gemlike flame, a homosexual or two trying to look blasted and corroded by inward sin. Painters of bile-green landscapes, cubist photographers, poets and iconoclasts, scorners of the bourgeoisie, makers of cherished prose, dream-tellers, correspondence school psychoanalysts, they had swarmed through Holly's apartment and eddied around her queenly shape with noises like breaking china. He remembered her in her gold gown, a Proserpine or a Circe. For an instant she was slim and tall in his mind and he saw her laughing in the midst of the excitement she created, and how her hair was smooth black and her eyes very dark blue and how she wore massive gold hoops in her ears.

He wrote the number down and tucked it in the pocket of the suit laid out on the bed. But when he had dressed and gone down and was walking up South Temple past Beehive House, Lion House, Eagle Gate, the old and new apartment buildings, he began to look at numbers with a feeling that approached suspense, and he searched not so much for the Merrill Funeral Parlors as for the house with the round stone tower. Finally he saw it, lifting across the roof of a mansion gone to seed, and in another thirty paces he could see the sign and the new brass numbers on the riser of the top porch step. It was the very house.

Quickly he looked around for landmarks to restore and brace his memory. Some of the old maples and hickories he remembered along the sidewalk were gone, the terrace rolled down with an unfamiliar smooth nap of grass. The porch no longer carried its sagging swing, and porch and steps had been renewed and painted. The door was as he remembered it, with lozenges of colored glass above it, and the door knob's massive handful was an almost startling familiarity. But inside all was changed. Partitions had been gutted out. The stairs now mounted, or levitated, a spiral of white spokes and mahogany rails, from an expanse of plum-colored carpet. Instead of the cupping old parquetry his feet found softness, hushedness. The smells were of paint and flowers.

He was eying the stairs when a young man came out of an office on the left and bent his head a little leftward and said softly and pleasantly, "Yes, sir. Can I help?"

Harris brought himself dryly back to what he had driven eight hundred miles to do. He said, "I'm Kimball Harris. My aunt, Mrs. George Webb, died day before yesterday at the Julia Hicks

Home. They telephoned me she would be here."

"We've been expecting you," the young man said, and put out his hand. "My name is McBride." A brief handshake, a moment when the young man regarded Harris with his head tilted. "Did you fly in?" he asked.

"Drove."

"All the way from San Francisco?"

"I slept a few hours in Elko."

"It wasn't so bad, then."

"Oh, no," Harris said. "Not bad at all."

In his mind was a faint amusement: this young man might have been left over from one of Holly's parties. He looked better equipped to write fragile verses than deal with corpses.

"She's in the parlor just back here," McBride said. "Would you like to see her? She looks very nice."

That would be young McBride's function, of course. He would be the one who made them look nice. "Maybe later," Harris said. "I expect there are some details we ought to settle."

"Of course," McBride said. "If you'll just step in here. We can look at caskets after a minute. You have a family cemetery plot, I believe? It will only take a minute for this. The details you can leave to us." He held the door wide, standing gracefully and deferentially back, and ushered Harris through.

A very few minutes seemed to settle the details. They rose, facing each other across the desk coolly glimmering in muted afternoon light. "Now would you like to see her?" McBride said.

Why, he takes pride, Harris thought. He probably stands back estimating his effects like a window dresser. Mister McBride, the Mortuary Max Factor. "All right," he said, "though it's not as if I had any tears to shed. I haven't seen her for twenty-five years, and she's been senile for ten."

McBride guided him around the unfamiliar stairs to where the plum carpet flowed smoothly into what had evidently once been a dining room. "She does look nice," he said. "Very sweet and peaceful."

Which is more than she did alive, Harris thought, and went forward to the table with the basket of chrysanthemums at its foot. To remind himself that this was his mother's sister, his last near relative, made him feel nothing. Not even a deliberate attempt to squeeze sentimental recollections out of the past and remember suppers at Aunt Margaret's, Christmas visits at Aunt Margaret's, times when Aunt Margaret had unexpectedly given him a quarter, made the wax figure any dearer or realer. His indifference was so marked that he separated it and noticed it, wondering with a tinge of shame if he was callous. He supposed that if he had been attached to the dead woman he might think her peaceful, touching, even terrible. All he could think as he looked at her was that she looked well-embalmed—but then she had probably been close to mummified before she died.

Old Aunt Margaret, never very lovable, never dear to him in his childhood, and in his maturity only a duty and an expense, thrust her sharp nose, sharp cheekbones, withered lips, up through the rouge and lipstick and was, if she was not a total stranger, only old Aunt Margaret, mercifully dead at eighty-three. Harris did not even feel the conventional disgust with young McBride, who tampered with the dead. Considering what he had had to work with, McBride had done reasonably well.

Back in the hall again, he stood looking up the spiral stairs, apparently as unsupported as the Beanstalk, and remembered a time when Holly and three roommates—which three didn't matter, they changed so fast—came down the old shabby steps arguing about the proportions of the perfect female figure, and he met them on the second landing and like a chorus line they raised their skirts and thrust out their right legs before him, clamoring to know which was the most shapely. An undergraduate Paris and four demanding goddesses. He had picked Holly: why would he not?

McBride was in the office doorway. "We've just redone the whole place," he said. "It was the home of a Park City silver king originally, but it was all run down."

Harris was still looking up the stairs. McBride's words were no more important than the decorative changes, but upstairs there was something that *was* important, that pulled at him like an upward draft.

"I used to know this house twenty-five years ago," he said. "Some people I knew had an apartment on the third floor."

"Really? The front one or the back?"

"Front. The one with the round tower window."

"Oh yes," said McBride. "We haven't done much to that yet—just painted it."

"I wonder," Harris said, and made a little shrugging deprecatory motion and felt irritably ashamed, like a middle-aged man recalling last night's revels and his own unseemly capers and his pawing of the host's wife. It was fatuous to want to go up there, yet he did.

"Go on up if you want," McBride said. "The only thing, there's a woman laid out there."

"Well, then . . ."

"That wouldn't matter, if you don't mind. She's . . . presentable."

For a moment Harris hung on the word, and on the thought that McBride's professional vanity was one of the odder kinds, and on a little fit of irritability that a corpse should intrude upon a sentimental but perfectly legitimate impulse. Then he put his hand on the mahogany rail. "Maybe I will."

The second-floor hall, at whose doors he had knocked or entered, was as much changed as the ground floor, but up the second flight of stairs he mounted into a growing familiarity. And he climbed against the pressure of a crowd of ghosts. The carpet ended at the stairhead; he put his feet down softly and held back his breath with the wild notion that he heard voices from the door of Holly's old apartment. Up these stairs, a hundred, two hundred, three hundred times, through how long? a year? two years? he had come with books or bottles or manuscripts in his hands and (it seemed to him now) an incomparable capacity for enthusiasm in his heart. From the high burlap-hung windows of the apartment inside they had let their liquid ridicule fall on the streets of the bourgeois city. He half expected, as he moved into the doorway, to see their faces look up inquiringly from chair and couch and floor.

But in the room there was only the dead woman, and she was not looking at him.

She lay on a wheeled table, with beside her one stiff chair and a taboret bearing a bowl of flowers, all of it composed as if for a macabre still life. Looking toward the windows across the woman's body he saw how the gray light of the afternoon blurred in her carefully-waved hair.

For a minute or two, perhaps, he stood in the doorway, stopped partly by the body and partly by the feeling of an obscure threat: he must summon and gather and recreate his recollections of this room; he was walking in a strange neighborhood and needed his own gang around him.

In Holly's time the tower bay had held an old upright piano, its backside exposed to the room like the hanging seat of a child's sleepers. Afternoons, evenings, Sunday and holiday mornings, there had been loud four-hand renderings of "Twelfth Street Rag," "St. Louis Blues," "Mood Indigo." On at least one Christmas morning they had even sung carols around it, syncopating them wickedly. That was the morning when he brought Holly the facsimile copy of *The Marriage of Heaven and Hell*—a mutinous book full of mottoes for their personalities and their times.

But what he remembered now, hanging in the doorway, was how in some lull in the bedlam that always went on there they had found themselves smiling foolishly at each other by the piano and she had put up her hands to his face and kissed him sweet and soft, a kiss like a happy child's. He realized now that he had recalled that kiss before, waking or sleeping, and that the memory of it had acquired a kind of caption, a fragment of the world's wisdom contributed to his adolescent store by a returned Mormon missionary: *"Das ewig Weibliche fuehrt uns hinan,"* that remembered moment said.

How they had flocked and gathered there, debated, kissed, lied, shocked and astonished and delighted each other, there in the tower with Holly at their center, there by the vanished piano: poets and athletes, Renaissance heroes, fearless Stoics and impassioned Epicureans and abandoned Hedonists, girls with the bloom on their loveliness, goddesses with Perfect Proportions, artists and iconoclasts, as delighted with their own wickedness as if it had meant something.

He felt the stairs in his legs, the years in his mind, as he went in softly past the woman who lay so quietly on her back, and when he had passed her he turned and searched her face, almost as if he might surprise in it some expression meaningful to this wry and confusing return.

She was a plain woman, perhaps fifty. McBride had not yet made her look nice with rouge and lipstick. She lay in a simple black dress, but she had a Navajo squash-blossom necklace around her throat. It struck him as a remarkable piece of realism—perhaps something she had especially liked and had stubbornly worn even past the age when costume jewelry became her. It gave her a touching, naïvely rakish air.

Yet she shed a chill around her, and her silence spread to fill the room. Hardly a sound came through the stone walls. In the old days there had always been the piano banging, the phonograph going, two or six or sixteen voices making cosmic conversation. And he never remembered daylight in the apartment. Holly had affected a romantic gloom; the windows were always shrouded by the artistically-frayed burlap, and the light was from lamps, most of them low on the floor and some of them at least with red globes in them. And always the smell of sandalwood.

Like a Chinese whorehouse. He shook his head, pitying and entranced, and sat down on the window seat overlooking the reach of South Temple. Directly across was a Five Minute Car Wash with a big apron of concrete and a spick dazzle of white paint and red tiles. In the times he remembered, that lot had held a Peewee Golf Course where men in shirt sleeves, women in summer dresses, young couples loud with laughter, putted little white balls along precise green alleys and across precise circles of green artificial grass and over gentle and predictable bridges and causeways into numbered holes.

"Look at them," Holly said to him once as they sat in the tower looking down at the after-dinner golfers moving under the bright floodlights. *"Toujours gai,* my God. Some day I'm going to build a miniature golf course with fairways six inches wide and rough all over the place. I'll fill the water holes with full-sized crocodiles and sow the sandtraps with sidewinders. How would it be to hide a black widow spider in every hole so that holing out and picking up your ball would earn you some excitement? What if you sawed the supports of all the little bridges nearly in two?"

Live it dangerously. It was strange to recall how essential that had seemed. Go boom, take chances. He touched the casement windows, thinking that this was the pose, sitting right here and looking out, that Holly had assumed when Tom Stead painted her in her gold velvet gown.

Probably that portrait wasn't anything special. It couldn't have been. The chances were that Tom Stead was painting signs somewhere now, if he hadn't drunk himself to death. But then, in this room, in the presence of its subject whose life overflowed upon them all, that slim golden shape with the velvet highlights was Lilith, Helen, Guenevere, *das ewig Weibliche*. And it was hardly a day before other girls, less fortunately endowed or graced, had begun dropping comments on how *warm* that Stead-Holly romance was getting, and hinting that there was hidden away somewhere a companion portrait—a nude.

Well, well, what a bunch of Bohemian puritans. Harris did not believe in any nude, or in its importance if there had been one, though at the time it had bothered him, and he had been malely offended, surprised that she would *lower* herself, you know?

Now, sitting bemused in the window, he reflected that what had truly shone out of that golden portrait, as out of Holly herself, was not so much glamour as innocence. Under the sheath she was positively virginal; if you cracked the enamel of her sophistication you found a delighted little girl playing Life.

Again he remembered the soft, childlike kiss by the piano on a Christmas morning, and he stood up so sharply that he startled himself with the sight of the dead woman. It *was* innocence. She could put away the predatory paws of college boys, twist laughing from the casual kiss, pass among the hot young Freudians as untouched as a nun, shed like water the propositions that were thrown at her seven to the week. There she sat in her gold gown by her window opening on the foam: a maiden in a tower.

He crossed the room and tried the bedroom door, wanting to look in on her intimately. In this room, now completely bare, aseptically painted, he had sat dozens of times when she was ill or when on Sunday mornings she made it a charming point of her sophistication to entertain in bed. While she lay propped with pillows he had read to her, talked to her, kissed her, had his hands fended away. The empty room was still charged with the vividness with which she invested everything. There was one night very late, two or three o'clock, when he had sat on one side of the bed and a mournful and lovesick jazz trumpeter had sat on the other, neither willing to leave the other alone there, and all that night he had read aloud into the smell of sandalwood the life story of a mad woman from Butte, Montana. *I, Mary MacLean,* that one was called.

What an occasion she made of it, laid up by flu, hemmed in by rival young men, covered to the chin in an absurd, high-necked, old-fashioned nightgown, taking aspirin with sips of ginger beer, laughing at them alternately or together with that face as vivid on the pillow as a flower laid against the linen. It was innocence. In that crackpot Bohemian pre-crash wonderful time, it was innocence.

How he and the trumpeter broke the deadlock, what had ever happened to the Tom Stead flurry, what had happened to any of Holly's string of admirers—all gone. She sent them away, or they quarreled at her over their bruised egos, or they grew huffy at finding her always in a crowd. Plenty of self-appointed hummingbird catchers, but no captures.

And yet, maybe . . .

Summer and winter, day and night, were telescoped in his memory. How old would he have been? Twenty? Twenty-one? It must have been near the end of Holly's reign in this apartment, before everything went sour and the delayed wave of the crash reached them and he left school to go to work and Holly herself went away. There was neither beginning nor end nor definite location in time to what he most vividly remembered. What they were doing, whether there had been a party there or whether they had been out on a date, whether she had roommates then or was living alone, none of that came back. But they were alone in a way they had seldom been.

They must have been talking, something must have led up to it, for there she was with the clarity of something floodlighted in his mind, Holly pressing against him and crying with her face against his chest, clinging and crying and saying—he heard only the refrain, not the garble against his chest—"Kim, Kim, get me out of here! I want to get out of this. This is all no good, I've got to, Kim, please!"

Both the tears and the way she clung excited him. But the game had been played so long by other rules that he went on in the old way, laughing, burlesquing gestures of consolation, patting the crow-wing hair, saying, "There there, little girl." Inanities, idiocies. . . . She wore an evening dress cut very low in the back, and he played his fingers up and down her spine. He slid his hand in against her skin, slid it further, expecting the competent twist and shrug and fending and the laugh that would mean the emotional fit was over. But his hand went on around, clear around, and with a shock like an internal explosion he found it cupping the frantic softness of her breast.

Even remembering, all his sensations were shocking to him. He remembered how smoothly the curve of her side swelled upward, how astonishingly *consecutive* her body seemed. Also, also, and almost with revulsion, how rigid and demanding the nipple of her breast. Innocence—he had never touched a girl there, never imagined, or rather had imagined wrong. Stupefied by the sudden admission to her flesh, made uneasy by the way she crowded and clung, he stood wrapping her awkwardly, and kissed her and tasted her tears, and thought with alarm and conviction of Tom Stead and the rumored nude, and was anguished with eagerness to escape.

He could remember not a scrap, not a detail, of how he got away. She offered herself passionately in his memory, and that was all. The Peewee Golfer putting his little white ball up the little green alley of his youth came suddenly upon the sidewinder in the sandtrap, the crocodile in the artificial lake.

Harris closed the door on the ridiculous and humiliating memory. It had begun to occur to him that he had been an extraordinary young man, and very little of what had been extraordinary about himself pleased him. Innocence? Well, maybe, though there were more contemptuous names for it. He had been a fraud, a gargler of whisky he would obediently not drink. A great yapper with the crowd, but when the cat stopped running, what a frantic sliding to a stop, what digging not to catch what he was after.

Weakly he tried to prop up the slack thing he had been. He told himself that it was a pose with all of them, the life that revolved around Holly was an absurd and perhaps touching and certainly unimportant part of growing up. Or was it? What might he be at this moment, would he have more or less to regret, if he had taken Holly at her passionate word, married her, lived it, as she was determined to live it in her innocence, dangerously?

The last time he saw Holly she was boarding a train for Seattle, on her way to Shanghai and a job they all publicly envied but would probably not have risked taking themselves. Her life, whatever happened to her, would not have been dull. And yet it might have been more thoroughly wasted than at that moment he thought his own had been.

He had played it the other way, not so much from choice as from yielding to pressures, and he had done the best he could with it. How would he look to Holly now, at this very minute? How had he looked then?

Like a bubble of gas from something submerged and decaying in deep water there rose to the surface of his mind one of Blake's proverbs of Hell that they had admired together that long-gone Christmas morning. It burst, and it said, "Prudence is a rich ugly old maid courted by Incapacity."

It shamed him to remember, though he half repudiated it. From the life of prudence he had got a wife he loved and respected, children he adored, a job he could do with interest and almost with content. He regretted none of them. But he stood here remembering that moment when Holly stopped playing make-believe, and it seemed to him that his failure to take her when she offered herself was one of the saddest failures of his life. The fact that he might make all the same crucial choices the same way if he had them to make again helped not at all; it did him no good to remind himself that no one could turn in any direction without turning his back on something. The past had trapped him, and it held him like pain.

Angrily he looked at his watch. Past five. Starting for the door, he passed the dead woman's table and saw her calm pale face, the skin delicately wrinkled like the skin of a winter-kept apple, but soft-looking, as if it would be not unpleasant to touch. What was her name, what had she died of, what had she looked like when she wore expression? Who mourned her, who had loved her, what things in her life did they regret or had she regretted? Would they think it disagreeable that a total stranger had been alone with her here staring into her dead face? And in that face what was it that the caution of death enclosed and hid?

The barbaric silver necklace seemed somehow to define her. What it said of frivolity, girlishness, love of ornament and of gaiety and of life, made him like her; the way it lay on the sober black crepe breast preached the saddest lesson he had ever derived.

He thought of how she had been transported and tampered with by McBride, and how further touches of disguise would complete her transformation from something real and terrible and lost to something serene, removed, bearable. Alone with her here, before the arrival of the others, before she went forth to be forgotten, he could feel a strange, real anguish for this woman he had never known, and a strange gratitude that he had been permitted to see her.

Gratitude, or something near it. And yet as he started for the door he threw a sick, apologetic glance around the room as quiet and empty as a chapel, and at the woman who lay so quietly at its center. He meant to tiptoe out, but he heard, almost with panic, the four quick raps his heels made on the bare floor before they found the consoling softness of the stairs.

(From Botteghe Oscure)

BIRD MAN

BY DAVID STUART

"*LISTEN!*" Becker said. "I'll guarantee he'll show up this spring, just like the rest of the birds."

"Here we go again!" Moreau said, shrugging his shoulders.

At the time four of us were sitting in the Café des Deux Magots, and Becker had finally switched the conversation onto his favorite topic—the Bird Man. I was the only one who had yet to see the fabulous creature, so Becker's performance was chiefly for my benefit. And what a performance! Not that the other two, Moreau and Augier, were any less insistent about the Bird Man's existence, they were just less theatrical. Becker punctuated his tale by cocking his head, hopping about the café—even climbing over the tables, if not prevented, and blasting out shrill rooklike caws. After each blast we'd see at least one café-sitter pick himself off the floor. It was ear-splitting entertainment, no mistake about that.

Then when we'd leave the café Becker would trot me across the street and into the St.-Germain-des-Prés churchyard to point out the spot where the Bird Man was to appear. Now the yard was grim and bleak, the wooden benches colder than pump handles, and the trees bare. "But spring," Becker would insist, "is only three months off."

Once a day for those three months I heard the tale of the Bird Man. Each time it was embroidered a bit more, but with each hearing I believed a bit more. The idea of a man's insanity taking the harmless twist of making him a bird fascinated me. So when at last the cold let up I commenced spending most of my time hanging around the churchyard. Becker was busy painting, getting ready a spring show. Even so, he managed to drop by several times a week to make sure my interest didn't flag.

"Don't be impatient," Becker said. "He'll come on, brother, like the aprocryphal roc!"

And one day he did.

I was alone in the yard, scratching some notes on the back of an envelope, when suddenly I heard a loud chirping. I looked up to see the Bird Man hopping along Rue de l'Abbaye, coming for the churchyard. He hopped through the gate and on to the far end of the yard where he continued his chirping. And almost at once the air was filled with birds—thousands of them. They settled around him. They covered the ground like a patchwork quilt. It looked as if every bird in Paris turned out for his welcome.

He was a tall, gaunt man, with piercing blue-black eyes that darted about like gnats around a rotting pear. The pupils were tremendous and looked artificially dilated. A knife-edge aquiline nose hooked over his thin, too-red lips: they were constantly pursed as he never stopped chirping. His fingers were long and brittle and the few nails not broken off short were cardboard thick and yellow. Over his thin shoulders he wore a cape of *mousseline* into which were woven feathers of a hundred different species of birds. Dirty chicken feathers were set beside fine ostrich plumes, duck beside egret, sparrow beside oriole, until the whole was a haphazard arrangement of colors and sizes. From his feather-covered, short, cotton pants shot a pair of bony, knotty-kneed, hairy legs. And around his ankles and covering his otherwise bare feet dangled rings of feathers like those worn in certain native dances. This costume was topped with a tuft of quetzal tail feathers thrust into his shaggy matted black hair.

Crouched down, sort of sitting on his heels, and with the feathered cape covering him, he really looked like a monstrous bird—like something out of Chagall via Roquefort. And the amazing thing was that the birds accepted him. He moved among them chirping and clucking. He was one of them. I know that I had only to lift my arm to send them all into the air.

"How about the phoenix!" Becker called to me. He was coming full tilt across the street carrying a loaf of bread in each hand. "He's the eagle! The king of birds!"

"He's that," I agreed. I took one of the loaves and we set to work tearing them into crumbs. "He's lost his marbles, too."

"Insane? He's the *only* sane thing in the world!"

There couldn't have been more than a split second between Becker's shout and the Bird Man's leap. He went high into the air, his cape spread like wings across his arms. And the birds rose with him and fluttered overhead until in some mysterious manner he signaled that danger had passed, when they returned to his feet.

"God. . ." Becker breathed ecstatically.

By now the churchyard was filled with spectators. A good hundred more were hanging on the surrounding iron fence. This group kept changing as the big green busses stopped at the corner to take some away and leave a new lot. A number of cars had lined up along the curb, the people standing on the fenders and engine hoods the better to see. Augier and Moreau elbowed their way through this crowd and stood beside us.

"You ought to stuff him and stick him in the next surrealist show," Augier said.

"Bag your lip!" Becker cracked. He placed the last crumb of his loaf in the middle of his palm and held it toward the Bird Man. "Here, birdie, birdie, birdie," he called softly.

Augier let out a howl you could hear twenty kilometers up the Seine. "Birdie, birdie! Holy Christ! You're both lunatics!"

The Bird Man cocked his head at us. Then he threw out his arms and flapped his feathered cape, and the birds went into the air with a great sound like the beating of waves on rocks. With a final glance at us he climbed onto the fence, dropped to the sidewalk, and hopped off down the street. He was out of sight in a very few seconds.

"You big-lip!" Becker yelled. "You've scared him off, you and your goddamn laughter!"

Becker was sore, like a Breton would be if you stood off and heaved rocks at his calvary. Becker actually holds birds in high awe, subscribing to all the mystical flapdoodle about them. In his paintings the *Good in Man* is represented by bird forms: he paints birds in battle, birds attacking and beating the hell out of men, amorous birds, and birds of God. For all that, he wasn't sore very long. When we left the yard he was off on a harangue about how the earth evolved out of the mundane egg.

In the next two months I saw quite a bit of the Bird Man. As the days grew warmer he came more often to the churchyard until by the end of June he was doing three shows a week. Moreau's and Augier's interests fell off early. But Becker was with me whenever he could take an afternoon off from his painting. It wasn't long before the Bird Man recognized me. He'd hop up and sort of squat at my feet, cocking his head and looking at me with one bright eye as he snapped up the crumbs I held on my palm. Actually he liked me better than he did Becker. Becker was overboard in his sympathy. He bent backwards too far trying to make him a friend. The Bird Man would suffer it just so long, then hop away to his feathered pals. Personally, I preferred him to stand a bit off: he smelled pretty sour, like the bottom of a bird cage.

As far as I could tell he spoke no language, unless you can call clucks, chirps, quacks, and gobbles a language. I tried him with the several languages I know, and even read him a chapter from the Koran in the original. For this last effort he gave me a couple of bird whistles. Finally I tried cursing. I dumped a load on him that would have made the most inarticulate jerk, and particularly one the size of the Bird Man, knock my ears down. He took it all like it was so much birdseed.

For the next month or so nothing particular happened. Then one roasting hot day in the middle of July something did. There were four people in the churchyard that day—the Bird Man, myself, a father, and his noisy little son. The boy was dressed in a sailor outfit and was armed with a variety of rackety toys—mechanical autos and tanks, a shovel and a pail (which from time to time he filled with gravel and dumped into his father's shoes), and a slingshot. The Bird Man and his flock kept an eye on the child and stayed well to the far end of the yard. The streets were empty except for a policeman who spent most of his time by the fountain, dipping his handkerchief in the water and wiping it over his red face. The sidewalk cafés on the shady side of St.-Germain were packed. Those on the sunny side were empty. I had sometime before given up the idea of writing and was half dozing in the sun. I couldn't quite get to sleep because each time I was about to pop off, the brat wound up one of his toys and sent it rattling over the gravel. And each time the birds would fly up into the trees where they'd wait till the spring-motor died.

Nevertheless, it would have been an agreeable afternoon had not the brat suddenly tired of his toys and taken up the slingshot. He singled out a bird that had wandered too far away from the others, loaded his slingshot, and proceeded to stalk the bird like a big game hunter after lion. I watched out of partly closed eyes as he pulled back on the rubber bands, never dreaming he'd fire. I noticed that the Bird Man had hopped out of his flock and was watching nervously as the bands stretched farther and farther back.

Suddenly the big game hunter let go. There was a dull thud, and the bird rolled over, its legs thrust into the air like a picture of Cock Robin in a children's book.

"I got him, papa!" the hunter squealed.

What happened next happened so fast I couldn't move for amazement. First the Bird Man pounced on the boy and with one whack sent him tumbling senselessly along the path. When he stopped rolling his legs didn't stick up in the air at all. They just flopped out like broken twigs. Then the Bird Man turned to the father, his arms whirling like blades of an electric fan. He was punching and clawing and pounding the startled gent's face all at the same time. And for the first time he spoke. All the while he was belaboring the father he was filling the air with healthy oaths. His voice was as shrill and penetrating as a peacock's. Later I remembered that everything he said was something I had used on him.

Now the Bird Man had the father on the ground and was kicking him into insensibility. Just as I started across to help the father, the red-faced policeman came roaring through the gate swinging his white nightstick. He clipped the Bird Man squarely on the head, smashing his tuft of quetzal feathers and sending him on his face.

I picked up the boy's pail and raced across the street and filled it at the fountain. I wiped the boy's ear where the Bird Man had clouted him, and cleaned the gravel from his face. Not wanting to move him for fear he was internally banged up, I left and started in on the groaning father.

"I'm going to call the wagon," the policeman said. "You stay here and see that fool doesn't escape." He ran across the street to the café and was back in a moment and we both worked on the father. By the time the wagon arrived the father and son had come to. But not the Bird Man. He was still face down in the gravel, his feathered cape covering his head. The brat was wandering around the yard rubbing his ear and bawling like a wounded calf. I wished the Bird Man had hit him harder. The father's eyes, puffy and swollen, were slowly closing. His face was pulped, and his clothes were hanging in ribbons.

The policeman and the wagon driver carried the Bird Man out of the yard and dumped him into the wagon. After taking all of our names, they drove off for the station.

"Can you and your boy get home?" I asked.

"I think so," he mumbled through thick blue lips. With that they left, the brat still bellowing and the father stumbling blindly along.

I looked about the yard. It was littered with feathers, and the boy's toys, like playthings forgotten when snow falls, were partly hidden beneath them. I took a last look at the dead bird: its legs were still sticking straight up. Then I went across to the café and had a double shot of Courvoisier.

The next morning Becker and I went to the police station. Becker was pretty much broken up over the mess the Bird Man had got himself into. And he was sore as hell at the father and son. "He ought to have killed them both, shooting a bird with a slingshot. The goddamn pigs!"

We asked at the desk what had happened to the Bird Man.

"He's gone. He was taken to an asylum last night. He should have been in one years ago. Imagine beating a small child!"

"He ought to have used a blunt weapon," Becker said.

"Sir? . . ."

A heavy-set, moustached chief—the type you can spot at one hundred meters—walked in. "Hello. I heard you from my office. I'm on my way to his rooms. Want to come along?"

Indeed we did.

We climbed into the chief's Peugeot and drove down Rue de Rennes, past the churchyard, and turned into Rue de l'Abbaye. Then we turned into Rue de Furstenberg and just beyond the Delacroix atelier we pulled up before an ancient, moldy white building.

"He lives here?"

"Yes. Has a room on the top floor," the chief answered.

"How do you know? I thought no one knew where he lived," Becker said.

"Oh, sure. We've watched him for years. But he's always been funny—up to now . . . Let's go. It's a good long hike. Watch the steps, they're about to collapse."

I could smell the room two floors below. And when the chief kicked open the door the stink roared out like a black cloud and almost knocked me flat. The room was matchbox in size. The faded blue walls were painted with yellow stripes running up and across the ceiling where they converged in the center at the lightless socket. The washstand was covered with dirty white oilcloth and shaped to resemble the porcelain drinking well in a bird cage. On the opposite wall was a similar oilcloth well partly filled with stale bread crusts. The floor was covered with a layer of dirt and crusts and filth three centimeters thick. The room was truly a bird cage on a grand scale. And smelled like one that hadn't been cleaned for fifty-two years. The chief and I held our noses, but Becker was beside himself with joy.

"It's unbelievable!" He went about the room poking into the wells, picking up scraps, and thoroughly enjoying himself in the crud. "Listen! Neither Lautréamont nor Ernst ever dreamed up anything to touch this. He's a genius—the master!"

"Let's get the hell out of the master's nest," the chief said, sounding like his nose was stopped with a summer cold. We had to drag Becker from the room. Had the chief let him, I'm sure he would have moved in and set up housekeeping.

During the next four months either Becker or I made it a point to look into the churchyard at least once a day. But the Bird Man was never there. His room had been boarded up and a sign reading *Closed By Order Of The Police* was nailed on the door, the sign they use to close a stew. We made inquiries at the police station: "Can't you at least tell us what's happened to him?" They couldn't. The papers had been mislaid, or lost. They didn't even know in which asylum he was. Nobody in his right mind will ever seek information from a French government agency—they're all like a Kafka novel in a diving bell. But as a last resort we called on several of them. The above statement still goes.

Then one day in the early part of November we saw him once again. It was a lovely day, a hangover from summer. The sun was bright and warm and there were a few leaves on the trees. Becker and I were sprawled out on the benches in the churchyard sopping up this last bit of sunshine. Two children rolled hoops around our benches and over our feet, but when we didn't provoke they grew tired and left us alone. I must have been dozing because when I heard the sound of footsteps on the gravel I sat up with a start. A tall, gaunt man dressed in a cheap blue serge suit was just sitting down on the bench opposite mine. I didn't recognize him until he looked up. Then I saw his eyes. The pupils were no longer so large, but they were still a piercing blue-black. And no one could have mistaken his nose, knife-edge thin and hooked like a macaw's beak over his mouth. For a moment he stared at me as though trying to place me in his memory. Then he looked down at the ground. I nudged Becker.

"What?" he asked, rubbing his eyes.

I pointed to the man on the bench.

"It's him, it's him!" Becker whispered excitedly.

For some time we all sat quietly. The man occasionally lifted his eyes to look at us, then turned them back to the ground at his feet. Some birds were hopping about the yard, but they went no closer to him than to us. The attraction seemed to have vanished. It was about this time that I noticed him suddenly sit rigidly on the bench and follow with his eyes a fat little sparrow. No part of the man moved but his eyes. They were like hunters hidden behind the blind of his body. Meanwhile the sparrow hopped jauntily up the path. Finally it stopped and cocking its head looked first at the man, then at us. Very slowly the man took from a pocket a crust of bread. He tore off a bit and held it out to the sparrow. The bird eyed the crumb, then hopped over and pecked at it.

I didn't even see his hand close. It worked with the speed of a hair trigger, because suddenly there the sparrow was in his fist, twisting its head this way and that, and chirping like mad. The man held it up and stared into its frightened eyes. I didn't look at Becker. But I could feel his tenseness as he sat forward on the bench. We were absolutely fascinated, like snakes by the fakir.

Seconds passed.

Then as suddenly as the hand had snapped shut to catch the bird, it snapped once again. There was a sound like the crushing of an empty matchbox, and the sparrow's head fell limply over the man's thumb. Then silence. I could hear Becker's furious heart pounding. I put my hand on his arm to stop him from leaping wildly on the man.

The Bird Man looked up, his face set and unsmiling. Very slowly he got to his feet and holding the dead sparrow out like a rare gift he walked across to me and dropped it in my hands. I looked up into his eyes. They were no longer piercing. Now they were a weak watery-blue, and slightly moist. A little drop of water on the tip of his nose sparkled in the sunlight.

(From New World Writing)

HERMAN'S DAY

BY HARVEY SWADOS

TOOTHBRUSH in hand, Herman Felton raised the lid of the ebony toilet seat and recoiled in dismay. Floating in the clear water a red and luscious mouth was looking up at him, lips parted sensually. He bent forward, peered down into the bowl, and saw a folded sheet of toilet paper bearing the imprint of someone's lips—Clara's? Betsy's? The price you pay for living with two women.

Now at least he was awake. But there are better ways to wake up, he thought, as he shuffled about, glaring at his gums in the mirror, running the razor cautiously around his Adam's apple, slicking the thin strands of hair anxiously into place; slobs, he thought, the best of them are such slobs that you can't train them to flush down the water. Lips in the bowl, hair in the teeth of the comb—he shook his head angrily as he knotted his tie (yellow, with green leaves and things that looked like streaks of lightning) and clipped it to his summer shirt with the initialed tie clasp that Clara had given him for his last birthday.

His wife and daughter were still asleep as he passed their closed doors on his way to the kitchen and a bowl of Grape-Nuts with milk and a dash of sugar. From beyond his own bedroom door, which he had closed earlier with a finesse born of years of experience, came the soft bubble of Clara's breathing, more relaxed and quieter than the strangled sound of her snores in the dark of the night. She would be waking soon, he knew. From behind Betsy's door there was no more sound than from her absent brother's.

She was there now, and she had always been a quiet sleeper, but the uncanny silence seemed to reinforce his uneasy suspicion that she had slipped away from him, despite all his efforts, as completely as Morrow, who had gone, left an empty, freshly-painted bedroom, without even a wave of the hand.

At the end of the hall a vagrant June breeze bellied the printed curtains of the half-opened window above the stairs. As it reached for him, he paused for an instant before going on with the day's work and found himself actually shuddering at the renewed memory of an incident of three or four years ago that had refused to lie dormant, but kept crawling to the surface like a fat worm after rain, called forth by the season, the early summer breeze, and the closed door of his daughter's room.

It was on a morning like this when they were still living in the Bronx, with Morrow away at college and Clara and Betsy still asleep in their rooms, that he had paused, eager for some sign of life, some moment of affection, before plunging into the salt and sweat of the subway. Without knocking, thinking that he might find her asleep or better still half awake and ready to throw her arms around his neck for a good-by kiss, he had opened Betsy's door and tiptoed noiselessly into her room. She was asleep, but something, perhaps the morning air quickening the gauze window curtains, perhaps only the exhalation of his breath, stirred her so strongly that at once she sat bolt upright, staring at him wildly as though he were an apparition from her dream that had refused to fade away with the night. She was completely nude, and as she sat up the sheet which had covered her fell away from the upper half of her body, revealing her torso to him in the pure morning light as he had never seen it before. The sun purled across her milky shoulders, touching the clavicles that were just now losing their sharp childish outlines and lighting her young breasts that were not much larger than apples and glowed with the same kind of verdancy. Herman's eyes were fixed on the little buds of her nipples, firm and hard, ready to be bitten. They were the most beautiful things he had ever seen, and although his ears were roaring and a giant hand was pressing on his chest, squeezing it so tightly that he could not breathe, he could not bring himself to turn his head. When at last he was able to look into his daughter's eyes, he was stunned at the expression he met there. There was nothing simple about it, it was compounded of emotions that he had never associated with Betsy before—pride, anger, voluptuousness, recklessness, and worst of all a calculating recognition of what she had seen in his face. In the narrowing of her shallow blue eye he could see a bold greeting of that force in himself of whose existence he had been absolutely unaware until this moment. She made no move to cover herself, but sat upright with her arms rigidly at her sides, her hands pressed into the mattress. "Haven't you got enough pajamas to wear?" he asked in a strangled voice. Before she could answer, he went on, "You look like a street woman, sleeping naked. Your mother is going to hear about this," and he closed the door without the smile or the hug that he had been hoping for when he entered the room. But he was never able after that to close his mind on the incident.

Clara has something to do with it, Herman thought as he spooned sugar carefully into his cereal. Betsy wouldn't have been like that when he opened the door, she wouldn't behave the way she did now, if she liked and respected her mother as a daughter should. For some reason that he couldn't fathom Betsy was incapable of understanding why he had married Clara, and why he still loved her. From time to time he had tried to explain what Clara meant to him, but it involved too much that he could not talk about freely—his immigrant childhood on the lower East Side, his dates with Clara on the evenings when he wasn't studying at Cooper Union, and his wonder at her smooth plump ease and her Germanic phlegm. But Betsy's reaction, when he did tell her that her mother had defied the entire Hamburger family to marry him before either of them was old enough to vote, was one of mingled incredulity and boredom, and of course he could hardly go on to explain that he had always felt grateful to Clara, and would continue to feel grateful, even after she had lost her figure and he had discovered that he was her superior in every quality save that of patience. Nor could he explain to his daughter how it was that love-making with Clara had never lost its original excitement, for even as she grew fatter there was a greater area for him to grasp and conquer and a more urgent proof required of his manhood and his brutal Russian superiority to the refined German Jews of her own family circle.

He placed the bowl in the sink and filled it with warm water, determined to shake off his morning mood; and indeed by the time he had picked the morning paper from the porch steps and backed the two-year-old Dodge out of the garage, he had pushed subjective matters entirely from his mind and was ready to concentrate on the business of the day.

He parked the car—it was his first, but he drove it without pride or affection, thinking of it only as a tool, not as a symbol of any kind—at the Long Island Railroad station three minutes before the express arrived, nodded briskly to the few familiar faces that boarded the train with him, and took his customary place in the last seat of the smoker, next to the window.

In ten minutes he had finished the first section of the *Times,* concentrating on General Rommel, General MacArthur, General Timoshenko and the news from Washington, and he was free to study the market quotations, with the first section tucked under his buttocks. Midway through the quotations he took a gold pencil from his inside jacket pocket, made some computations on the margin of the newspaper, and then had to pull out a leather notebook to transfer the notations to a more practical place. From the market page he flipped to the business opportunities department, checking the capital and commodities offerings that might have some bearing on his immediate situation. He looked up, genuinely surprised, when the train ground to a halt in Penn Station—it seemed to him that he had left his house only a few minutes ago.

In the taxi there was no time for work, or even thought, for he was at the Empire State Building in a few minutes, while he was still sorting out the papers in his briefcase. He took the elevator to the eighteenth floor and walked down the hall to the office of his accountant.

The receptionist looked up from her tabloid and smiled at him. "Hello, Mr. Felton. How's the family these days?"

"All right." It struck him that service help were getting more Goddamned familiar every day. If you smiled back at them they felt encouraged to start asking you questions about your family, simply because they were privileged to overhear private conversations that they shouldn't be listening to anyway. He said curtly, "Is he in yet?"

"He'll be here any minute. But Mr. Wax is in. Do you—"

"I don't want Wax. I'll wait for Gelbhorn in his office. Get me long distance on his phone in the meantime."

"Surely."

As he entered Gelbhorn's office the phone began to ring. He took off his jacket and hung it neatly over a chair, then sat down at Gelbhorn's desk and picked up the phone. "Hello, long distance," he said. He waited for the click that meant the switchboard girl had cut the connection for herself. "Get me Allentown, Pennsylvania, please. I want to talk person-to-person to Warren Staley."

"There may be a delay in getting through to Allentown."

"Yes. All right. Here's my number—you can call me when you're ready."

He was reading off Gelbhorn's number when the accountant walked in, tossed his heavy briefcase on the desk, opened his tie, and took out two cigars. Herman pronged the phone and made a perfunctory gesture of rising.

"Stay there, Herman. I'll take this chair. After all, I should have come to see you. You're stripped for action already, I see."

"It's going to be a scorcher. I read it in the *Times*. You could have had an air-conditioned office—I don't know why you had to go and stick yourself in the Empire State Building."

Gelbhorn shrugged embarrassedly. Herman knew why he didn't remove his jacket—he was ashamed of his fat breasts, about which Herman had teased him on more than one occasion. "After all," he said, "I'm not on my own. There were four other men to consider. Tell me," he added hastily, "what do you hear from Morrow?"

Herman hesitated. How much could he know? He forced himself to wait until he could speak without revealing any emotion. "He's in the middle of it, the way he wanted. He's my only son, I wish him nothing but the best, but he brought it on himself. I only wish he knew what he was doing to his mother."

"She should be proud. How *is* Clara?"

"She worries—it gives her insomnia."

"What do you expect? It's no joke, not knowing what your boy is going through. And there's no end in sight, no end. What's with the little beauty?"

"Betsy? She's high-strung, very high-strung. You've only got the one girl, Alex, and she's just starting high school, so you don't know what I mean. But you have to take my word for it that the war is like a cancer on these young people. Don't think Hitler isn't doing a job on me, just because I'm sitting here smoking a cigar."

"What do you mean?"

"What do I mean?" Herman felt his face grow hot with anger. How smug this man was, with no son in the army or in a jam, no daughter exposed to a thousand different temptations, not even a business of his own to worry about, just the account books of businesses which would give him an income regardless of what happened to them. With an effort of will he said calmly, "Betsy is restless. She doesn't get it from me or from Clara. It's in the air. It's Hitler's fault. She wants to go away. Can I send her away, aged eighteen? That she's still innocent is already a miracle. She goes to summer session at college, Benedict College, to keep a little busy. Maybe she'll be a scientist."

"Maybe she'll get married one of these days," Gelbhorn suggested coyly.

"To who? To a soldier? Over my dead body. That much Hitler isn't going to get. Come on, let's get to work."

"Listen, Herman." Gelbhorn took several folders from his briefcase and cleared his throat. "You're setting up so many corporations I can't even tell them apart myself. This latest one—"

"There's going to be more." Herman looked at his accountant with open contempt. "Are you a C.P.A. or what? If you want to go back to Second Avenue and do the candy stores' books instead of mine, just say the word."

"That's not the point. I'm not complaining for myself, I'm enjoying every minute of it, even when I have to stay up all night. I just want you to be sure that you realize how complicated things are already. The Alro Corporation has seven directors, five of them are on the board of the Watertite Corporation, four of *them*—"

"I know all that. All I want from you is to keep us legitimate."

"It all depends on how you define it. Right now anything is legitimate, but the war isn't going to last forever, Herman."

"Maybe you ought to tell that to Hitler."

"Don't kid. When it comes to renegotiate all the contracts you have, the government is going to want to know what went where, and why, and how come it had to be so complicated."

"That's what I'm paying you for. Right? So your education

shouldn't go to waste. Remember this—all these years I've been trying to get on my feet, the tax set-up has been rigged against me, and in favor of the big fellows. Could I charge machinery and equipment off against contracts the way they did? You know damn well I couldn't. All the corporations that have had big profits going back to 1936 pay smaller taxes than me, because the excess profits tax is rigged for them and against me, the way it goes back five years or more and lets them write everything off. Well, it's not going to be that way any more. This time I'm going to write things off, and when it's all over I'm going to be one of the big ones. They'll pin a medal on me when the war's over, watch and see."

"Medal or no medal, does every company have to have a different fiscal year ending? Every one? How am I going to explain that?"

"Alex, if you want to start worrying about things like that now, it's all right with me. But don't bring me your problems—I've got other things to worry about. You were the one that explained to me how we could build up a good credit position that way. If stuff can disappear over the year end of one company and not be picked up until after the other company starts in, why not? I want Alro to look very strong when it ends this fiscal year, so we can borrow capital from it for Watertite for expansion. We can clean that up for the statement period and then reloan it right away after the statement period, can't we?"

"But like I explained to you at the time." Gelbhorn hesitated, then got up and walked to the window. "If you can make it look like there's more assets than there are with different fiscal year endings, you can also hide assets that way too."

"Fine."

"It's easy for you to say fine, but you can always plead ignorance. I'm the one that'll have to do the explaining."

Herman Felton placed his cigar carefully in the ash tray and looked up at Gelbhorn. "I'm going to make you happy, Alex. I'm waiting for a call from Allentown. There's a nice old-time American manufacturer who's going on the rocks because he can't get material to make porch awnings and umbrellas. It's an established business, in the same family for three generations, but they've got no contacts with Washington. Without contacts you can't get contracts. Staley Awnings are willing to make a deal, Alex. I think you belong on their board of directors with me. I want to set the officers' salaries at $12,500 per annum. You'll earn it, Alex, I know you will—and Minnie will be pleased when you tell her."

Gelbhorn opened his mouth to speak, but just then the phone began to ring, and he said nothing. He looks like a fish, Herman thought, like a big fat goldfish with glasses on; he was so pleased with this fancy that he let the phone ring four times, with his hand on the receiver, before he picked it up.

"Yes, this is Mr. Felton. Hello, Mr. Staley, how are you?" he smiled into the telephone. "I'm all set at this end. Not just a subcontract, a prime contract from the Navy, no less . . . Isn't it great? We'll have to straighten out about the waterproof backing that we were talking about, but my chemist says not to worry. I want you to start thinking about labor supply for a second shift, Mr. Staley. It won't be easy, but I've got confidence in you . . . The union may be able to help us out when we explain how desperately the stuff is needed." He winked at Gelbhorn, who had seated himself once again and was laying out the folders on the desk. "I'll be out tomorrow after lunch with my attorney, Mr. Scharf, and my accountant, Mr. Gelbhorn. You want to expect us about two-thirty p.m.? Fine, we'll iron out the last wrinkles and shake hands on the deal . . . Hitler is going to be sorry we ever got together, Mr. Staley . . . See you tomorrow. Good-by."

"Have you really got the contract, Herman?"

Herman shook his head sadly at Gelbhorn. "Sometimes I think you have no faith in me at all. What do you think I'm knocking myself out for in Washington, three, four times a week? What do you think Hennessy's brother, the congressman, is doing all this time—writing love letters to his constituents?"

"I've got to hand it to you. If the Navy's got faith in you, Herman, I suppose I should have, too."

"That's what I like to hear. Now come on, Alex, let's get to work. I want to have all the figures at my fingertips for the Alro board meeting tonight. I don't anticipate any objections, but it doesn't hurt to be prepared."

Gelbhorn spread out the papers he had removed from his briefcase and they set to work. Within five minutes Herman was so deeply absorbed in the corporate problem of the organization which he had fathered, midwifed, nursed, and was now leading to maturity that he was startled and annoyed at any evidence that Gelbhorn had any other interests—the ringing of his telephone, the sighing of his breath, the impatient sparking of his cigar lighter. For several hours they worked steadily and uninterruptedly, with Gelbhorn occasionally calling a girl for computing on her calculating machine. As time went by Herman felt an ecstasy warm and rich as wine rising within him; the figures slipped into place like tumblers in a lock, and it seemed to him that he was not only master but creator of a situation that held the promise of infinite fulfillment and infinite happiness for himself and his family.

Even though he knew that they were caught up at last it came as a rude interruption, almost a shock, when Alex Gelbhorn scraped back his chair and said, "Thank God that's out of the way. Listen, Herman."

"I'm listening."

"Wax and I are going to eat downstairs in Longchamps. Maybe we'll bump into Brody there—you know, the district Treasury man. It wouldn't do you any harm to get next to him. You want to join us?"

He replied contemptuously, "Hennessy's brother has got Brody in his hip pocket. What do I have to buy him meals for?"

"I didn't know that."

"There's lots of things you don't know. Maybe," he added cruelly, "you'd be a little more alert if you didn't eat such heavy meals."

Gelbhorn flushed. Herman refused to change the subject or turn his head away, but continued to stare at his accountant's sloping, narrow shoulders, his broad feminine hips, his thick and ungainly thighs. "People are suffering, Alex," he went on coldly. "They can't all stuff themselves at Longchamps. Maybe you should make every day meatless Tuesday."

"We can't all be wiry like you. It's the way you're born."

"Fat isn't born, it's made." Herman Felton gathered up his paper and briefcase, slipped into his jacket, and threw away his cigar.

"You're sure you won't join us?"

He shook his head. "I've only got time for a quick bite. I can't spend a couple hours cracking jokes."

"Well," Gelbhorn said weakly, as he showed Herman to the door, "it's up to you."

"Give my regards to Wax. And to the rest."

"I'll do that."

"And you'll be ready to go to Allentown with Hennessy and me in the morning, right?"

"Do you think we'll be back tomorrow? My wife likes to know."

"It depends on how things work out. Your wife shouldn't worry, you're a big boy now. And listen, please have ready the figures on maximum gift allowances. Don't give me the old cost-plus stuff—I want some figures, because Scotch comes high and I've got to give out a couple dozen cases in Washington next week. We'll go over it during the trip."

"Sure thing, Herman." As though he were already thinking of the chopped sirloin and the congenial company at Longchamps, Gelbhorn said more genially, "Remember me to Clara and the cutey-pie. And the best of luck to Morrow—next time you write—I don't care what you say, he's a great guy."

Herman's mouth tasted sour as he descended in the elevator. He squeezed a pep-o-mint lifesaver from a pack in his pocket and popped it into his mouth. What did that last crack about Morrow mean? It was utterly uncalled for. He walked rapidly west on 34th Street, ignoring the crowds and thinking what a hell of a business it was, that you had to stand for personal remarks from a bookkeeper just because he knew the family and handled the accounts. If you were cold, they wouldn't stick their necks out for you, and if you were friendly they took advantage of it and started to give you advice on how to run your life. But as he breasted the crowds, feeling the rush of life around him as no more than the air that he breathed or the leather under his feet, he began to berate himself for his narrowness. Gelbhorn was not a bad person, simply a coward, and if he had no imagination, at least he was willing to work hard and do his job. He'll be ready tomorrow, I can count on him for Allentown, Herman thought, and he felt himself warming toward Alex, for after all most of the people that you had to deal with were not only cowardly but stupid and lazy too, and ready to cut your throat if you made the mistake of unbuttoning your shirt. At least Gelbhorn was loyal—or at least, Herman thought wryly as he reached Sixth Avenue and swung north, he would be as long as you could show him a rosy future, a summer place on Lake Mahopac, a good college for his daughter, a big car when the war was over . . . How easy it was to satisfy some people, how easy to keep them in line!

But the strain, he thought, the strain was something that people like Gelbhorn could never understand, not in a million years. How could the average schlemiel know what it meant to carry on your shoulders the war, Hitler, a son who wouldn't listen and had to do the opposite of what was best for him, and then had to get caught with his hand in the cash register like a cheap crook, a daughter who listened but looked at you with God knows what kind of expression on her face, as though she was daring you to say something else, as though she loved you but wanted to prove it by doing things that would make a father's hair stand on end. The worries were bound to keep piling up higher and higher for anybody with guts enough to want to keep climbing. The higher you climbed, the more family worries. The thought was enough to annoy a man of gold.

He determined to close his mind to his family. Allentown, the board meeting, you had to keep your eye on the ball, especially if it was the eight-ball. because it was the softies, the ones who couldn't concentrate, who wound up behind that old eight-ball. That he knew as he knew the palm of his hand—if you allowed yourself to be distracted, you were lost. Morrow and Betsy were big enough already; he could help them most by tending to his business.

He turned into a vegetarian restaurant that was satisfactory if only because the waiters had no excuse to cry into your soup about shortages, passed the cash register and nodded to the owner who was chewing rapidly on some small object that made his little beard bob up and down, sat down at an empty table for two near the door, and ordered a vegetarian veal cutlet without looking at the menu.

All around him they were eating, and Herman found himself wondering how people could live like this, stuffing, gorging, shoveling food into their mouths as if they were eating their last meal, as if everything was going to disappear at two o'clock and they had to cram down everything they could before then, as if they didn't have a thought, a vision, an ideal, except gluttony. It was enough to make you hate everybody, Herman thought, stabbing at the cutlet with his fork, because they were worse than animals really, when you considered that animals could never know any better. But how do I know, he thought, that they have no visions? Am I unfair?

He raised his head from his plate. A saintly looking gentleman with a flowing beard was seated across from him, toying with a bowl of chopped vegetables and sour cream and chatting with an adolescent boy who wore earlocks and a skull cap. His spirituality was somewhat marred by a white streak of sour cream that lay across his mustache and beard like a bandage. What about him? Did he think about the war, about the Jewish people in Europe? What about the couple over by the mirror—a plump, rosy-faced blond Jewish boy in an army uniform and his girl, who looked like somebody's stenographer and nothing else, both of them grinning at each other like idiots and stuffing their faces with pancakes as though they hadn't eaten in weeks. What about them? Was she worried about anything besides getting enough jelly to put on her pancakes? Did he want to be a hero like Morrow? Did he ever think, late at night, what boys like Morrow were going through so he could sit safely and stuff himself? What about the tall, shadowy, skinny man who sat behind them gumming his imitation chopped liver? A health nut, a vegetarian, a spiritualist, a crank who took the BMT out to Coney Island every day, even in the dead of winter, so he could strip down and swim in the surf; he probably earned his living in some dingy, badly-lit store, pasting stamps on approval sheets to mail to other nuts who collected little pieces of paper, subscribed to strength and health magazines, and drank strained carrot juice. Did he have a woman, or just secret dreams? Did he ever stop to realize what the world was coming to, the mix-ups, the pain, the misery of trying to be responsible, a father, an executive? Suddenly behind the skinny nutrose-eater, in the long mirror bolted to the wall behind him, Herman Felton caught sight of his own reflection, another character pushing artificial food into his face.

He stared absently at himself just as he had glanced at the others. His face wasn't any different—narrow, high-domed under the thin strands of plastered-down hair, his lips pursed secretively even when he forked mouthfuls of fake cutlet past his false teeth, his eyes colorless behind the glittering steel-rimmed spectacles, his small animal nostrils dilating at the restaurant odors, all in all looking like a subway rider, a nonentity, a solitary eater who cared about nothing but smoothing out the belly wrinkles. The others could look up from their plates too and see him as one of them; they would never know who he was, what he had on his mind, how the war and his family were pressing on his chest like hot bricks. Which means, he said to himself as he gulped down his coffee and picked up the check, that I don't know anything about them either.

Nobody knows anybody else, he reflected as he left the restaurant. It was still impossible to believe that all of them, the stamp collector, the stenographer, the rabbinical student, lived for anything more than the moment or the immediate appetite; because if that was true then they would all be trying to do something better with their lives. It would show in their faces, it would have to, and the world would be a better place to live in. But some of them must have deep feelings, he thought; maybe not as deep as mine, but still deep enough so that the rabbi suffered for the Jews in Europe and the stenographer suffered for her boy friend who would have to fight for his country. And maybe even the health nut thought about his father sometimes, and about all the fathers that were struggling and suffering all over the world. It had to be, or otherwise you might just as well commit suicide because it wouldn't be worthwhile to go on living on such a planet.

Just the same, he thought, if you wanted to get ahead in the business world you had to act as though everybody was an enemy, a potential enemy at least, whether he was your own brother-in-law or a business partner that you played rummy with, and regardless of whether he was smart or dumb you had to go on the assumption that he was in the game for what he could get out of it and nothing else. If you figured that a man was a bleeding heart or had a grudge against Hitler or wanted to make the world safe for democracy he'd have the knife in your ribs, right up under the armpit, the minute you stretched our your arm to pat him on the back.

He had never burdened Clara with any of this—she was the way she was, too soft and good to know about the cutthroats, and there was no sense in exposing her to something that was alien to her family and her upbringing and that she didn't even have to know about, as long as he was around to take care of her. With the children it was different. Their troubles were still ahead of them, they'd been protected and coddled all their lives although they didn't even realize it, and who else if not their father had the responsibility of showing them what the world was really like? It was all very well, he thought as he crossed Seventh Avenue and bore down into the heart of the garment district, to bring up your children to believe what they were taught in Sunday school; but the world was a little different from that. If they didn't find out about it from their father, they'd only have to learn from the bitterest experience.

The trouble was that it was so hard to know how to do it, and where to stop once you had begun. If you simply talked about life in a general way, or if you used a newspaper article about suicide, illegitimate babies, bankruptcy, the torture of Jews in Europe, race riots, or chiselers getting fat with ration coupons, black market deals, and war contracts, the chances were that Betsy would say, "Oh, Daddy, what are you worrying your head about that stuff for? Haven't you got enough problems with your own business and your own wayward family?" Or that Morrow, who really understood better than his sister what you were driving at, even if people didn't think he was as quick on the uptake, would lift his black sullen head if you pressed him for a comment, and say in his own peculiarly cold and cutting way, "I can take a hint. I won't bring you home any bastards, I'll keep my nose clean, and I'll watch out for the gentiles."

The other way, the way that he really wanted but was somehow afraid to carry through because God knows what it would lead to, was to talk to them about his own problems and the empire that he was building up out of nothing. Betsy loved it, her eyes would gleam as soon as he began to explain even the simplest details of a merger or a board meeting, showing how you had to be on your toes, how you had to watch out for your "friends" that were trying to get the best of you, how you had to plan in advance and keep one step ahead of even the people who were supposed to be working with you and for you. "Oh, I'm proud!" Betsy would cry, as she leaped forward to kiss him on the forehead, her warm breath steaming his glasses. "I'm so proud of my shrewd daddy." She was *too* proud, that was the point that he couldn't explain to anyone, not even to Clara, because he was afraid to admit what it meant. There were times when he suspected (and he hated himself for the suspicion) that she took such delight in hearing about his business because she felt a direct connection between his success and the things that she would be able to have. In a sense that was what he wanted her to feel, how could he deny it? But it implied a kind of selfishness that it was frightening to think about, especially when you matched a new pair of high-heeled shoes or a party dress against the strain that you could actually feel in your heart muscles when you put your own nerve on the line against the authority of Navy officers, procurement officials, and tax agents.

But Betsy, with her childish daydreams about yachts and coming-out parties, didn't really connect them to her father's world. Her pride in his success, Herman reflected, was only a kind of wonder at her daddy's ability to outwit and outmaneuver men whose names she read in the papers, men who were themselves as shadowy and unreal as the yachts and society parties of which she day-dreamed. And there was the rub all over again. How could you know beforehand that your daughter would admire most of all those characteristics which maybe you weren't even sure you had yourself, before you started talking about your business life? And was that to be the final result of all your hopes and dreams, that she would seize on just those questionable things, things that you *had* to do whether you liked them or not, and take them as proof of your ability to beat the world and as principles by which to live? Once, just once, he had tried to point out to Betsy that she was mistaking his meaning, that instead of trying to understand what a mean and bitter world it was, she was picking out and glorifying certain methods which he was forced to use in order to close a deal —but when she replied, "I'm only taking you at your word, if you didn't act the way you do you wouldn't be so successful and you wouldn't be my daddy, and that's why I think you're the smartest man in the United States," he had given up, and he had never raised the question again.

With Morrow it was different. He didn't drink it in at all, just sat there with either a bored expression as though his thoughts were a million miles away, or what was worse a twisted smile on his face that broadened as you spoke until by the time you got to the climax of how you were freezing out a tricky partner or putting one over on a government inspector, his lips were pulled back tight like a wolf's, exposing his long white teeth in a malicious sardonic grin that was enough to make your skin crawl. The funny part of it was that he had always been a quiet boy, not wild and imaginative and rebellious like his sister, and it had always been taken for granted that he would go into business himself when he grew up, ever since the time he had made enough selling green-painted box scooters to the kids on his block in the Bronx to buy a two-wheeler bike. He had gone off to Wharton Business School, without ever having been expelled or suspended from high school as Betsy would be a few years later, and without a lot of crazy nonsense about wanting to be an explorer or a physicist like Betsy. He had even seemed grateful that his father was sending him to the best school of its kind at what was in those days still a personal sacrifice. Sometimes Herman thought that it might even have been better if Morrow had gone out for a team or shown some sign of kicking over the traces for a while, like joining the Young Communist League at college, the way Bert Adler's boy had done.

As it was, Morrow had gone quietly through college, bringing average marks home from Philadelphia and occasionally a classmate for a week end in New York. Even the friends whom he brought home on week ends were such ordinary boys that Herman had more than once confessed to Clara, "I swear to you I can't remember their names or even what they look like five minutes after they leave the house." From all appearances, therefore, Herman should have had every reason to expect that Morrow would get his degree in business administration and then go to work for his father, starting as a stock clerk or a runner and moving up as he earned it into a junior executive's job in one of the corporations that would give him a draft exemption.

And yet Herman knew—he had always known—that there was no more real possibility of Morrow's fitting into a routine like that than there was of his landing on the moon. There was a dark stubborn streak deep within him like a vein of coal or iron—if you ever struck it you would recoil from the force of its resistance, and you would know that it would be futile ever to try again. What was Morrow after? Nobody really knew, sometimes you could wonder if he knew himself—but he wasn't going to just drift, not with that sharp mocking glance of his, and the quick darting way he moved his hands.

When he got a job with a food broker (the father of a classmate, but nevertheless a legitimate employer) six weeks after commencement exercises, Herman told himself that he was pleased. Able only to dream vague and horrible nightmares of what might have been, he told Clara that he was thankful that now Morrow would be living at home and maybe having a good influence on Betsy, and that with luck he could move up to a position that would qualify him for draft exemption.

Nobody was prepared for the quiet frenzy with which Morrow attacked his job, studying the food business on week ends with library books, staying on late to do extra work, and within seven weeks wrenching a promotion and a raise out of his new employer.

When he realized what Morrow's energy and application could have meant to the furtherance of his own expanding affairs, Herman could not hide his intense disappointment at the way they were being wasted in a stranger's business; and he only made it worse by trying to put it into words one day and getting in reply a cold grin from his son, a heartless grin that suddenly revealed the depths of their rivalry. It was no consolation that Betsy too looked at Morrow as a betrayer, because if she really disliked her brother, it was for the wrong reasons.

Then came Pearl Harbor. On Monday morning, December eighth, Morrow walked out of the house without a word and joined the army, without discussing it, without asking advice, almost as if he had deliberately desired to prostrate his mother and infuriate his father, and just when his father was pulling wires for a deferment.

It was inevitable after that, Herman realized, turning west on 36th Street into the lunch-hour crowds of garment workers who filled the sidewalks on the sunny side of the street to the curb, eating early hot corn on the cob wrapped in newspaper, playing pitchpenny against the walls, arguing about the war, and sunning themselves while they picked their teeth, leaning against the parked trucks and the pipe racks loaded with garments, it was inevitable that Morrow should curse and frustrate his efforts to get him into Officers Candidate School, or to keep him from being shipped overseas—both objectives which Herman was convinced he could have accomplished if only his son had given him the minimal cooperation of keeping his mouth shut. But no, he had to break things up like an anarchist, just to show that he could do everything himself. He had gotten the commission on his own, all right, he had even made First Lieutenant in a big hurry, but what good did it do him out in the North African desert, what good did it do him now that he was in the worst trouble you could possibly have in the army, charged with falsifying his accounts and doctoring company books?

Herman had seen an article on Morocco not long before in the *National Geographic* while waiting his turn at the dentist's, and the bright Kodachromes and glossy pages of text had seemed so incontrovertibly authentic that the article—together with a strong remembrance of Adolph Menjou spitting sand in *Beau Geste,* which he had watched holding hands with Clara in the early years of their marriage—gave him what he felt was a reasonably accurate picture of the land in which his son, supposedly battling Adolf Hitler to the accompaniment of cheers from family and friends, was misappropriating funds for dark purposes of his own. North Africa was picturesque, filthy, and backward, Herman knew, and he knew also that a combination like that was a trap and a corrupting influence which had to be fought as if it were a living enemy.

In a way Herman was grateful that North Africa, the army, and Hitler had conspired to bring his son so close to disaster, for it was a disaster—as distinguished from being wounded, God forbid, or captured—that he himself could avert. He was fairly sure that it could be handled successfully without Morrow being ruined, although you had to use caution and tact with army officers. They liked the same good things as politicians or any other human beings, but it was a question of approach. If they weren't handled in the right way the whole thing could be hopeless.

Herman was feeling a little better when he reached his building, just as he always did, regardless of the weight of his burdens or the pain in his heart, because it was like coming home. There were people like Gelbhorn who thought he was demeaning himself by remaining in the garment district, married to his original business and his little beaverboard office although he had long since outgrown both. They would have preferred, for his comfort and their reflected prestige (and Herman knew that he was fighting time, bucking against the day when his expanded interests would force him to open a suite maybe in a hotel), that he acquire right away a fancy new office in a fashionable building, the way older men sometimes went out and got themselves glossy blond wives and then set them up in apartments on West End Avenue where they would never have lived if they'd followed their own inclinations.

But what fun was that, he wondered as he jabbed the bell of the scarred old elevator, compared to the constant reminder of your early days that surrounded you here, or to the secret knowledge that now you could buy and sell the whole damned building and everybody in it if you wanted, and that the rest of the tenants didn't even know that you were any different from them, not any richer, or smarter, or more ambitious.

Suddenly he started to laugh, standing among the familiar fabric smells in the familiar lobby; thinking of the other tenants reminded him of a conversation that had taken place the previous winter between the super and Ben Jacobson, a converter who rented the fourth floor.

Herman and Jacobson had been standing in the lobby, just like this, waiting for the elevator, except that the radiator was bubbling and the floor was streaked with mud and slush. When the super brought the creaking elevator up from the basement and slowly, reluctantly, opened the door, Jacobson stepped in first and said angrily (but throwing a wink at Herman), "Say, what's about sending up some heat to the fourth floor? Do my workers have to freeze all winter?"

"Mr. Jacobson," the super replied stolidly, "it's not as easy as it sounds. This is a seventy-five-year-old building."

"So last year it was seventy-four years old—but we had heat!"

Herman was still smiling when the super pulled open the elevator door. They rode slowly to the fifth floor in the companionable silence that Herman liked, and as soon as he stepped out into the long room filled with the noise of his women at their machines, he felt quite at peace with himself.

He nodded to the forelady and climbed the three steps into his partitioned office. Here, with the safe at his side, the window at his back and the glass door separating him from the women whose fingers danced now at their machines for the war effort—"And I admire them for it," he told Clara, "they're doing their part"—he could do his best and most productive work.

It was something you could hardly admit to anyone, but there were actually moments when he felt closer in spirit to the working women outside his office, none of whose names he knew, many of whom spoke languages that he couldn't even understand, than he did to Clara or Betsy, either of whom might be sitting now in some ice-cream parlor, sipping a soda through a straw and staring into space.

He unbuckled his briefcase and concentrated on his work. First, before all, was the problem of contact work in clearing up Morrow's trouble. It could be just as dangerous to see too many people as too few. Since he had already decided to go on to Washington from Allentown, Herman made two lists, occasionally consulting the references he had been collecting since Morrow's induction into the service. On one list went the titles, and where possible the names, of those who could directly alter his son's fate. The other had to be composed of those who, while they could not change the course of the prospective court-martial, could exercise a secondary influence, such as keeping it out of the papers—which was just as important in the long run to Morrow and to the family.

When he had finished, Herman walked the length of the floor to the water fountain, where Bessie, his bookkeeper-secretary, was arguing heatedly with the forelady.

"That cold fish?" the forelady was saying, her back to him. "He'd strangle his grandmother for a buck."

"Let's break it up," he said, and observed with pleasure how the forelady's ears turned white, frozen with fear that she had been overheard. "Bessie, there's a few things I need."

His secretary touched her glasses nervously and marched in step with him to her office. Something in her taut look, like a bird ready to fly off the branch of a tree, told him that she was due to start telling him about her father's illness and the doctor's weekly visit, but now he had headed her off and she was afraid to start in on him.

"Get my lawyer on the phone. Get me reservations for Allentown for tomorrow, and then I got to be in Washington from there. I want my stuff, all the mail, everything, waiting at the desk for me when I get to the Statler. I'll have some letters for you in a while."

For the rest of the afternoon he worked steadily, not noticing the sunlight slowly retreating from behind his shoulders, or doing anything more than scan the letters that Bessie placed before him for his signature. Mostly he worked by phone, and it still gave him a guilty pleasure, like buying Primadoras by the box, to keep two telephones going with long-distance calls, and without bothering to tell the operator to notify you when your three minutes were up, either.

The telephones were indispensable to the conduct of Herman's affairs. In the course of the afternoon there were calls to and from

Scharf, his lawyer, who would be picking Herman up later to take him to the board meeting; Bagby, the Allentown attorney who was just a little too eager to get in on everything; Richardson, manager of the Morton Grove plant, full of loud bluster (probably phony, with his hints about a Navy "E") about new departmental quotas and plant production records; Sowerby or Sourbee or something like that, the kid at the South Carolina mill who was fresh out of school like Morrow, but had sense enough to promote his engineering deferment with long-distance calls to the boss and prove that he was making a big thing out of his job; and Slutsky, his tailor, who promised to get around the no-cuff regulation for Herman's sharkskin suit. He'd better, Herman mused, as he swiveled around in his chair.

For each phone call, and there had been many today, some so brief that they had only needed a yes or no, he used one sheet from the scratch pad bearing the inscription *From the desk of Herman Felton,* which the printer gave him at Christmas. Those calls which only required doodling, like Slutsky's, were crumbled and thrown into the wastebasket. The others he carefully filed in his briefcase which never left his side, not even when he went to the men's room. At the end of the day he could tell how things had gone by comparing the pile in the wastebasket with the stack of sheets that were to be saved.

Today hadn't been bad. He glanced at his Omega watch and called out to Bessie, "I'm going downstairs to wait for Scharf. You can lock up when you're through."

She clumped off to the ladies', and as soon as the iron door had slammed behind her, he picked up the telephone once again. Waiting for the ring, his ear ached, and he felt himself straining to tell who would be home to answer.

"Hel-lo." It started high and low, lazy and tired. Clara. "Hello Clara," he said. And then he couldn't keep from asking, "Is Betsy home?"

Softly, unhurriedly but implacably, like a great river flowing on and on, Clara's voice washed against his ear: "She never comes home from school until late at night, I think personally she's got a boy friend, it may be that Burley fellow, but still if it was him he'd bring her home, as it is she comes in at all hours and sneaks into her room without talking to me . . ."

Herman was unpleasantly aware, holding the receiver away from his sore ear, that he had really called on the off chance that Betsy would answer, and that he didn't have any desire to listen to Clara. Nevertheless just at this instant he was overwhelmed with a different kind of loneliness; now it was his business life, and not the children, that was preventing the indulgence of the impulses which he and Clara had had to suppress or muffle under a blanket all through the years. But he heard his own stranger's voice saying curtly that he had to attend a board meeting, that Clara should not wait up (for what, he did not say), that he would take a late train home, that he would have to leave in the morning for Pennsylvania. He did not point out, however, that it would have been easier for him to stay in town overnight at a hotel . . .

Outside the street was quiet, hot and breathless. The sun was already hidden behind the tall warehouses of the West Side. There was something frightening and unnatural about the silence, as if everyone had run from plague or bombs and left him alone in the city. But Herman was always uneasy when the street was empty and the workers had gone home; he was glad to see Scharf pull up to the curb in his Chrysler, which looked like a long hearse in the deserted block.

Herman liked his lawyer. Scharf was neither a blabbermouth nor a coward, he liked money and knew how to make it, and he understood Herman better than anyone else did. An older man, but not too old to take chances when the odds looked good, he was frank enough to tell Herman that he got a real pleasure out of watching him operate. The only trouble was that he was so much like Herman in so many ways that his moral support became suspect (just as Herman sometimes mistrusted his *own* enthusiasms); and there were moments when Herman was afraid to confide in Scharf because it was like talking to himself about his own ultimate ambitions—which was something he dreaded giving way to, knowing somehow that beneath the self-praise and flattery there might be opposition, scorn, even contempt.

Herman clambered into the car and said, "It's getting a little hotter, Ruby."

Scharf replied without preamble, "I kicked a guy out of my office today. He was asking questions about you."

Herman felt his heart race just a little as the car swung around the corner. "Government?"

Scharf shook his white head, laughing silently. "Some crazy kid.

He came in with a phony line about your credit status, but the only reason I listened to him at all before I threw him out was that his name was Traynor."

"Is that good?" Herman felt relaxed now, and leaned back comfortably.

"A long line of famous lawyers had that name. This kid knew it—he claimed to be the last of the line. Maybe he is, I don't know about that. I've just been wondering two things. What he wanted, and how he got ahold of your name."

"Maybe Betsy. I think she mentioned a name like that once, but who can remember? The hell with it. Tell me, Ruby, you think it looks all right for tonight?"

"Depends on how they eat." Scharf laughed and showed his long yellow teeth. "You know what Napoleon said about an army marching on its stomach. Scharf says a board of directors marches on its bromo-seltzers. If they like the dessert they'll eat out of your hand, like squirrels. Besides, what the hell, why are you worrying? It's all cut and dried. You've got to worry about the outside stuff, not these free loaders."

Actually the dinner was not too good, but they ate out of his hand, anyway, just as Scharf had said. He talked through the meal, giving what he called an informal report. By the time coffee was served in the paneled private dining room of the hotel, all these relatives and noch-schleppers were ready to vote up anything he recommended. Even Gelbhorn's brother-in-law Morton, a little zero who thought he was a big man, and Clara's cousin Irving, a shyster who actually claimed to know more law than Scharf and more business than Herman, even they went along, led on perhaps by the smell of big money that Herman had to dangle before them the way you dangle a bloody shirt under a bloodhound's nose.

So when Scharf presented him with a cigar in a glass tube, Herman nodded his thanks and whispered, "It's going almost too good."

"Why not?" Scharf hardly bothered to lower his voice. "They sniff money. Wake up, Herman. They're taking five per cent of the risks, and you're taking ninety-five."

Scharf was right. Herman resolved to get tougher with all these outstretched hands. Minutes were being taken by a silent secretary, and it was only necessary for him to speak somewhat more frankly than usual to get at least the outlines of the truth on the record. He waited patiently until the mulatto waiters had closed the doors behind them; then he plunged into an explanation of the proposed merger that covered not only its financial possibilities, which he had touched on during dinner, but also its legal hazards. It was good to see some of those red overstuffed faces turn pale—it made their final support all the more enjoyable.

Still, Herman's elation was mixed with disgust with these paper capitalists for their greed, which it was so easy to exercise behind the barricaded safety of their positions; and with disgust for himself too, for his own squeamishness, and for having to rely on, to cozen, to flatter them, even while they mixed avarice with cowardice.

"It's written all over your face," Scharf said as they walked out to the parked Chrysler. "Look ahead, don't even think about them until the next time you need them to say yes. They don't count, they just live off you. Keep your eye on the big thing."

Yes, of course, Herman nodded, but maybe even Scharf didn't understand how it affected you, having to wade through mud in order to be able to reach up to the stars. If I had known right from the start, Herman reflected, from the very first days when I made up my mind that I was far enough ahead of the crowd to head for the top, that in order to get there I would have to waste years with slobs, perhaps I never would have been willing to make the sacrifices, perhaps I would have settled for a different kind of life.

Always in the back of his mind, buried so far back that he rarely dug it out to examine it unless prodded to it by Betsy's giddy ambitions, was an ideal of a better society, peopled with gracious, learned and well-bred men and women of wealth, in whose presence he would be a little ill at ease but still convinced that he was worthy of belonging if only he tried hard enough, made so much money that it became a thing it was no longer necessary to mention or even think about, and brought up his children to take their legitimate place as full-fledged members of that society.

And yet something, something that seemed to have to do with the way he was working at it, was drawing his children away from the future that should have been theirs and into an uncharted country that filled him with dark and gloomy forebodings. As the future which he had envisioned became the present, he found it peopled with men and women who could be related to his half-conscious preconceptions only in their titles and positions. The rear admirals, colonels and corporation executives with whom he mixed on terms increasingly approaching equality were not as *different* as he had thought they would be; sometimes he felt that they differed from the people with whom he had grown up, and who now sat on boards with him, only in the superior confidence and cunning that came with more money and more power.

Where were the good people? Somewhere, he had to believe, was the society for which he and all genuinely ambitious people must yearn; but the more he pushed on into hitherto mysterious territory the more it seemed to recede into a future which it was difficult even to conceive. And in order to get there you had to cut throats, you had to push your stiffened arm into the faces of the weaklings, like the football runners in the newsreels.

"You've got a tendency," Scharf explained, as he drove the Chrysler up the ramp into Penn Station, "to press too hard. Time yourself, save the pressure for the really tough ones."

"I can't let up, Ruby. If I don't press, who will?"

"Tonight you didn't have to. Tomorrow you probably will."

"You talk like I should be able to turn it on and off."

"That's exactly what I do mean." The old lawyer stopped the car and squinted at him unsmilingly. "If you don't learn how, you'll wind up with a coronary, and for what?"

"I'm healthy."

"If not that, some little nobody, out of all the two-bit enemies you've been making, is going to figure that it's only practical for him to save his own neck by breaking yours."

"I'm no movie actor, I can't play I'm friends with people I wouldn't have in my house."

"Try. It won't hurt. Meantime, I'll expect a call from Allentown. The papers will be drawn up before you get to Washington. I'll shoot them down to the Statler as soon as I hear from you."

"Thank you," Herman said primly. "Thanks for the lift."

"Give my regards home."

"And mine," Herman called over his shoulder as he plunged ahead into the railroad station without looking back.

When he eased himself into his accustomed seat in the train's last car, he felt that it would be possible to squeeze out a little more work before the day finally came to a close. With a kind of bitter good intention he opened his briefcase and took out the Allentown papers.

But the figures blurred before his eyes. How much he could take out of just this one deal alone nobody knew, but it was phenomenal. A hundred thousand would be nothing, if the war lasted—Betsy would be stupefied, maybe she would be even more flabbergasted if she knew that he couldn't even count it any more than you could count the stones in a pyramid, or want to try, because it was the whole effect you were after. The beauty part was that, if you could get the Gelbhorns of this world to handle this right, there was just as much in it after the war ended as before, if you could go by the renegotiations after the last war.

The car clacked dully over the rails, and Herman found himself slipping into a half-waking dream, in which Ruby Scharf, together with fat Gelbhorn, had gone over to the other side, ratted on him, and was dickering with Morrow, who explained that his uniform meant that he was an officer of the court, not of the army. And then he really fell asleep, fell asleep so hard and so deeply that he no longer even dreamed.

He awoke two stops before his station, thinking with relief, at least I didn't dream about women. But his forehead was wet with sweat and he had to wipe his face with a handkerchief before descending into the cool night air.

Once in his Dodge, Herman was suddenly as keen and alert as he had been early in the morning, with the windwing opened wide and flushing sweet air into his face. He headed for home full of inexpressible expectations, like a child running downstairs on Christmas morning not knowing what wonderful things might be in the stocking. But from the street the front of his house was dark. He rolled the car into the garage and entered the house through the kitchen door.

In the silence he could hear the uneven throb of the refrigerator (it sounded as though it had a bad heart) and the steady dry snake-like rattle of the electric clock that hung on the wall next to the stove. Without turning on the light, he took a bottle of milk from the refrigerator. The inside light dispelled enough of the darkness for him to make out a looming contorted mass in the sink: dirty dishes.

"Oh, for God's sake," he said aloud. He capped the milk bottle without drinking from it and put it back on the shelf.

He walked quietly upstairs, his thirst gone, and skipped the squeaky second step after the landing. For a moment he stood outside Betsy's room at the head of the stairs, listening so hard that his eardrums seemed to pop as though he had climbed a mountain.

There was no sound. No line of light glowed under her doorway; she wasn't reading in bed, or writing her mysterious letters. Was she asleep, then? Was she lying in the dark, staring up at the moonbeams laddered against the ceiling by the venetian blind? Or was she still out, necking in some roadhouse with a draft dodger or a cannon fodder soldier, while he stood outside her door, shaking with fear for her?

The fingers of his outstretched hand, suspended just above the doorknob, began to tingle exactly as though his hand had fallen asleep in a cramped position. He withdrew it then and continued on past his own bedroom where Clara lay, doubtless sound asleep (which made no difference: as soon as he came in and sat down on the edge of the bed to take off his shoes, she would roll over slowly and sigh, in her high feminine wheeze, "Hello, Herman. Tired, honey?").

He proceeded to the bathroom, where he turned on the light switch and undressed rapidly, leaning against the side of the tub and stacking his clothes neatly on the pearl-topped hamper as he removed them. Naked save for his shoes and socks, he flexed his arms briefly, then took his pajamas from the hook where he had hung them in the morning and squirmed into them. With a toothbrush as shaggy as John L. Lewis's eyebrow, he scrubbed his teeth, using the up-and-down motion the *National Geographic* dentist had shown him. He took out his little bridge and scrubbed it too, and finally applied a few drops of pomade to the thin strands of his hair.

Now, prepared to meet his wife at last, he squared his shoulders, adjusted his pajamas, and closed the door on the bathroom refuge. It was one o'clock in the morning.

(From The University of Kansas City Review)

I GOT A FRIEND

BY MARK VAN DOREN

"I *GOT* a friend goes with me where I go. Tells me what to spend, what not. Saves me every time—would lose my bottom dollar but for him."

"You mean just money?"

"No, mam, not just money. Anything you give away and don't get back—he knows."

"Feelings, honey?"

"Anything don't come back home in cash—I mean that. He knows, he tells me."

"Where's he now, that friend?"

"Right here."

"Inside your head?"

"No, mam."

They walked along the levee, and he watched the river for barges, steamboats, anything with lights that showed a minute through the fog. He listened when a whistle blew, or when one deck hand sang out to another, over black water that smelled of engine oil. She looked at only him—a head taller, his arm held fast in hers. She had seen him for the first time at Portsoaken's, Beer and Dancing. She never let him go from that hour on. He said he could get back to the tug by his own self, but she said no, she'd take him. He didn't ask if it was safe for somebody like herself, going off alone then to where she lived. He didn't ask her where that was, if with her family, if what.

"You never answered one thing, honey. When does the *Dorothy*

O. tie up here next time? When you coming back up empty?"

"Told you, didn't know. Don't know."

"What's the name for?"

"Old man's wife. She died."

"He good to you?"

"He don't say much. Not bad."

"Is *that* it?" For he had stopped, and was looking down a plank that connected with the river. The far end of it melted into a dark thing of no great size, hard to see between two lanterns, fore and aft, that rose and fell a little. The plank, from where they stood, from where she studied it, seemed like it might be slippery. It wasn't raining, but there was a soft wet wind. Her arms felt clammy to herself.

"That's it."

He started down, but she held on to the buttons at the bottom of his sleeve.

"Honey, is the friend here now?"

"Sure is." He didn't make much effort to get loose.

"What does he say about a kiss? Somebody's got one ready to give back. Worth just the same—you tell him there won't be a nickel lost."

He listened, but not to her. It might be for someone down there that had heard her, and would laugh. It might be for the friend.

"What does he say, honey? You can leave me then—this time. But I won't promise not to keep an eye on what goes up the river, full or empty. Next week, next month—I'll watch."

Perhaps it surprised him, the light quick way she gave him back his kiss. And then disappeared—again so light and quick that after a few steps down the plank he turned around, came up again, and started following her along the levee, in the black fog that made her footsteps sound farther away than they were, like watch ticks in cotton. Except that they weren't so close together. She took a longer step than most did—not so long, so slow as his, but free and swinging, like the way she danced.

Nobody bothered her, and soon she turned off toward town. He followed her till he could see the street lights and one neon sign, and a bus where the sign was, a blue bus with people in it. Then he came back, and this time disappeared himself down the whole length of the plank; and in the morning there was no tug there.

She didn't meet it when it tied up two weeks later, in the middle of a bright afternoon when everything was plain to see. He looked up on the levee and there wasn't any woman there. It would have been funny if there had been, but he took a look.

Nine o'clock, and he was at Portsoaken's again; and soon enough he saw her, dancing with a sawed-off man that wasn't half her match. She saw him too, and when the music stopped came over where he was.

"Hello, honey. Where's your friend?"

He considered a minute. "Somewheres here."

"Not right behind you? Not that handsome fellow—"

He turned before he thought; she had to laugh. "How about you dancing this with me?" The band had started up again.

They didn't talk much, then or any other time that night, till she was taking him, the way she did before, along the gravel wall that kept the river to itself. There wasn't any fog, so they could see the *Dorothy O.* before they got clear to it.

She slowed down, suddenly, and stopped. "You didn't ask me if I knew when she came in."

"Did you? Thought you didn't."

"Because I wasn't there to wave? I knew all right."

He started, but she held him back. "Honey, did you hope I wouldn't know?"

He had an answer ready. "Your own business. None of mine. Either way's all right."

"Tell me, though. Why did you follow me that evening? I heard you, quiet as you tried to step. A funny sound, your big feet in the fog." She mimicked what she remembered, shuffling her own feet, stamping on the ground. "Like that. So I felt safe. That your idea? Worried about me, honey?"

He didn't admit it.

"Was it the friend's idea too? Didn't he tell you it was wasting time? Shoe leather? I could push him in the river." She stooped, picked up a rock her foot had kicked, and threw it past him. There was a weak splash.

"You leave my friend alone."

She had taken his arm again, but she let it go. "You think he likes you better than I do—knows better what is good and bad."

"He never told me wrong, that man."

She felt for him and found him. "What did you come for then?"

"Where to?"

"Portsoaken's."

"Dance. The same as you."

"But not *with* me? You didn't ask about the one I was with when—didn't even ask his name."

"You got him all the time. That's good."

"Honey, you don't mean it.

"Sure I do."

He said it as if he might not mean it after all; he said it confidentially, in a low voice, for only her to hear. But she was already slipping off.

He heard her, then he didn't. She might be waiting for him to come and find her in the dark.

He stood there quite a while before he went on to where the tug was, bobbing between its two clear lanterns, fore and aft.

The third time was not till a month later, and then he didn't even find her at Portsoaken's. He studied all the girls, and not a one of them was her.

He was standing there, watching both doors, when a woman in a red dress, not very young, not very old, came to him through the crowd and said: "You looking for somebody?"

"Nobody special, mam." And still his eyes went round the room.

"Well, if it's who you walked home with twice, she told me to tell you she won't be here any more. Said to look out for you and tell you."

His eyes were on her now. "Why's that?"

She seemed a bit afraid.

"Why's that, mam?"

"Well"—she still hesitated—"there's somebody don't want her to come here. She met somebody."

"When? How far back?"

"Now that I couldn't say."

"A little runt?"

"Guber? Oh, no. Who'd pay him any mind? This is somebody got to have her to himself. No strangers—that's it. Someone steady."

"Who?"

"She don't bring him any more. She met him here, but they don't come since he decided—"

"Ever seen him your own self?"

"No. It's almost like they run off and got married. I don't know a soul that sees him. Or her, hardly, since it happened."

"What happened?"

"What I said."

"She all right?"

"Why not?"

"Where is she? Where's her house?"

"Now that she didn't want you told." She seemed afraid again. "She said—"

"What street?"

"I promised. But I *can* say, it's only a little piece from Fourth and Market. She might be going to the drugstore now, there on the corner."

He didn't thank her.

The drugstore was about to close. There was only one customer in it—the last booth on the street side, where you could see in. She was by herself, but she was getting up. The proprietor had turned off most of the lights.

If she saw him standing by the door she didn't show it as she paid her check. Then she came out, and there he was.

"Hello, honey."

He fell in with her, going up Fourth Street. "You can't call me that."

"Why not, honey?"

"Somebody don't like it."

"Who? Oh, *him*. He wouldn't care. He knows me—it's my way of speaking."

"Always was?"

"Since I could walk. You been to Portsoaken's? Get my message?"

"What you think?"

"What *you* think?"

"Going home now?"

"Maybe. How's the *Dorothy O.?*"

"All right. You live here on this street?"

"It's safe. Don't worry, honey."

"Don't you call me that. Not any more."

She turned her head away and laughed. "I'll tell my friend. He minds a lot of things, but never that."

"Like going to Portsoaken's?"

"Like meeting you."

"Me?" He stopped. "How does he know?"

"He knows."

She hadn't stopped, and he caught up with her. "Listen. Was that woman telling me some lies?"

"I don't know all she said."

"Well—"

"I got a friend, if that was it. I don't waste time on strangers now. I don't waste anything."

They had gone a block beyond the last street light before she said: "From here on, honey, don't you follow me."

"Listen." He took hold of her arm. "How could this happen when—how could it happen so damn fast? Where is he? Your house? Do you and him—"

"Same house, honey. Same downstairs, same up. He's good looking. A little taller than you, honey. Not better looking, but he stands a inch higher in his shoes."

He shook her, hard. "What did you go do it for?"

"Do what? He did it. A friend of his, he introduced him to me, then he did it. He worked fast. It didn't take him long. We're in the same house now. Same table, bed."

He slapped her, and she screamed: "Look out! There he is behind you!"

He turned around. There was nobody between him and the street light, nobody taller than he was, or shorter.

She laughed and cried—one sound—and he looked back at her again. Back quick, and saw her holding both her cheeks. Of course one of them hurt.

But she was laughing too. "You great big fool!"

"Listen!" He stepped closer. "Don't you—"

"Big dumb fool! Honey—don't you see? I fell for *your* friend. My friend now."

He didn't say a word.

"You didn't bring him with you this time, did you? He didn't tell you this time not to give yourself away. You did, all right. I guess I know what hit me."

"Shouldn't done that."

"He ought to been there, ought to told you how to keep that big paw to yourself. It gave you flat away. He's been with *me,* though. Ever since last time he's been with me. You miss him?"

"Yes, mam. I couldn't—"

"Couldn't keep from thinking of me, honey? Same thing. Now I'm glad. Give me a sweet kiss."

He did, and then they went down to Portsoaken's.

(*From The Atlantic Monthly*)

THE SCALE ROOM

BY GEORGE VUKELICH

THE SKINNY personnel man left me with the chunky man in the long white coat. "This is your foreman," the personnel man said and he gave the foreman some papers and walked away.

"Call me Al," the foreman said studying out the papers. "I'll take you down to Supply and we'll get you fixed up. You got anything at all of your own?"

I didn't know exactly what he meant. "I've got work clothes," I said. "Safety shoes."

He wrote something on the papers. "Okay," he said, "I'll get you fixed up."

I followed him out of the green office into the hot-smelling cement stair well with the greasy black pipe railings.

"It gets pretty sloppy in the kill," he said as we clattered down the steps. "Water and stuff. You need rubber boots and a rubber apron for sure."

"How much do they cost?"

"Oh, seven, eight bucks. Boots and apron." We were back on the first floor.

"I only have two bucks on me," I said and stopped.

"That's okay. You just sign for the stuff, and the company will take it out of your first check." He pushed in on a wide steel door stenciled SUPPLY ROOM. There was a small one-armed man behind the counter reading the morning paper.

"Fingers," Al said as the one-armed man looked up, "I got a new man here. Can you fix him up?"

"Sure, Al." The supply man folded his paper and pushed it down the counter. "For the kill?"

"Yeah," Al said. "Find him a good pair of boots though. I don't want him getting wet feet."

The one-armed man reached down and slung up a knee-long pair of shiny black boots on the worn metal counter. The boots smelled like new army raincoats. "Try these on for size," he said, shoving the boots at me. "Better take off your shoes first. You wear the boots without shoes."

"What color apron do you want?" the supply man asked.

"I don't know," I said, untying my street shoes. "What's the difference?"

"Price mostly," the supply man smiled, and bent himself over a paper pad on the counter, holding it firm with his elbow stump in order to write with his right hand. "Black, brown, yellow, and olive drab. Brown's the cheapest."

Al nodded at me.

"Okay," I said. "Brown."

He threw a tight brown rubber square on the counter top. "You want me to give him some knives?" he asked the foreman.

"No, he won't need no knives," Al said. "He's gonna push hogs for John."

The supply man asked for my name and the foreman pushed a piece of paper across the counter. "Take it off this," he said. "You'll never spell it otherwise."

The supply man squinted and half uttered my name. "That's bohunk, ain't it?"

"That's right," the foreman said.

The supply man smiled. *"Cocko ti,"* he said to me.

I finished pulling on my left boot and stood up working my toes in the stiff cold rubber casing and I wondered how many people there were in this place who could say "How are you?" in Croatian.

"Dobro," I said.

"Give him a cap too and you can go back to your newspaper," Al said.

"Size seven and a half," I said.

The supply man got out a white cap with a black visor and shoved his paper pad at me. "Sign it any place on the bottom. Put your locker number down too." I took his Eversharp and wrote my name. As he gave me the duplicate carbon he grinned at the foreman. "Say hello to the Dago for me, Al."

"Come on," Al said as I swept up my stuff. "Let's go up where the working people are."

The foreman made me a hog-pusher right off the bat but it was a full four weeks before my body accepted the job. By that time the hog kill was into the busy season because the farmers sold out their pigs for the winter months and the company ran in a night shift and hired all the men it could get and that's when Big Wayne came to work in the cooler gang with the Dago.

The hogs had just started into the resin bath up the line on our first night and Old John and the Dago and I were sitting on the greasy wooden bench in the scale room when Al came back with the big blond boy. "This is Wayne, Dago," he said. "He's your new man for the coolers."

"Hello," the big boy said and he put out his right hand before he saw the hook that encased the Dago's wrist. He stood there awkwardly.

"Where's your gloves?" the Dago snapped. "You'll freeze your goddam hands off in the coolers."

The big boy looked at Al.

"The supply room was out of his size. I'll get him some."

The big boy lowered his hands because Old John and I were staring at them. The hands were big.

"I'll be okay," he said. "I'm used to a lot of cold anyway."

Dago was struggling his one heavy black mitt onto his left hand and he stopped and looked up at the new man.

"Your ass," he said.

They stood facing each other until Al finally said again that he would find Wayne some gloves, and then Jumbo came in and everybody started in on him as usual.

Jumbo was not too smart and he talked through his nose and though he was thirty years old he had always lived with his mother who was a widow and drank up all of Jumbo's pay checks. It was a standing joke how she waited by the Number One gate on Fridays and he signed over the pay envelope to her and then she would go off to the Railroad Tap to have it cashed.

He would be in the coolers until his strength gave out. He was like a little boy with his strength. Dago had to watch over him constantly or the jokers on lard pulling would have Jumbo ramming his fists into the cement block walls to show what a punch he had.

"You cooler gang?" he asked Wayne now, surveying out Wayne's brawn.

"Yeah," Wayne said.

"Me too," Jumbo said and shoved out his hand. "Shake."

Wayne took the hand and it was obvious that Jumbo was intending to impress him with that nut-cracking grip. Their hands were locked waist-high only momentarily. In a flash Wayne had spun Jumbo around, the dummy's arm bent tightly into the small of his shoulder blades. As he arched backward to relieve the pain pressure on his arm, Wayne gently and firmly crashed him onto the wet steel floor mat under the scales. I think Jumbo's scream was more surprise than anything else. Wayne flung his arm free.

"Whattaya, tough guy?" Dago said evenly.

Wayne was wiping his hand on his overalled thighs and working his fingers. "Your ass," he said to Dago.

The hogs started coming into the scale room then and Old John and I went to work and our new night gang walked slowly down the steaming gambrelways into their coolers.

The scale room was in between the hog kill itself and the coolers. Up at the other end of the sprawling, clattering, sharpening, cutting water-floored building the hogs came into the shackling pens day and night and were lifted screaming onto the gambrelways into the kill. Heads down and hanging in close ranks, they looped and circled and came around the big plant on the continuous overhead track into scald baths and resin baths and wash baths past the waiting men with axes and saws and the razor knives. The hogs were burned and stripped and gutted and emptied out and washed and cleaned and all their cutaway parts dropped down metal chutes in the floor to bins below where they were processed into soaps and fertilizers and meat products and hundreds of things.

They say that the company used every part of the pig except the squeal and that there were company scientists working on that so that the foremen could save their own voices in the hell noises of the kill.

The automatic overhead track became manual at the scale room and my job was to push the hogs into the room by hand onto the overhead scale; and when there were ten, Old John would click a knob on the electric scale and the scale would record the weight and number of hogs and then clear itself for the next weighing. Old John also punched out the figures on an adding machine set in a waterproof pedestal. Then I would push the entire ten onto the automatic track for the coolers and they would click and clatter away into the misty passageways bound for the Dago's gang, and they would be routed to the proper coolers to set and harden before the next day when the meat cutters began on them.

The average weight for ten hogs was around fifteen or sixteen hundred pounds and the big trick was to move them out fast so the ones coming in didn't pile up in a bunch at the end of the automatic track.

On the night shift we were to come in at three and work straight through until about seven for a half-hour dinner break.

The stick men took it easy in the kill because there were new men on the line and the hogs came in so slowly that Old John stuck his head out a couple of times and looked down the line to see if there had been a breakdown somewhere.

"Petersen said they got five thousand on day shift," Old John said. "We'll be lucky to get thirty-five hundred out tonight." I chewed my gum and didn't say anything. John looked worried.

"Lots of bad cuts coming through," he said pointing to the carcasses split in two up the backbone dangling loose from the clotheshangerlike gambrels. I worked the pieces of them carefully onto the scale rail and he filled his mouth from the Copenhagen box in his adding machine drawer. "Bad cuts," he snuffed. "Lots of new men."

He clicked the scale knob and punched on his adding machine and I pushed all the bad cuts onto the cooler track.

They stopped killing at six-fifteen and forty-five minutes later I pushed the last two hogs onto the scale rail and let them hang and Old John worked his adding machine and I took off my apron and washed off the blood and hosed down my boots.

The cooler gang along with Al was waiting when Old John checked his figures.

"Eighteen hundred sixty-two," he said solemnly. "Eighteen hundred sixty-two."

"You bastard," Dago said, "I bet that breaks your heart."

"We'll get thirty-five hundred," Al said. "They're gonna kill thirty-five hundred tonight." He looked at Dago and over at Wayne who was washing down his boots with our hose. "I couldn't get any gloves for him," he said to Dago. "How's he doing?"

"Ask him," Dago said. "They're not my hands freezing."

"It's okay. I been in colder places," Wayne said.

Dago wasn't smiling as he nudged me with his cold hook and we walked out to the locker room to get our lunches.

"That bastard," Dago said with the crumbs falling from his lips. "Got his big goddam hands into everything already."

"Who?" I said.

"That Wayne. Four bolognas he ate already. I ought to kick Jumbo's head in."

Jumbo looked up from the locker-room floor. "I didn't do nothing."

"You showed him where the bologna was. You ate one in front of him. What the hell did you expect him to do, watch you eat?"

Jumbo munched on his hard-boiled egg. "I told him not to eat any," he said.

Big Wayne came around the corner of the steel aisle then and opened his locker and took out his lunch. "That's right, Shorty," he said to the Dago as he sat down. "Jumbo told me not to eat any sausage," he smiled, "and then he ate one."

Dago was burning. He was touchy about his height and he was touchy about Jumbo's intelligence and he was especially touchy about this new man. "I don't want any trouble with the front office," Dago said. "They start getting big short counts in their meat packs and the first guys they'll hit is the cooler gang. They'll have so many guards walking through this place, you'll think it's the First National Bank."

"I don't think they miss a few little sausages," Wayne said.

"Listen, smart boy," Dago snapped. "You been on this job four hours and already you swallowed down four bologna rings. That's a pretty good average. I wouldn't exactly call that a few little sausages."

Wayne unwrapped a sandwich and began to chew. "I left enough for you, Shorty. Us big men need to eat big meals."

"I'm telling you now so you get it straight."

"I got it straight," Wayne smiled. "Straight from the horse's mouth."

I didn't know what was going to happen for a minute and finally to my relief nothing happened and I started chewing again. We ate without talking and balled up our lunch bags and started in to smoke. Jumbo was humming a polka tune. Wayne got up and closed his locker. "I don't want to be hard-nosed, Shorty," he said. "I just don't like being horsed around, that's all."

"Nobody's horsing you around," Dago said.

"That's right," Wayne said. "Nobody is. I wouldn't know the guy who owns this place if I saw him. But one thing I know is that he ain't working in the hog kill or in the coolers."

Dago dragged on his cigarette and didn't say anything.

"Do you own this place, Jumbo?" Wayne asked suddenly.

"No," Jumbo said, "no, I don't own this place."

"Does Shorty?"

Jumbo stared and blinked slowly around at Dago and couldn't speak.

The Dago threw down his cigarette and closed up his locker and started back by himself up to the hog kill.

Wayne sat down again and shook another cigarette from his plastic pack. "Stop me if I'm wrong," he said, "but I thought Al was our foreman."

"Al is the foreman," Jumbo said nodding his head.

"What the hell is Shorty bucking for, then?" Wayne said and his question was directed at me.

"He's sort of in charge of things in the coolers," I said. "Al can't be all over every minute."

"Well, that Shorty is sure all over, only he's not gonna be all over me."

I shrugged and field-stripped my cigarette and Wayne stared at me. "You been in the infantry, huh?"

"Yeah," I said and got to my feet.

"Korea?" Wayne asked.

"The old war," I said, "Europe."

Wayne nodded. "I was Korea myself. We almost starved in Korea. Maybe that's why I'm so hungry all the time." He dragged on his cigarette. "Goddam Shorty reminds me of the army; Watch the Hook, we used to say. He couldn't pull this crap in the army."

I didn't tell Wayne that the Dago had been with the 32nd Red Arrow against the Japs at Buna in '42 and that he had two hands up until then. I slammed my locker door shut and spun the combination lock.

"We go by working people," Jumbo said. Wayne snapped him a salute.

"Yes, sir, general," he said.

"General Jumbo," Jumbo smiled.

"Dumbo Jumbo," Wayne said.

Jumbo saluted us gravely and we walked slowly in behind him as he marched back up into the hog kill.

It was nine-thirty before I saw the Dago again. He came out of the Number Two cooler with a pail hanging from his hook and he dumped it on the blood-slick floor under the scale rail. It was salt.

"Thanks," I said spreading it with my boot. "It was getting pretty slippery."

Dago set the pail in the corner and started pushing hogs in to me. "You seen Wayne?" he asked.

"Not since supper," I said. "I thought he was working on the cooler gang."

Dago scowled. "You and me both," he said.

He swung his hook into the hanging belly of a hog and spun it viciously. "He took off about eight o'clock for the infirmary. Said his hands hurt him." He shifted the gum in his mouth. "That's not all that's gonna hurt him when he gets back."

Old John shuffled over and stood listening.

"You and Jumbo been alone back there?" I asked.

"You goddamned right we been alone," Dago said.

Old John shook his head. "That's Big Wayne, huh?"

"Big Wind," Dago said. "I'll give him something to blow about. Bastard doesn't deserve hands." He pulled in the number ten hog and picked up his pail. John clicked his scale knob, and after I pushed the pigs onto the cooler track, Dago entered the streaming passageway, shuffling slowly behind the hogs on the gambrelways.

When we hit the twelve-minute break for a smoke Al came back to quick-check the totals with Old John.

Dago and Jumbo came out of the coolers and took off their gloves, their faces tight and red with cold. Jumbo's nose was running and Dago told him to blow it in our paper towels on the wall rack.

"Where's Wayne?" Al asked.

"In the john," Dago said.

"How's he doing?" Al asked.

"Peachy," Dago said. "He's doing peachy. Got a great pair of hands."

Dago poked me in the ribs with the hook and we walked out to get our smokes. "Two more sausages he ate," Dago said as we sloshed along the deserted line.

"That's a lot of bologna," I said.

"He's gonna screw it up for everybody," Dago said as we entered the john.

Wayne came out of a stall tying on his apron.

"I told you you weren't supposed to bring your apron in here," Dago said and he was angry.

"You're always telling me something, Shorty," Wayne said. "Are you the latrine orderly or something?"

"They're not my rules," Dago said.

"They're not mine either," Wayne said. "You know where you can stick the rules." He started out the door.

"You gonna wash your dirty hands?" Dago snapped.

Wayne stopped. "You gonna make me?" he asked firmly and then went out through the door.

We washed our hands in silence. Dago didn't say anything for the rest of the break and we walked back through the moving line again without speaking.

After the break, Dago opened the steel doors and I switched the overhead track into the front cooler and Dago came out carrying another salt pail on his hook for me. Then he filled up the empty pail with boiling hot water and disappeared back into the gambrelways.

Jumbo and Wayne could push hogs right from the scale room now, and I wandered over to the wide doorway and stood surveying the empty smoking cooler room. Dago motioned to the corner and there behind the pinned-back steel door was the water pail with a bologna ring in it. I took off my gloves and broke off a piece of the sausage. It was hot, cooked-tasting, and juicy. I nodded to Dago and he jerked his head over at Old John. I wandered back to the scales and Old John shuffled over to size up the cooler too. He stepped aside next to Dago as Wayne and Jumbo pushed in a load and Wayne saw him and the pail. The bulge in Old John's mouth was too big to be tobacco.

Wayne stooped and fished out the sausage in his big hand. "I'll be goddamned," Wayne said.

Dago swung his hook and clipped the bologna ring cleanly out of Wayne's grasp. "Keep your goddamned filthy hands to yourself," Dago said.

Wayne brought up his fists and moved on the Dago.

"When I leave one for you it'll be in the john bowl," Dago said.

Wayne lunged at him then, but at that moment Jumbo cracked Wayne from the side with his great forearm and the blond head flung back and the left temple slammed into the steel door and Big Wayne crashed onto the slime floor. Jumbo and Old John looked like they wanted to run. Dago bent down over Wayne and felt with his good hand and then looked up at me. "Help me move him," he said. "John, don't let them hogs pile up."

John scurried away.

"Jumbo," Dago said dumping the hot-water pail, "fill this with salt and bring it back."

"Salt?"

"Come on, move," Dago said. "Salt!"

He picked up the remainder of the bologna ring and slipped it inside Wayne's heavy shirt. He told me to button it in and I did, and then we dragged Wayne's body out of the cooler entrance and onto the steel matting under the hanging hogs. There were at least thirteen pigs jammed up on the scale rail already and John was waving frantically. Dago rolled Wayne's head to the left with his foot and then he kicked over the heavy wooden bench and began to yell. Uprighting the bench immediately, he broke out into the hog kill screaming for Al and for a doctor and for help.

They had pulled Wayne off to one side and were looking at him when Jumbo came back with the salt. "I got salt," he said. Al looked at him and at the blood-slick floor.

Dago sprinkled the pail under the hogs and we pushed them off together. They were piling up like a log jam and Dago screamed for Jumbo.

"What's wrong with Wayne?" Jumbo asked.

"He's dead," Dago said.

"Dead?" Jumbo stopped and stared at the long body. "Dead?"

"Come on, get these hogs out of here," Dago screamed again. "Wayne had an accident."

The doctors had the body taken away and some men from the

front office came to ask us questions while the last of the hogs tracked in off the line, and then two city police detectives arrived and talked to us in the locker room until after midnight. Al came in with a slip of paper and gave it to the detectives. One of them worked Wayne's combination and opened the locker and looked through his street clothes.

We just sat there until we were aware of Jumbo slumped in the corner—sleeping. The detectives looked at him and at Al. The foreman ran his finger in a tight circular motion around his ear.

"This place could do it to anybody," one of the detectives said.

"Tomorrow he will probably want to know where Wayne is," Al said.

"That's a dumb question all right," the detective said. Then he said that was all and we could go home. The Dago shook Jumbo awake.

"Huh," Jumbo said.

"We can go home now," Dago said.

"I dream," Jumbo said. "Big Wayne and me going work good together."

Dago stared at him and dropped his hand from Jumbo's shoulder.

"Big Wayne and me," Jumbo said. "Good cooler gang." He got to his feet and punched Dago's arm. "We going work good with you, Wayne and me." He scooped up his lunch bucket and Dago watched him dully. In Dago's eyes I could see the long, long smoking cooler rooms and the endless, endless tracks of warm hanging bodies coming in from the screaming hog kill.

"General Jumbo," Jumbo said and I saw Dago was looking into my eyes for something.

I buttoned up my mackinaw and fell in beside Dago and then the two of us walked slowly in behind Jumbo as he marched proud and swinging down past the time clocks.

(From Harper's Bazaar)

GOING TO NAPLES

BY EUDORA WELTY

THE *"POMONA"* sailing out of New York was bound for Palermo and Naples. It was the still warm September of a Holy Year. Along with the pilgrims and the old people going home, there rode in *turistica* half a dozen pairs of mothers and daughters. If Mrs. C. Serto, going to Naples, might miss by a hair's breadth being the largest mother, Gabriella Serto was beyond dispute the largest daughter. But she was not the youngest—she was over eighteen. And how she did love to scream! From the time the *Pomona* began to throb and move down the river, she regaled the deck with clear, soprano cries. As she romped up and down after the other girls, screaming and waving goodbye to the Statue of Liberty, a hole broke through her stocking and her flesh came through like a pear.

Before land was out of sight, everybody knew that whatever happened during the next two weeks at sea, Gabriella had a scream in store for it. It was almost as though their ship—not a large ship at all, the rumor began to go round—had been appointed for this. "Why do I have to be taken to Naples! Why? I was happy at home in Buffalo, with you and Papa and Aunt Rosalia and Uncle Enrico!" she shrieked along the passage—where of course everybody else, as well as the Sertos, was lost.

"Enough for you it is *l'Anno Santo,*" said Mama. "Hold straight those shoulders. Look the others."

The others were going to pair off any minute—as far as pairing would go. There were six young girls, but though there were six young men too, they were only Joe Monteoliveto, Aldo Scampo, Poldy somebody, and three for the priesthood. As for Poldy, he was a Polish-American who was on his way now to marry a girl in Italy that he had never seen.

Every morning, to reach their deck, Mrs. Serto and Gabriella had to find their way along the whole length of the ship, right along its humming and pounding bottom, where the passage was wet (Did the ship leak? people asked) and narrow as a school room aisle; past the quarters of the crew—who looked wild in their half-undress, even their faces covered with black—and the *Pomona* engines; and at last up a steep staircase toward the light. Gabriella complained all the way. Mrs. Serto, feeling this was the uphill journey, only puffed. On the long way back to the dining room—downhill—Mrs. Serto had her say.

"You saw! Every girl on ship is fat"—exactly what she said about school and church at home. "In *Napoli,* when I was a girl, your *Nonna* told me a hundred times, 'Little daughter: girls do well to be strong. Also, be *delicata.*' You wait! She'll tell you the same. What's the matter? You got pretty little feet like me." Mama framed herself in the engineroom door, and showed her shoe.

But not every girl coming into the dining room had to pass seven tables to reach her own, as Gabriella did—bouncing along sideways, with each table measuring her hips again as briskly as a mother's tape measure; while Joe Monteoliveto, for example, might be looking her way.

"You are youngest of six daughters, all beautiful and strong, five married to smart boys, Maria's Arrigo smart enough to be pharmacist. Five with babies to show. And what would you call every one those babies?"

The word rushed out. "Adorable!"

"*Bellissimo!* But you hang back."

"So O.K.! If you wouldn't follow me all the time!"

"I know the time to drop behind," said Mama sharply.

On deck all day, where she could see all that water, the smoother the ocean looked behind, the more apprehensive Gabriella felt: tourist deck faced backwards. She yelled that she wished the ship would turn around right where it was and take her back to the good old Statue of Liberty again. At that, Mama cast her eyes heavenward and a little to the left, like St. Cecilia on the cake plate at home, won on stunt night at the Sodality.

"Walk!" said the mothers to their daughters.

"You hear, Gabriella? Get up and walk!"

There was nowhere to go but in a circle—six of them walking arm-in-arm, dissolved in laughter; Maria-Pia Arpista almost had to be held up—especially when they wheeled at the turns and Gabriella gave her scream. For every time, there were the same black shawls, the same old caps, backed up against the blue—faces coming out of them that grew to be the only faces in the world, more solid a group than a family's, more persistent than faces held fast in the memory of floating to nearness in dreams. On the best benches sat the old people, old enough to be going home to die—not noticing of the water, of the bad smells here and there, of where the warnings read *"Pittura Fresca,"* or when the loudspeaker cried *"Attenzione!"* and the others flew to the rail to learn the worst. They cared only for which side of the boat the sun was shining on.

On the last bench on one side two black men sat together by themselves. They never said a word, they did not smile. Their feet were long as loaves of bread, and black as beetles, and each pair pointed outward east and west; together their four feet formed a big black M, for getting married, set out for young girls to fall over.

"Why you put your tongue out those black people? Is that nice?" said Mama. "Signora Arpista, your Maria-Pia needs to sit down, look her expression."

But by the third day out, Maria-Pia walked with Joe Monteoliveto, and her expression had changed. So did Mama's—she stepped up and joined Maria-Pia's mama, a few paces behind the new couple's heels, where she would get in on everything.

Gabriella took a long running jump to the other side of the deck. And there, only a little distance away, stood Aldo Scampo, all by himself, as though the breeze had just set him down. He stood at the rail looking out, his rich pompadour blowing. The shadow of the upper deck hung over him like a big jaw, or the lid of a trunk, with priests on it.

As Gabriella drew near, slowly, as though she brought bad news, he leaned low on his elbows, watching the birds drop into the water where the crew, below, were shooting guns through the portholes. Except for white frown marks, Aldo's forehead was all bright copper, and so were his nose and chin, his chest, his folded arms—as if he were dressed up in somebody's kitchen dowry over his costume of yellow T-shirt and old army pants. The story Mama had of Aldo Scampo was that he was unmarried, was *Californese,* had mother, father, sisters and brothers in America, and his mother's people lived in Nettuno, where they partly owned a boat; but as he rattled around in a cabin to himself, the complete story was not yet known.

Pop—pop—pop.

These were the small, tireless, black-and-gold island birds that had kept up with their ship so far today that Gabriella felt like telling them, "Go home, dopes"—only of course, having followed for such a long way, by now they could never fly all the way back. (*"Attenzione!"* the loudspeaker had warned—all for some land you couldn't see, the Azores.) Another small body plummeted down before Aldo, so close he might have caught it in his hand. Did Aldo Scampo, mopping his radiant brow, know how many poor little birds that made?

Like a mind-reader, he turned brilliantly toward her; she thought he was going to answer with the number of birds, but when he spoke it was even more electrifying than an answer; it was a question.

"Ping-pong?"

She screamed and raced him to the table.

This must have been the very moment that Aldo Scampo himself gave something up. Until now he had not had more than a passing glance for the girls who went walking by in a row with their chocolate cigarettes in the air. Like Joe Monteoliveto before him, he had brooded over La Zìngara, the popular passenger said to be an actress; there she was now, further down the rail, talking to an almost *old* man. As Aldo and Gabriella pounded past her, La Zìngara—thin, but not one could say how young—leaned back into a life preserver as though it were a swing. Her lips, moving like a scissors, could be read; she was talking about the Jersey Highway.

While Aldo went begging the balls from the children, Gabriella seized her paddle and beat the table like an Indian drum. In a moment, many drew near. Up to now, Gabriella's only partner had been a choice between a boy of nine, who had since broken his arm and would have to wear a sling to see the Pope, and the Polish-

American fellow, who was engaged. Both, of course, had beaten her—but not as she would be beaten today! And her extra-long skirt, made by Mama in a nice strong red for the trip, rocked on her like a panoply as she readied herself for the opening ball, and missed it.

Everybody cheered. Even if she did not miss the ball, Gabriella was almost certain to fall down; finally, rushing in an ill-advised arc, she did collide with a priest, a large one, who was down from above to see how things in *turistica* were going. He rolled away in his skirts like a ball of yarn and had to be picked up by two of the three for the priesthood, while Gabriella clapped her hands to her ears and yelped like a puppy.

Everybody had begun to wonder if Gabriella could help screaming—especially now, after three days. It was true her screams were sometimes justified, out on a ship at sea, and always opportune—but there were also screams that seemed offered through the day for their own sake, endeavors of pure anguish or joy that youth and strength seemed able to put out faster than the steady, pounding quiet of the voyage could ever overtake and heal.

Only her long brows were calm in her face with its widened mouth, stretched eyes and flying dark hair, in her whole contending body, as though some captive, that had never had news of the world, land or sea, would sometimes stand there and look out from that pure arch—but never to speak; that could not even be thought to hear.

The evening after her overthrow at ping-pong, the dining room saw Gabriella come to the door and for a breath pause there. There was an ineffable quality about Mrs. Serto's daughter now. An evening after a storm comes with such bright drops—so does a child whose tantrum is over, even the reason for it almost, if not quite, forgotten. Through large, oval eyes whose shine made them look over-forgiving, she regarded the dining room now. And as she came through the door, they saw appearing from behind her Aldo Scampo, almost luminous himself in a clean white shirt.

As she and Aldo started hand in hand across the room, there was a sudden "Tweeeeet!" Papa, an old man from the table farthest back in the corner, blew a tin whistle whenever he felt like it—his joke and his privilege. Immediately everybody laughed.

Was it on every boat that tried to cross the ocean that some old fellow and his ten-cent whistle alerted the whole assembly at the most precious moments? Papa was an outrageous, halfway dirty, twice-married old man in an olive-green sweater who at each meal fought for the whole carafe of wine for himself and then sent the waiter for another. On top of his long head rose a crest of grizzly hair. A fatherly mustache, well-stained, draped itself over the whistle when he blew it. His black eyes were forever traveling carelessly beyond his own table. And just when it was least expected, when it was least desired, when your thoughts were all gentle and reassured and forgiving and triumphant—then it would be your turn: *"Tweeeet!"*

Gabriella and Aldo, after stopping dead in their tracks—for there was something official about the sound—marched to their separate tables like punished children. But by the time Gabriella had reached hers safely, she was able to lift her face like a dish of something fresh and delicious she had brought straight to them; and Mrs. Serto smiled her circle round: Mr. Fossetta, for Bari; Poldy, who was engaged; and Mr. Ambrogio, for Rome.

"Dressed up!" said Mama, a gesture of blessing for all falling from her plump little hand. Mama was even more dressed up. They had on silk blouses.

"We've been strolling, with Maria-Pia and Joe!" And Gabriella took her seat on Mama's right hand.

Tonight, the dining room felt, the missing sixth should have been at that table. Between Poldy and Mr. Ambrogio waited the vacant chair and spotless napkin of one assigned who had never come. Even if appetite had gone, he should have shown his face to complete the happiness of a mother.

Later that very night, Gabriella was fallen against Mrs. Serto on the rearmost bench on deck, trying not to watch the flagpole ride, while at gentle intervals her mother gave her a little more of the account of the bride's dress reported to be traveling on this ship in the Polish-American's cabin. Without those screams, the *Pomona* sailed in a strange, almost sad tranquillity under the stars, as in a trance that might never be broken again. So there had come a night, almost earlier than they had expected, when they all had their chance to feel sorry for Gabriella.

Between tea and dinner time next day, everybody who was able was sitting about on the benches enjoying the warm sea. All afternoon, with the sun going down on their backs, they had been drawing nearer and nearer the tinted coast of Spain. It grew long, pink, and caverned as the side of a melon. Chances were it would never come close enough for them to see much: they would see no face. But to Gabriella, the faces here on deck appeared bemused enough. Beside her, sitting up on their bench, Mama seemed to be asleep, with Mrs. Arpista, beyond her, also asleep; the two maternal heads under their little black buns nodded together like twin buoys in the waves.

Only the two black men looked the same as always. Not yet had they laughed, or asked a single question. Not yet had they expressed consternation at mealtime, or a moment's doubt about the course of the ship. Their very faith was enough to put other passengers off.

Aldo Scampo, like a man pining to be teased, was reading. He lay sprawled in the solitary deck chair—the one that the steward had opened out and set up in the center of the deck to face everybody, and labeled "Crosby"—very likely the name of the unattached lady who could not speak a word of Italian. All afternoon Aldo had held at various angles in front of his eyes a paper-back book bought on board, *The Bandit Giuliano, Dopo Bellolampo*. Or else he got up and disappeared into the public room to drink cherry soda and play cards with three little gray fellows going to Foggia.

When Aldo was about to open that book again, Gabriella rose from Mama's bench, took a hop, skip and jump to the chair, and pulled Aldo out of it. He came down to the deck floor on hands and knees, with a laughable crash.

She dropped beside him to make a violent face into his. Aldo, as though he drew a gun from a holster, placed a toothpick between his lips. On the softly vibrating floor, ringed around with the well-filled benches, they knelt confronting each other, eyes open wide. Just out of range, the ship's cat picked his way in and out the circle of feet, then, cradled in a pair of horny hands, disappeared upward.

It did not matter that the passengers on the warm *Pomona* deck had heads that were nodding or dreaming of home. It took only their legs from the knees down to listen like ears and watch like eyes—to wait dense and still as a ring of trees come near. The sailors softly beating the air with their paintbrushes, up in Second

Class, could look down and see them too, over the signs *"Pittura Fresca"* hung on ropes festooning the stairs.

Aldo's hands and Gabriella's interlocked, and their arms were as immobilized as wings that failed. Gabriella drove her face into Aldo's warm shirt. She set her teeth into his sleeve. But when she pierced that sleeve she found his arm—rigid and wary, with a muscle that throbbed like a heart. She would have bitten a piece out of him then and there for the scare his arm gave her, but he moved like a spring and struck at her with his tiny weapon, the toothpick between his teeth. In return she butted his chest, driving her head against the hard, hot rayon, while, still in the character of an airy bird, he pecked with his little beak that place on the back of the neck where women no longer feel. (Weren't all women made alike? she wondered: *she* could no longer feel there.) She screamed as if she could feel everything. But if she hadn't screamed so hard at Aldo yesterday, she wouldn't have had to bite him today. Now she knew *that* about Aldo.

The circle was still. Mama's own little feet might speak to them—there they rested, so well known. For a space Mama opened her eyes and contemplated her screaming daughter as she would the sunset behind her.

"Help! He's killing me!" howled Gabriella, but Mama dropped her eyes and was nodding Mrs. Arpista's way again.

Aldo buried his face in Gabriella's blouse, and she looked out over his head and presently smiled—not into any face in particular. Her smile was as rare as her silence, and as vulnerable—it was meant for everybody. A gap where a tooth was gone showed childishly.

It lifted the soul—for a thing like crossing the ocean could depress it—to sit in the sun and contemplate among companions the weakness and the mystery of the flesh. Looking, dreaming, down at Gabriella, they felt something of an old, pure loneliness come back to them—like a bird sent out over the waters long ago, when they were young, perhaps from their same company. Only the long of memory, the brave and experienced of heart, could bear such a stirring, an awakening—first to have listened to that screaming, and in a flash to remember what it was.

Aldo climbed to his feet and set himself back in his chair, and Gabriella went back to her mother, but the *Pomona,* turning, sailed on to the south, down the coast of Europe—so near now that Father's vesper bell might almost be taken for a little goat bell on shore. The air colored, and a lighthouse put up its arm.

Even the morning sky told them they were in the Mediterranean now. They could see it glowing through the windows of church, waiting for Father to come and start Mass. In the middle of the night before, they had slipped through the Gates of Gibraltar—even touched there, so it was said. While everybody was asleep, the two black passengers had been put off the boat.

"They're going to the Cape Verde Islands," Mrs. Arpista cried to Mrs. Serto two rows ahead. "They don't know nothing but French."

"Poveretti!" Mrs. Serto cried back, with the sympathy that comes too late. "And where were their wives, *i Mori?"*

"My sweetheart and I are going to have a happy, happy Christmas," Poldy announced, rubbing his hands together. His straw-blond hair was thin enough to show a baby-like scalp beneath.

"So you never seen your girl, eh?" remarked Mr. Fossetta, a small dark father of five, who sat just in front of him. All the Serto table sat together in church—Mama thought it was nice. Today they made a little square around her. At her right, Poldy locked his teeth and gave a dazzling grin.

"We've never seen each other. But do we love each other? Oh boy!"

Mr. Fossetta made the abrupt gesture with which he turned away the fresh sardines at the table, and faced front again.

Poldy reached in his breast pocket and produced his papers. He prodded under the elastic band that held them all together to take out a snapshot, and passed this up to Mr. Fossetta.

"Yes, a happy, happy Christmas," said Poldy. "Pass that. Why *wouldn't* we be happy, we'll be married then. I'm taking the bridesmaids' dresses, besides the bride's I told you about, and her mother's dress too, in store boxes. Her aunt in Chicago, that's who gave me the address in the first place—she knows everything! The names and the sizes. Everything is going to fit. Wait! I'll show you something else—the ticket I bought for my wife to come back with me to the U.S.A. on. Guess who we're going to live with? Her aunt."

Everybody took a chance to yawn or look out the window, but Mama inclined her head at Poldy going through his papers and said, "Sweetest thing in the world, Christmas, second to love." She suddenly looked to the other side of her. "You paying attention, Gabriella?"

Gabriella had been examining her bruises, old and new. She shook her head; under the kerchief it was burgeoning with curlers. Here came the snapshot on its way from the row ahead.

"Take that bride!" said Mama.

"Hey, she's little!" said Gabriella. "You can't hardly see her."

Poldy reached across Mama as though she were nothing but a man. That golden-haired wrist with its yellow-gold watch was under Gabriella's nose, and those golden-haired fingers snatched the picture from her and Mama's hands and stuck it at Mr. Ambrogio, behind.

"Wait, wait! There went who I love the best in world," said Mama. "Little bride. Was that nice?"

"We haven't got all day," said Poldy. "Gee, I can't find her ticket anywhere. Don't worry, folks, I'll show it to you at breakfast."

"She knows how to pose," said Mr. Ambrogio politely. He was a widower of long standing.

"All right, pass it."

At that moment, who but Aldo Scampo elected to come to church! Just in time, as he dropped to his knee by the last chair in the row, to be greeted with Poldy's bride stuck under his nose.

"Curlers!" hissed Mama in Gabriella's ear. She gave Gabriella's cheek one of her incredibly quick little slaps—it looked for all the world like only a pat, belonging to no time and place but pure motherhood.

There Aldo studied the bride from his knees, sighting down his blue chin before breakfast.

"O.K., O.K., partner!" said Poldy, his hand on the reach again, as Father came bustling in with fresh paint on his skirts (*he'd* been standing at the rail overhead); and there was quiet except for two noisy, almost simultaneous smacks: Poldy kissing his bride and snapping her back under the elastic band.

"You stay after Mass and confess sloth, you hear?" whispered Mama.

Gabriella and Aldo were looking along the rows of rolled down eyelids at each other. They put out exactly simultaneous tongues.

By nine o'clock, Gabriella and Aldo were strolling up on deck;

so was everybody. Aldo pushed out his lips and offered Gabriella a kiss.

"Oh, look what I found," said Mrs. Serto from behind them, causing them to jump apart as if she'd exploded something. She had opened a little gold locket. Now she held out, cupped in her pink palm, a ragged little photograph, oval and pearl-colored, taken from its frame. "Who but my Gabriella as a baby?"

Gabriella snatched it, where Mama bent over it smiling as at a little foundling, and tucked it inside her blouse.

"No longer a child now, Gabriella," announced Mama to the sky.

"Somebody told me," Aldo said, "it's nifty up front."

"Cielo azzurro!" said Mama. "Go 'head. *Pellegrini, pellegrini* everywhere, beautiful day like this!"

Three priests strolled by, their skirts gaily blowing, and as Joe Monteoliveto ran their gamut, juggling ping-pong balls, Mama held Gabriella fast for a moment and whispered, "Not the prize Arpistas may think—he leaves the boat at Palermo."

"Keep my purse," was all Gabriella said.

The long passage through the depths of the ship, that was too narrow for Mrs. Serto and Gabriella to walk without colliding, seemed made for Gabriella and Aldo. True, it was close with the smell of the sour wine the crew drank. In the deepest part, the engines pounding just within that open door made a human being seem to go in momentary danger of being shaken asunder. It sounded here a little like the Niagara Falls at home, but she had never paid much attention to *them.* Yet with all the deafening, Gabriella felt as if she and Aldo Scampo were walking side by side in some still, lonely, even high place never seen before now, with mountains above, valleys below, and sky. The old man in the red knit cap who slept all day on top of that box was asleep where he always was, but now as if he floated, with no box underneath him at all, in some spell. Even the grandfather clock, even the map, when these came into sight, looked faceless, part of a landscape. And the remembered sign, so beautifully penned, on the bulletin board—"Lost, a golden brooch for the tie, with initials F.A."—it shone at them like a star.

By steep stairs at the end, they came out on an altogether new deck, where the air was bright and stiff as an open eye. It was white and narrowing, set about with mysterious shapes of iron wound with chains. No passenger was in sight. Leaning into the very beak ahead, with her back to them, a *cameriera* was drying her hair; when she let it loose from the towel it blew behind her straight as an arm. A sailor, seated cross-legged on an eminence like a drum, with one foot bare, the blackened toes fanned out like a circus clown's, sewed with all his might on a sock with a full shape to it. All was still. No—as close as a voice that was speaking to them now, the *Pomona* was parting the water.

"Wait—a—minute," said Aldo still looking, with his hands on his hips.

So this was where Miss Crosby came with her book. Still as a mouse, she was sitting on the floor close to the rail, drawn up with the book on her knees.

"Don't bother her, and maybe she won't bother us," said Gabriella. "That's how *I* treat people."

Aldo reached in his hand, and took the picture away from Gabriella, then sat down cross-legged on this barely slanting floor to see what he'd got.

At last he hit his leg a slap. He said, "They took one of me the same age. They had me dressed up like a little St. John the Baptist. Can you beat 'em?"

Gabriella had been standing behind him, where she could see too. Suddenly she grasped a length of the hem of her skirt and blindfolded him with it. Aldo threw up both hands, the hand with the snapshot releasing it to the milky sea. The uncovered part of his face expressed solemnity. Like all blindfolded persons, he was holding his breath. Gabriella couldn't see his face; hers above it waited with eyes tight-shut.

A moment went by, and she jumped away; that was all that had come to her to do. Aldo promptly wheeled himself around, one leg flailing the deck, and caught her by the ankle and threw her.

She came down headlong; her fall, like a single clap of thunder, was followed by that expectancy in the air that can almost be heard too. The *cameriera* bound down her hair, and the sailor put on his sock; as if they'd been together a long time, they disappeared together through the door, down the stairs.

Neither Gabriella nor Aldo stirred. They lay, a little apart, like the victims of a passing wind. Presently Aldo, moving one finger at a time, began to thump on the calf of Gabriella's leg—1, 2, 3, 4—

while she lay as before, with her back to him. Intermittently the 1, 2, 3, 4 kept up, then it slowed and fell away. Gradually the sounds of the dividing sea came back to Gabriella's ear, as though a seashell were once more held lifted.

She turned her head and opened her eyes onto Aldo's clay-colored shoe, hung loose on his sockless foot. Far away now was his hand, gaping cave-like in sleep beside her forgotten leg. Past the pink buttress of his jaw rose the little fountain, not playing now, where his mouth stood open to the sky. He lay there sound asleep over the Mediterranean Sea.

Gabriella stayed as she was, caught in an element as languorous as it was strange, like a mermaid who has been netted into a fisherman's boat, only to find that the fisherman is dreaming. Where no eye oversaw them, the sea lifted and dropped them both, mindless as a cradle, up then down.

Even when La Zìngara clattered out on deck, with a spectacled youth at her heels, and, seeing Aldo, gave the sharp laugh of experience, Aldo only shut his lips, like a reader who has just licked his finger to turn a page. But Gabriella sat up and caught her hair and her skirt, seeing those horn-rims: that young man was marked for the priesthood.

With the pop of corks being drawn from wine-bottles, La Zìngara kicked off her shoes. Then she began dancing in her polished, bare feet over the deck. ("Practicing," she had replied with her knife-like smile when the mothers wondered where she went all day—furiously watching an actress rob the church.) She made the horn-rimmed young man be her partner; to dance like La Zìngara meant having someone to catch you. In a few turns they had bounded to the other side of the deck.

"Excuse me," said a new voice. Miss Crosby had unfolded herself and come over on her long legs. Speaking across the sleeping Aldo as though she only called through a window, she asked, "What do you call those birds in Italian?"

"What birds?"

"There! Making all that racket!" Miss Crosby pointed out to sea with her book, *First Lessons in Italian Conversation*. "Ever since we've been passing Sardinia."

"Didn't you ever see seagulls before?"

"I just want to know the Italian."

"I gabbiani," said Gabriella.

In a moment, Miss Crosby made a face, as if she were about to grit her teeth, and said, *"Grazie."* She went away then. Gabriella crossed her legs beneath her and sat there, guarding Aldo.

Three members of the crew presently materialized, one raising his gun toward the birds that were flying and calling there, shifting up and down in the light.

"No!" cried Aldo in his sleep.

In two minutes he was up shooting with the sailors, and she was merely waiting on him.

"Terrible responsibility to be coming into property—who knows how soon!" said Mama.

"It's nothing to be sneezed at," said Gabriella. A white triangle of salve—Maria's Harry had tucked that into her suitcase—was laid over her nose; the rest of her face still carried a carnation glow.

Just those three sat propped on the back of the rearmost bench—Gabriella, Aldo Scampo and Mama. They could see the long blue wake flowing back from them, smooth as a lady's train.

"Look at the dolphins!" cried Aldo.

"Where, where? Wanting their dinner. A terrible responsibility," said Mama. She ran her loving little finger over the brooches settled here and there on her bosom, like St. Sebastian over his arrows. If she had had to slap Gabriella at the lunch table for getting lost on her morning walk, all was *delicato* now. Nice naps had been taken, tea was over with, and real estate in the vicinity of Naples had come up in conversation.

"And tomorrow, Gala Night," said Mama. "Am I right, Mr. Scampo?"

"Yeah, Mrs. Serto, I guess you are," said Aldo.

Mama slipped down from between them to her feet, her fingers threw them a little wave that looked like a pinch of salt, and she began a last march around deck. Her opposite turn was the public room, where her friends would by now be collecting, the *indisposti* propped deadweight among them but able to listen, and the well ones speculating peacefully out of the wind.

When Mama passed the bench again—really her farewell time, and then she would leave the sunset to young sweethearts—all seemed well. With the obsessiveness that characterizes a family man, Aldo was drumming a soft fist into Gabriella's plump young back, which held there unflinchingly, while her words came in snatches with the breath cut off in between.

"Nothing to be sneezed at—We'll have to wear paper caps—and dance—"

The wake of the ship turned to purple and gold. The dolphins, in silhouette, performed a rainbow of leaps. Gabriella screamed and her laugh ran down the scale.

Mama bowed herself into the public room, where the mothers were expecting her, the full congregation; and taking the seat by Mrs. Arpista, she continued with the subject she loved the best—under its own name, now: love.

But the day of Gala Night broke forth with a trick from the Mediterranean. Its blue had darkened and changed, and here and there at the edge of things could be seen a little white-cap. Father did not look too cheerful at Mass, and among other messages coming in from either side to Mama was the one that Aldo Scampo himself had not been able to rise. When a wave was seen at the glass of the porthole, looking in the dining room at lunch, Mama retreated upward to the public room, with Gabriella to sit by her side; and through the afternoon she declared herself unanswerable for the night.

But when the dinner gong was sounded, Mrs. Serto found she could raise her head. She believed, if she were helped to dress up a little . . . After she had pinned and patted Mama together, Gabriella got out of her skirt, into her blue, and up on her high heels; then she guided Mama down that final flight of stairs.

And when they had crossed the dining room to the Serto table, one of the old, old ladies was sitting in Mama's place. Was it simply a mistake? Was it a visit? She was far too old to be questioned. Every little pin trembling, Mama sat down in Gabriella's place, which left Gabriella the vacant one with Mr. Ambrogio between them. The first thing the waiter brought was the paper hats.

The old lady put on hers, and so did they all after her. Gabriella's was an open yellow crown, cut in points that tended to fall outward like the petals of a daisy. But poor Mama could not take her eyes away from the old lady who sat in her place.

She was a Sicilian. With her pierced ears and mosaic ear-drops, the skin of her face around eyes and mouth like water where stones have dropped in, her body wrapped around in shawls and her head in a black silk rag—and now the paper hat of Gala Night atop that, looking no more foolish there than a little cloud hanging to a mountain—their guest was so old that her chin perpetually sank nearly to the level of the table. She treated their waiter like dirt.

He was bringing every course tonight to the old lady first, instead of to Mama, and with a croak and a flick of the hand the old lady was sending it back—not only the *antipasto,* but now the soup. She wanted to see something better. Their waiter treated her dismissals with respect—with more than respect; some deeper, more everlasting relationship was implied.

And suddenly, as the *pasta* was coming in, their long-missing table mate chose to make his appearance. Another chair had to be wedged between the old lady's and Mr. Fossetta's where he sat down, with pale cheeks, snow-white hair, and mustaches that were black as night. He looked at them all in their paper caps. His first words were to demand, "Is it true? There is no one for Genoa but me?"

Mama looked back at him, in a little soldier hat with a tassel on top, and said, "This boat is *Pomona,* going to *Napoli.*"

"And after *Napoli,*" said he, "Genoa." A paper cap was put in his hand by the waiter, and he put it on—it was a chef's cap—and lowered his head at Mama. "Genoa I leave only on holiday. Only for pleasure I travel. Now I return to Genoa."

"Please," said Mr. Ambrogio politely, "what is there in Genoa?"

He was handed a calling card. Mama's little hand asked for it, and she read to them in English: "C. C. Ugone. The man to see is Ugone. Genoa."

"For one thing, is in Genoa most beautiful cemetery in world," said Mr. Ugone—and did well to speak in English; otherwise who could have understood this voice from the north tonight? "You have never seen? No one? Ah, the statues—you could find nowhere in *Italia* more beautiful, more sad, more real. Envision with me now, I will take you there gladly. Ah! See here—a mama, how she hold high the little daughter to kiss picture of Papa—all lifesize. See here! You see angel flying out the tomb—lifesize! See here! You see family of ten, eleven, twelve, all kneeling lifesize at deathbed. You would marvel how splendid is Genoa with the physical. Oh, I tell you here tonight, you making a mistake to leave this boat at Naples."

Mama returned Mr. Ugone's card.

"I go to Rome," Mr. Ambrogio said.

"Say, mister," said Poldy. "What you say sounds worth coming all the way to Italy to see."

"Signore," said Mr. Ugone, turning toward Poldy—he had to lean across Mr. Fossetta and his *pasta*—"you will see this and more. Oh, I guarantee, you will find it sad! You want to see tear on the little child's cheek? Solid tear!" Mr. Ugone made a gesture of silence at the waiter coming with the fish. *"Ecco!* Bringing the news! Is turned over, the little boat. Look how hand holds tight the hat. Mmm!"

"No sardine!" said Mama, ahead of the old lady, but there was no need of warning. The waiter had dropped his tray on the floor.

But Mr. Ugone, with his untoward respect for Poldy, went on above all confusion. *"Signore,* we have in Genoa a sculptor who is a special for angels. See this tomb! Don't you see that soul look glad to be reaching Heaven? Oh! Here a sister die young. See her dress—the fold is caught in the tomb-door—*delicato,* you accord? How she enjoin the other sister she die too, before her wedding day. Sad, mmm?"

"Say!" said Poldy.

"Gabriella, you please listen to me, hold tight that hat!" said Mama. "You shake your head and it goes round and round."

"I show you," said Mr. Ugone to all, "the tomb my blessed mother."

Back in the corner, old Papa had been fixing his eye on Mr. Ugone for some time. Now he blew his whistle.

"Go ahead," said Poldy. Mr. Ugone had stopped with his napkin over his heart. "He does that all the time—we're used to it."

"Of course," said Mr. Ugone, "other beautiful things I can show to you in Genoa. I enjoin you direct your attention to back of old wall where Paganini born."

"Say, what are you?" Gabriella asked him, holding her crown on straight.

"Who's Paganini?" said Poldy.

But Mr. Ugone, who had never quite taken his eyes off Papa, waiting there still in that red engineer's cap with his whistle raised, now rose to his feet. With the words, "Also well-known skyscraper!" flung to them all, he suddenly left them—almost as though he hadn't ever come.

Mr. Fossetta brushed off his hands, and poured more wine around. Under cover of Mr. Ugone's departure, the old lady stole a roll from Mama's plate, and Mama watched it disappearing into that old, old mouth.

But Mama remained throughout the evening just as nice to the old lady as Gabriella was nice to Mama. Even when the old lady described the Cathedral of Monreale from front to back, and more than one time said, "First church in the world for beauty, Saint Peter second," Mama only closed her eyes and gave a brief click of the tongue.

"Mama," said Gabriella, "are we coming back home on this boat too?"

"No more *Pomona!*" said Mama. "We come home *Colomba*. By grace of Holy Mother it will not rock—beautiful white boat, *Colomba.*"

"You are full of thoughts too." Mr. Ambrogio turned to Gabriella. "I am still missing my tie-pin. Do you feel I will ever find it?"

"Who knows?" said Mama. "You never know when you find something. That's what I tell my poor daughter every morning she wants to sleep late the nice bed."

"Ah, it could have been lost into the sea—before we start, who knows? Standing to wave at friends, from the rail—'Goodbye! Goodbye!' " and Mr. Ambrogio half rose from his chair to wave at them now.

"But you're *wearing* a tie-pin!" said Poldy, and laughed loudly at poor Mr. Ambrogio, who sat down; and it was true that he was doing so, and true too that he had been showing them from the first night out the way he had said goodbye to all those friends he had in America.

"It is my second pin, not my first. Only a cameo." Mr. Ambrogio's feelings were hurt now. He was going eventually home to Sicily but certainly he wanted his first pin for his audience with the Pope. He asked not to be given any of the fish, which the waiter now brought in for the second time.

The boat lurched. A black wave could be felt looking in at the nearest porthole, out of the night.

"Ah, the Captain this boat—has he anywhere a wife?" cried Mama, and rolled her head toward the old lady, who gave no answer.

Poldy at once took out his papers. Hadn't Mr. Ugone's card at the table been enough?—even supposing it had not been Gala Night, with *gelati* somewhere on the way. Now Poldy was finding an envelope he had never brought out before, with an address written on it in purple ink—a long one.

"What town in Italy is that?" he demanded, and passed the envelope back and forth in front of Mr. Fossetta's eyes. Mr. Fossetta, with one sharp gesture of the hand and a shake of the head, went on taking fish bones out of his mouth.

"Can't read? That's the town they're taking me to get married." Poldy beamed. "My sweetheart and her brother, or cousin, or whoever comes with her to meet the boat in Naples, they'll take me there. How about you, can you read?" he asked Mr. Ambrogio, but on the way to him the envelope had reached the old lady, who deposited it in her lap.

Poldy only shouted to the waiter, "Gee, I'll take another plate of that," pulling him back by the coat. It was not only Gala Night that Poldy asked for second plates—it was every night. He enjoyed the food.

"If," Mr. Fossetta remarked ostensibly to Mama, with something a little ominous in his voice, "if she has a brother, then it will be her brother come to meet him."

"Only daughters have I ever been sent!" cried Mama—then gave an even sharper cry.

Through the dining room door, arriving at the same time as the veal course, Aldo Scampo had entered like a ghost. Tentatively, not seeming to see with his eyes at all, he made his way through the dining room with all its caps, past the Serto table without a sign. Even after he had sat down safely in his own chair, who could speak to him? He was so white.

Papa, however, blew his whistle. This time he stood up to do it.

And instantly, another old man—the old man in the red knit cap who slept in the day by the ship's engines and had not exchanged for a paper cap tonight—rose up from the other side of the room and answered Papa, with mumbled words and the vague waving of an arm. He thought somebody had been insulted. Papa blew the whistle back at him, and then carried away at meeting opposition at last, blew without stopping—"Tweet! Tweet! Tweet! Tweet!" The argument filled the dining room to its now gently creaking walls.

The head steward himself came to Papa's table—his first visit to the back of the room. Everybody but the other old man, and the old lady who was crushing a crust, like a bone, between her teeth, grew hushed.

"What is the meaning of this whistle?" asked the steward.

Old Papa, with his head cocked and in the voice of a liar, told the steward that once a little boy, long ago, was going away to America from Italy. Papa's left hand dived low and gave the air a pat. On such a big ship—and his right hand poked the whistle into the girth of the steward—the little boy might have been lost. But his papa said to him, "Never mind. Whenever you hear this" —and before the steward knew it, the old man had blown it again, "Tweeeeeet!"—"Papa."

Aldo Scampo moved out of his chair and started silently out of the room the way he had come; only his yellow, pointed crown was crumpled like the antlers of a deer where, as he rose up, he had had to clutch his head.

"No *gelati?*" many called sorrowfully after him through their laughter.

"Why did he think he had to come, anyway?" Gabriella shrieked as he staggered past her. "Who's Aldo Scampo?"

"Champagne! *Gelati!*" For here came out the trays, sparkling all over, radiating to every table. Jumping up, Poldy raised his glass. "To my wedding!" he cried to the room, then swallowed the champagne without a stop.

Mama first pulled him down, then rose herself with her own arms stretched empty, like a prophetess.

"Mama! It's Gala Night," said Gabriella, joining her hands and looking into her mother's face.

Mrs. Serto, with a tragic look for all, toppled upon her daughter. Gabriella, struggling up just in time, caught her beneath the arms and then bore her, leaning, from the dining room. As they passed table after table, people who were eating *gelati* rose spoon in hand, paper hats a-bob on their heads, to make way.

It was thought an anti-climax, showing lack of appreciation of the night's feelings, that Gabriella came straight back. The *frutti* was just appearing. Crowned a little nearer to the ears, as though by one last sweep of a failing hand, she took back her real place at the table, where she ate her own *gelati* and then her mother's, and drank both glasses of champagne.

The old lady—as though she were the waiter's own mother, or the V. M., thought Gabriella—finally accepted his bowl of fruit, and Gabriella was allotted, from her fork, a little brown-skinned pear.

It was this old lady who remained last at the Serto table. When the others excused themselves, she was still dropping grapes into her mouth, like a goddess sacrificing a few extra tribes. Scarcely an eyelid flickered from above.

Upstairs in the public room, when the three-piece band began playing "Deep in the Heart of Texas" to start the dancing, an unexpected trio of newcomers turned themselves loose on the girls. Two looked like, and were, the radio operator and the man who brought the bouillon around the deck in the mornings; another, who had the mothers guessing at first, was placed as the *turistica* hairdresser, seen daily, after all, standing in his doorway. Then Mr. Ambrogio, who had softly perfumed himself again since dinner, with the thin little widow from Rome went arrowing bravely down the floor; she was the usually distracted mother of those divine, but sometimes bad, little children.

Gabriella stood in the door, in her blue dress mounted with ruffles from which the little pleats had still not quite shaken out —and suddenly she was asked to dance by Joe Monteoliveto. Maria-Pia was out of it too, then; there was no one who could not fall by the wayside tonight and have a stranger appear in his place. Joe wore on his head a pink stack like a name-day cake, with a cherry on top. Gabriella gave him her hand. Out on the floor, under the stroke of the riding ship, they began circling together as easily as if they had sailed many a time across the sea, and were used to the waves and the way to dance over them.

Tonight was Gala Night, that was the reason—and partners were not real partners, the sea not the sea Mama had had in mind, and paper lanterns masked the lights that climbed and fell over their heads; and there was no colliding with the world. The band went into "Japanese Sandman," and as Gabriella went swinging in the arms of Joe Monteoliveto the whole round of the room, a gentle breath of wonder started after her, too soft to be accusation, too perishable to be hope. Dancing, poor Mrs. Serto's daughter was filled with grace.

The whole company—mothers banked around the walls, card players trapped at the tables, and the shadowy old—all looked her way. *Indisposti* or not, of course they knew what was happening. Once more, slipping the way it liked to do through one of life's weak moments, illusion had got in, and they were glad to see it. How many days had they been on the water!

The mothers gently cocked their heads from side to side in time, the old men re-lit their tobacco and poured out a little *vino.* That great, unrewarding, indestructible daughter of Mrs. Serto, round as an onion, and tonight deserted, unadvised, unprompted, and unrestrained in her blue, went dancing around this unlikely floor as lightly as an angel.

Whenever she turned, she whirled, and her ruffles followed—and the music too had to catch up. It began to seem to the general eye that she might be turning around faster inside than out. For an unmarried girl, it was danger; but some radiant pin through the body had set her spinning like that tonight, and given her the power—not the same thing as permission, but what was like a memory of how to do it—to be happy all by herself. Their own poor daughters, trudging uphill and down as the ship tilted them, would have to bide their time until Gabriella learned her lesson.

When La Zìngara arrived, and took Joe Monteoliveto away in the middle of a waltz, Gabriella spread both arms and went on dancing by herself. Lighter than ever on her toes, as the band swung faster and louder into a new chorus of "Let Me Call You Sweetheart," and the very sides of the room began tapping and humming, she began whirling around in place in the middle of the floor.

Arms wide, toes in, four, six, ten, a dozen turns she went, all blue, and kept whirling; and at the end, as the cymbal crashed, she stopped. The ruffles ran the other way once, and fell into their pleats. The *Pomona* rose and fell, like a sigh on the breast, but Gabriella held her place—not falling: smiling, intact, a Leaning Tower. A shout of joy went up—even from those that the spectacle of an un-grasped, spinning girl was bound to have made feel worse. "Bravo!" shouted Father, standing dangerously on a chair.

It was the stunt Gabriella was famous for in the St. Cecilia Sodality.

Whistles with toy balloons attached arrived on a dining room tray, and were blown in every direction.

"May I have the pleasure of the next?" Mr. Ambrogio asked Gabriella, moving a saffron handkerchief over his brow above dilated eyes.

Poldy, in the end, broke up the evening—he did not dance—by rushing in pretending to be Gene Autry on horseback and shooting an imaginary pistol at all the girls and all the boys and at all the lights in this room afloat in the night at sea.

It was as though they'd *forgotten* Palermo!

Everybody, at sun-up, crowded to the rail to turn one concerted gaze, full and ardent, on the first big black island rocks. They pointed fingers that trembled up at crags, into caves. They smiled on a man they had surprised in his frail little craft with the pomegranate-colored sail, far out in the early morning under the drop of some cliff. How fast now they were slipping through the silver light! Shafts of the clearing sun forked down from battlements higher than the ship was. The mist lifted and revealed something dim and green sliding near, something adored.

Smiling, they turned and admired one another. Everybody was dressed up for Palermo—not only the Sicilians, who would be reaching home. Gone were the shawls except on the oldest ladies—those were eternal. All about were the coats and hats of city streets; new stockings flashed in the light. Gone were the caps—there had been a felt hat on the grayest old grandfather since six o'clock in the morning.

Gabriella, though not specially in honor of Palermo, had got back into her blue. Only Aldo must still be untouched by where they were. Back in the canary sweatshirt, he was spread out in Miss Crosby's chair, not even looking when a passing cave was hailed at Giuliano's, and Joe Monteoliveto, with Maria-Pia pulling on his coat-tails, nearly fell overboard trying to see who was in it.

As they were being tugged into the harbor, it looked at though Palermo itself could wait no longer on the *Pomona*. One by one, bobbing out on the water's altered green, appeared tiny rowboats, and out of them presently came small, urgent cries. The boats worked their way nearer and nearer the ship, shirtsleeved arms shot up from them like flags, cries turned into names, and suddenly everywhere at once there was welcome. One boat was bringing thirteen, all fat, still unrecognized, one man in shirtsleeves rowing, the rest in a frenzy of waving.

"Enrico!"

"Achille!"

"Rosalia!"

"Massimiliano!"

The little old lady who had invited herself to the Serto table on Gala Night was all ready to disembark. She was the one with the limp. She made her way around deck like a wounded bird on the ground, opening her mouth now and then to scream "Fortunato!"

And suddenly she was answered from the water: "Pepi-i-ina!"

Mama, rushing to look out by first one side, then the other, was wildly excited. Her crisis last night had done her good. She was dressed as though for Sunday. She easily found *Signora* Pepina's relative for her—that was his boat. No, it was that one!

"Fortunato!"

"Fortunato! I see him!" Mrs. Serto could be heard above all the rest. "Fortunato and seven. Have no doubt. It is he."

"Why couldn't he wait? We'll get there soon enough," said Gabriella.

"He is the rower!" Mrs. Serto swung her purse in a wild arc; now her crucifix, having come unpinned once but discovered thus by Mr. Ambrogio, was pinned back all crooked.

"Francesco!"

"Pepi-i-ina!"

"Massimiliano!"

"But where is Achille?"

"He has had heart attack!" screamed Mama fearfully.

In the dock—now in plain view from shipboard—a fight was going on among those who had been patient enough to wait on shore; a big man in a straw hat who had got past the rope was struggling in the hands of the police. Here, crowded to the *Pomona's* landward side, the passengers could hear the warm, worldly sound of fisticuffs traveling across the last reach of water, the insults rolling and falling on solid ground.

"Francesco!"

"Assunta!"

"Achille, Achille, Achille!"

"Pepi-i-ina!"

"Ecco, ecco Pepina!" screamed Mama. "Must we tell you which one she is!"

In the background, by the flagpole. Maria-Pia Arpista and Joe Monteoliveto were trying to say goodbye. Maria-Pia was weeping into a handkerchief, and Joe was so swallowed up in a winter suit —the one from whose sleeves he had nearly fallen out—as to look entirely different from last night.

"Moto perpetuo." A little man smiled at Gabriella, stirring the air with his black-nailed finger. He knew her.

Gabriella nodded to him. She set her shoulders and posed beside her mother, frowning out from under her Buffalo hat, facing the dock.

"Fortunato, he is your brother?" Mama was asking the old woman at her other side. "Your nephew? Cousin? He was never your husband?

"He is all I have," the old woman replied.

La Zìngara managed to be the first from *turistica* to disembark. She went swaying down the gangway, arms outstretched—secretly for balance, Gabriella felt, but outwardly to extend a tender greeting. Below, with his arms also outflung, waited, alas, a country clown, with red face and yellow shoes. La Zìngara had saved for this moment those two thin but brilliant red foxes that bit each other around her neck, both with blue eyes.

"Well, there *she* goes," said the voice of Aldo, a yawn all through it. He had wandered to the rail where the three for the priesthood stood.

Gabriella did not even look at him. From Maria-Pia she had heard what all the boys called La Zìngara among themselves—*Il Cadavere.*

"You will see tomorrow," her mother told her with a nod. "It will be much more than this. These are only Sicilians. Why don't we go 'head to Naples?"

Gabriella screamed. "Where's the fire? What's going to happen when we do get there?"

"L'Anno Santo, l'Anno Santo," said Mama. "But listen." She pulled Gabriella to her. "If you don't pay attention, you be like Zìngara some day—old maid! You see her neck? Then you cry for somebody to take you even to *Sicilia!* But who? I'll be dead then, in cemetery!" Mama gave a cross little laugh and pushed her away.

At last the Sicilians were all off the boat, and all their trunks and boxes and bundles had been flung down behind them, with the electric toasters and irons tied on like Christmas tags. The struggling and shouting and claiming ceased on shore, kissing and embracing fell off, and the final semaphores from the shirtsleeved arms were diminishing away. Once more the *Pomona* throbbed and moved in blue water.

"When did that Joe Monteoliveto sneak off the ship?" wondered Mama aloud, not yet going inside. "He never said goodbye to me."

This sunset was the last. Gabriella stood at the flagpole and looked off the back of the ship; it moved smoothly now as by magic.

Once—she couldn't remember how long ago—there had been some country they sailed near—Africa—with mountains like coals, and above, the scimitar-and-star of evening. The country had vanished like the two black men who got off in the night for Cape Verde. The moon and star tonight looked as though they had never been close together in their lives, to hang one from the tip of the other to go down over the edge of the world.

Was now the time to look forward to the doom of parting, and stop looking back at the doom of meeting? The thought of either made sadness go leaping and diving, like those dolphins in the water. Gabriella would only have to say "Goodbye, Aldo," and while she was saying the words, the time would be flying by; parting would be over with almost before it began, no matter what Aldo had in store for an answer. "Hello, Aldo!" had been just the other way.

"What d'you think you see out there?" came Aldo's voice. "A whale?"

Reflecting the rosy light, a half-denuded stalk of bananas at his feet—for Aldo Scampo had slipped off the boat in Palermo and back on again, without a word to anybody—he was where you could find him still, in the old place, eating away and turning over pages he could hardly see any longer.

She made her way slowly to his chair and sat down on the arm of it, and like a modest confession let out the weight of her side against his shoulder. He offered her a bite of his banana. Tiredly and quietly, in alternation, they ate it. His book dropped to the floor; the toe of her shoe found it and drew it under the chair. Her heel went down, almost without her knowing, on the idealized, dreaming, and predatory face of that Sicilian bandit.

"Almost over now," said Aldo into the evening.

Their thoughts had met. Curtained into her bed that night, and after Mama had fallen silent, Gabriella could go to sleep thinking of those three words. Just now she dropped her head and put a kiss on Aldo somewhere, the way she would upon a little baby.

Near them, there was a patter of applause. Without their noticing, the nightly circle of sitters had gathered outside tonight, on the warm apron of deck—their ranks thinned now, since Palermo, by a number of the solidest. The clapping was for old Papa, who had come forward to sing.

His verses were like little rags that fluttered on the wind from his frail and prancing person. He carried a willowy cane. He had saved his paper hat, which showed against the first stars, jutting like a rooster's crown. So he must have known all along he would sing on the last night.

He stepped back and came forward again, tapped his cane, and sang a verse; retired, and came back with a new one. His voice was old and light, a little cracked. Each time, they gave him back the chorus, sitting in close array, moved in nearer together than ever on the benches and on the floor, a row reclining against billowy knees and another leaning on billowy shoulders behind, as if for some strange, starlit group-photograph, to be found years later in a trunk. A girl went to the well for water, Papa sang, and a traveler jumped out and surprised her, and she dropped her pitcher.

Mama's benchful moved in closer to make room for Gabriella and Aldo. After they sat down, they joined in the chorus with everybody. Whatever the verse, it was the same chorus—in Buffalo, in New York, in California, in Naples, perhaps even in Genoa. As the song went on, Aldo turned his head and on Gabriella's moving lips returned her kiss.

If only that had been the goodbye! But here they still were. Mama in the next instant rapped Aldo's skull with her knuckle—the crack of her wedding ring went out all over the Mediterranean night. Mama was still not speaking to Aldo for his ruining Gala Night for her. He obediently caught up with the song. Everything was in darkness now—there were only the *Pomona's* lights and the stars.

Presently Mama called out to ask the time of Poldy; but Poldy was stretched on a bench nearby, face-down on his sleeve; his hair had turned to silver.

"Time for my Gabriella to say goodnight," announced Mama anyway.

"I'm not sleepy!" said Gabriella.

Old Papa tapped. This is for me, thought Gabriella, and stood up. Mama flew up beside her, boxed her ears, and pulled her out of Papa's way, calling to them all, "My youngest! Look once more my baby Gabriella! Tomorrow she will be in Naples!"

"Goodnight!" they said, the women all embracing Gabriella and one another. "The last night—the last!" Mama kissed Mrs. Arpista back and cried, "In Naples, who knows what will happen?" Gabriella waved her hand at Mr. Ambrogio. Speechless, he rose.

"Don't fall down the stairs!" called Aldo after her in an odd, discordant voice, as from a distance over the water.

But old Papa, tapping his cane, brought in his circle closer. He could sing the night to sleep.

When the *Pomona* came in sight of land, it was sunrise. Sailors were lifting away tarpaulins, and hauling ropes and chains over the feet of a crowd, while joking indecipherably among themselves; for this once-secret, foremost deck had by now been discovered by everyone.

The body of the sea had been cut off. The *Pomona* sailed among dark, near islands, like shaggy beings asleep on one arm or kneeling now forever. Far ahead, Vesuvius, frail as a tent, almost transparent, lifted up under the morning. Gabriella watched it coming nearer and nearer to her. At last it was exactly like the picture over the dining room mantel at home, which hung above the row of baby photographs and the yellow one of Nonna with the startled eyes under a mound of black hair.

Tightening her hand to a fist, Gabriella banged herself on the chest three times under Aldo's eyes. Holding his eyes wide open to keep himself awake gave him an expression of indignation.

"Man Mountain Dean!" she wailed at him. "I'm a big girl now and I want my nourishment!" This had never failed to bring a laugh from the girls in Sacred Heart typewriting class.

But that breakfast was the one *Pomona* meal Gabriella could never remember afterwards; though she could see the tablecloth stained like a map with old wine. Surely she and Aldo had sat there, where neither had ever sat before, and eaten one meal together, in the hue and cry of what was about to happen.

Arriving in Naples was not so simple as being welcomed to Palermo. Only officials came out on the water to meet them, speeding direct by motor and climbing up on board. *"Attenzione!"* was broadcast every moment; everybody was being herded somewhere, only where? Mama, who could find the heart of confusion wherever it moved, constantly darted into it, striking her brow. And then, up in First Class as they stood in line to wait, the man who had charge of the S's couldn't find something he needed, his seal. Then Poldy's passport was lost—by the *Pomona,* not Poldy—and there was much running about, until all at once the spelling of his name, hailed through the room, seemed to clear up business everywhere. The feeling ran strong that landing would be soon. Mr. Ambrogio steered two of the ancient shawled ladies, like old black poodles, one on each arm, outside on deck and started a line at the rail. But Aldo Scampo still reclined in one of the overstuffed chairs, hideously yawning.

Half an hour later, with everybody watching from high on board, the docks of Naples in a bloom of yellow sun slid directly under their side. They could hear the first street sounds—*they* had awakened them!—the whipping of horses, the creaking of wooden wheels over stones, the cry of a child from somewhere deep in the golden labyrinth.

The gangway was an apparatus of steps and ropes. As it dropped like an elephant's trunk from the height of the ship, streams of Neapolitans came running toward it across a sweep of walled-in yard floored over with sun, with yellow trees stirring their leaves and buildings whose sides danced with light.

"Hey! Naples smells like a kitchen!" cried Gabriella; for all that couldn't be helped in life had stolen over her, sweet as a scent, just then.

"Not the kitchen on *this* boat!" said Aldo beside her.

"Where's Nonna?" screamed Gabriella.

The first passengers, the priests, were already descending, fast as firemen down a pole. Then a shower of nuns went down.

And down rushed Mrs. Serto headlong. She flew from Mr. Ambrogio, who wished to offer her his arm, as if she'd never seen him before. She clopped down the slatted steps like a little black pony, her spangled veil flying. Then all were let loose!

And where was Mama now? Gabriella frowned down over the rail, and could recognize nobody in the spinning crowd but Mr. Fossetta. Looking flattened, taking long steps, he seemed already making for Bari, dressed in a Chicago overcoat, long, thick and green, with a felt hat over his eyes and his lips pushing out a cigar. He looked bent on demonstrating that the most intimate crowd, when the moment came, could tear itself apart, hurry to vanish.

Where was Aldo? He was still behind her, breathing on first one side of her, then the other—breathing as he took the coats both out of her arms, hers and Mama's. She was left at the head of the ladder with only her purse and the pasteboard box for the hat she had fastened on her head.

"Now?" she asked him.

"See Naples and die!" he said loudly in her face, as if he had been preparing the best thing to say.

She took a step down, and the gangway all but swung free. Everything moved below, travelers and relatives running in and out of each other's arms, as if rendered by the devil unrecognizable; a band of ragged boys with a ball; a family of dogs, another of blind and crippled people, and what looked like generations of guides and porters, in hereditary caps; and now moving in through the big arched gate (an outer rim of carriages, horn-blowing taxis, streetcars and cars reached around the Piazza beyond) a school of nuns with outstretched plates, all but late for the boat. Loudest of all, a crowd of little girls all dressed in black were jumping up and down shaking noisy boxes and singing like a flock of birds, *"Orfanelli, orfanelli, orfanelli—"* Then she felt Aldo's step behind her shake the whole scene again, as if they were treading the spokes of a wheel, and now it began to turn steadily beneath them.

"Poldy!" Aldo hailed him from the air. "See Naples and die, Poldy! Where's your girl?"

Poldy was running up and down the dock pitching a ball with some little boys of Naples. He wore the feathered hat, the bright yellowish coat with the big buttons that had galvanized them all so on the first day at sea, before they knew all about him. He shouted back, "Oh, she'll find me! I sent her a whole dozen poses!"

Poldy's and Aldo's laughs met like clapped hands over Gabriella's head, and she could hardly take another step down for anger at that girl, and outrage for her, as if she were her dearest friend, her little sister. Even now, the girl probably languished in tears because the little country train she was coming on, from her unknown town, was late. Perhaps, even more foolishly, she had come early, and was languishing just beyond that gate, not knowing if she were allowed inside the wall or not—how would she know? No matter—they would meet. The *Pomona* had landed, and that was enough. Poor girl, whose name Poldy had not even bothered to tell them, her future was about to begin.

"Watch me!" Poldy, just below, was shouting to the little boys. "I'll teach you how to throw a ball!"

But he turned his shining face upward and threw the ball at Gabriella. It only struck the *Pomona's* side and bounced back; all the same, she dodged and swayed, and Poldy covered his head with his sleeve in imitation shame, while the little urchins stamped up and down beside him, laughing in a contagious-sounding joy like the *orfanelli's*.

"Rock-a-bye baby!" she yelled down over their heads. "On the the tree top! When the wind blows—"

Aldo, coming out of the family coats, put a grip around her neck for the last time. But even while he did it, instinct, too, told her she could not scream that way any longer. She was here.

"Ecco! Ecco!" came Mama's own voice, wildly excited. *"Mamma mia!"* There she was, halfway across the yard.

And where she pointed, almost in the center of everything, was a little, low, black figure waiting. It was the quietest and most substantial figure there, unagitated as a little settee, a black horsehair settee, in a room where people are dancing.

"But she doesn't look like her picture!" cried Gabriella. And her foot came down and touched something hard, the hard ground of Naples. Out of it came a strange, rocking response—as if the earth were shocked, on its part, to be meeting their feet. Then the coats were bundled in her arms.

"O.K.," said Aldo. "Got to line up my stuff and try for a train. Goodbye, Mr. Ambrogio!" he shouted. "Don't let 'em try to keep you over here!" And off he went, at an odd trot.

"We shall never meet again!" Mr. Ambrogio, standing at the foot of the gangway now with his arm raised like a gladiator, had found words. Then, raising the other arm too, he half ran through the moving game of ball, to be gathered in by some old ladies—just like the ones he'd been escorting across the ocean. But in his consideration he did not even knock down Poldy's stack of suitcases and cardboard boxes, neat as a little house in the thick of the disembarkation.

"Gabriella Serto! You want to stay on ship?" Mama had seized her and was taking her through the crowd. "Think who you keep waiting! You want to go to Genoa?" Mama was first pushing her ahead, then pulling her back and showing herself in front.

"Mamma mia!"

"Crocefissa!"

Mama threw herself forward and arms came up and embraced her.

Then Mama herself was set to one side by a small brown hand with a thin gold ring on it. And there was Nonna, her big, upturned, diamond-shaped face shimmering with wrinkles under its cap of white hair and its second little cap of black silk. So low and so full of weight in all her shawls, she not only looked to be seated there—she was. Amply, her skirts covered whatever she was resting on.

Nonna drew Gabriella down toward all her blackness, which the sun must have drenched through and through until light and color yielded to it together, and to which the very essence of that smell in the air—of cinnamon and cloves, bananas and coffee—clung. Raising Gabriella's chin, Nonna set a kiss on one of her cheeks, then the other. Nonna's own cheek, held waiting, was brown as a nut and soft as a rose. She gave Gabriella an ancient, inviting smile.

"Si," she said. *"Si."*

As Nonna began to address Gabriella, the very first words were so beautiful and without reproach, that they seemed to leave her out. Nothing had prepared Gabriella for the *sound* of Nonna. She couldn't understand a word. Her gaze wavered and fell. A little way off in the crowd she saw the feet of Miss Crosby, raised on tiptoe beside a suitcase. *She* had learned only one thing the whole way over, *i gabbiani*. And there, poor Maria-Pia Arpista, rigid as though bound and gagged, was being carried off by a large and shouting family, who were proudest of all of the baby's coming to meet her. But Nonna had not finished already? Here was Mama rushing her off to the Customs.

Afterwards, there was Nonna watching for them in her same place, as they came out of the shed with their baggage behind them. The porter in a kind of madness—he was an old man—had thrown their trunk over his back, taken their suitcases, and then had seized the coats as well, and even the little hatbox that had been swinging since early morning on its string from Gabriella's finger, like a reminder. Now she had nothing but her purse.

And there apart stood Papa. Nobody had come to meet Papa. Even as Gabriella saw him, he was deciding not to wait. Bearing on his cane, still in the same old olive-colored sweater—why should she have expected that hole to be sewed up by this morning?—he walked, with nothing to carry, away into the widening sunlight as if he had blinders on. He's only come home to die, thought Gabriella. All the way over, *he* might have been the oldest and the poorest one. Mama pretended not to see him go. Her curiosity about Papa had long been satisfied: he had nobody: she knew it. It was the punishment for marrying twice.

Nonna, when they reached her, said calmly. "We will wait one little moment longer. A dizziness—it will pass."

Mama crossed herself, and laid her instant, tender hand to Nonna's cheek. The porter just as instantly shed every bit of the baggage to the ground.

Gabriella raised her eyes to the empty *Pomona* standing over them still—not empty, for Mr. Ugone still rode aboard, with Genoa yet to come. She could actually see him at that minute, standing at the rail with his cigar in his hand; but he did not see her. His gaze was bent and seemed lost on Poldy—still playing there with some of the little urchins, so that the docks took on the echoing sound of a playground just before dark. Maybe the surest people, thought Gabriella, are also the most forgetful of what comes next. All around was the smell of yellow leaves.

"Look who I see!" cried Mama, without ceasing to pat Nonna's cheek. "Mr. Scampo! Ah, I thought we had seen the last of him. On board ship—poor *mamma mia!*—he was passionately running after our Gabriella. It was necessary to keep an eye on her every minute."

"Her fatefulness is inherited from you, Crocefissa, my child," said Nonna.

"All my girls have been so afflicted, but five, like me, married by eighteen," Mama said—pat, pat, pat.

Aldo was coming toward them slowly, with his strange new walk of today, almost hidden by a large number of hopeful porters attacking him like flies from all sides. He did not wave; but could he? He was loaded down. Gabriella did not wave herself, but suddenly missing the old, known world of the *Pomona,* she gave one brief scream. Nonna bent a considering head her way, as though to place the pitch.

"That she gets from her father," said Mama. "The *Siracusano!"*

"Ah," replied Nonna. "Daughter, where is my little fan? Somewhere in my skirts, thank you. . . . With the years he has calmed himself, Achille? You no longer tremble to cross him?"

Gabriella said absently, "She should've seen him hit the ceiling when I flunked old typewriting."

"Per favore!" cried Mama to her. "Quiet about things you know nothing about, yet! Say goodbye to Mr. Scampo."

Aldo had pulled a disreputable raincoat over his thick, new brown suit; even now he wore no hat, and his hair was down in his eyes. In addition to two suitcases he was carrying something as tall, bulky, and toppling as a man. It towered above his head.

Mama said, "If you think this fellow looks strong, *mamma mia,* I tell you now it is an illusion. He is delicate!"

"Only on Gala Night," protested Gabriella. "That's the one and only time he faded out of the picture. And so did you, Mama."

"We stop first thing at Santa Maria, to thank Holy Mother for one thing she saved you from!" Mama said. She shook her head one way, Nonna nodded hers in another.

"Hey! What you got in that thing, a dead body?" cried Gabriella to Aldo in good old English. She went bounding out to meet him.

"Watch out!" said Aldo, who seemed to have to walk in a straiight line, by now, or fall. "You got nothing but just one trunk and those suitcases? You're luckier than you know."

"You watch out who you bump with that funeral coffin."

"You watch out how you talk about what I got. This is a musical instrument." With Gabriella there in his path, Aldo had to come to a full stop. The porters closed in in fresh circles of hope. "A cello," Aldo said, embracing it. Even one ear was being used to help hold it. "And after I rode it all the way in the bed over mine on the boat, the Naples Customs grabbed it right out the cover and banged the strings and took a stick and knocked all around inside it! I bet you heard it out here."

"What did you have in it?" called Mama.

"My socks!" Aldo shouted at Gabriella. "All my socks that my aunt knitted! It's going to be *cold* in Italy this winter!"

"Aldo, don't yell," said Gabriella. "That's my grandmother."

"Oh, yeah. She looks pretty well to me," said Aldo. "She ought not to've tried to meet a boat in Naples, though."

"Mother—excuse me—Mr. Scampo, a shipboard acquaintance," said Mama.

"Il Romeo? Il pellegrino, Signor Scampo?" murmured Nonna serenely. She moved a glistening black silk fan back and forth in front of her now, in a way that seemed to invite any confidence.

"I'm just saying goodbye to Mrs. Serto and Gabriella, ma'am," said Aldo.

Gabriella had clapped her hand over her mouth. She cried, "Aldo! Did you hear her? *Romeo!* First Mama thought you were Dick Tracy or somebody, the time you spent studying crime the whole way over—now Nonna is asking if you're not a pilgrim!"

"And what did *you* ever think I was?" Aldo stared at her rudely, clasping his burden round in that clumsy and painful way that made him look as though *he* were the one to wonder how people ever parted.

"Yes, *Signore?"* said Nonna. "Perhaps you will tell us?"

"Well, ma'am, what I came to Italy for, since somebody really *asks* me, is study cello in Rome under the G.I. Bill," said Aldo. *"Musicista, Signora."*

"Sfortunato!" exclaimed Nonna, and gave a familiar-sounding click of the tongue.

"I already have a son-in-law in Buffalo the same!" cried Mama.

There Aldo stood before the three of them.

"Hey, Aldo. Want to see our trunk real quick?" asked Gabriella gently. She moved over to it, and the porter swept off the coats, unveiling it. The Serto trunk stood there—its size, shape, and weight all apparent, also the rope that went around it and the original lock that nobody trusted, and the name "Serto" painted on the lid in the confident lettering of a pharmacist. It did not matter that the hand of Customs had gone romping through it—it was restored now to the miracle of ownership.

"It's full of presents, I can tell you," said Gabriella.

Advice arrived almost like gratitude upon Aldo's face, as pride had come upon hers. "Then keep your eye on it till you get it home," he told her. "A fellow in New York told me they'll steal them even from over your head, in Naples. With a kind of tongs, very nifty. Running around over the rafters of the Customs shed, or even hanging over the gate as you go out. Everybody here knows about it, and don't even try to stop it."

"Shame," said Mama. "That's not nice about Naples."

And again, as Nonna spoke to him too, he was pulled around in a daze.

"My mother is telling you, Mr. Scampo, the human voice alone is divine," said Mama with her little chin up. "Not the screeching of cats. She is telling you there still may be time to set right your mistake—she sees you so young. Of course, in *Napoli,* she once sang with Caruso."

Nonna was looking up at Aldo. No two smiles were the same in her face. Aldo had now turned dark red, and his head hung.

"Well, goodbye, Aldo," said Gabriella in English, and he looked up already startled, as if to see someone he had never expected to see again.

"Be good," he replied formally, and momentarily setting the suitcases down, he shook hands with them all, even their porter, who joined the circle.

"Goodbye, Mr. Scampo! Maybe we all meet at St. Peter's on *Ognissanti*—who knows?" said Mama. That was what she'd said to everybody.

As Aldo staggered away, Gabriella reached out her hand and with her fingertips touched his cello—or rather its wrinkled outer covering, at once soft and imperious. It was like touching the forehead of an animal, from which horns might even start; but indeed, the old lady's withered and feminine cheek had felt just as mysterious to Gabriella's kiss. Aldo's back grew less and less familiar with every step, while the porters like a family of acrobats were leaping and crying in chorus, *"Stazione! Stazione!"* all around him. They all saw him pass, unrobbed and unaided, through the archway into the big Piazza, and away into the sliding life of the streets, and then Mama brought her handkerchief up to her face like a little nosegay of tears. *She* was being the daughter—the better daughter.

But Nonna was still the mother. Her brown face might be creased like a fig-skin, but her eyes were brighter now than tears had left Mama's, or than the lightning of bewilderment that struck so often into the eyes of Gabriella. Surely they knew everything. They had taken Gabriella for granted.

"Come now," Nonna said.

She stood up. She was smaller than Mama. She came only to Gabriella's shoulder. But as she turned around, a motion of her hand, folding shut the little fan and pointing away with it, told them they were none of them any too soon. She stood perfectly straight, and could have walked by herself, though Mama, with a little cry, seized hold of her. Gabriella took her place a step behind. The porter once more—he, one man, all alone, and possibly for nothing—shouldered the backbreaking luggage of women, to which now something extra was added—the little rush-bottomed fireside stool on which the old lady had been sitting. They all set off toward the gate.

Only for the space of a breath did Gabriella feel she would rather lie down on that melon cart pulled by a donkey, that she could see in the street ahead. Then the melons and the arch of the gate, the grandmother's folding of the fan and Mama's tears, the volcano of early morning, and even the dangerous voyage behind her—all seemed caught up and held in something: the golden moment of touch, just given, just taken, in saying goodbye.

The moment—bright and effortless of making, in the end, as a bubble—seemed to go ahead of them as they walked, to tap without sound across the dust of the emptying yard, and alight in the grandmother's homely buggy, filling it. The yellow leaves of the plane trees came down before their feet; and just beyond the gate the black, country horse that would draw the buggy shivered and tossed his mane, which fell like one long silver wave, as the first of the bells in the still-hidden heart of Naples began to strike the hour.

"And the nightingale," Mama's voice just ahead was beseeching, "is the nightingale with us yet?"

BIOGRAPHICAL NOTES

Bowen, Robert O. Mr. Bowen was born in Bridgeport, Connecticut and is thirty-five years old. He served in the Navy from 1937 to 1945, and after World War II he attended the University of Alabama where he studied writing with Hudson Strode and earned a Bachelor's and Master's degree. Mr. Bowen spent a year at the University of Wales on a Fulbright grant, and has published three novels — *The Weight of the Cross, Bamboo,* and *Sidestreet.* His short stories, poems, articles, and reviews have appeared in *The Western Review, Prairie Schooner, New Ventures, The Beloit Poetry Journal,* and other quarterlies. At present Mr. Bowen teaches writing at Cornell, is an editor on *Epoch,* and is finishing an anthology of essays for college students.

Cardozo, Nancy. She was born in 1919 in New York City and, except for summers in New England, spent most of her childhood there. "I attended the Dalton School and Swarthmore College, have travelled in France and Mexico, and lived and worked in places as remote from each other as San Diego, Terre Haute, and Monhegan Island. I have been writing since I was twelve years old — first poetry, some of which was published in *Scribner's, Poetry, The Yale Review,* and little magazines." Her short stories have appeared in *Redbook, Charm, Seventeen, The New Mexico Quarterly, Mademoiselle,* and *The New Yorker.* She lives with her husband and two small sons in a little Connecticut town.

Chaikin, Nancy. She was born and grew up in Brooklyn. At the University of Michigan, where she graduated in 1945, she worked in short fiction writing with Alan Seager and won two Avery Hopwood awards — for short stories and for essays in literary criticism. "This last award led me straight to the door of the *Saturday Review of Literature* and the Book-of-the-Month Club, for whom, after graduation, I did book reviews and reading. In 1946, I was married to Marvin Chaikin, a communications engineer, continued the reviewing until after the birth of our first child, a little girl (now seven) named Robin. Then I attended Columbia's fiction workshop under Martha Foley for a year and a half, until just before the birth of our second child, Peter (now four). I live in Great Neck, Long Island, with husband and children, dividing time, quite unequally and never consistently, between family and writing. My first published story, "The Climate of the Family," was reprinted in the 1952 edition of *Best American Short Stories* and this story, like that one, was written for workshop criticism. I hope to have more stories, some novels, and, perhaps, another child. The last item I should find it infinitely more simple to produce than either of the other two!"

Cheever, John. Mr. Cheever was born in Quincy, Massachusetts, in 1912 and has written a great many short stories. He lives in that part of northern Westchester that is bounded by the Hudson River and is so active in civic and religious affairs that he would be indistinguishable from the more responsible members of the community if he didn't always wear old tennis sneakers. He is a member of the faculty of Barnard College, and his work has been represented in many previous editions of this anthology.

Connell, Evan S., Jr. Mr. Connell was born in Kansas City and attended Dartmouth College, the University of Kansas, Stanford, and Columbia. During World War II, he spent about two and a half years as a Naval Aviator. He has published stories in *American Mercury, Flair, New World Writing, Today's Woman, Tomorrow,* and several other magazines, and has had stories reprinted in *Prize Stories of 1949* and *1951,* in addition to receiving prizes in several story contests — the Edith Mirrielees award at Stanford, a second prize in the 1948 Midwestern Writers' Conference contest, and a second prize in the National Five Arts contest. "A couple of years ago I received a Eugene Saxton award to enable me to continue work on another novel which, as of this date, has not been successfully completed. I have worked at a considerable number of ordinary jobs, such as reading gas-meters, delivering ice, clerking in a shipyard, etc., to substantiate my income from writing. When *Best American Short Stories 1955* is published, I shall probably be living in San Francisco where all my evenings and Saturdays are spent in life-drawing or painting. I have illustrated some of my own stories and recently was asked by the editors of *The Paris Review* to illustrate the work of another author. My primary interest has always been in the graphic arts."

COOGAN, JOSEPH P. Mr. Coogan was born in Philadelphia in 1920 and attended a parochial grammar school and LaSalle College. He left college after two years to enter the Army and served three and a half years in the Medical Corps, Infantry, and Special Service. "My Special Service stint was with Maurice Evans' Pacific Entertainment Section where I wrote and acted in Army shows, and my most dangerous Army mission was acting the Player Villain in the *G. I. Hamlet*." After his discharge in 1946, Mr. Coogan took Martha Foley's short story class at Columbia, wrote his first short story for a class assignment and sold it to *Collier's*. He free-lanced in New York for a year, then went back to college for his Bachelor's and Master's degrees. He taught for a while, then quit to take a job editing scientific manuscripts and writing promotional material for Smith, Kline and French Laboratories in Philadelphia. "I married Jeanmarie Dunn, an ex-editor of *The Ladies' Home Journal*. Beautiful. Have two children, Kevin (age two) and Ellen (four months). Kind of beautiful." Mr. Coogan's stories have appeared in *Collier's, The Ladies' Home Journal, Four Quarters, Bluebook, The London Daily Express, The London Evening Star*. One story was broadcast as an "outstanding short-short" over NBC network. His other writing jobs have included writing routines for M.C.'s and night-club acts, and radio scripts. "The nadir of my career came when I wrote a one minute radio commercial for a free haircut. Haircut terrible. Commercial not so good either."

CURLEY, DANIEL. Mr. Curley was born in 1918 in East Bridgewater, Massachusetts. He has Bachelor's and Master's degrees from the University of Alabama. During the war, he welded in the shipyards in New Orleans and Boston, and later worked as a reporter for Dodge Building Reports in New York. He taught at Syracuse University for seven years, and is now at State Teachers' College at Plattsburgh, New York. Mr. Curley has published in *Accent, The University of Kansas City Review, New Story, Perspective, Harper's Bazaar, The Atlantic Monthly*, and *The Kenyon Review*. "I have about four novels that I rewrite in succession, and they may be getting close to being publishable. I am married and have four daughters — Sean, Deirdre, Caitrine, and Aillinn."

EASTLAKE, WILLIAM. "I grew up in the farm country of New Jersey and moved to California where I was drafted for World War II. I served four years, mostly on the Western Front. After the war, I attended the Alliance Française in Paris and contributed to the small European magazines. When I got back to the states, I decided that I preferred the ranch and Indian country of northern New Mexico — and now I have a small cattle ranch between the Apache and Navajo Reservations." Mr. Eastlake has published in *Accent, The Hudson Review, Quarto*, and *Harper's Magazine*. He has just finished a novel called *Indian Country*.

ELLIOTT, GEORGE P. Mr. Elliott lived in California since the age of eleven but was born in Indiana in 1918. He has recently moved to Ithaca, New York. After receiving his M.A. in English from the University of California, he had "the usual variety of jobs for a writer," from surveyor's helper to bureaucrat to union business agent to taxicab driver. His poems and short stories have appeared in several of the little magazines during the past nine years. His short stories, "The NRACP," "Children of Ruth," and "Faq," appeared in *The Best American Short Stories* 1950, 1952 and 1953 respectively. Last year he spent studying the modern staging of poetic drama, along with the poet James Schevill, on a fellowship from The Fund for the Advancement of Education. Previous to this he taught English at St. Mary's College and lived in Berkeley with his wife and daughter.

HYMAN, MAC. Mr. Hyman was born and raised in Cordele, Georgia. He attended Duke University and afterwards served in the Army Air Force for three years. "I went to Duke to try to learn how to write, got married, tried writing and did so little with it that I started out on a bunch of different jobs — shipping clerk, ice cream stand manager, laundry-truck driver, schoolteacher, and finally back into the Air Force for another three years. Been back out this time for about two years, back at writing again." Mr. Hyman published the novel, *No Time For Sergeants,* by Random House, in 1954. He had previously written one other which has never been published. "*The Hundredth Centennial* is my first paid-for short story. Had a hard time getting it published, too — took as long as it did to get the novel published. Still doing what I call writing, but I don't know yet which direction it is going in." Mr. Hyman is the father of three children and continues to make his home in Cordele, Georgia.

LA FARGE, OLIVER. Mr. La Farge was born in New York City in 1901, and educated at Saint Bernard's, Groton, and Harvard. He was a full-time anthropologist until 1929, and part-time since, when his principal occupation became writing. Mr. La Farge made three expeditions for the Peabody Museum of Harvard to do archaeological work in the Navajo Reservations, in the general area described in his story in this anthology. He is a Fellow of the American Anthropological Association and of the American Association for the Advancement of Science. His previous publications include *Laughing Boy,* Pulitzer Prize novel for 1929, and a number of other works of fiction and general nonfiction as well as several anthropological monographs. His work now in progress is a book based on reminiscences of life on a Spanish ranch in New Mexico in the 1920's.

MALAMUD, BERNARD. Mr. Malamud was born in Brooklyn forty years ago. He attended CCNY and Columbia. After college he worked at odd jobs, then began to teach evening school and write during the day. "After five years in Greenwich Village, my wife and I moved to Corvallis, Oregon, where I combine teaching with a writing career. I am an assistant professor in English at Oregon State College. My novel, *The Natural,* was published in 1952 by Harcourt, Brace." Mr. Malamud has contributed short stories to *American Mercury, Commentary, Discovery, Harper's Bazaar, Partisan Review,* and other magazines. This is his second appearance in *The Best American Short Stories.*

MERRIL, JUDITH. She was born January 21, 1923, and attended school in New York, Boston, and Philadelphia. She has worked one time or another as package wrapper, book salesgirl, busgirl, waitress, curtain examiner in a factory, and editor. For a while she was "ghostwriter to a ghostwriter"; then began using her acquired knowledge of Americana to sell her own articles to magazines. From there she drifted into writing fiction — Western, detective, and adventure. Her first science-fiction story, "That Only a Mother," was so enthusiastically received that she has since devoted herself almost exclusively to this field — her favorite, in any case. Miss Merril has edited six anthologies of science fantasy and written four novels; two under her own name, and two in collaboration with C. M. Kornbluth, under the joint pseudonym of Cyril Judd. Her short stories have been widely reprinted.

MIDDLETON, ELIZABETH H. She was born in Framingham Centre, Mass., in 1902, and went through high school there. In 1925 she graduated from Vassar College, and was married that same year to Dr. William D. Middleton. Most of the time since then has been spent raising a family of six children, in many different places. At present she lives in Madison, Wisconsin. "My husband is retired, and I work part time in a laboratory at University Hospitals, but set aside every evening for writing. One novel, *Judith,* is 'going the rounds.' Another, *The Prisoners,* is almost completed. A few short stories have been published in the past, but not many. The best two are "Four Eagle" which appeared in *Frontier* and in *Midland,* and was later included in an anthology, and "The Hungry Winter," a story for young people, which has also been anthologized and been reprinted four times. I think this about covers it."

MUDRICK, MARVIN. Marvin Mudrick was born in Philadelphia in 1921, and educated at Temple University and the University of California, where he received his Ph.D. in 1949. He has been teaching there since and is now an assistant professor of English. He served in the United States Army Air Forces, primarily in the Southwest Pacific Area, from July, 1942 to December 1945. He taught English at Temple University. Mr. Mudrick has published one book, *Jane Austen: Irony as Defense and Discovery,* Princeton University Press, 1952, and a number of articles and reviews in *The Hudson Review* and *Shenandoah;* he has delivered literary-critical papers at annual meetings of the English Institute, the Modern Language Association, and the Philological Association of the Pacific Coast as well as the Institute of Humanistic Studies for Executives at the University of Pennsylvania. "The Professor and the Poet" is his first piece of fiction.

NEMEROV, HOWARD. Howard Nemerov was born in 1920 in New York City and educated at Fieldston and Harvard. His wartime service was as pilot with RCAF, FAF and USAAF. Since then he has been teaching first at Hamilton College and now at Bennington. He has published three books of poetry, *The Image and the Law; Guide to the Ruins* and *The Salt Garden;* and two novels, *The Melodramatists* and *Federigo, or The Power of Love.* His work has appeared in *The New Yorker, The Atlantic Monthly, The Hudson Review, The Kenyon Review, The Sewanee Review,* and *Partisan Review.*

O'CONNOR, FLANNERY. Miss O'Connor was born in Savannah, Georgia, in 1925. She graduated from the Georgia State College for Women and later took courses for two years in creative writing at the University of Iowa. A number of her short stories have appeared in various magazines. Miss O'Connor is the author of a novel, *Wise Blood.* A collection of her short stories has been published recently in book form under the title of *A Good Man Is Hard to Find.* She lives on a farm near Milledgeville, Georgia. "My people could come from anywhere," she says, "but naturally since I know the South, they speak with a Southern accent."

SHAW, IRWIN. Irwin Shaw was born in Brooklyn. His writing career began in high school; at Brooklyn College he was involved simultaneously in play-writing and football. Upon graduation he began to write serial dramatizations of comic strips for radio, the success of which gave him the necessary leisure to write two plays. One of them was the memorable *Bury The Dead,* produced on Broadway in 1936 when the author was twenty-three. Since then, in addition to writing occasional motion pictures for Hollywood, he has written several more plays, principally *Salute, Siege, The Gentle People, Sons and Soldiers,* and *The Assassin.* His short stories have appeared in many magazines but most frequently in *The New Yorker* and he has been represented in previous volumes of *The Best American Short Stories* and in a number of other anthologies. Three collections of his short stories have been published by Random House — *Sailor Off the Bremen, Welcome To the City* and *Act of Faith.* He is also the author of two novels, *The Young Lions* and *The Troubled Air.* During World War II Mr. Shaw saw service in Africa, England, France and Germany, first as a private and later as a warrant officer.

STEGNER, WALLACE. Mr. Stegner was born on a farm near Lake Mills, Iowa, in 1909. His childhood was spent in many places, North Dakota, Washington, Saskatchewan, Montana, Utah, California, Nevada. He attended grade school in a little frontier town in Saskatchewan and high school and college in Salt Lake City. He did graduate work at the Universities of California and Iowa, receiving the degrees of M.A. and Ph.D. from the University of Iowa. He now teaches creative writing at Stanford University. In 1937 he won a Little, Brown novelette contest with *Remembering Laughter.* He is the author of a number of books, the latest being *Beyond the Hundredth Meridian,* a biography of John Wesley Powell. His short stories have appeared in many magazines and have been reprinted in *The Best American Short Stories.* His home is at Los Altos, California.

STUART, DAVID. David Stuart had been running a bookstore in Hollywood, and then went to Paris with his wife for five years. While there he worked at the American Theatre of Paris as an actor and did some writing and some plays. He sold several short stories to an Italian magazine in 1951 and made a picture in Norway which later played at the French Festival. Prior to that he spent about two years writing for Orson Welles at RKO. He collaborated on a motion picture for Welles which was never produced. He also has run a jazz record shop, and during the war he flew for ATC. Most of his writing has appeared in experimental art and surrealistic magazines. He is now working on a novel and resides in Hollywood.

SWADOS, HARVEY. He started life in Buffalo, New York, where he went to public schools until, at the age of fifteen, he entered the University of Michigan. While he was still in college one of his stories was reprinted in *The Best American Short Stories,* then edited by Edward J. O'Brien. He engaged in a variety of jobs, the two most fascinating, according to him, being a census taker in New York and a bartender in New Orleans. After the war, in which Mr. Swados served in the Merchant Marine, he settled in New York City and worked for a public relations firm. At the same time he wrote short stories and book reviews. His novel, *Out Went the Candle,* was published last year. With his wife and three small children, Mr. Swados is now in Europe.

VAN DOREN, MARK. Mark Van Doren was born in 1894 on a farm near Hope, Illinois. He was educated at the University of Illinois and Columbia University, and has taught English at Columbia since 1920. From 1924 to 1928, he was literary editor of The Nation. Best known as a critic and poet, his *Collected Poems,* published in 1939, was the winner of a 1940 Pulitzer prize. Among his other works are the books of poetry, *Spring Thunder; Now the Sky; Jonathan Gentry; Our Lady of Peace* and *New Poems,* and two novels, *The Transients* and *Windless Cabins,* published in 1935 and 1940 respectively. He is also the author of several critical studies and editor of a number of anthologies. His most recently published books have been *The Short Stories of Mark Van Doren* in 1950, and *Spring Birth and Other Poems* in 1953. His stories have appeared in previous collections of *The Best American Short Stories. Nobody Say a Word, and Other Stories* was published by Henry Holt & Company in 1953, and *Selected Poems* in 1954. Mr. Van Doren is a resident of New York City.

VUKELICH, GEORGE. "I was born in South Milwaukee, Wisconsin, in 1927, and raised overseas during World War II in the ETO." Mr. Vukelich studied under Mari Sandoz and Robert E. Gard at the University of Wisconsin and graduated from the Academy of Radio Arts in Toronto, Canada. His past jobs have included "hustling in my father's poolroom, garbage collecting, truck driving, hod carrying, dish washing, hog pushing, radio continuity writing, announcing and DJ-ing *The Promised Land,* a Jazz Poetry late evening show which was a big boon to local TV." At present he is reviewing books for the *Milwaukee Journal* and free-lancing while working on a novel, *Fisherman's Beach,* for Houghton Mifflin Company. Mr. Vukelich has published in *Idiom, The Beloit Poetry Journal, Botteghe Oscure, American Poetry Magazine, The Armenian Review, The Atlantic Monthly,* and *The Sign.* "I am married to a Madison girl and have one daughter, Julia Lea, aged 14 months. To them I credit my little start: also to my father who had the wisdom to skip out of Yugoslavia at the age of 21. He credits his start to my Romanian mother."

WELTY, EUDORA. Born in Jackson, Mississippi, Miss Welty is a graduate of the University of Wisconsin and has done postgraduate work at Columbia University. She has held various publicity jobs and was copy reader for the *New York Times* Book Review Section for a short time. *The New Yorker, The Atlantic Monthly, Harper's Bazaar, Harper's Magazine, Accent,* and other magazines have published her stories. Her work has been reprinted in previous volumes of *The Best American Short Stories.* Her novels include *The Robber Bridegroom, Curtain of Green, Delta Wedding,* and *The Ponder Heart.* Miss Welty lives in Jackson, Mississippi.

THE YEARBOOK OF THE AMERICAN SHORT STORY

JANUARY 1 TO DECEMBER 31, 1954

ROLL OF HONOR

1955

I. *American Authors*

BALLENGER, WALTER
Mindine Ramones. Prairie Schooner.
BENCHLEY, NATHANIEL
Trick or Treat. New Yorker.
BETTS, DORIS
The Sympathetic Visitor. Mademoiselle.
BOWEN, ROBERT O.
A Matter of Price. Prairie Schooner.
BRODKEY, HAROLD
State of Grace. New Yorker.
BUTLER, CLAIRE MCGRATH
Who Lives Alas Away. New World Writing.

CARDOZO, NANCY
The Excursionists. Mademoiselle.
CHAIKIN, NANCY G.
Bachelor of Arts. University of Kansas City Review.
CHEEVER, JOHN
The True Confessions of Henry Pell. Harper's Magazine.
The Day the Pig Fell Into the Well. New Yorker.
The Country Husband. New Yorker.
COATES, ROBERT M.
Accident at the Inn. New Yorker.
CONNELL, EVAN S., JR.
The Fisherman from Chihuahua. Paris Review.
COOGAN, JOE
The Decline and Fall of Augie Sheean. Ladies' Home Journal.
CURLEY, DANIEL
The Day of the Equinox. New Mexico Quarterly.
A Young Girl's Fancy. University of Kansas City Review.

DEJONG, DAVID CORNEL
Those Who Eat Dragonflies. Southwest Review.

EASTLAKE, WILLIAM
Little Joe. Accent.
ELLIOTT, GEORGE P.
Miss Cudahy of Stowe's Landing. Hudson Review.
Brother Quintillian and Dick the Chemist. Western Review.
ELLISON, RALPH
Did You Ever Dream Lucky? New World Writing.
ENRIGHT, ELIZABETH
The Operator. Harper's Magazine.

FROSCHER, WINGATE
The Younger Brother. University of Kansas City Review.

GALLANT, MAVIS
Going Ashore. New Yorker.
GOLD, HERBERT
The Man Who Was Not With It. New World Writing.
GORDIMER, NADINE
The Smell of Death and Flowers. New Yorker.

HALE, NANCY
The New Order. New Yorker.
HALL, OAKLEY M.
The Crown. Epoch.
HUTCHINSON, ROBERT
The Foxhound. Southwest Review.
HYMAN, MAC
The Hundredth Centennial. Paris Review.

JOHNSON, DUNCAN
The Home. Sewanee Review.

KHANZADIAN, ANITA
No Time to Argue. Armenian Review.

LA FARGE, OLIVER
The Resting Place. New Yorker.
LANGDON, JOHN
The Bullet in My Father's Neck. Virginia Quarterly.

MADISON, JOHN
First-Class Heel. Southwest Review.

MALAMUD, BERNARD
The Magic Barrel. Partisan Review.
MERRIL, JUDITH
Dead Center. Fantasy and Science Fiction.
MIDDLETON, ELIZABETH H.
Portrait of My Son As a Young Man. University of Kansas City Review.
MILLER, JAMES E.
The Colonel Dudley Company, Inc. Prairie Schooner.
MUDRICK, MARVIN
The Professor and the Poet. Shenandoah.
MCCULLOCH, ELIZABETH
Your Birthday All Day. Charm.

NEIMAN, GILBERT
Death in the South. New Mexico Quarterly Review.
NEMEROV, HOWARD
Yore. Hudson Review.

O'CONNOR, FLANNERY
A Circle in the Fire. Kenyon Review.

PENDERGAST, CONSTANCE
The House on Gerard Street. Accent.

ROBINSON, ROSANNE SMITH
Miching Mallecho. Epoch.
RODDAN, SAMUEL
A Sunday Picnic. Canadian Forum.
ROTHBERG, ABRAHAM
The Red Dress. Epoch.

SAUL, GEORGE BRANDON
What Came of an Argument. New Mexico Quarterly.
SHAW, IRWIN
Tip on a Dead Jockey. New Yorker.
SHORE, WILMA
The Painter. Antioch Review.
SMITH, JOHN CAMPBELL
The Evening. Charm.
SPINGARN, LAWRENCE P.
The Pond. Colorado Quarterly.
SPROREL, KATHLEEN
A Fine and Private Place. Kenyon Review.
STEGNER, WALLACE
Maiden in a Tower. Harper's Magazine.
STUART, DAVID
Bird Man. Botteghe Oscure.
SWADOS, HARVEY
Herman's Day. New World Writing.
SYLVESTER, WILLIAM
The Death of Francisco. New World Writing.

THOMAS, DYLAN
The Followers. New World Writing.
TODD, ROBERT E.
A Decent Burial. Epoch.

VAN DOREN, MARK
I Got a Friend. University of Kansas City Review.
VUKELICH, GEORGE
The Scale Room. The Atlantic.

WANKLYN, CHRISTOPHER
Mistral and Mermaids. Paris Review.
WEBBER, GORDON
The Kite That Flew Away. New World Writing.
WELTY, EUDORA
Going to Naples. Harper's Bazaar.
Spring. Sewanee Review.
WESELY, DONALD
Chipper and the Frog. University of Kansas City Review.
WILNER, HERBERT
The Bandaged Man. Epoch.
WOOLF, DOUGLAS
The Third Doorman. Interim.

YAFFEE, JAMES
Only A Crazy Man Has Daughters. The Atlantic.

II. *Foreign Authors*

CARUNUNGAN, CELSO A.
My Father's First Son. The Sign.
CHEKHOV, ANTON
An Unpleasantness. Charm.

DANESHVAR, SIMIN
A Letter Home. Pacific Spectator.

LOWRY, MALCOLM
The Bravest Boat. Partisan Review.
NEWBY, P. H.
The Clerkly Salamander. Harper's Bazaar.

ORTESE, ARINA MARIA
Family Scene. New World Writing.

WHITE, ROBIN
White Bhagavather. Colorado Quarterly.

DISTINCTIVE VOLUMES OF SHORT STORIES

Published in the United States

1954

Betts, Doris
The Gentle Insurrection and Other Stories. G. P. Putnam and Company.

Bottome, Phyllis
Man and Beast. Harcourt Brace and Company.

Bunin, Ivan
The Knotted Ears and Other Stories. Chekhov Publishing Company.

Chekhov, Anton
The Woman in the Case and Other Stories. British Book Centre.

Collins, Wilkie
Tales of Suspense. Library Publishers.

Derleth, August
Time to Come. Farrar, Straus and Cudahy.

Engle, Paul, and Martin, Hansford, Editors
Prize Stories: The O. Henry Awards, 1954. Doubleday and Company

First Prize Stories: The O. Henry Awards
Introduction by Harry Hansen. Hanover House.

Foley, Martha, Editor
The Best American Short Stories, 1954. Houghton Mifflin and Company.

Geist, Stanley, Editor
French Stories and Tales. Alfred A. Knopf.

Howe, Irving and Greenberg, Eliezer, Editors
A Treasury of Yiddish Stories. Viking Press.

Irwin, Margaret
Bloodstock and Other Stories. Harcourt, Brace and Company.

Jones, Katharine M., Editor
New Confederate Short Stories. University of South Carolina Press.

Lagerkvist, Par
The Eternal Smile and Other Stories. Random House.

Lawrence, Leland W.
The Family Book of Best Loved Stories. Hanover House

Lee, Vernon
The Snake Lady and Other Stories. Grove Press.

Lohan, Robert, and Lohan, Marie, Editors
A New Christmas Treasury. Stephen Daye Press.

Merril, Judith, Editor
Beyond the Barriers of Space and Time. Random House.

Moskowittz, Samuel, Compiler
Editor's Choice in Science Fiction. McBride and Company.

Onis, Harriet De, Editor
Spanish Stories and Tales. Alfred A. Knopf.

Patchen, Kenneth
Fables and Other Little Tales. Jargon Publications.

Peery, William W., Editor
Twenty-One Texas Short Stories. University of Texas Press.

Pick, Robert, Editor
German Stories and Tales. Alfred A. Knopf.

Sansom, William
Something Terrible, Something Lovely. Harcourt Brace and Company.

Sloan, William M., Editor
Stories for Tomorrow. Funk & Wagnalls.

STEGNER, WALLACE, and SCOWCROFT, RICHARD, Editors
Stanford Short Stories. Stanford University Press.

TALBOT, DANIEL, Editor
A Treasury of Mountaineering Stories. G. P. Putnam and Company.

TAYLOR, ELIZABETH
Hester Lilly and Twelve Short Stories. Viking Press.

TAYLOR, PETER
The Widows of Thornton. Harcourt, Brace and Company.

WELTY, EUDORA
Selected Stories. Modern Library.

WILLIAMS, TENNESSEE
Hard Candy, a Book of Stories. New Directions.

DISTINCTIVE SHORT STORIES IN AMERICAN MAGAZINES

1954

I. *American Authors*

ADAMS, SAMUEL HOPKINS
Grandfather's Criminal Career. New Yorker, Mar. 27.

ALDERMAN, LOIS
The Circle. University of Kansas City Review, Autumn.

ALPERT, HOLLI
The Darkness. New Yorker, Oct. 16.

ANGOFF, CHARLES
Reunion at Midnight. University of Kansas City Review, Spring.
Dr. Feivel Charney. Arizona Quarterly, Summer.

ASHBAUGH, DICK
Never Pick Up Strangers. Chatelaine, Oct.

BALLENGER, WALTER
Mindine Ramones. Prairie Schooner, Spring.

BENCHLEY, NATHANIEL
Trick or Treat. New Yorker, Oct. 30.

BERWICK, DONALD
Peekaboo. Colorado Quarterly, Winter.

BETTS, DORIS
The Sympathetic Visitor. Mademoiselle, March.
I Can Understand Pilate. Mademoiselle, Dec.

BISSELL, RICHARD
Candle Salad. Atlantic, Dec.

BLUESTONE, GEORGE
The Ascent of Corey. Epoch, Winter.

BOWEN, ROBERT O.
My Grandfather Benbow. Prairie Schooner, Spring.
A Matter of Price. Prairie Schooner, Summer.

BOWEN, TRUE
The Moment of Truth. New Mexico Quarterly, Autumn.

BOYD, CATHARINE
The Convertible. Canadian Home Journal, Oct.

BRADBURY, RAY
The Wonderful Death of Dudley Stone. Charm, July.

BRENNAN, MAEVE
The Servant's Dance. New Yorker, May 22.
The Stone Hot Water Bottle. New Yorker, Nov. 27.

BRODKEY, HAROLD
State of Grace. New Yorker, Nov. 6.

BROOKBANK, RICHARD
The Invisible Wall. Fantasy and Science Fiction, Aug.

BUTLER, CLAIRE McGRATH
Who Lives Alas Away. New World Writing, No. 5.

CABLE, MARY
The Birth of Aphrodite. New Yorker, Sept.

CALHOUN, LORRAINE NAUSS
The Cerineral Picnic. New Mexico Quarterly, Summer.

CARDOZO, NANCY
The Excursionists. Mademoiselle, Nov.

CARROLL, SIDNEY
Who Is Mr. Dean? Collier's, Oct. 29.

CASSILL, R. V.
The Puzzle Factory. Epoch, Spring.
The Inland Years. Western Review, Spring.

CHAIKIN, NANCY R.
Bachelor of Arts. University of Kansas City Review, Spring.

CHEEVER, JOHN
The True Confessions of Henry Pell. Harper's Magazine, June.
The Day the Pig Fell Into the Well. New Yorker, Oct. 23.
The Country Husband. New Yorker, Nov. 20.

CLOSSER, MARY JO
Malay Boy. University of Kansas City Review, Summer.

COATES, ROBERT M.
Accident at the Inn. New Yorker, June 19.
COLEMAN, LONNIE
Noblesse Oblige. The Volusia Review, No. 1.
CONNELL, EVAN S., JR.
The Fisherman From Chihuahua. Paris Review, Fall-Winter.
COOGAN, JOE
The Decline and Fall of Augie Sheean. Ladies' Home Journal, Oct.
COREY, MARILYN
The Pure in Heart. Mademoiselle, August.
CURLEY, DANIEL
The Day of the Equinox. New Mexico Quarterly, Summer.
To Ask the Hard Question Is Easy. Kenyon Review, Autumn.
A Young Girl's Fancy. University of Kansas City Review, Winter.

DAVIDSON, KAY
The Boy and the Bull. Everywoman's, Oct.
DAWKINS, MARY LUCILE
Pop the Blue Moon. The Pacific Spectator, Winter.
DEAL, BORDEN
Daniel. Virginia Quarterly Review, Autumn.
DEALEY, TED
Reunion. Southwest Review, Autumn.
DEASY, MARY
Reward of Virtue. University of Kansas City Review, Summer.
DEJONG, DAVID CORNEL
Those Who Eat Dragonflies. Southwest Review, Autumn.
The Most Beautiful City. Yankee, Nov.
DEMING, BARBARA
The Siege. Charm, Nov.
DERBY, MACK
The Sixth Midnight. This Week, Oct. 31.
DEVRIES, PETER
Slice of Life. New Yorker, Mar. 27.
DOUGHTY, LEGARDE S.
Aunt Amelia's Retreat. Arizona Quarterly, Winter.
DOWNEY, HARRIS
The Clown. Epoch, Fall.

EASTLAKE, WILLIAM
Little Joe. Accent, Autumn.
EATON, CHARLES EDWARD
A Morning Walk. Northern Review, Dec.-Jan.
Balloons of São Joad. Talisman, No. 5.
Green Cross in the Sky. Four Quarters, Nov.
EDWARDS, KATE F.
The Reception. Georgia Review, Fall.
ELLINGSON, MAMIE
The Real You. Ladies' Home Journal, Oct.
ELLIOTT, GEORGE P.
Mrs. Cudahy of Stowe's Landing. Hudson Review, Spring.
Daemon Lovers. Quarterly Review of Literature, Vol. 7, No. 4.
Brother Quintillian and Dick the Chemist. Western Review, Autumn.
ELLISON, RALPH
Did You Ever Dream Lucky? New World Writing, No. 5.
ELLISON, RICHARD
The Dorset Giant. Virginia Quarterly Review, Spring.
EMBREE, CHARLES
Them Monumental Blues. Esquire, Aug.
ENRIGHT, ELIZABETH
The Operator. Harper's Magazine, May.

FARRELL, JAMES T.
Danny O'Neill Was Here. Commentary, Dec.
FINLETTER, GRETCHEN
The Young Man Who Came To Visit. Harper's Magazine, Dec.
FONTAINE, ROBERT
The Wrong Way Home. Prairie Schooner, Summer.
FOOTE, ELLIS
A Day for the Rain. New Mexico Quarterly Review, Summer.
FOWLER, MARY DEWEES
A Delicate Constitution. Woman's Day, May.
Man of Distinction. Accent, Summer.
FRANCIS, H. E.
The Journey of Ann Bliss. Four Quarters, Spring.
The Fence. Prairie Schooner, Fall.
FREILICH, IRVING
Three Lives. Quarterly Review of Literature, Vol. 7, No. 4.
FROSCHER, WINGATE
The Younger Brother. University of Kansas City Review, Spring.

GALLANT, MAVIS
Poor Franzi. Harper's Bazaar, Oct.
Going Ashore. New Yorker, Dec. 18.
GILL, RICHARD T.
The Secret. Atlantic, April.
The Ten-Dollar Bill. Atlantic, Oct.

GLEN, EMILIE
Cain to Cain. Shenandoah, Spring.
Perish Poetry. Four Quarters, Nov.
GODWIN, TOM
The Cold Equations. Astounding Science Fiction, August.
GOLD, HERBERT
A Celebration for Joe. Antioch Review, Fall.
Help These Days. Accent, Winter.
The Man Who Was Not With It. New World Writing, No. 6.
GORDIMER, NADINE
The Smell of Death and Flowers. New Yorker, May 15.
GOTTLIEB, NAOMI R.
Young Knighthood. Arizona Quarterly, Autumn.
GOYEN, WILLIAM
The Geranium, Mademoiselle, April.
GRAU, SHIRLEY ANN
Joshua. New Yorker, Feb. 20.
GRAVES, JOHN
The Laughter from the Western Islands. Colorado Quarterly, Winter.
GREENE, PATTERSON
Sandals and Shade. Charm, Dec.
GROVE, EDGAR J.
Don't Joggle Me. Paris Review, Spring.

HALE, NANCY
How Would You Like to Be Born . . . University of Kansas City Review, Summer
Miss August. New Yorker, Sept. 18.
The Secret Garden. New Yorker, Oct. 2.
The New Order. New Yorker, Nov. 27.
HALL, JAMES B.
A Try from the Gulf. Harper's Bazaar, Oct.
HALL, OAKLEY M.
The Crown. Epoch, Spring.
HAMMEL, MARGARET
The Aunts. Charm, Dec.
HANLON, BROOKE
The Summer Children. Ladies' Home Journal, Oct.
HARROLD, JOHN
Just Out of the High-Rent District. Esquire, Aug.
HERBERT, WALTER T.
Word of Fear. Georgia Review, Spring.
HERBST, JOSEPHINE
Hunter of Doves. Botteghe Oscure, XIII.
HERVELCKE, EDWIN
Authority. Arizona Quarterly, Summer.
HUTCHINSON, ROBERT
The Foxhound. Southwest Review, Autumn.
HYMAN, MAC
The Hundredth Centennial. Paris Review, Fall-Winter.

JACKSON, SHIRLEY
The Order of Charlotte's Going. Charm, July.
JEROME, V. J.
The Word. Masses & Mainstream, June.
JOHNSON, DUNCAN
The Home. Sewanee Review, Summer.

KAPLAN, CHARLES
The Advancement of Learning. Antioch Review, Spring.
KAUFMAN, SUE
An Act of Human Kindness. Collier's, Jan. 8.
KELLY, EVERETT
Here Comes Roscoe. Epoch, Spring.
Moment. Epoch, Winter.
KHANZADIAN, ANITA
No Time to Argue. Armenian Review, Spring.
KRETSCHMAN, LOUIS
A Father's Ordeal. Redbook, Nov.

LA FARGE, OLIVER
The Resting Place. New Yorker, Oct. 16.
LANGDON, JOHN
The Bullet in My Father's Neck. Virginia Quarterly Review, Summer.
LANGIS, ISABEL
Have You Heard About Lucy? McCall's, May.
LAVIN, MARY
Limbo. Atlantic, June.
LAWRENCE, LARS
The Hungry Ones. Arizona Quarterly, Autumn.
LE FEUER, HARRY, JR.
A Summer's Tale. Quixote, Spring.
LIEBERLING, A. J.
The Dog in the Millpond. New Yorker, Oct. 9.
LUNDY, JO
Morgan. Virginia Quarterly Review, Spring.
LOGAN, ANDY
The Interview. New Yorker, Nov. 7.
LYNDS, DENNIS J.
The Island. Interim, Vol. IV, Nos. 1 & 2.
LYONS, AUGUSTA WALLACE
Prince Charming, Montrealer, Dec.

McCarthy, Mary
A Charmed Life. New Yorker, Oct. 9.
McCoy, Esther
The Hidden One. Arizona Quarterly, Autumn.
The Best Chess in Cuernavaca. New Mexico Quarterly, Autumn.
McCulloch, Elizabeth
Your Birthday All Day. Charm, Feb.
McKelway, St. Clair
The Shooting at Forty-Seven. New Yorker, March 13.
McNeilly, Mildred Masterson
One Man Missing. Collier's, Jan. 8.
McNulty, John
An Old College Chum. New Yorker, Oct. 9.
Madison, John
First-Class Heel. Southwest Review, Spring.
Malamud, Bernard
The Magic Barrel. Partisan Review, Nov.-Dec.
Manning, Harvey
Frolics of the Fellaheen. Interim, Vol. IV, Nos. 1 & 2.
Marine, Gene
When The Sky Is Black. Prairie Schooner, Fall.
Marquis, Lucian
The Revenge. Pacific Spectator, Summer.
Marsh, Willard
Astronomy Lesson. Yale Review, Summer.
Martin, Placide
The Incantation of This Whitems. University of Kansas City Review, Spring.
Mathesen, Richard
Descent. If, May.
The Test. Fantasy and Science Fiction, Nov.
The Doll That Does Everything. Fantastic Universe, Dec.
Merril, Judith
Dead Center. Fantasy and Science Fiction, Nov.
Middleton, Elizabeth H.
Portrait of My Son As a Young Man. University of Kansas City Review, Autumn.
Miller, James E.
The Colonel Dudley Company, Inc. Prairie Schooner, Spring.
Morris, Wright
The Safe Place. Kenyon Review, Autumn.
Morrison, William
G'rilla. Beyond, Jan.
Morton, Frederic
Happiness Is Not So Hard. Esquire, Jan.
Moss, Philip
To The Mountains. Commentary, Nov.
Mudrick, Marvin
The Professor and the Poet. Shenandoah, Summer.
Muheim, Harry
The Train to Trouble. Colorado Quarterly, Spring.

Neely, E. J.
When Spring Comes. University of Kansas City Review, Winter.
Neiman, Gilbert
Death in the South. New Mexico Quarterly Review, Spring.
Nemerov, Howard
Yore. Hudson Review, Winter.
Norris, Hoke
Handyman. Prairie Schooner, Summer.

O'Brien, Edna
The Splendor and the Speed. Everywoman's, Nov.
O'Connor, Flannery.
A Circle in the Fire. Kenyon Review, Spring.
A Temple of the Holy Ghost. Harper's Bazaar, May.
The Displaced Person. Sewanee Review, Autumn.
Olsham, Ruth
Murder. Epoch, Spring.
Owens, William A.
In Thine Own Blood. Southwest Review, Spring.

Patton, Frances Gray
Miss Dove and the Maternal Instinct. Ladies' Home Journal, Oct.
Papashlivy, Helen
The Day the Water Came Under the Door. Everywoman's, May.
Parrott, L. M., Jr.
Edwina. Quixote, Spring.
Pendergast, Constance
The House on Gerard Street. Accent, Winter.
Peters, Roberta Engle
The Edge of Twilight. Colorado Quarterly, Summer.
Plageman, Bentz
The Great BB-Gun Crisis. Charm, July.

Rikhoff, Jim
The Beasts in the Forest. Quixote, Spring.

Riter, Faye
The Gifts. Yale Review, Spring.
Robinson, Rosanne Smith
Miching Mallecho. Epoch, Spring.
Roddan, Samuel
A Sunday Picnic. Canadian Forum, Sept.
Rothberg, Abraham
The Red Dress, Epoch, Fall.
Ryan, Anne
Ludvica. Paris Review, Spring.

Saroyan, William
The Rearward Dog. The Armenian Review, Autumn.
Saul, George Brandon
What Came of An Argument. New Mexico Quarterly, Summer.
Scott, William R.
Judy and the Iceman. Saturday Evening Post, Oct. 23.
Shahade, William
Two Short Tales, Western Review, Spring.
Slaiman, Mortimer
Who's Better? Kenyon Review, Summer.
Shaw, Irwin
Tip on a Dead Jockey. New Yorker, March 6.
Shore, Wilma
The Painter. Antioch Review, Fall.
Smith, John Campbell
The Evening. Charm, April.
Spingarn, Lawrence P.
The Pond. Colorado Quarterly, Autumn.
Sproul, Kathleen
A Fine and Private Place. Kenyon Review, Summer.
Stegner, Wallace
Maiden in a Tower. Harper's, Jan.
Stern, Richard G.
Cooley's Version. Kenyon Review, Summer.
Stockdale, Joseph G.
Sailor from Nowhere. Argosy, March.
Stolz, Mary
The Flirt. Seventeen, April.
Stuart, David
Bird Man. Botteghe Oscure, XIII.
Swados, Harvey
Herman's Day. New World Writing, No. 5.
Sylvester, William
The Death of Francisco. New World Writing, No. 5, April.

Taper, Bernard
Inge. The Pacific Spectator, Winter.
Taylor, Peter
The Dark Walk. Harper's Bazaar, March.
Thomas, Dylan
The Followers. New World Writing, No. 5, April.
Todd, Robert E.
A Decent Burial. Epoch, Winter.

Uhr, Leonard
The Jungle Down the Drain. New World Writing, No. 5, April.

Van Doren, Mark
I Got a Friend. University of Kansas City Review, Spring.
April Fool. Ellery Queen's Mystery Magazine, April.
Viereck, Peter
8 Times 8 is 88. The Volusier Review, Vol. I, No. I.
Vukelich, George
The Scale Room. The Atlantic, June.

Wade, John Donald
The Very Pulse. Georgia Review, Fall.
Wanklyn, Christopher
Mistral and Mermaids. Paris Review, Summer.
Weathers, Winston
The Matador. Arizona Quarterly, Autumn.
Silver in My Pockets, Boots on My Feet. University of Kansas City Review, Autumn.
Weaver, John D.
A Soft Answer. Harper's Magazine, Sept.
Webber, Gordon
The Kite That Flew Away. New World Writing, No. 6.
Welty, Eudora
Going to Naples. Harper's Bazaar, July.
Spring. Sewanee Review, Winter.
Wesely, Donald
Chipper and the Frog. University of Kansas City Review, Summer.
Wilkins, E. M.
Serenade to the Bidders. P. S., No. 2.
Wilner, Herbert
The Bandaged Man. Epoch, Winter.
Wilson, Ethel
The Birds. Northern Review, Oct-Nov.
Wilson, William E.
A Work of Art. Colorado Quarterly, Summer.
Woodcock, Louise P.
Cat's Got His Tongue. Woman's Day, Oct.

WOOLF, DOUGLAS
The Third Doorman. Interim, Vol. IV, Nos. 1 & 2.

YAFFEE, JAMES
Only A Crazy Man Has Daughters. Atlantic, Sept.

YARROW, JULIA
The Counting. Arizona Quarterly, Winter.

YOUNG, MARY JO
Welcome Home, Marie. Seventeen, April.

YOUNG, JEFFERSON
The Princess. Shenandoah, Spring.

II. *Foreign Authors*

AKUTAGAWA, RYUNSOKE
Autumn. Shenandoah, Winter.

BORGES, JORGE LUIS
Death and the Company. New Mexico Quarterly, Autumn.

CARUNUNGAN, CELSO A.
My Father's First Son. The Sign, Nov.

CARY, JOYCE
A Good Investment. Harper's, Dec.

CHEKHOV, ANTON
An Unpleasantness. Charm, Feb.
Saintly Simplicity. Charm, April.

DAHL, ROALD
The Way Up to Heaven. New Yorker, Feb. 27.

DANESHVAR, SIMIN
Narges. Pacific Spectator, Spring.
A Letter Home. Pacific Spectator, Winter.

DAVIS, LYDIA
Flat Tire in Rarotonga. Atlantic, Sept.

DE URIBE, IRENE HAY
Sois Rage O Ma Doulem. Accent, Summer.

DUNSANY, LORD
In The Mojave. Harper's Bazaar, February.

GOLDO, BENITO PEREZ
Torquem Ada in the Flames. Harper's Bazaar, 1954 — Nov.

GARY, ROMAIN
The Lute. Harper's Bazaar, Sept.

GLANVILLO, BRIAN
Miss Lawrance Will Be At Home. New World Writing, No. 6.

GORDIMER, NADINE
The Scar. Harper's Magazine, March.

HAMASDEGH
Oh, For Those Good Old Days. The Armenian Review, Spring.

HOCKENHULL, JACK
The Glass Wanderer. Quixote, Spring.

JACOBSON, DAN
The Break. Commentary, October.

JAMESON, STORM
The Mask. Harper's, November.

KUNIKADA, DOPPO
Spring Birds. Pacific Spectator, Summer.

LOWRY, MALCOLM
The Bravest Boat. Partisan Review, May-June.

MANKOWITZ, WOLF
The Finest Pipe Maker in Russia. Atlantic, Nov.

MOORE, JOHN
Sunfish. Charm, July.

MORTIMER, JOHN
Nature Study. Harper's Bazaar, July.

NEWBY, P. H.
The Clerkly Salamander. Harper's Bazaar, May.

O'BRIAN, PATRICK
The Slope of the High Mountain. Harper's Bazaar, January.

O'CONNOR, FRANK
The Face of Evil. New Yorker, April 3.
The Sissy. Mademoiselle, May.
Lost Fatherlands. New Yorker, May 8.
Don Juan's Apprentice. Harper's Bazaar, August.
The Tram. The Atlantic, October.
The Ladies of the House. Harper's Magazine, October.

O'FAOLAIN, SEAN
Childybawn. New World Writing, No. 5, April.

OLIAJI, NARIE
Piya Bina Nalun Awat Chain. Pacific Spectator, Autumn.

ORTESE, ANNA MARIA
Family Scene. New World Writing, No. 5.

Panter-Downes, Mollie
Their Walk of Life. New Yorker, Sept. 12.
The Willoughbys. New Yorker, Oct. 2.

Radcliffe, Garnett
The Elephant Ride. Esquire, Nov.

Sansom, William
A White Lie. Harper's Magazine, June.

Singer, Isaac Bashevis
From the Diary of One Not Born. Partisan, March-April.

Tucci, Niccolò
Last Stand. New Yorker, April 17.

Watney, John
First Term. New Yorker, June 5.

Warner, Sylvia Townsend
Wherefore, Unlaurell'd Boy. New Yorker, June 12.

White, Robin
White Bhagavather. Colorado Quarterly, Autumn.

Wong, David T. K.
The Vase. Pacific Spectator, Spring, 1954.

Yessayan, Zabelle
My Uncle Hachik. Armenian Review, Spring.

ADDRESSES OF AMERICAN AND CANADIAN MAGAZINES PUBLISHING SHORT STORIES

Accent, Box 102, University Station, Urbana, Illinois
Adventure, 205 East 42nd Street, New York City
American Jewish Times Outlook, 603–4 Southeastern Bldg., Greensboro, North Carolina
American Magazine, 250 Park Avenue, New York City
Antioch Review, 212 Xenia Avenue, Yellow Springs, Ohio
Argosy, 205 East 42nd Street, New York City
Arizona Quarterly, University of Arizona, Tucson, Arizona
Armenian Review, 212 Stuart Street, Boston, Massachusetts
Atlantic Monthly, 8 Arlington Street, Boston, Massachusetts
Beyond, 421 Hudson Street, New York City
Black Mountain Review, Black Mountain College, Black Mountain, North Carolina
Bluebook, 444 Madison Avenue, New York City
Botteghe Oscure, Redazione, Botteghe Oscure, Via Botteghe Oscure, N. 32, Rome, Italy
California Quarterly, 7070 Hollywood Boulevard, Los Angeles, California
Canadian Forum, 16 Huntley Street, Toronto, Ontario, Canada
Canadian Home Journal, Richmond and Sheppard Streets, Toronto, Ontario, Canada
Catholic World, 411 West 59th Street, New York City
Charm, 575 Madison Avenue, New York City
Chatelaine, 481 University Avenue, Toronto, Ontario, Canada
Collier's, 640 Fifth Avenue, New York City
Colorado Quarterly, University of Colorado, Boulder, Colorado
Commentary, 34 West 33rd Street, New York City
Commonweal, 386 Fourth Avenue, New York City
Cosmopolitan, 57th Street and Eighth Avenue, New York City
Country Gentleman, Independence Square, Philadelphia, Pennsylvania
Dalhousie Review, Dalhousie University, Halifax, Nova Scotia
Discovery, Pocket Books, Inc., 630 Fifth Avenue, New York City
Ellery Queen's Mystery Magazine, 570 Lexington Avenue, New York City
Epoch, 252 Goldwin Smith Hall, Cornell University, Ithaca, New York
Esquire, 366 Madison Avenue, New York City
Everywoman's, 31 West 47th Street, New York City
Family Circle, 25 West 45th Street, New York City
Fantastic, 366 Madison Avenue, New York City
Fantastic Universe, 471 Park Avenue, New York City
Fantasy, 175 Fifth Avenue, New York City
Fantasy and Science Fiction, 570 Lexington Avenue, New York City
Folio, English Bldg., Indiana University, Bloomington, Indiana
Four Quarters, La Salle College, Philadelphia, Pennsylvania
Four Winds, 3 Liberty Street, Gloucester, Massachusetts
Galaxy, 421 Hudson Street, New York City
Georgia Review, University of Georgia, Athens, Georgia
Golden Goose, Box 583, Sausalito, California
Good Housekeeping, 57th Street and Eighth Avenue, New York City
Hairenik Weekly, 212 Stuart Street, Boston, Massachusetts
Harper's Bazaar, 572 Madison Avenue, New York City
Harper's Magazine, 49 East 33rd Street, New York City
Hudson Review, 439 West Street, New York City
Inferno, P.O. Box 5030, San Francisco, California

Interim, Box 24, Parrington Hall, University of Washington, Seattle, Washington
Jewish Forum, 305 Broadway, New York City
Jewish Horizon, 154 Nassau Street, New York City
Kansas Magazine, Box 237, Kansas State College, Manhattan, Kansas
Kenyon Review, Kenyon College, Gambier, Ohio
Ladies' Home Journal, Independence Square, Philadelphia, Pennsylvania
Maclean's, 481 University Avenue, Toronto, Ontario, Canada
Mademoiselle, 575 Madison Avenue, New York City
Masses and Mainstream, 832 Broadway, New York City
McCall's, 230 Park Avenue, New York City
Merlin, English Bookshop, 42 rue de Seine, Paris VIeme, France
Montevallo Review, Alabama College, Montevallo, Alabama
Montrealer, 770 St. Antoine Street, Montreal, Quebec, Canada
New Mexico Quarterly, Box 85, University of New Mexico, Albuquerque, New Mexico
New World Writing, 501 Madison Avenue, New York City
New Yorker, 25 West 43rd Street, New York City
Northern Review, 2475 Van Horne Avenue, Montreal, Quebec, Canada
New Liberty Magazine, Toronto, Ontario, Canada
Pacific Spectator, Box 1948, Stanford, California
Park East, 220 East 42nd Street, New York City
Paris Review, 2 Columbus Circle, New York City
Perspective, Washington University Post Office, St. Louis, Missouri
PS, 2679 South York Street, Denver, Colorado
Phylon, Atlanta University, Atlanta, Georgia
Prairie Schooner, 12th and R Streets, Lincoln, Nebraska
Quarterly Review of Literature, Box 287, Bard College, Annandale-on-Hudson, New York
Queen's Quarterly, Queen's University, Kingston, Ontario, Canada
Quixote, Box 536, Cornwall-on-Hudson, New York
Redbook, 230 Park Avenue, New York City
Saturday Evening Post, Independence Square, Philadelphia, Pennsylvania
Seventeen, 488 Madison Avenue, New York City
Sewanee Review, The University of the South, Sewanee, Tennessee
Shenandoah, Box 722, Washington and Lee University, Lexington, Virginia
Sign, Monastery Place, Union City, New Jersey
Southwest Review, Southern Methodist University, Dallas, Texas
Talisman, P.O. Box 255, San Jose, California
This Week, 420 Lexington Avenue, New York City
Today's Family, 295 Madison Avenue, New York City
Town and Country, 572 Madison Avenue, New York City
University of Kansas City Review, University of Kansas City, Kansas City, Missouri
Upstream, 1539 Tennessee, Lawrence, Kansas
Virginia Quarterly Review, One West Range, Charlottesville, Virginia
Vogue, 420 Lexington Avenue, New York City
Western Review, State University of Iowa, Iowa City, Iowa
Zero, 138–52 Elder Avenue, Flushing, New York